TEAL ROSE

*For the little girl in the back of
the classroom reading reading romance books and
dreaming of grown folks business.*

TRIGGER WARNING

This book contains profanity, sexually explicit scenes, violence, assault, infidelity, poisoning, death, and blood.

CONTENTS

THE GODDESSES

Milmera
Goddess Of The Moon

Ghilphine
Goddess Of Dream

Juna
Goddess Of Judgment

Zadia
Goddess Of Life & Death

Youna
Goddess Of Fertility

Qroaris
Goddess Of Vengeance

Thetris
Goddess Of War

Uona
Goddess Of Peace

Chapter 1
Kaydian
1923

The sun was unbearable today. It made me wonder if it was against us. I turned to my right, and Delphine Pourciau's freckled pale skin was already sunburnt from the treacherous sun. But she didn't have a care in the world as she twirled around in the sunrays, giggling. Her smile stretched so wide across her face that I thought she might be delirious. I shook my head while she sang, "I'm free" over the soft noise of the flowing water. I looked at her long pale blonde hair that was in a French braid today and smiled. It's not every day that we get to run away from our hectic lives, my princess duties, and her farming duties.

I hummed the song embedded into my mind as I returned my attention to my drawing. Using my granite stick to trace the slight curves of Delphine's slender body against the Upper San Jacinto River, I blended the gray lines until they darkened. Older Drake Elms trees that shielded us away from the craziness were turning to a shade of persimmons as I ran my hand over a lush dark green carpet of medium blades of grass. The noisy whistling ducks provided us with enough sound as they roughhoused with the blue herons that flocked to the water area. I glanced at the little brown ducks and smiled. Nature is very territorial. It reminded me of humans, full of bark but no real bite.

The wood of the tree I leaned on dug into my back, which I knew would leave red marks on my soft, golden-brown skin. I needed to focus on the drawing now. But my mind kept straying. My eyes rolled on their own accord because I knew if I didn't finish this drawing now, I probably wouldn't complete it until next year. I will have to hide my illustration from my mother because she would complain about me being a contumacious child. My father would shake his head and call me stubborn even though I was twenty-five years old. Rolling my shoulders, I hear my mother's imposing voice say, "Am I raising a queen or a petulant human?"

I love my mother and our family's history, but sometimes I wish I wasn't bound and tied to the throne. The pressure sometimes felt like a metal anvil dropped on my chest. Blowing out a breath into the balmy Houston air, I looked at my drawing. Everything was perfect to my liking except for the main piece, Delphine.

I looked up to capture my lanky, breathtaking friend.

Immediately, I should have known Del was up to no good because her high-pitched squeals went silent. There, my friend stood by the edge of the river. Del had everything on full display. If anyone walked by, we would definitely be brought to the castle for punishment.

But I still looked on, paralyzed with slight jealousy, as I watched her small, perky breasts bouncing as she ran towards me. Carefree as the day she was born. My back went rigid as I prepared for Del to pester me about getting into the water with her. Even though I mentioned to her before we got here that I wouldn't participate in any shenanigans today. But no, my little, bustling friend never listens to me.

"Kaydian!" she shouted. Her hand wrapped around my arm with the pencil. "Come in the water with me. It's not too hot for once."

I tried to break her hold on me, but one thing about Delphine is that she is determined to have her way. And she has a grip that will make you do whatever she says.

"Del, I can't. What if someone spots us and reports us back to my parents? They would punish us." I chastised. "Put on your clothes, Del."

I nervously glanced around. My heart pounded in my chest as if I thought someone would pop out of the wooded area.

"KD! Come on." Her delicate hand dug into my wrist as she called me by the nickname she picked out for me when we first met. I was about to cast magic out to see if anyone was nearby. But Delphine tsked and said, "No magic, KD. Now come on, we will be fine. You know your mother will probably find us here if she even sees a hint of green in the air, and that will be the end of our day."

She narrowed her robin egg-colored eyes to my emerald-colored ones. I opened my mouth to protest, but came up short. Del decided she had had enough of my worrying for the day. She turned and pulled me along to where she'd unclothed. With a sigh, I mimicked her, and soon, I was naked as the Houston sun warmed my skin.

Sometimes it was better to give in to Delphine.

My arm snaked out to cover my full, perky breasts, and my hand covered my mound. Crossing my thighs together, covering what my small hands couldn't. I prayed to the goddesses that no one would catch me naked. The coven would have a field day if word was caught.

I watched Del's smile return to her face, and it was almost like those colds that humans get from being near each other, contagious.

Del took off running at top speed into the blue river, and I followed suit. Del was right. The water was lukewarm and inviting as I swam to the deep part. Dunking my head under the water, I forgot about the magic spell I cast this morning that got my long, coily, curly black hair straight. Although I was a descendant of one of the first witches, my hair was still wild and uncontrollable. Ms. Kincaid would always mutter, "That child needs a good whoopin'," in her thick Texan accent after she witnessed the aftermath of me wetting or sweating out my hair. When I came up for air, I watched Del spin in the water.

I shouldn't be surprised Del was itching to get out of her farm clothing, which was a far cry from the colorful array of outfits she normally adorns. It was hard to imagine how her parents got her to do any work on their pig farm. But somehow, they did.

Swimming closer to the small island that divided the river into two parts, I turned back just before the riverbed threatened to skin my knee. I dunked myself under the water, keeping a lookout for Del's legs as my marker for where I should return. I swiveled my head from left to right, but I didn't see a skinny pair of legs. All I could see were the river fish and rocks that lined the riverbed. My lungs burned as I retreated to the surface, breaking the clear water as I came up for air. Wiping my face clean of salt water, some still managed to get into my mouth. I cringed and spat out what remained of the salt water.

"Del!" I yelled as my eyes readjusted to the world again.

"Kaydian Thibodeaux! You better get your narrow tail out of that water at once."

The water rippled around my trembling body when I heard my mother's commanding voice. And I almost contemplated submerging my head back under the water.

Queen Celestine Thibodeaux stood by the grass edge of the water in all of her glory. She is stunning, to say the least. Her perfectly coiffed black curly hair was in a high bun today. Her blue tweed A-line dress matched her pumps and her white handkerchief in her hand as she clutched the cloth for dear life. Emerald eyes, like mine, narrowed in on me. I could have seen her scowl from Florida and could tell I was in for it.

I knew father wasn't home yet from the way she dressed. If he found her, or any of the coven, dressed as humans, he would have been beyond annoyed. So, I guessed it wouldn't have been that bad until I looked next to her and saw Sir Michael Reid, the right-hand man for our family. His cold, obsidian eyes gave me the death stare as he turned to face the tree I had occupied. I looked over to see a scarlet Delphine as she tugged on her oversized dirt-ridden work pants, shirt, and farming leather boots.

All I could do was muster an apologetic look at Delphine, but she held her head to the ground. My mother blatantly ignored her, as she has done on multiple occasions. Her hawk-like eyes were trained on me, heating my face in shame. Hurriedly, I got dressed as Sir Reid walked back to my mother and handed her my canvas.

Shit.

"I-I can explain—" I stammered, but she silenced me before I could finish.

"I have repeatedly told you to quit spending time with this silly hobby of yours," she said as I cast my eyes on her narrowed eyes. "You're dismissed," she said to Delphine.

I shot her another pitiful look, but she still had her head tucked into her chest as she turned and shuffled away. A part of me wanted to run after her and hug her for my mother's cruelty, but I knew better. That would earn me extra training time with Sir Reid and a lashing. With my head held down, I put on my clothing.

This was my fault. I knew it was too good to be true. When I snuck out today, I was extra careful because the lack of sound in the castle made me uncomfortable. Or so I thought. I didn't hear the bellows of Ms. Kincaid's stern voice, which had ricocheted off the columns when she spoke. Nor did I hear my mother fussing with Ms. Kincaid, our family's steward.

"I'm sorry, ma'am."

It was a pitiful apology, but I wanted to be on her good side since she was a bit high-strung from being separated from my father. She, and every royal, suffered from the madness that occurs when we are separated from our fated mates for too long. My mother needed some Cliff Fieldcress tea. The little red bitter plant that my father found saved us more times than we can count. Mated royal witches used Cliff Fieldcress tea to keep the severance frenzy away while their mates were away for days on end. In some cases, it helped with glut. As if our lives weren't hard enough, we have to add separation madness to the list. This affects the female witches more severely than the male.

My mouth formed a word to curse Youna, my goddess, the progenitor of the Thibodeaux family. For once, I wanted to be free from the confinement of being a princess.

When I looked up, I saw her glare at me, and before I knew it, my hand found its way to my hot cheek as she returned her arm to her jutted hip. The slap stung my soul, but the pain vanished like a whisper with the power of my magic. My throat ached with the sob I refused to let out. No good would come of it. I wouldn't get any sympathy from my mother now.

"Drawing is for humans. Would you like to go live with them since you're so similar?" she stated in our royal language that the covens have long since forgotten.

A little voice inside of me screamed, "Yes!" but common logic told me to humble myself and act like I have sense. In our world, if you didn't possess magic, then you were not worth our time. Hence why witches and other supernatural's chose to live their lives away from them.

"I apologize," I said, my voice soft and meek. Whenever I took out my drawing supplies, my mother's voice would become cold, and her expression hard, her disgust for my hobby unmistakably clear.

She wouldn't understand painting and reading, which took me out of my bleak reality. It was the only thing that was keeping me from...

"You spent almost all day out here when you could have been training with Sir Reid."

"I know. I'm sorry," I said hurriedly again, waking from my thoughts.

She gave me one last hard look and hugged me. Suddenly, I was surrounded by the heady, floral scent of her Chanel number twenty-two perfume, her latest obsession. I bite back a smile. She despised humans, likening them to be just as useless as a door with no handle, but she loved to dress and shop in their stores. As she pulled away and kissed my forehead, she gave me her famous childhood southern motto, "You know that hurt me more than it hurt you."

I huffed and shook my head in disbelief.

Sir Reid simply let out a curt grunt.

My mother and I walked back to the castle on the makeshift path Delphine and I had made. She cursed softly, muttering that the pebbles and dirt would have to be cleaned from her shoes and clothing when we returned. Sir Reid, the stoic warrior, just muttered that he wished we would find a better hobby. So that when he had to hunt us down again, it wouldn't have to be down a dirt road. I almost mentioned that it's 1923, and we're in Houston, not New York City. Also, if my father wasn't such an old-fashion witch, we could have cars and paved roads like the humans, but that would have most definitely gotten me thrown into the dungeon.

As we walked along my dusty path, my mother noted the thicket of the forest on both sides of the path.

"These bushes will be the death of me!" She exclaimed.

My mother rambled on about the woods and how my father needed to allow the gardeners to cut it down. Sir Reid was in front of us, swinging his sword, cutting the stubborn branches that would stab us if we walked near them. My father loved the older trees. While my mother always pleaded for him to get rid of the overgrown bushes, my father would say, *"Not everything old needs to be removed, Cele. Plus, they're the best secret keepers because they can't talk...well, to us, that is."* That would earn him an eye roll from both my mother and me. He always had a saying for everything, especially about secrets. My mother claimed to hate when my father brushed things off, but I always saw the sparkles in her emerald eyes. I hated the idea of it being there, but was grateful for the coverage it had provided for Del and me for the past year. It was the best hiding spot until I ruined it because I hadn't searched the area. If I had, then I would have felt my mother's pulsating magic and Sir Reid's stifling magic before I allowed Delphine's overzealous nature to persuade me.

After a ten-minute trek on the dusty path, we reached the lush grassy area with the Thibodeaux castle right in the center of the secluded countryside of east Houston. It was unbeknownst to humans, which wasn't hard to imagine since they didn't have any magic to survive, making it through the woods that encircled the coven. Iris, begonias, and buttercup flowers clashed against the Blackstone castle. The black roof made it ominous, according to some of the coven members, and I had to agree with them for once. Dark-trimmed windows decorated the walls of the castle. No matter how much I begged my father to update the castle to something more modern so we could appear more approachable, he would just laugh and say, *"You, young witches. When will you learn that the old way is the better way!"*

It was exhausting trying to reason with him.

My eyes roamed around the front of the castle to see if my father was back from his visit to the South American coven of the cast out witches. Usually, when he was outside, the gardeners would bury themselves in the shed until my father disappeared. Breathing a sigh of relief when I saw no signs of him, I escaped my father's wrath again. A smile appeared on my face before I could stop myself. When Sir Reid turned his vast frame around, his black eyes found mine. He raised his eyebrow as if he could hear my thoughts.

He probably could, the tortuous bastard.

"How annoying. I ruined my new dress!" My mother jabbered—she had slowed down to dust herself off.

"I can run into town to buy you a new one, Mother."

She leveled me with a dark stare when I turned to her. Smiling sheepishly, I turned back around to walk behind Sir Reid.

As we shuffled to the castle, Sir Reid stopped to speak with one of the garden's attendants, Mr. Sawder. I waved to him, and he returned it, his glove covered in grass stains that matched the ones on his clothing. I wasn't in the mood to carry on with our typical conversation, so I reminded him to take breaks and not overwork himself. That earned me a bright smile from the garden attendant and a smirk from my mother.

Walking the rest of the way to the colossal-sized black metal door. The guards opened the heavy door with a grunt, and I rushed in before my mother could catch up to me.

"Kaydian!" my mother called from just beyond the door. "Quit all of that running. It's unladylike!"

"Give me a break," I muttered. I'd rolled my eyes one too many times at her repetitive declaration.

Upon entering the foyer, my feet couldn't take me fast enough through the gray tile floors and white walls that told our family's arrival in North America thousands of years ago. In my mother's words, *"We were here before the Humans knew how low on the totem pole they were."* I shook my head as I rushed past the dining hall, where we used to host the Royal's gatherings. To the right, behind the white brick wall, were stairs that would take me to my haven, my wing of the castle. I rounded the wall and avoided the black-painted wooden staircase banister. The last time I held onto it, I ended up with splinters in my palm, which was fun as I reopened the wounds to get the tiny pieces of black wood out.

Secretly, I dreamed of the day we could renovate this place to resemble the human homes in Houston. But I would never say those words out loud. My mother had long since banned the coven from interacting with humans, calling them nothing more than useless food for the vampires. I would hate to be the witch that got caught. They would be cast out without their magic. And not even I was exempt from those rules. But Del and I found ways to escape without being caught.

For now!

I was halfway up the cold, gray stone stairs to my haven, where I could escape my mother and Sir Reid. As my foot touched the last step, I heard the one voice I had hoped to evade. Cursing, I mentally banged it against the white brick wall. In my mind, I knew it was too good to be true.

How lucky would I be if my ancestors would throw some help in my way?

"Kaydian Thibodeaux, where have you been?" My father called out.

Chapter 2
Kaydian

Hello, Father," I said, placing a smile on my face and standing tall.

My father, Braxton Thibodeaux, was no one you wanted to meet in a dark alley. He stood almost as tall as the seven-foot columns that decorated the old castle. I guess that's the only thing I inherited from my dad. His dark umber skin glistened against the inner ward's white walls. My father's murky brown eyes sparkled with amusement as if he knew I had just got caught red-handed. His wide smile that struggled to contain his teeth opened and damn if I'm not crazy, but I found myself with a large one as well. It's one thing about my father. Whatever mood you were in before seeing my father never lasted. I don't know if he cast a spell on himself, making him likable, but whatever it was, it was working.

I retreated down the steps, and into my father's waiting bulky arms. His velvety skin enveloped me in a hug. He smelled like the cinnamon and sweet oranges that were sold in Tou-Sin Square. My mother, who just caught up with me, comes to a stop when she sees me and my dad together. She stood there with a hand on her hip and arched one of her perfect eyebrows as she waited to see if I would come clean. I wouldn't. I tried to shrug away from him, but not before he planted a kiss on my head and turned his attention to my mother, placing a kiss on her cheek.

They kept their public display of affection minimal to nonexistent. My parents were fated mates. The greatest gift the goddess had bestowed on their royals. Unlike the coven witches, royals were bound to another kindred magical spirit—a fated bond. And a royal who fails to find a mate by their twenty-fifth birthday would fall under the curse of glut.

Long after, the goddesses returned to the otherworld and, before the three sisters rose, watched over the covens and their descendants. As the years turned to centuries, the greedy offspring turned from their fate and became hungry for power, with no guidance or desire to follow the rules. They wreak havoc with their potent magic, killing the other royals and copulating with anything that breathed. After Qroarisa, Goddess of Vengeance, the family almost became decimated. The goddesses decided that power was better shared than hoarded. With their primeval magic, they cursed their bloodline, making sure that either they share their magic or suffer the consequences.

That was the first of our ancestorial stories that were drilled into us from a young age.

Fortunately for my parents, they met each other before the "Awakening." The vexatious term caused my insides to distort. The Awakening was a pinnacle life event for witches. When we reach a certain age, our magic becomes more vehement as it reaches out to connect to its tethered mate. Coven witches, they are able to choose their mates or stay alone.

Heat blossomed across my face as I thought about the memory clearing my throat.

"Alright, lovebirds." I shook my head as I watched the pair.

One of our maids slipped into the foyer and stopped in front of us. Her skin, which reminded me of gypsum, flushed scarlet red all the way to her ears. She bowed slightly, and my mother dismissed her. She scurried off without a second glance. *Poor girl.* My parents kiss will most likely spread around the castle. I can almost hear the loud pitch of her voice when she reminded us that intimacy in public was egregious, and we had an image to uphold.

"So, where have my two favorite witches been?" he questioned.

I looked at my mother, who peered at my father with glazed-over eyes. The tip of her nose was the color of berry Fae wine, red, as she bit back a smile and stared up at my father. She was almost in a trance-like state. Which always made me wonder about my mother's reaction. We were taught about the effects of being with your fated mate, being overly infatuated, but watching my mother's interaction seemed… wrong for a reason I couldn't comprehend.

"Well, we just came back from a walk around the castle," I said hurriedly as I switched the conversation. "I'm going to head for my room. I will be out of commission for a while."

When they didn't protest, I counted my blessings. Sailing up the old gray stone stairs, my thick thighs protesting after the long trek home, which probably gave me a good chafe. Taking a sharp left, I headed to my wing of the castle. The stark white walls gave way to burnt orange walls that held some of my paintings and drawings my parents allowed me to showcase. I hightailed it down the long corridor, passing my gold and white sitting room to the right. My second prize possession was my personal library filled with magic books that dated back to when my ancestor, Goddess Youna, walked the earth. Not stopping, I pushed through to the last door, my heavy wooden door, and I was greeted… with chaos. The colorful array of dresses and garments litter the floor. My underwear drawer, which was once neatly organized, was now ransacked as some of my panties hung from the black four-poster bed. I'd forgotten I pushed the little writing desk to the far side of my room, and the light wooden chair toppled over in my attempt to make space for me to climb out the window. I would neither confirm nor deny that I caused this mayhem. Kicking some of the clothing to the side, I barreled past my lilac walls with my white Oushak carpet that covered the barely seen oak flooring. A light breeze sent the thin white curtains fluttering as I made my way to my bathroom.

I threw open my bathroom door and closed it. Not wanting to take a chance of having my mother or Ms. Kincaid waltzing into my bathroom, I sent my magic out to magically lock the bathroom door. My magic was like a warm kiss from a lover, subtle but powerful, as it swept through me and flowed out of me like the river, I once swam in. Covering the bathroom door with its soft green hue, it simmered and dispersed when it re-enforced the door with a click. A soft sigh left my mouth as more of my magic shot out to start the shower I needed. I could feel the salt from the river that coated my hair. It left my brown skin ashen, like I had just taken a run into the flour bags in the kitchen pantry. Ms. Kincaid surely had a fit when I ransacked the pantry one summer when I was six.

As I got into the warm shower, my magic prepared for me. The warm water fell down from the makeshift waterfall, draining into the tub. I stood under the water, every inch of my tall body covered. My hair, which swept my butt when dried, touched the back of my upper thighs as the water made the coily curls flatten against my skin. Using my favorite lavender soap, I scrubbed myself until the salt was gone from my hair and my skin. My magic dissipated as soon as my foot hit the warm bathroom tile.

My father refused to allow the coven to study outside of the village to learn about plumbing, possibly the only thing worthwhile from humans. His excuse was, *"Why do we need plumbing when we have magic?"*

On any other day, the housekeepers would use their magic to prepare my bath and get me ready for the day. But nothing feels better than doing it yourself. When I was prepared for bed, I broke my magic hold on my bedroom door. The pink and deep red shade of the setting sun filtered through my large bedroom from the window as I looked to see Seraphina and Lucifer, my dragons. Old dark trees covered their blue and red shiny bodies.

A low whine came from the dark shadows of the wooded area. It sounded like Sera was hurt. With my breath hitched in my chest, I searched the area. And when my eyes landed on the spot, I finally saw my two dragons. I froze against the windowsill. If anything happened to my babies, I would kill whatever hurt them. My magic warmed and waited, ready to transport me to the area, until I saw Luc's shiny blue scales shimmering in the moonlight, unlike Sera's red scales that blended in with the dark shadows. Luc stood behind Sera, his mate, as she presented herself to him. Her spiky tail laid at her side.

At least someone is having a good time.

My mother said Youna blessed me with them as a gift because they saved my life when we first met. At ten years old, I was adventurous and loved to see how far I could push myself. One day, while visiting the Pourciau farm, Del and I decided we could climb the biggest tree that surrounded the back portion of the farm. To no one's surprise, I was winning as I ascended the tree without a care in the world. The tree's rough bark dug into the soft flesh of my unprotected hands and the inside of my legs. Pushing myself up the ancient tree, my instincts told me I should have stopped a few inches back and declared myself the winner, but I was a hardhead. The need to be at the top crippled the fear I had when I looked to see Del struggling to match my pace. Del gasped, which caused me to glance back and notice her pale skin was the color of the red hydrangea that surrounded the trees.

Of all the days for this to happen, I had my emerald ring on as punishment for almost burning the coven's drunk with my powers. So, no magic to help me out of this situation.

My eyelids shut closed and waited for the pain that would land me in the infirmary for the next couple of weeks. However, it never came, as my back connected with something soft enough to break the fall but hard enough for it to draw a soft oomph from my mouth. A low grumble shook my slight frame, causing my eyes to spring open. Turning to the nightmare tree, Del was flushed against the tree trunk. The red flush she had was replaced with a deathly sick look that painted over her tearful face.

My mouth dropped open to heckle her, saying I couldn't hurt myself even with my ring on. Yet the words died on my tongue as the hard surface vibrated underneath me. I caught Del out of the corner of my eye as she made shooing noises out of her thin lips. Her body remained firmly planted against the tree. At what Del was shooing, I'm not sure, but I took a chance and looked. The grassy, muddy mixture normally found in this area was replaced by smooth blue iridescent scales that occluded half of my view. My clumsiness kicked in as my body rolled off the blue object, and my back hit the muddy grass with a thump. When my eyes finally opened, I was greeted by Seraphina, sharp teeth inching closer to my body. The bright redness of her eyes shined like the red rubies my father kept in his office. She was decorated with spiky scales over her head, which continued down her back to her barbed tail. If I had fallen on her, I probably would have died right then. If only my magic wasn't drained by my ring, I wouldn't be so afraid. That's what I said to myself as warm liquid drenched my legs, my underwear, and the white tweed skirt as I urinated on myself. This is how I died, not fighting or saving the day, but by being eaten by dragons in my now soiled skirt. My parents would die from secondhand embarrassment.

As Seraphina drew closer, I prepared myself to be eaten. My chin held high, and my eyes stared at Seraphina's advancing razor-sharp teeth as her mouth stretched wide. She stopped right as I felt the smooth skin of her snout rub against my stomach and inhaled deeply. I had long forgotten about Lucifer when he gently nudged Seraphina with his blue snout. Unlike Seraphina, Lucifer was the color of sapphire with spiky scales that littered his head. Contrasting the fiery pits of Seraphina's eyes, Luc's was bright yellow, like the canaries I once saw traveling with my father in the western Sahara. Later on, I learned Luc's scales on his body appeared smooth until provoked, then those scales rose and became just as sharp as Sera's.

Lucifer was definitely the nicer dragon out of the fated pair. He followed Sera and rubbed his snout over me and lightly rested his gigantic head on the ground next to me. I didn't know what else to do but to reach out and pet his giant head like a dog. It wasn't long before Sera laid next to me and placed her horny head close to me as well. That's how Mr. Pourciau and Del, who escaped, found me on the muddy ground with my urine-soaked clothes, petting my babies.

If I had thought wetting myself was funny, then seeing Mr. Pourciau run to save me takes the cake. He came running, huffing and puffing as his pudgy stomach juddered and swung from side to side as he yelled stop to the two dragons. I fell into a fit of giggles as I watched Mr. Pourciau and Del stumble when Luc turned his head around and bared his pointed teeth at them. It wasn't until I pulled my damp, muddy body from the ground and told them what happened that they unglued themselves from their fence. Both were two sweaty messes as they scampered into their home.

Sera and Luc hadn't left my side, not even when we walked home with my now yellow and dirt brown outfit.

I used the term babies loosely since Sera was seventy-seven years old and Luc was eighty-two years old at the time, according to Sir Reid, when he contacted the only person who was familiar with the era when dragons roamed the earth freely—

PSSSSTTT!

My head swiveled as I searched for the annoying sound.

"Princess Kaydian! Down here," the voice, unfamiliar to me, whispered shout.

The dark blue sky was barely visible, casting everywhere that didn't have the floating magic lamps into a pitch-black shadow, including Luc and Sera's forest. With my eyes squinted, I could hardly see the person in the bushes who was disturbing me.

"Well, come out of the dark before I send my magic to find you!" I yelled out into the shadows.

Rustling from the tall Oakleaf Hydrangea bushes that lined the side of the castle wall under my window drew my attention. Whoever was in there must be a mad person. My stalker jumped out of the bushes, and I rolled my eyes instantly. Why does this night have to end in misery?

"Oh, hello, Raynaud." I tried to hide the annoyance in my voice.

"Hello, Princess Kaydian," he said as he stepped into the light where his sleepy brown eyes shone. "I was finished with the garden and wanted to see if you would like some help with your...Peony."

By the Goddess!

My eyes shuttered closed as I shook his words out of my head. Raynaud Dando III was the head gardener's son who had just recently started working for us. Before that, we attended the same school together, but in different areas. The Royals and the Coven had separate classes and connecting buildings. Raynaud was a homely looking fellow. He had soft doe like brown eyes that overtook his plain features. His nose was a bit hawkish on his wide face, but by far, it was not the worst-looking nose I've seen. There was a ruby tint to his ivory skin. Raynaud's gray garden suit was smeared with dirt and grass. When we first met, he would follow me around carrying my books until the professors caught him roaming the Royal section of the school. When he couldn't follow me anymore, he started bringing me gifts and leaving them with the housekeepers to sneak upstairs to give me. He was a sweetheart...just a tab bit simple. The more I stared at Raynaud from my window. I knew I wasn't annoyed to see him because he had become my biggest helper. What he lacked in looks, he made up in...being a good fuck.

He's made me scream all eight goddess names more times than I can remember, even if he couldn't make me come. Not that anyone can because the goddess gave that special moment to our fated mates only. But I couldn't stop myself from trying to ease the ache.

Sex among the coven witches wasn't something we shied away from, but it had to be behind closed doors.

"No, Ray, I'm quite busy right now. Maybe you can ask me next week."

"But Kay—"

The look I leveled him would rival Sera's fiery glare.

"Princess Kaydian." Raynaud shuffled on his feet. "It's been a minute, and I just wanted to make sure your n-needs are being met."

Maybe I'm a terrible witch as I leaned over the window seal, allowing my full breast to be pushed up in my blue nightgown. His ivory skin turned red under the lamp's soft, dim hue.

"I'm sorry, Ray. Have a good night."

Quickly closing the window finalized my answer. My white curtains fluttered after I gave one last glance at Sera and Luc, making sure the two rambunctious duos were okay. I waited a minute and then glanced out the window. Ray was almost clear across the lawn as he made his way to the other side of town. The bitterness in my mouth made me wince. I hated being mean, especially to Ray. He would make a wonderful mate for someone one day.

It would be wrong for me to rob him of finding true love. All for what? To be in a loveless relationship with someone as screwed up as me.

I wasn't that cruel.

To be the last descendant of Youna, Goddess of Fertility, and haven't found my other half, which, among Royals, was a fate worse than death. In the back of my mind, I knew the coven was counting down the days until I went mad from the curse of glut. I didn't care... at least for today.

A soft knock on my door made a curse fall from my lips.

"Kaydian, can I come in?" My mother's voice called out. I guess my mom was here to reign in my punishment.

"Come in, Mother."

My mother had changed out of her tweed suit and into her cashmere robe. The tawny-colored robe complimented her golden soft skin.

She already had her bonnet and house slippers on. And Ms. Kincaid wasn't by her side as usual.

"Can we talk?"

"Yes, of course."

She approached me as I sat on the cold white sheets. Her back was straight, and her head held high in the air. Even when she's in her bathrobe, a regal air surrounds her. I don't believe my mother knew how to relax as she sat down next to me, her mouth painted with a small smile.

"Let me help you with your hair."

"You want to help me with my hair?"

The perplexed look on my face must have bothered my mother. Her smile slipped just a tidbit. And I opened my mouth to apologize, but the sad look in her green eyes told me the damage was already done. So, I nodded instead and turned with my back toward her like I'd done so many times before when I was younger. Nowadays, we barely have time to say hellos. Dividing my hair into two parts, she quickly made work of my long, coily curly hair.

"When are you going to make Ms. Kincaid cut your hair, Kaydian?"

"Mmm, maybe when never come around," I joked. If we were facing each other, I would have poked out my tongue at her.

My mother chuckled, and I would have loved to see the sparkle in her green eyes. These were rare and bittersweet moments since she was always sidetracked with her queen duties. I loved those times, even though they were so far and in between. She produced lavender-scented hair oil and rubbed it onto my scalp. When she was done, she took my silk headscarf and wrapped my hair.

"I know you don't want to cut your hair, but it's laying on your butt. Soon, it's going to be tripping you when you walk."

I turned around and gave her a half-cocked smile. "You're so adorable when you're mothering," I taunted while playfully pinching her cheeks.

She rolled her eyes at me. "Kaydian, I came in to talk to you as well."

Oh yeah, time for the real deal.

"Are you taking your Stoneseed root?"

Stoneseed root was used to dim our unquenchable desire to procreate, especially our line of descendants. I religiously drink the bitter tea mixed with the healer's magic to help prevent my dear ancestral gift, which left me like a panting dog if I didn't drink it every month. It's also what my mother took and her mother's mother. Although I was thankful for it, I hated that I couldn't experience my magic when it was at its purest when I was with my mate, with no strings holding me back.

"Yes, I'm due for another cup tomorrow."

"Good, and judging from that garden boy steaming off from beside the castle, you need to stay on top of it," she said as she dug into her robe pocket and handed me the bitter tea packet.

My face was feverish as I opened my mouth to refute her claims, but she cut me off.

"Listen, I was young once. Before your father and I were ready to be serious, we fooled around the Bayou a bit. Plus, you weren't exactly discreet. I knew I taught you how to close a door with or without your magic." I don't think she saw how I tried to hold back the acid that threatened to come up. Her lips pulled in between her teeth as she bypassed the fact that she'd heard me having sex. There was something unsettling about my mother knowing that information. Her eyes filled with sparkles as she looked off into the distance. "Yes, I had fun. I even found a half-troll in the swamp, and...well, I learned something valuable that night. But that's neither here nor there. I know we're hard on you, but it's because we expect more from you."

I blinked and blinked again. My mouth went to open, but I couldn't come up with anything. From my silence, she might have mistaken it for a need to remind me of the tale she drilled into my head.

She continued, "Don't tell me you forgot, Kaydian..."

Of course, I wouldn't forget.

My mother used to tell a fairytale that seemed so far-fetched, even for her, almost every night. The short end of the story was one of the goddess's descendants will bring "unity" to all the supernatural community. I used to soak up that story any time my mother would tell me it. However, as I got older, I found it harder to believe that this would transpire. Thanks to my father and the implementations he enacted throughout the North American supernatural community, the mere thought of unity seemed like a mockery.

"Of course, I couldn't forget the story you told me almost every night until I was in my teens," was the first thing my stunned mind could think of as I processed everything she had just spilled.

"Good, because—" my mother said.

"The sooner you come to terms with it. The better," I said, cutting her off before she could venture down a path I wasn't in the mood for. Shaking her head, her sigh of defeat filled the room.

I continued, "And let's not glide over the fact that you had sex with a mixling! I—that's forbidden!"

"Hush, that's between you, the troll, and I," she said as she got up from the bed. "Yes, I'm glad I had the experience, but nothing beats your father."

She laid her hand on my cheek. The soft touch of her velvety skin soothed my heated cheek as a warmth washed over me in waves, leaving my eyelids fighting to stay up. Finding the little groove in my bed, I fought the yawn that I struggled to keep inside, but it ended up winning the fight.

"T-Tha..." I tried to get out before another yawn broke free from me. "Thank you for helping me."

"You're welcome, my emerald moon," she said as she walked toward my door. "Will you think about going on a date with one of the royal heirs?"

My eyelids grew heavy as my mother's frame doubled and tripled in my watery vision.

"Mmmm, maybe. One date won't hurt," I thought I said before my eyes drifted close, and all I could hear was her light steps retreating out of the door.

Chapter 3

Kaydian

When I woke up the next morning, I was invigorated. My body felt more rested than I had been in a while. The surge of my magic coursing through my veins made me eager to start the day and confront my mother for using her mear magic.

My mother possesses a special type of magic that no one else has unless you've given birth. Humans called it Mother's Touch, but we called it Mother's Magic, or if you're from New Orleans, like my mother is, Mear La Magie...Mear Magic for short. Humans have this saying *"it takes a mother's touch to calm an infant or to soothe a child"*. Little did they know that magic is real. From my royal classes and my mother's teachings, this type of magic announces itself when the birthing mother's milk finally comes in. And it never leaves them, either. It just doubles the mother's magic watching over her child from deep within the mother, even when they're older.

Throwing off the warm comforter and slipping into my slippers, I got ready for the day. I placed on my favorite long white dress that hit my shin, which was rare, with a faux waistband. The puffy sleeves of lace made me itch, but I loved the dress. I brought it on a rare trip to Houston with my mother. After slipping on my short white Mary Jane's,

I decided to leave my curly hair out. Dressed and ready for the day, I rushed to the dining hall for breakfast.

My body gloated out the door with my wide smile plastered on my face. This euphoric feeling that I woke up with this morning led the way as I speed-walked down the gray, cold steps to the dining hall, all while never losing my pace. My long hair swung from side to side as I walked down the staff corridor.

"Your Highness…" one housekeeper said as I passed one of the many rooms that lined the long hallway. The young man looked at me like I had grown a second head out of the tip of my nose. His bushy black eyebrows met his nonexistent hairline, and his steel gray eyes looked bugged as if filled with unshed tears. He stood glued to the doorway as he shuffled on his feet.

"I'm sorry, I didn't see you in the way," I apologized.

"I-It's no problem, your Highness. Are you okay?" He stuttered while he threw me a shaky smile.

I stopped to peer at the nervous housekeeper and thought about his question. "Yes, of course, I'm okay. What's your name?"

"I wasn't sure, your Highness…" he replied over his words as he inched closer to the door. "My name is Arnold…Arnold Winchester, my family is one of the farmers in the village."

Are we going to take that from this insignificant maid? Let me out so I can kill him…maim him and hang him—

For Youna's sake, the cursed voice would have killed this man for nothing.

Blinking my eyes until the dark voice settled into its locked room in the back of my mind. The constant reminder of the imminent future that awaits me. I tried to lock the voice of the curse away, but that was easier said than done right now as the cursed voice continued to invade my mind. It had been four months since I'd felt the slow drawl of the curse. As its claws dug into the wet flesh of my mind, changing the basic structure that makes me who I am. And with no solution to end my evident downfall.

Too overwhelmed with shock and shame, I did something very out of character, even for me. I hugged him. When I pulled away, he was rooted to the floor, his eyebrows scrunched together, and then had the nerve to shake his head. "No. It's alright, your Highness," he said, holding his arms out.

I tried, I thought as I continued the long white hall to the dining room. He must be new. They're the only ones that act as if the world is ending when I'm nice to them.

This boost of energy and my magic had my blood singing as I ran into the dining room with an infectious smile plastered on my face. My parents, who stopped mid-sentence, mouths twisted before noticing it was me. My father's eyes widened as if he had seen a mermaid walk into the dining hall, which would be very rare since he poisoned most of the North American Mermaids. And if we were being honest, he was the reason every supernatural being was basically extinct. Whether it was Fae, Shifters, demons, and any others that stood in his way. Only the vampires managed to escape his wrath. His cup with his black coffee was hung in mid-suspension. While my mother, whose corner of her mouth twitched as she moved her hand to her mouth to hide her impending smile.

"Kaydian, I'm taking it you slept well?" my mother asked.

When she removed her hand from her mouth so she could articulate, it was in its usual firm line, but her emerald eyes flickered with amusement.

Such unqueenly behavior, I should say, but I valued my life.

"Yes, I did," I replied as I sat across from my father and next to my mother. The hall walls were painted red like the blood moon, with a dark-brown wood batten wall that met the others halfway. Our dark-brown wood table seated fifty coven members and royals at a time. *Joys of Joy*. The only time my thick thighs appeared small was in this seat while my feet were planted on the gray-colored floors.

My mother sat at the head of the table because she held a higher rank than my father. Even though they ruled equally, my father was considered a baron. He was the only remaining one after the war between the royal covens and the opposition, which was headed by my father's remaining family. My father's position was lower than a royal, but just a tad bit more powerful than a coven witch. Their role in our world was to bridge the gap between the coven and the royals.

Over the centuries, their role dwindled as the coven became more reliant and loyal to the royals. Deeming the baron's only purpose was to be lucky enough to be a royal's fated mate. My father was one of the few chosen ones, and he used his position to fit him. Every coven has a reigning royal ruler, be it a queen or a king. Next would be their heirs, whose role is to be their shadows. While learning, overseeing some of the coven's positions, and waiting for our day to come to sit on the throne. And then we have our right hand and our army, which wasn't a lot. Sometimes, after his trips, he would sleep and sequester himself to the royal wing for days before he reappeared.

With my arms crossed under my breast, my top lip hitched to one side as I threw my mother a distasteful look, but was unsuccessful as it turned into an outright giggling fest. My mother joined in after a minute while my dad looked on and slowly shook his head. Even though I felt the magic waning, it still wasn't enough to allow me to be mad at my mother.

"I guess your mother slipped a bit of her magic in with her Mears Magic." My dad sighed and ran his long hand over his short brown hair. He was sporting a rough morning beard that made him look older than his hundred years.

"How was South America?" I asked, deciding to change the subject.

My dad shifted in his seat, clearing his throat as he fidgeted with the white coffee cup.

"The problem was taken care of before I got there. You know, the cast out witches want to be seen from time to time. I can't complain because I get to come back to my girls early," he said.

Another question was on the tip of my tongue, but the clacking of shoes against the concrete floor drew my attention. The sound made the hair on my arms stand up. It was one of the new housekeepers that was drawing her feet into the dining hall. Her red-rimmed brown eyes cast down onto the silver serving tray, or should I say, the shaking serving tray. Her tawny brown skin was flushed. My mother and I glanced at each other for a moment before the Housekeeper placed the silver tray down with a thud that made us flinch. The movement sent some of the fluffy eggs and a strip of bacon onto the silver tray.

I was in her shoes one time.

When I was younger, my mother made Ms. Kincaid teach me etiquette lessons after I knocked Sir Cross, the European coven leader, and his son, Liam Cross, right on their ass.

I placed my hand over the housekeeper's hand. They were small and rough under mine. She looked so young when she turned to me. Her big brown eyes nearly popped from her sockets.

"It's okay," I said, offering her a smile. "What's your name?"

Her small hand trembled in mine. "I-I'm not to be heard or seen, your Highness."

"Meh, enough with that highness shit! What's your name?" I pondered as the heat from my mother and father's gaze scorched me. I knew a stern lecture would follow after the young housekeeper leaves.

Her eyes shifted to my parents before she said, "My name is Clarissa Manet, your Highness."

"It's okay, Clarissa. Thank you for bringing my breakfast. Give Chef Dubois my compliment—"

Before I could finish, Clarissa turned and nearly tripped over herself, trying to run away.

Poor Girl.

My stomach gurgled a little too loudly for my liking, reminding me I hadn't touched my breakfast. I wasted no time devouring the fluffy eggs, seasoned bacon—thank you, Del—buttered toast, grits with butter, and freshly squeezed orange juice. My parents continued with their talks about coven matters. Supposedly, I should have been paying more attention, but the food and my stomach had other plans for me. If there was one thing I loved more than drawing, it was eating.

After I cleaned my plate, I placed all the glassware onto the silver tray and was about to leave when the white edge of a notebook page peeked out from under the tray. I thought it belonged to Clarissa, so I pulled it out before my mother could see it and excused myself from the table. By that time, all of my mother's magic had vanished, so I didn't have to worry anymore. As I made the turn toward the housekeeper's area, I opened the busy door to the kitchen and saw the housekeeper's lithe body at the kitchen sink, cleaning the pots from this morning's meal.

I cleared my throat, and if I had thought she was nervous before, she definitely looked petrified as her tawny skin turned ashen. Clarissa looked like she'd seen death at the door with its bony finger making the come hither sign. The other five kitchen attendants stopped in their tracks as they bowed their heads to acknowledge me. I hated this. The staff feared breaking many rules my parents erected and walked on eggshells throughout the castle. Even holding their head down as they walk through the halls.

"Your High-Highness, what are you doing here? Was the food not to your liking? Did I not make your eggs fluffy enough? I—" cutting off poor Chef Dubois before he had a complete and utter breakdown.

"Chef Dubois, your food is nothing but the best in the south. I just wanted to give something to Clarissa."

Chef Dubois looked ready to pass out. "Y-Y-Your Highness, whatever Clarissa did, please forgive her! She's my niece, and I wasn't hard enough on her during training," he pleaded.

Clarissa stood by the overflowing sink. Her brown eyes bounced between Chef Dubois and I. Overreacting must be a family trait.

"Clarissa, may I have a word with you?" I questioned while ignoring Chef Dubois as he twitched, and the other kitchen attendants pretended to be busy cleaning the kitchen.

Oh, brother! Can't I do one good deed today?

Clarissa hadn't moved one inch from the sink, but I saw fat tears welling up in her eyes, so I took matters into my own hands. My shoes clicked as I walked over to her, dodging some attendants who were too busy trying to eavesdrop. As I grabbed Clarissa's tiny wrist and dragged her into the Housekeeper's hall. She dropped to her knees and begged for forgiveness.

"Please forgive me, Your Highness... If you plan to fire me, can I at least have time to gather my things before I leave?"

I exhaled. "I wanted to give you your paper. You forgot it under the tray. That's it."

Her head popped up, and she stared at me with her big, brown, watery eyes. "It's not mine, your highness. I-I did a favor for Merrell. They asked me to slip that note to you. They promised me that I wouldn't get caught. But I was so nervous because this is treason, and if I'm c-c-caught—"

I scratched the inside of my wrist, a nasty habit when I'm nervous. Merrell owned the town's books and art store, affectionately called Merrell's magical corner. For the life of me, I couldn't understand why they couldn't have waited until I made my way into town on Friday as usual.

"It's okay, Clarissa. I won't tell anyone."

She all but kissed my shoe as she pulled her petite frame up from the floor and ran back into the kitchen, leaving me just shaking my head. My parents have never created an environment of fear. They just demand respect, and if you cross that boundary, I would hate to be in that person's shoes. Clarissa made me cringe because I'd always wanted to make friends with the younger housekeepers, but they were always too afraid of me. Pushing back my unruly curls, I read the note from Merrell.

In the black square

Merrell's letter seemed indecipherable to understand, but the code name of our favorite painting was a beacon. A jolt of happiness bolted through me as I flew through the castle. The infectious smile painted on my round face probably made me look crazy. Bursting through the heavy front doors and stepping onto the wet lawn. I thanked Youna that I threw on the flat Mary Jane shoes. The wet sucking sound of my shoes leaving the wet ground caused me to wince. These were my favorite pair of shoes, and I knew I'd ruined the white fabric. My magic will do over-time to clean them and the little splashes of mud on the bottom of my dress.

"Your Highness, quit running in the yard! It's wet. You might slip and fall!" The gardener yelled out. If I had to guess by the squeaky voice, it was Raynaud's father, Raynaud Dando II. Luckily, the coven, or like my parents called them, common witches, typically brew potions, and because of their limited powers, I didn't have to worry about his power stopping me.

I should have been more discrete, but I didn't care.

Pain raked my lungs, which threatened to take me out, while the muscles in my thighs contracted, but I was determined to make it to the square before I collapsed. As Tou-sin drew nearer, I started losing momentum with each step. All thanks to my thunder thighs—and my ass as well. My calves screamed with each hard step I took on the small, muddy hill that the castle sat on. I was almost there. The last muscle contract caused me to stop as I reached the back entrance of Tou-sin Square, both hands on my knees, bent over and sucking in air like a madwoman. Sweat dripped from my back down the sides of my breast. This made me realize that I'm not ten years old anymore, and even though I could get away with training with Sir Reid, I could barely make it to the square.

Several minutes went by as I gathered my sweaty body against the orange-brown brick building. With time being of the essence, I pulled myself from the wall, making sure no one was around. Wordlessly, my inner voice echoed the incantation word, SeilqofeiII, transformation, in my mind. In the royal tongue, summoning my magic, which hummed with excitement. The green aura hit the Houston sun, making my usual deep green seem lighter as it whirled around me, enveloping me in its warmth and love. My magic and I are one, and I belong to it as much as it belongs to me. One may exist without the other, but would be an empty shell. Wincing at the slight pinch as my face contorted into someone else made me frown. I hated this part. Sadly, I had to hide because the Golden Army and our house guards patrolled every corner of Tou-sin Square. If they even caught a whiff of me in the square heading toward the Books and Arts store, my parents would know, and I definitely would be punished with my ring for months on end.

When the transformation was done, I used the alleyway to enter the square because it was closer to Merrell's. Big mistake! I had to turn sideways to squeeze between the two narrow old buildings. Even that was a fight, as I used my hands, which were the color of espresso coffee now, to guide me out of the tight alleyway. The rough texture of the wall was like a grater as it scratched my back and the palms of my hands. It smelled like horse manure and urine. I was halfway through the blasted alleyway when I sucked in my soft stomach, which only slightly helped me as I pushed through. No more bread for me. The light from the sun was close as I gave a last quick tug and slipped out of the deathtrap alley and right into a man who just so happened to be passing by.

"Hey, are you stupid?" His face was in a scowl, and his orange eyes narrowed at me. If he knew I was the princess, he would have begged me for mercy.

"I'm sorry I didn't—"

"I don't care! Watch where you're going next time," he scoffed and walked off, leaving me standing there with my jaw on my chest. The nerve of the asshole! My magic flickered and churned as I fought to control my emotions. **Kill him! Make an example of him.** The dead voice shouted in my head as my balled-up fist dug into my thighs. If I wanted to reach out and strike him down for being rude, I would have to force my magic to choose between what was most important. String the man alive or holding up my transformation spell? I couldn't force my magic to do two major spells at once.

Don't let him get away, Kaydian! Let me take over and avenge our name.

I watched as he disappeared down the long road of Tou-sin Square. My jaw clenched as he continued to walk without a care as he bumped into other witches in the crowded square. A part of me let him go because I had better things to do than to get caught by the guards for skinning him alive. And I didn't want to give the voice the satisfaction. *Fucking men!* When you found a good one, best believe there were a hundred foolish ones that followed.

I won't let this ruin my day. A coven member who watched the interaction stopped to see if I was okay, and I smiled while I nodded at her before excusing myself. The square was bustling with witches, young and old. A couple perched on the white stone statue of Youna placed in the center of the square for display. Both of them were rosy colored, as their lips were locked together as they blocked out the crowd. A slight heat singed the tips of my ears. There wasn't any confusion. They were bonded together, and I felt intrusive as I stood there wishing it was me.

"They're so adorable," an elderly coven woman sighed beside me.

A light breeze blew her floral perfume around me. "They are," was all I could reply as I excused myself.

My family insured the coven members had no need or want to go into Houston. Every store was tucked into a medium size orange-brown building with black pointed roofs that appeared to be endless. Uniformed just like my parents liked it—well, everything except for the windows. That's where the most colorful decorations were placed to draw in witches and served as a type of resistance to the strict rules.

Tou-sin was scorching hot, as there were none of the mammoth-sized elm trees to shade the square. It was sad because the colorful variety of horses tied up at the hitching post suffered the most. My father would only accept your feet and magic as the modes of transportation. Even though he knew the common witch couldn't use their magic to travel, so they didn't have a choice in the matter. It felt like we were ten decades behind the humans. At least they have cars and paved roads! I didn't know why or how my mother gave my father such free range over making the rules. I continued on the brown dirt road and blended into the crowds.

Merrell's magical corner store was on the opposite side of the square and near the end, where if you blinked, you'd miss it. It was almost as if my family knew I would have an addiction to the arts, because if I could, I would have the quaint store right next to my bedroom. As I crossed the street to the aging bookstore, my mouth widened, and all of my teeth were on display as the colorful storefront inched closer. Merrell had placed every color known to the goddesses in the window. Merrell had tons of photos of new books and art supply flyers enticing the art fanatics, such as myself, to come in.

If my father was here, he surely would have met Youna quickly.

My heart pounded, and the heat from the sun had nothing to do with the blood that rushed to my face as I placed my hand on the metal doorknob and opened the purple door. Merrell was my spirit twin, an artist with a passion for books. The bell dinged loudly in my ear as I entered and was greeted with the warm citrus scent Merrell loved. The faint, harsh turpentine aroma wafted through the tiny store, which led me to believe Merrell had opened the wooden door in the back to let the fumes out. Soft music filled the quaint store. A soft click came from behind me, making the door chime ring once more. Merrell never kept the door open because it would invite unwelcome guests, such as my father.

"Merrell!" I called out in the shop. There were a couple of ladies in one of the five rows of packed bookshelves that stopped and peered at me with their faces turned up at me for interrupting them. One lady had her blonde hair in a high bun that appeared dry and brittle. Her black dress was almost see-through, like the flappers I'd seen once in Houston. The second lady had a beautiful brown afro of curls that matched her light brown shirt. She paired it with a dark blue skirt that almost touched the ground. The last lady looked familiar, but I couldn't quite place her face. She wore a plain white shirt and black trousers. Her white socks could be seen from a mile away.

I rolled my eyes at the witches after they gave me their backs to stare at.

"Hello, how may I help you?" Merrell peeped their head out from the row closest to the back stockroom.

Before they recognized me, I grabbed them and dragged them into the tiny back room. Merrell wanted to protest, but I spoke first.

"Fire and Ice make everything nice," I said, speaking our secret phrase.

Merrell's frown softened, and a cheesy smile spread across their face.

"Princess Kaydian, I was about to turn you into a toad," they joked.

Matching their toothy smile as I hugged them. Merrell was just as tall as me, so we saw eye to eye. Literally, I can see all the yellow flecks in their aquamarine eyes. Today, they had green hair that hugged their shoulders with lots of frizzy curls, a style Merrell loved. Their lips were red, clashing with their green eyeshadow. They had on a yellow dress that had seen better days and no shoes—a common thing for Merrell. I shook my head. Some things never changed, and I was glad Merrell never did. They took off their glasses, which were tethered to a gold chain, and it bounced against their chest. Merrell, like some covens, preferred everyone to use their, theirs, them, themselves, or they to identify them. Everyone respected that even my parents, who made a rule, the only rule I probably agree with, that anyone who disrespected this rule would be sentenced to time in the dungeon or become a part of the cast out witch's coven in South America.

Okay, maybe I am turning into my mother. The thought made me run my hand down my face.

"I would love to see you try, Merrell," I teased. "You know Sir Reid would have my ass if he heard I was turned into a toad. He would just say…"

"Bloody child!" we said in unison and chuckled.

Merrell was the closest thing I had to a friend outside of Del. I love them with all of my heart. They opened my mind up to so many avenues within art that I loved, like introducing me to painting.

"Did the canvases come in?" I asked, as my eyes misted.

I've wanted these canvases for a while now, but unfortunately, Merrell didn't have them stocked. They were, however, able to sneak out of the village to retrieve them from Houston.

Merrell just nodded and pulled me into the stockroom. We didn't get far because the room itself was as big as the dungeon cells underneath the castle, cramped. They came to a halt in front of two canvases made with a primer that would protect them from rotting. An important lesson I learned one day when I went to retrieve one of my old canvases and it crumbled in my hands.

Sadly!

"Oh, Merrell, they're gorgeous!" I said, even though I knew that was silly since, technically, they appeared to be like all of my other blank canvases.

"I know, right!" Merrell's light green eyes danced as they stared at the blank canvas. "And they're all yours. Luckily, this time, you wore your white dress with your magic pockets."

"Honestly, I forgot about the canvases, but it must have been the goddess Juna who helped me pick this dress," I said as I thanked Juna, Goddess of Judgment.

The magic pocket is something my fourth great-grandparents had created to bind to your clothing to help protect them from the witch hunters, a group of humans who knew of our existence and hunted us down. The thought was for them to strip out their clothing, hide the clothing, and then wait in their pockets until they thought the coast was clear. Luckily, they destroyed the last of the hunters, and we hadn't seen or heard from them again.

Humans! For goddess' sake.

Merrell smiled and said, "Whatever the case, I'm just glad. You have a knack for the arts, and I want to nurture it whenever or however I can...even if that means going head to head with your father."

Honestly, I think Merrell would drag my father, all seven feet of him, through the muds of the bayou. A haughty smirk found its place on my face. And soon we were laughing. The stitch in my side found its home again as we woofed down the air like we were drowning.

I loved Merrell.

"Merrell, thank you for getting this for me. I truly appreciate it."

"Wait, I got a little something extra for you." They produced a small paperback book and handed it to me. The tears welled in my eyes as I read the cover. "I couldn't have risked going into the big bad human world and not get you this new book."

"The Transformation of Phillipé," I read out loud.

"It's a historical romance novel," Merrell said, as they wiggled their eyebrows at me.

My arms circled their thin body as I breathed in Merrell's book mixed with the peppermint scent. I wanted to stay longer and read it with them, but the longer I was gone, the more my parents would become suspicious. Hurriedly, I tried to tuck the two canvases and the book into my magic pocket, sliding the snacks I had long since forgotten about to the side to make room. I made a mental note to stop binging on snacks because that was why my thighs always tried to start a fire when I walked.

"Get on now," Merrell said, as they shooed me. "I don't need to see the dragon come down here looking for you...and I'm not talking about the ones in the dragon's wood."

Shaking my head as I slipped out of the backroom, I was about to approach the back door. Normally, I would never eavesdrop, but when I passed the row with the gossiping witches, I heard one of them mention my father's name. This made me pause, so I took cover behind the end of the row closest to the exit.

Curiosity killed the cat, yes, but I wasn't a cat, and I just wanted to listen for a few seconds.

"Yes, you know the king visited me after he came home from his trip," the witch with the brittle blonde hair said, as I watched her smile and twirl the strands of loose hair coyly.

The two other ladies gasped and fell into a giggling fit.

"Again, Francesca?" The familiar one mentioned. She had her back to me with her hands on her narrow hip.

"Oh yes, we spent the day together..." she paused. "With me on top of him."

The acid in my stomach seared my throat. The gall of this common bitch—not a witch, to say this about my father.

"Francesca!" both women whisper shouted, which sent them into another giggling fit.

"That's so scandalous but not surprising," the lady with the curly afro said. From my angle, between the small space that separated the shelves, I could see the haughty smirk formed on her nude-colored lips.

"What do you mean, Sophie?" The familiar one asked.

"Well, Amanda. King Thibodeaux has fallen into my bed once or twice before," Sophie said with a shrug of her wide shoulders.

"Am I the only one who hasn't fucked the King?" Amanda asked.

How many times will our father dearest embarrass us? He is nothing but a lust-drunk baron.

My dark voice had a point, but I tried my best to block it. The other two witches nodded.

Amanda snorted, but I couldn't see her face. "What would the great Queen Thibodeaux say if she found out?"

"Well, we were just doing our rightful duties and servicing our king. It's our duty to make sure all of his needs are met," the swamp blonde said. I wanted to wipe the ugly smile off her face.

These women were committing treason out in public...right in front of me. My blood boiled as they continued to heckle about my father. The stinging sensation from the rounded edges of my nails stinking into my palms didn't help one bit as I grappled with losing control of my magic. **Let's slice their throat open, then they won't be able to speak on dear old father again.** My rational brain went as I muttered, "My father wouldn't lie down with these whores." My father wouldn't do that...

"It's not like we hadn't heard the rumors, Amanda. Our king loves to dip his bejeweled staff into any and everything. Mermaids, the Fae..." Sophie said with a wave of her small brown hand.

"You think it's true?" Amanda asked. Curiosity blossomed in her deep voice.

"Why do you think the king and the Golden Army went around America basically eradicating all the other supernaturals?" Sophie tapped her brown sandals on the wooden floor.

"He wouldn't roam if he had it good at the castle, would he?" Francesca wondered. "Maybe if we told her the truth, she would get her head out of her ass and leave. I could take over as queen."

Amanda snickered. "What about our dear princess?"

"Well, everyone knows she's a flight risk, or should I say a psycho risk," Sophie said as she threw back her head and laughed. "How long do you think it will be before the curse sets in? She'll be a looney case soon. It's sad really. She's twenty-five and still hasn't found her mate. Alone and abandoned by Youna...I couldn't imagine being the descendant of the goddess of fertility and can't even find a mate to procreate with. What a waste of the goddess genes."

I wasn't usually a weak woman, but the bitter words made tears spring out of my eyes. My actions were not driven by foolishness. Well, not always. I knew the coven gossiped about me not finding my fated mate and the ticking time bomb of my downfall, but hearing it out loud in public made something tick inside of me.

"I give it another year. She'll be done for, and then I can comfort King Thibodeaux with my pussy on his beard—" the blonde bitch Francesca said, but I've heard enough.

Magic fed off of your emotions. If you weren't careful with it, you could burn down the earth with it, and at this very moment, I was beyond being careful. **Let's play with them, Kaydian.** The voice echoed in my head. My magic, no better than the dark voice, wanted to watch as the three witches' skin turned to charcoal as they beg for mercy on their knees with their skin falling off the bone. **Let's lace their blood with their tears and watch how they beg us, the mateless psycho, for their lives.** With my eyes closed, I prayed to Youna. My insides shook as much as the witches did when they laughed. **Then, we can draw what was left of the pathetic excuse of witches out to the square and mount them on the statue of Youna as an early sacrifice.**

No, No, No! I felt myself slipping into the dark part of my mind, and I would definitely kill everyone in the store. Even the group of kids I heard in the background chuckled as they spoke. My hands found the edge of the bookshelf as I felt my magic slip away, bringing my true identity back to the forefront. A loud bang followed by more bangs filled the store as the books fell one by one from the tremors that ran through me. The disturbance caused the three gossiping bitches to stop, and Merrell stuck their head out to see what the problem was.

"Princess Kaydian, Your Highness!" Merrell called out.

"One...Two... Three...Don't mess me up today!" I bellowed at the voice in my head.

Time stopped as I stood in the tiny shop, but when I looked up, Merrell was saying a chant to help soothe me while the three gawking bitches stood there watching. Their brown and blue eyes bulged from their ugly faces. My hands ached from how tightly I had gripped the shelves. When I locked the darkness in the corner, I unwrapped my hands from the shelves as I pulled away and waited in silence.

Would the Golden Army come and haul me back to the castle? A minute or two passed before I decided I was in the clear, and my racing heart finally calmed down. They would have been here the moment my magic rippled in the air if that were the case.

"Princess Kaydian, are you okay?" Merrell asked. Their voice was barely above a whisper.

"I'm fine, Merrell. Thank you so much." I said while I touched the back of their hand, which rested on my shoulder.

I gave them a tight smile, which they knew was fake. I'm glad I didn't slip into a total meltdown. That was the main thing. Turning my attention to the three nosy witches.

"Francesca, Sophie, and Amanda," I said. My voice shook on the last note, but I cleared my throat and straightened my back. "You were in public speaking about my father, who you know shit about. If the rumors were true, I would chalk it up to my father being senile to lie with y'all."

My formal teaching slipped just for a moment as I fought to find the right words.

"My father would never look twice at you hapless hags. You're jealous." Pausing, I looked at the three wide-eyed fools. With a smirk on my face, I continued, "If I hadn't known better, I would have thought how three pathetic humans had found their way into Tou-sin."

Francesca's trembling teeth played in tune with the music in the room as she looked poised to sprint out the door. If I were a betting royal, I would say she would have left her friends for dead. The young kids and teens had gathered at the end of the bookshelves.

"You- you're right, my Highness. We were just gossiping and lying..." She licked her thin, chapped lips as she stumbled over her words. "Forgive us, we're just bored—"

"Bored peasants, you meant," I corrected her.

"Yes, yes, your Highness." Amanda's shrill voice made me want to silence her forever. "We're just bored peasants... nothing we said was true. Please—"

"Thank you for agreeing with me, Amanda. It seems only you have enough sense between you and your daft friends." I turned my attention to the other witches. "How about this? I will allow Sophie to plead your case."

A glance between the three pairs of shaking limbs as uncertainty and a small slice of hope filled their closed-off circle. Sophie's once tan skin had turned gray, like the books on the floor behind her. Her once curly afro now laid flat on her sweat-drenched skin. She tried to take a step back, hiding from my view, but Amanda and Francesca pushed her to the forefront.

"I—Your Highness. We...um...yes, we deserve a second chance because," she paused, rubbing her hands together quickly. I thought she would start a fire in Merrell's store. "We mean no harm. We will go back to our jobs and keep our heads down. And never speak again about today or your Majesties."

Miss Sophie wasn't as confident and brave as she was when she had the nerve to speak on my father's name.

"Thank you, Sophie. I know you defend yourself and your friends to your mental capability. Loyalty to Thibodeaux means more than any friendship or pathetic apology. Don't worry your ditsy little head. When you and your little friends are wasting away in the dungeons, then you'll have enough time to gossip about my father."

Amanda's and Sophie's loud sobs made the children snicker as their alligator tears, mixed with snot, dipped down their faces. They were all talk, no action as they clung onto one another.

"Your Highness, may you take pity on them? They may be foolish, but—" The doorbell chimed and interrupted Merrell.

My glare was lasered on the three flighty bitches until I heard the heavy, deep baritone voice of Sir Reid.

"What's the meaning of this?" The deep timber of his voice bounced off the walls.

His tone broke the silence that fell over me. I had to turn this around in my favor.

"Sir Reid, take these three witches into the dungeon, separate cells." A wicked smile crossed my face. "They will be held for treason."

"M-My Highness, please—" Sophie stumbled.

I held my hand up to stop her blundering. Poor Merrell stood to the side. Their eyes bounced back and forth between us.

"Are you sure, Princess Kaydian?" Sir Reid asked low enough that only I could hear.

When I turned to him, his inky black eyes were already focused on me. As much as I complained about Sir Reid, I knew he had my back—well, unless it was something that would make my parents send me to the underworld. His armor covered his scared back, which held our family's promised gem, the emerald. I stared at the Marquise-shaped emerald and wondered if I was overreacting. Probably, but I was too far gone.

"Yes, throw them in the back of the dungeons for now," I said with a nod.

"As you wish, your Highness," he said, bowing slightly.

Sir Reid snapped his fingers. The ends of my hair fluttering against me were the only indication he listened. Sir Reid, like the others in his family, was gifted a more powerful magic than the coven members after they took an oath to Youna to protect and serve her descendants until our line dies—which, by the look of things, it may stop with me.

Two of the Golden Army men marched into the tiny store, shaking the shelves more than my magic had done. Their golden armor was out of place in the tiny shop. Our family crest, a Norman-shaped symbol with a picture of Youna and her emerald eyes as she's surrounded in a green halo, is stamped into the chest of the breastplate as a shining honor. The only signs you can tell there was a witch in the suit were their gold-rimmed eyes that glowed in the darkness of their helmets.

"Take them to the back of the dungeons," Sir Reid ordered, while nodding at the two soldiers.

"Please, your High—" Amanda pleaded.

"Only the graciousness of Queen Thibodeaux can save you now," Sir Reid said, silencing the three pathetic grinches as they cried out of the tiny store. With just Merrell, Sir Reid, and me in the tiny store, the weight of the day wore me down. I hugged Merrell and apologized. They were shaken, but they understood I had to make an example of them.

As we left the tiny store, my shoulders finally relaxed. Sir Reid walked ahead of me, and I couldn't help but become suspicious of him not complaining about my actions, but I kept my big mouth shut as I stared at the gleaming emeralds that lined the back of his armor. If only the coven knew that those pretty gems were painted to hide that one thing that was associated with our family was the same thing that could drain us of our powers. I could still remember the time my mother and I stayed in her office painting some of the new diamonds for the guards.

Just another secret to keep.

It wasn't until we were almost to the guard door that my silent, menacing companion turned around, placing his hand on my shoulder and steadying me before I tripped backward. Even though I was five ten, he still towered over me. The muscles in my neck ached as I craned to look at him.

"Before we go in, you should hand me the book and canvases in your pocket."

I had one shot to play it cool. Relaxing my face and putting on my best smile.

"I do not know what you're talking about?"

With an eyebrow arched, I waited for his reply. To tell you the truth, between the scorching sun on my back and the blazing stare from Sir Reid, I didn't know what made my heart pound faster. I couldn't phantom the thought of enduring the three brittle witch's situation just to lose my gifts.

Where is the justice in that?

"We can play dumb, or we can stop wasting each of our time, your Highness." He folded his enormous arms. "Either way, your mother will find them and take them away."

"Please, Sir Reid..." I begged, and I'm not above it. Especially for my art equipment. I got on my knees, my white dress be damned, "I've had a bad day, and this will make up for everything."

Sir Reid's blank face stared down at me as I groveled on the floor. In the back of my mind, I knew this would lead nowhere, but I was determined. The gardeners and the guards at the door stared at me as if I undressed and went running through the front lawn...maybe I was going mad, like those witches said.

"Your mother knew you went to Merrell's store. If you were paying attention, you would have seen the magic shield she had put up. You were too busy with your head in the sky! And I had to come fetch you as if you were some petulant child."

My shoulders slumped as I dragged my hand down my face. Of course, I hadn't seen the shield. My mother had way too many tricks up her sleeves for me to count. Biting my lip, I fought the urge to lash out in defiance. What good would that ever do? My frown deepened at the thought. If I ever get the chance to have children of my own, they won't have to conform to their parents' rigid ways, because I would change every prehistoric rule in the coven. Reluctantly, I stood up and reached into my magic pocket to take out the canvases. Sir Reid's hand shot out to capture my prized possessions. He rolled those black abyss eyes and proceeded into the castle.

At least he hadn't taken the book as I stifled my silent winning victory over the brute.

When we walked through the door, my mother and father stood, perched at the door. My mother's beautiful large lips were serried together. My father tsked his disappointment—the irony.

"I know, I know..." I mumbled as I tried to walk past them.

"Kaydian Thibodeaux!" my mom said as I cursed in my head.

Slowly, I turned around to see her waiting outstretched hand. The tiny hope I had all but disappeared as I knew what she wanted, the book.

Youna!

I'd taken my poor goddess's name in vain way too many times, I thought. Digging into my pocket and placing the book in her hand, I groaned. This was worse than being sliced by Sir Reid's knife.

My mother turned the book over in her hand and read the title, "The Transformation of Philipé ...he's attracted the attention of a dashing new suitor..."

"We should have gotten rid of that store and Merrell." My father's deep voice washed over me like a cold sweat.

Wiping the mist off of my top lip, "Father, now that's a bit extreme. Merrell's store is not only beneficial to me, but also to the young witches in town."

My father and my mother stared at me as if I had lost my mind, which I couldn't fault them for. It was my careless neglect that caused me to be in this mess.

There, in the middle of our foyer, I wished I could die. The mist of sweat broke out on my forehead. I couldn't even drag myself to look at my parents or Sir Reid. As if it were second nature, I turned and ran up the steps to my safe haven. Away from the embarrassment, the gossiping witches, and losing the only thing I was looking forward to getting my hands on for weeks.

Chapter 4

Kaydian

"...**I**'ve been waiting for you," I whispered as he kissed the fleshy skin between my neck and my shoulder. That part always made my back arch, causing me to whimper his name—or the name I dedicated to him, Red, since every dream started from this point. With the view of his copper-colored ringlets as they burned a trail down to my dripping core. His face was shrouded in mystery except for the soft, wet trail of kisses and his muscular scarlet-hued arms.

"Red... please," I begged, as the lines between sanity and insanity blurred. The burning sensation that steered itself from my chest pooled in my stomach, making me delirious. His mouth was an inferno as it wrapped around the tightened peak of my nipple while his other cerise hand ran down the soft curvature of my belly. His touch felt like a heated feather as it roamed over the soft brown curls on my mound. One of his fingers found my inundated lips that waited for his touch. Slipping a long finger into me as his tongue abandoned my achy nipple, he dragged it to its neglected twin. I think this is what my curse of glut must be. A long punishment as this man—or whatever he may be, tortured me with his slow, meticulous fingers that dipped inside of me. For what I was being punished for, I hadn't the slightest clue.

I opened my mouth to yell his given nickname, but nothing came out but a pleading cry as he pinched my little tender clit between my nether lips.

YOUNA! I cried out shamefully.

My mind was murky as my auburn-headed lover, Red, placed his fiery face over my plump pussy mound, inhaling my scent. The heat in my lower stomach pooled into my pussy as he continued to tear me apart mercilessly with his thick fingers. My bed was damp underneath my body. There's no hope for these thin white sheets. His face was nose deep in my pussy as he moaned, lapping at my juices from my lips. He sounded needy and almost demonic. The noise hit a nerve in me as I arched for him. If he didn't stop playing with me, I would die right here in my dreams.

I couldn't take it anymore as he rubbed his face against my soaking pussy. Didn't he know I wanted him to play with my pussy, not on top of it. I reached to push him lower, and, like every time since these dreams had started, my hand glided through him. My red-haired mystery man could touch me, but not vice versa. A frustrated moan fell from my lips because I wanted more. But I couldn't, so I pushed myself against him until he got the message.

That wicked mouth of his captured my swollen clit, and I levitated off the bed, planting my feet and lifting my pelvis. I'd gone mad. I thought I heard him calling my name, but that would be a first. He added another finger to my greedy little pussy as he bit and teased the swollen bud. What else could I do but cling to the dampened sheets as I contorted and shuddered? Another free finger that played in my wetness slipped into my forbidden area as he called my name in a panic voice. That was all it took to send me to the edge of the cliff...If he can just keep going, maybe I can...

"WAKE UP, KD!" Del whispered shout. I jolted, waking to Del standing over me. Her small hands were on my shoulder as she held me, shaking me as she tried to turn my brain into an omelet until I woke up.

"I'm up, Del! If you sway me anymore, I'll be comatose."

She gave me a pathetic smile and said, "We're not human, so that's not possible." She wiped her hand off on the dry part of my sheets. "Why are you so wet? Were you having a nightmare?"

I rolled my eyes at her, but before I could tell her to give me a minute, Del threw the sheets off my slick body. My white nightgown was bunched up at my stomach, dampened with sweat, and my fingers were still deep inside my wet cunt. The throbbing, aching feeling had tampered down to a dull thud but never satiated. The luck of the unmated psycho, I guess.

"Oh," Del said. Her blue eyes roamed my body as her gaze dropped to my fingers.

Del had seen me naked countless times before and caught me masturbating, but we never talked about it because she thought it was useless for me to touch myself since I couldn't have an orgasm without my fated mate.

"*Nothing beats the real thing,*" she would say afterward.

How does she know what the "real" thing feels like if she's in the same boat as I am? Del didn't have to spend countless nights wondering how it would feel to have the release my high-strung body needed. I could only thank the goddesses who made sure their descendants couldn't enjoy the highs of sex with just any random witch. Just thinking about it made me roll my eyes.

I quickly pulled the two fingers out of me, fisting the wet hand, and got up from the wet bed. My face was as fiery as the Texas sun was in August. Del stood there. Her eyes glued to my breasts. I'm sure she could see right through the gown. I gathered the sheets from the bed and dumped them into the corner. Del's face was the same color as her ruby dress.

"Are you okay, Del?" I'm not sure what's going on with her.

"I-I'm good." She cleared her throat and turned to my little desk in the corner. "Seems you were good...I guess."

"Yeah, I guess...it sucks to be twenty-five and still mateless. On top of that, my fingers don't even scratch the stupid itch." A sad giggle left my mouth as I imagined every royal had found their mate at thirteen, which was early enough to enjoy their life together before the bonding ceremony.

"Have you ever thought maybe your mate is um..." Del rubbed her hands up and down her thighs, which meant she was going to say something ridiculous. "Maybe they're mermaids."

Del's smile flattered when she saw the appalled look on my face. She knew better than I did that being mated to a mixling or another super-natural was like disowning our coven. In my mind, I knew she meant well. Del never wished ill on me, but the thought of being mated to another supernatural being that wasn't a witch made the hairs on my arms stand. My hand shook while I scratched my wrist.

"Well...I...I mean, it would be better than a wolf!"

I stood rooted to the spot in front of Del. My mouth dangled open as I wondered if my best friend had lost every bit of common sense she had. Being mated to a wolf was almost akin to turning your back on your coven. That would be the last thing I needed. There were whispers and stares that made the hair on my arms stand. Some days when I walked into Tou-sin and wanted to scream at the top of my lungs that I knew I was cursed. But I stayed up all night thinking about my misfortune. My room was hazy, with my magic covering the entire area. Fine sheen lined Del's forehead before she took her hand and wiped the salty sweat away.

"Are you mad? I think you may have transported your brain to one of your pigs on the farm."

Just the thought of that possibility was absurd.

"Well, wouldn't it be better than going demented? Or being alone? I mean, how can you cheat fate?"

"My goddess! Fate be damned. Del, you have said some stupid shit before, but this..." I shook my head and fold my arms across my chest. "I would rather go mad than lie with a dog or a fish!"

"Sorry, I didn't mean to offend you. Honestly, it was the first thing I thought of when I saw you...I just...it would beat masturbating without an orgasm," Del said sheepishly.

I couldn't help but squirm under her watchful eyes.

How embarrassing? How could I explain to my best friend that some figment of my imagination evaded my dreams every Friday night for the past year? I was pathetic. Maybe my parents were right to be worried about me. Maybe my ancestor pissed off the other goddess, and now they seek to take their revenge out on me.

"Quit living in your head," Del said as she gazed at me. Her face was still scarlet as she sat on my now bare bed. The red sleeveless flapper dress showed off her freckled back. Her usual braided hair was out and in a low bun with silver trinkets in her hair.

"Anyway, go get washed up, and let's forget about this conversation. We're going out!"

"No, Del. I can't get into trouble again."

It had been two weeks since my mother confiscated my canvases and my book. Since then, I had been on the straight and narrow. No wondering out. No sneaky side remarks. As I tried to be the best Thibodeaux princess, I could be. I attended meetings, hearing hours and hours of coven squabble about the desire to control more land than they needed and what supernatural being crossed them that week. I drifted in and out of the mundane conversation of the typical royal weekly gathering.

"You won't get caught, KD. Everyone's locked away. I barely had to hide to sneak up here."

"Del…"

"KD, a new movie theater opened up downtown! We *have* to visit."

A new movie theater…in our backyard. I've only read about the Isis theater once in the newspaper, which I snuck in from my last outing into town. It was risky, but worth it.

In the middle of my room, in my damp nightgown, I fought with my conscience. For two weeks, I've been good. So, maybe Youna and the other goddess gave me some leniency. Chewing on my bottom lip as I shuffled from one leg to the next.

Del faced me. "Listen, if anything happens, then you can transport us home."

"My mother would know if I used my magic to teleport us from the city to the castle," I said, as I headed to the bathroom to take a quick shower. Before I closed the door, I told Del to wait while I washed. I made quick work of cleaning up my sweaty body and found myself back in the room with Del fifteen minutes later. My mind warred with the decision to sneak out. I couldn't—I mean, I could, but *should* I was the question.

For a new movie theater…maybe an hour wouldn't hurt, right?

"Let's go," I said, with my mind made up. I'll worry about everything as it comes.

Del jumped up and hugged me. Her smile was infectious as we covered our mouths and squealed. With a flick of my wrist, my magic sprung out and opened the enchanted room only I had access to. As the door creaked open, we dashed into the small room, which acted more like a storage or getaway room for the royals. Pushing the mess of used canvases, and the books scattered around the room, I threw some of the unwanted clothing on the floor as I searched for the dress that mirrored Del's. After a minute of digging through the canvas and my stack of romance novels I stilled needed to read, a light blue flapper dress appeared under the piles of books. Tugging it on, I paired it with a white patent shoe with a welted sole. It was my last white pair of shoes that weren't desecrated with mud. I beckoned my magic to control my coily hair, placing it into a high bun that made my neck sore because of the weight. Maybe my mother was right! I need to cut my hair. Shaking my head as I reentered my room, I put on the necklace and ring that I had grabbed on my way out of the closet. The nagging feeling deep in my chest tried to work itself to the surface.

We're only going to be gone for an hour or two. That's it, no more or less. That's what I promised myself as I grabbed the little white purse on top of the dresser. "I'm ready."

Del turned from the window and smiled. Her round apple cheeks lightened to a slight hue of pink. A vast improvement from earlier on.

"You look beautiful, KD. As usual!"

"We look beautiful." I corrected her. Del was too hard on herself sometimes. "Okay, how are we going to sneak out? Should we use Sera and Luc?"

"No, your mother will surely hear them, especially Sera. She's wider than the Mississippi River!"

Point taken.

"But we have to go through the servants' corridor to get to the escape tunnels. Usually, Ms. Kincaid turns in for the night early on Sundays."

Del's face pinched and twisted. She hated the escape tunnels, but unless we wanted to go the long route, this was the only way.

"Fine," she exhaled.

"Once we're out of the village, then at least we can clean the mess off of our dresses and teleport to the movies."

"Yes, let's go. We're losing time. It's seven thirty!" Del said.

"Okay, let's go," I said, as I stuffed the soiled bedding into the laundry basket.

We took off our shoes to prevent the clacking noise of our heels against the tiles and entered the oddly silent hallway. Maybe Del was right. Maybe we can get away tonight with no one knowing. But I won't celebrate until we've reached the end of the putrid tunnels.

With Del's clammy hand in mine, we hugged against the white wall that leads to the servant's staircase, which is past my parent's wing for a good reason. Stopping every few seconds to shush Del, who kept gasping as we sneaked away. Especially as we approached my parents' hall. Since I was leading our little getaway party, I sped our pace before the white walls curved into the soft tan-colored walls of my parents' hall. My heart thumped chaotically against my chest. The faint green color of my mother's protective shield covered the hall entrance. I tugged Del's hand to come along as I thought the coast was clear to cross the large entryway. Del moved so slowly I had to pull on her skinny arms. We were midway across when one of my parents' doors popped open. My heart logged into my throat as I pushed a wide-eyed Del back to the wall we just vacated. My hand shot out to cover her mouth as she was about to gasp when she almost tripped over her feet.

"She's been on her best behavior lately, but I'm still worried she won't be ready to do what she needs to do..." My mother's soft voice filled the hall.

"She will, Your Majesty." I heard the familiar deep southern honeyed voice of Ms. Kincaid replying to my mother. If you didn't know her voice, you would think she was my grandmother.

So much for her being asleep by now.

When I peeped around the corner, my mother was in another robe. This time in a deep green color like our magic. Ms. Kincaid was still in her work attire. The plain gray house dress was starched and flared at the knee with a white apron tied at the waist with her gray flat shoes. The gray dress stood out against her dark brown skin. Ms. Kincaid's shoulder-length gray and white coily hair was pulled back into a pony-tail today. She stopped aging in her forties, which was a tossup with the coven witches, but she looked younger. Without me seeing her face, I knew her hazel eyes would be attentive and assessing my mother, or anyone else, in her presence. Just like Sir Reid, she was another loyal member of the family who tied their servitude to Youna and her descendants.

She spun around to search the hall entrance. Luckily, I pulled back in the nick of time as I silently thanked the goddess for the plain white walls.

"What is it?" my mother asked.

"...nothing, I guess. Just me being paranoid," Ms. Kincaid replied.

"Oh, there goes my mischievous little queen!" The fresh voice that joined us said.

With my hand over my heart and Del's hand forgotten, I waited until my heart stopped pounding and the soft click of a door locking before I popped my head into the hall to see if the coast was clear.

Clenching my teeth, I whispered. "What's the matter with you, Bernadette? I told you to quit sneaking up on folks."

"Oh, Youna, not now!" Del said under her breath. "Tell her we're on a mission now."

"My! My! My! Del sure is anxious tonight!" Bernadette's thick country accent boomed. Luckily, I was the only one who could see or hear her.

Bernadette, or the annoying mess I nicknamed her, stood on the other side of the hallway with her hands on her hip as her foot tapped away. She tilted her partially severed skull as she tsked. It was almost as if she had enough of my foolishness. The tattered "white" apron she was murdered in had turned red as the blood moon. Her fingers, which used to be the "best" in the village, were chopped to the last joint, leaving behind short stubs. Luckily, her murderer didn't hack off her thin legs as well. That would have been too much of a blessing for me.

She was the last person I wanted to see now. Not that she could utter a word to anyone... besides my mother. This was the ugly side of being the only family with necromancy abilities. One of my great-grandmothers had long since instilled in us to just use our magic to block the wayward ghosts away, since sending them to the underworld would leave us weak and vulnerable for long periods of time. After a while, they stopped begging for our help, muttering we were useless hags. Bernadette pops up from time to time, invading my privacy and my space. When I first met the crazy ghost, she had found her missing fingers and dropped them in front of me. She pleaded for me to kill the wife of her lover who she was allowing to pass her a bit more than flour in the pantry. When the wife found out and made her suffer, forgoing the sharp butcher knives for a dull old bread knife. The wife took her hostage in the tunnels beneath the castle and took her time hacking at her body, one ligament at a time, until she was found dead. Sir Reid mentioned if he hadn't known better, he would have sworn the wife was going to eat her.

I think the wife had kept her partially hacked skull as a souvenir because they never found it.

"Bye, Bernadette!" I whispered, shooing her away until she faded into the castle's wall, but not before she muttered, "Foolish girl."

"Do I even want to know?" Del asked.

Shaking my head as I took hold of her hand, I told her to be quiet as we ran across the hallway and down the old cement stairs, blackened by all the usage over the years. When we reached the bottom of the stairs, all the doors were shut. It was smooth sailing down the long hallway and past the castle guard, who always had something smart to say to me. The sound of his soft snores echoed off the walls. I made a mental note to keep this information in the back of my mind for the right time. When we reached the dark metal door that led to the tunnel, I held the latch in my hand and gently lifted the heavy bronze bar. Pushing slowly, the door creaked and groaned. Del looked at the lone guard in the hall.

"He's still knocked out. Shoes, KD." She pointed out before I stepped out onto the brick pavement.

Thank Goddess, she remembered. I would hate to think what I would have stepped on in these tunnels. The rank smell hit us hard, leaving us both gagging and choking. It smelled like something died down here recently—make that several things.

"Let's just run for it. I don't see anyone at the end of the tunnel."

Del nodded her crimson head. *Poor Del.*

Chapter 5

Kaydian

With her hand in mine, we took off running. Our shoes clacked against the brick floors. The escape tunnels, or what I called the death tunnels, were built when my fifth great-grandparents made the east side of Houston our home. There were two of them in total. The one we traveled through now led to the Humble, Texas area. The other led out to Bear Lake River and to the countryside of Texas.

There was a thicket of bushes and trees that protected our village and kept us hidden on both sides. It wasn't until my fourth great-grandparents that they added Manchineel trees, wild parsnip, and Japanese spirea from around the world to prevent some of the intrusive humans from wandering into the village. You would think humans had enough common sense to stay away, but we once watched a couple of humans lost in the area rub against the manchineel tree and the wild parsnip. They died that day in the wood area. Their skin turned bloody red while they scratched at themselves until they peeled away their epidermis. The earth greedily accepted the offering of their nourishment. Del, the castle guards, and I stood there and watched them wither away in three day's time. We took bets on how long they would last, and the castle guard won. I had to give him a pint of my father's special witch's brew, and Del helped me—well, I had to use my magic to send what little of their remains were left back to their home. Bits and pieces of their skin remained until the earth took that as well. And even to this day, I can smell a hint of that metallic scent when we enter the area.

Finally, we made it to the small grassy area before the small river that led to the San Jacinto River. On the other side is the human trap forest.

"Del," I whisper shout. Del was about to edge out of the dark tunnel. Instinctively, I grabbed her arm and pulled her back. She opened her mouth, but my free hand snapped it, silencing her.

Del was never aware of her surroundings, and she was even clumsier than I. Luckily, we fit each other as I looked out for her. If I didn't, the guard—a golden guard at that would have caught her. To the coven witch, you wouldn't be able to hear their light footsteps, but I knew the soft crunching sound that blended in with the wind rustling the scattered leaves was a guard patrolling. I waited until the last soft step seemed muffled by my heightened hearing. My head stuck out the tunnel to see not one but three golden army soldiers circling the castle. If we didn't move now, we would have to wait because the next set of guards was due to walk this way in two minutes.

I yanked Del forcefully. A slight oomph left her lanky body as we ran to the river, and I thanked the goddesses it hadn't rained today, so the ground was dry except by the riverbank.

"Hurry, Del, take your shoes off, and let's cross."

With our shoes off, we hopped along the familiar stones, left and right, onto the dull brown and gray riverbed rocks. Their flat edges stuck out of the water. It was a path we remembered as we used to race to the other side. When my foot touched the weeds on the other side of the river, I almost cried. Now we needed to cross over my mother's shield, and then the hard part would be done.

Unlike humans, the shrubs and plants didn't affect witches, so we could easily move and re-fix the plants to cover our footsteps. Del and I maneuvered the half acre pathway to the shield with ease until we reached the dimmed red barrier of my mother's blood shield that only I could see. Unlike the magic shield she placed around the bookstore, this one was more for safety than anything else. It took our blood and protected the owner and everyone inside of it by keeping out anyone who would mean us any harm or kept them from seeing inside the village. The humans could cross the barrier, but they would be met with a long and agonizing death when they get into the forest.

After we crossed the blood shield, I almost dropped onto the grassy dirt. We made it without getting caught or having to put a guard to sleep. We did it! Our eyes connected, and Del's grin spread across her face.

"See? Easy peasy." She nodded.

"Okay, maybe you were right. The goddess is showing me mercy for once."

"Oh, hush." Del waved her hand at me.

Snorting, I grabbed her wrist a bit more securely than last time. I hated teleporting with anyone not royal. They always become sick. The very first time Del and I teleported, she upchucked her lunch onto my black dress. It was the only time I've ever cursed at Del. Some days, I can still see the atrocious yellow marks on any of my black dresses with the chunks of ham and mashed potatoes.

My mouth twisted into a frown as I threw her a sullen look. Before she could complain, my magic slipped from my fingers as it curled around my body. The green warmth of my magic slipped away from me, and Del shivered against my frame as my magic embraced her body. Del's small blonde hairs raised as her skin grew goosebumps the moment my hand touched hers.

The brown, green, and pitch black night blended as one, as the picture of the countryside of Houston twisted before our very own eyes. My stomach twisted in knots as my magic pulled and stretched, cutting a thin slit of white light into the dark night. My arm shot out, shielding my eyes as together we stepped into the slit of light and into the dark back alleyway of the Majestic Theater. Fixing my bun that got ruined in the portal, I watched poor Del with her hands on the red brick building, heaving as the remainder of her dinner hit the ground. The pungent smell of acid and bile perfumed the air.

Magic is personal and doesn't like to be shared. It leaves the other individual in a state of frigid cold and can kill the person who's been left in its presence for too long. Like my father's cousin, Layla, who was frozen after one of the goddess descendants developed an unnatural obsession with her. The royal shackled her to the bed and wouldn't let Layla go. Her captor would use their magic to keep Layla alive. I forgot the young royal's name, but she was beautiful and mateless, and decided she was going to keep Layla. It was a horrible story. My father was the one to find the royal lying in what was Layla's frozen, shattered remains. He never mentioned what happened next, but said the royal was kicked out of the coven.

Poor Layla. I thought as I worked in tandem with my magic to soothe Del's back. Hopefully, it won't be as bad when we return home.

"Are you okay, Del? Or do we need to go back home?"

Del straightened her lanky body as she tried not to hold her stomach. Her eyes shut out the world as she took several deep breaths through her nose. I offered her the lone mint in my bag. She thanked me and threw the white candy into her mouth.

After a minute, she opened those pretty robins at me, "No, we're not going back home. Not after I threw up my dinner. Let's go!"

Holding both of my arms up in surrender, I followed her. I am not one to complain, but if Del passed out, I would be beside myself. We wouldn't be able to use magic because we're surrounded by humans. I would have to drag her away, and I knew that would cause trouble I couldn't afford to get into.

"Del, I think I need to use a transformation spell tonight."

"What? Why?"

"You remember we're going to be amongst humans? You and I are not equal in their world. I wouldn't be able to sit with you without causing an uproar, and I would hate to have to kill every single person in Houston out of rage."

Del's eyes widened as she nodded, and her pale skin turned a pinkish hue. An "Oh, yes. You're right. Stupid humans." Left her plush red lips.

Commanding my magic to change to fit in again for the second time this month irked my soul. My magic trembled inside my chest as it fed off the anger. The little sweat that formed on my top lip had nothing to do with the Houston stifling summer night heat. When the slight pinching sensation was over, I turned to Del.

Del's lips thinned out, and she shook her head.

"I hate this." She chewed her bottom lip. "Maybe we should just do something else?"

"No, I already changed my appearance. It can't be that bad. Why waste my magic?" I said with a bit of an edge in my voice to keep the bile that threatened to spill out of my mouth at bay.

Pulling out the small mirror from my bag, I nearly blanched. The image that stared back at me was disheartening. Skin as pale as Del's, with a ruby tint to my newly thin lips and sunken cheeks. My black hair turned the color of rust, which made the light green eyes stand out. The once twinge of excitement was stomped out. This felt wrong in every shape, way, and form. Closing my eyes, I waited until the spark of my magic died down. It took a while before I was able to process the change. It's only for an hour or two, but it felt like a slap to my Youna's face for changing the features she had passed down to me.

I grabbed her small wrist, and we raced through the alleyway to the front of the theater. Yes, I forgot about how life outside the village could be. That was my fault. Nothing I could do would change the ugly hearts of people.

Skidding to a stop when we rounded the corner, both Del and I stood with our mouths hanging open.

Del's voice seemed far away as she muttered, "Wow, it's beautiful."

Beautiful indeed. The front of the building was painted white to stick out against the boring red brick buildings surrounding it. Two small windows held workers on either side of the building where people lined up to get inside of the theater. Shoving Del, I pointed to the massive, blinding white marquee, stating the last show of the night would start in ten minutes. If we didn't hall ourselves inside now, we would miss the show.

When we managed to unglue ourselves from our spot, we hurried to buy our tickets. Inside, the lobby was teeming with people. Everyone had small white bags filled with popcorn. The buttery scent wafted through the lobby. Del had returned with our own bags before we hurried into the medium-sized auditorium. The section where we were seated had red plush seats with gold trim on them, matching the walls and the floors. From our seats, we had a clear view of the full stage, which was twice the size of the small Isis theater across town. The space was divided into two different sections. The floor seats were for people who looked like Del, and the balcony section was for people who looked like me. My gaze traveled to the balcony section to see a handful of beautiful black couples and families. Warmth spread through my face as I realized I would've been focused on sitting apart from Del because of the humans' hateful views. My magic flickered slightly before I caught myself slipping.

"Are you okay? You're almost as red as my dress. We should leave. This isn't fun anymore, KD," Del said, her eyes filled with worry.

My sweet Del was nothing but a kind-hearted individual. Sometimes, I couldn't believe my luck that the goddess gifted me with her.

I placed my hand over hers and squeezed it with a small smile on my face to comfort her. "I'm warm here," I said, but knowing Del, like the freckles on the back of my hands, she wouldn't stop worrying until she knew I was truly okay.

A humph from behind us made our heads swivel around as I let go of Del's hand. A plump man with a balding hairline frowned as he looked toward the balcony.

The slender young woman who accompanied him turned her long, pointy nose at us as he placed his stubby, small hand in her lap. "Disgusting. I can't believe they're allowed here." The woman scoffed.

A match made in heaven. They were both ugly on the inside and out. It took all of my willpower not to turn them into a pile of shit.

"Let's just watch the performance and go home," I said through my foreign lips.

Pathetic Bastards

After two minutes, the lights dimmed, and the play commenced. Ten minutes into the play, I forgot about the turmoil that had brewed inside of me and got lost in the performance. The play was about a man who tried to save a woman from some evil villain. It wasn't a romantic play like I would have wanted, but I enjoyed it. Del and I laughed until tears sprung from our eyes, rolling down our dresses. We had to wipe our faces with the spare tissue I found in my purse.

The lights flooding the dim theater brought me back to reality and reminded me of the repugnant couple behind us.

"Thank God it's over," the woman behind us said. "We should speak to the owners, Frank. He shouldn't sully the theater already by entertaining...everyone."

How would it be if we sliced them up, young princess? We could hang their innards from the ceiling! YES.

No, No, No. I repeated as my hands found the metal edge of the chair. My mind was foggy with the voice's desire. I tried to take deeper breaths to control the grisly voice, but my body shook worse than the floor of the theater as people left.

"Darling, you're right. I could only imagine if the owners knew I was the mayor's advisor. They might think twice about who they allow to patronize their business," the man said.

Let us out to play, Princess.

"Are you okay? You're sweating bullets," Del said from beside me. Worry was thick in the air in our little area as everyone gathered their things.

I don't claim to be a good person. Quite the contrary, I walk a thin line between good and madness. And tonight, the madness won the fight when a sheath of darkness washed over my trembling body. As I turned to the plump man and his hawk nose date, I threw them a wide, unfamiliar smile, one that would make me look as angelic as the angels the humans worship. Waving at the couple, my magic seeped out, and I watched as it did, entering their noses and into their body. Too bad Del couldn't see it until they started to choke and gasp as I curled my fingers into my palms, tightening my magic hold on their trachea.

Yes, Yes, YES! Make them suffer.

"Someone help them! They're going to die..." I heard other patrons cry out.

The atrocious couple blended in with the blood-red seats of the theater. Their stubby and skinny hands clawed at their necks as if that would give them relief. Bright scarlet lines marked their pale skins like hives. It reminded me of some of my paintings, jagged and cruel but beautiful all the same. **More! More!** The voice rang out from deep inside of me.

The audience attempted to revive the couple on the theater floor. I fought an inside battle to keep the giggle lodged in my throat from bursting out, but failed as it came out, and everyone turned their head toward me. Del noticed my balled-up fist, which kept my magic tight around their windpipe. She placed her small hands over mine in an attempt to save the couple, but I couldn't stop.

"Kaydian, that's enough. I think they learned their lesson," Del whispered in my ear.

Their clawed hand movements became impeded as the faintly blue-lipped couple was on the verge of going into the underworld. The theater's employees and the audience's muffled cries ricocheted off the blood-red walls. Del pinched my side, and the world came crashing into me as I landed on earth. Luckily for them, Del gave the offending couple a second chance at their pathetic life. As soon as my magic dropped, the couple fought for air and cried on the dirty floor. I watched their skin rescind to its original color.

Only when Del touched my arm and said, "Let's go." I turned to her and nodded.

Ten minutes later, with a smirk plastered on my face, we stepped out of the theater and into the dark alleyway. I was walking toward the back when I noticed Del stopped. She stood there in the dark. The sequins on her dress stood out like Lucifer's scales.

"Come on, Del. Time to go home. I think we had enough fun for the week," I said.

"Are we going to skip over what just happened in the theater?" Del asked. It was then I noticed the deep frown painted on her face. "You know I hate the sight of blood or…. killing."

Opening my mouth, my initial thought was to tell her the truth. A moment of weakness sent me spiraling into the darkness. "I'm sorry, Del. It was a mistake. I let my guard down for a second too long and…" I stopped mid-sentence, fidgeting with the end of my dress.

"It happened then." Del paused. "It's becoming more frequent… maybe we should tell your mother at least."

Holding my hands up, I say, "Absolutely not. She has enough on her plate. No need to worry about something that can't be fixed." Del opened her mouth but closed it as I continued, "Let's get home. Nothing good will come for us fighting."

Silence fell between us in the dingy alley as I waited for her response. I knew Del like the back of my hand. Shifting to her feet, Del looked down at the floor.

"Del…" I said sternly.

"Can we do one more thing?" She had her hands behind her back.

"Lemon Johnson, the jazz player, is playing at a club in Frenchtown. Thirty minutes. That's all I'm asking for, and then we can go."

I rolled my shoulders and sighed. Del always had some type of trick up her sleeves, like my mother. It was already nine-thirty, and I didn't want to push my luck. However, as I stood there watching, Del folded her hands together with her mouth in a ridiculous pout, pleading and begging.

"I brought some of the Fae wine we couldn't finish from the last coven meeting," Del said, pulling out the small flask filled with the purple Fae wine. "Please," she cried as she jingled the tempting juice in front of me.

And I folded. I mean, who could turn down free Fae wine?

Lemon Jefferson was playing in the Fifth Ward of Houston, an area I've only ventured into once when I was younger. Before we step through the portal, I undid the transformation spell eagerly. Poor Del almost had whiplash on how fast I changed back, but she had said nothing except, "Thank Youna! I missed you." And I shared that sentiment.

When we stepped through the portal, we ended up on a dead-end street. Little brown and white brick homes lined both sides. The one streetlight on the block flickered and dimmed, casting the homes in a dark shadow. All except for one home at the corner of the neighborhood.

"I think that's the home," Del said after wiping her mouth with the back of her hand.

"Del, I thought you said it was a club?"

"Beggars can't be choosers," she said eagerly, causing me to roll my eyes.

Disrespectful common witch! The voice said. Squeezing my eyes shut, I counted to four until I felt the darkness recede. "Let's go then and make the best of it then."

The brown "club" appeared to be the size of Merrell's magical corner, as we stood on the front porch of the home. A small white paper was stuck on the door. "Lemon Jefferson playing tonight," it read. I wasn't sure about Del, but I was nervous. When we opened the door, a thick cloud of smoke greeted us. If we were humans, we would've coughed up a lung. My eyes squinted against the fog and made do with the only light in the medium-sized home that barely lit the center. Mr. Johnson was on a small stage in the back of the home, and several wooden tables with chairs lined the walls. People dancing in the cramped space by the door stopped when they saw us. All eyes gawked at Del, and she flushed ruby red under their observation. But as usual, we ignored it and pushed our way into the dark room of sweaty folks. I spotted an empty table by a door, tugging on Del's arm. We made our way to claim the old, rickety table and seats. When we dumped our belongings onto the chair, two human men spotted us from their table and came to us. *Already?* If there was one thing I hated more than anything, it's humans.

"Hello, ladies, what brings you to the Hole?" The taller man of the duo said. "My name is Malcolm, and my friend here is Yves. We've never seen y'all here."

He was beautiful for a human. He leaned so close I could smell the brown liquor on his breath that mingled with his sweat. His tawny skin glowed against his white dress shirt. Malcom's glasses took nothing away from his light brown eyes as he watched us over the rim. His hair was slicked back in waves. The light brown slacks fit snugly against his solid frame, and black dress shoes finished his look for the night. He was an inch or two shorter than me, but I guess that's the norm for humans.

"We traveled here from across town to check out Lemon Jefferson. We wouldn't miss it for the world," I said as Del's hand flew up to her mouth, hiding her giggle.

Nosy bastard.

"Sorry, my best friend isn't in a great mood tonight," Del said as I threw her a pinched look. "My name is Delphine, Del for short. And Kaydian, KD for short."

There wasn't a lot that made us mad when it came to Del, but right now, I wish I could magically sew her mouth shut.

"Kaydian, that's a beautiful name," Yves said, smiling.

Not to sound vain, but Yves was plain for a human. He wore a tweed white suit that stayed buttoned over a white dress shirt, even though you could see the sweat stains seeping from his suit. He was petite, standing next to Del, and he appeared mini next to me. Yves's bald, so you could see the sweat collected on his shiny head. His brown mustache was saturated and stuck to his lip.

Yves continued, "Ladies, let's get some drinks and hit the dance floor."

I would rather have Sera's dinner than go anywhere with Malcom and Yves. Malcom had a glint in his eyes that made the hair on my arm stand. Even without knowing him, I knew he was full of himself.

"No, thank you, Yves, but you guys have a good time," I responded.

"Come on, KD," Del said as she grabbed my hand, begging me with her enormous eyes. "Let's go dance!"

"Don't be a party pooper, KD. Let's go!" Malcolm pleaded with his hand open for me to take.

Biting my cheek, I shook my head at his outreached hand. His charming smile turned downward as he took back his hand.

"Seriously, KD. This is a once-in-a-lifetime show. Let's not waste it," Del said over the music. My heart raced to the beat of the drums from the stage as I shook my head. I felt down for refusing, but I would rather not make a fool of myself. Del tried three more times to get me to budge, yet I was nothing but stubborn. With a huff and a couple of swigs of Fae wine, she ambles off onto the crowded dance floor with Malcolm and Yves.

What was supposed to be a thirty-minute stop, has now turned into almost two hours. I hate to admit it, but dancing outside of the choreographed dance routine taught in the palace wasn't my forte. However, I enjoyed the upbeat music. Sweat, beer, and Lemon's baritone voice permeated the tiny room. The thickened air in the home filled with an electric energy that kept everyone moving. Lemon Jefferson had everyone up and dancing erratically, except for me. Firmly planted, I stuck to swaying in my seat, enjoying the music while watching Del, Malcolm, and Yves dancing until they called it quits, returning to the table with drinks in their hands.

To say I was uncomfortable was putting it lightly as I shifted in my seat, and everyone around the table noticed. *Just perfect.*

"What's eatin' ya?" Malcom asked as he took sips of the dark brown liquor in his cup.

"Nothing. It's just really late, and we should get going, Del," I said, but I might as well have been speaking to the air.

Del was so far up Yves's body that they could have been classified as Siamese twins. Her skin was flushed pink since she guzzled the fae wine until there was nothing left.

"Come on, KD. Don't be like that. Aren't you having a good time?" Malcom wondered. His hand found my thigh and gave it a slight squeeze. "Maybe we can get out of here and get to know each other properly."

Stupid foolish imbecile!

Staring at the foreign hand on my thigh, my mind wandered. I could take a lot of things, but someone, a human no less, invading my space, caused a slow death. **Yes, burn him from the inside out!** Maybe my dark doppelganger had a good idea for once. Before I could think about my actions, I grabbed the back of his intrusive hand. My magic, which boiled under my skin, set out to heat the piece of wasteful flesh attached to its owner. Malcolm's teeth grind, and he hissed as his soft, unmarred skin turned a bright shade of red that reminded me of the ruby band sign above the stage. Yellow boils formed all over his hand, and it took all my strength not to pop them. **More! Kill him.** My hidden voice screamed, and I didn't disappoint. Red open wounds formed once my magic overheated the boils that stretched with fluids and popped. Blood dripped from his hand and mixed with the clear fluids. I couldn't help but admire the color mixing.

The gall of him to touch us. Stupid human!

Exactly! ME! Kaydian Thibodeaux, future queen of the fucking North American Coven.

The fresh scent of metallic copper drifted through the stale air. It made the corners of my mouth pull into a smile, especially when the droplets of blood splattered on the wooden table and floor. One by one, I watched as it fell like snow. It was a beautiful thing to witness.

Malcolm jumped from his seat. His thick thighs hit the old, rickety wooden table, sending our drinks crashing onto Del and Yves. His injured hand flared in the air as he howled over the background music, drawing everyone's attention. Mr. Jefferson and his band stopped the music to watch the drama unfold. I would be a fool to say their watchful eyes didn't make my insides quiver. It wasn't typical for me to show out in the human world. Much less a crowded club.

"You evil witch!" Malcolm screamed while holding his bloody hand. "You did this to me!"

Now is my time to shine. I willed my magic to make tears flow from my eyes as I clutched my chest.

"Why little ol' me? How could I do such a thing?" I said as I summoned my best Creole accent, like my mother. "Maybe the god that you love so much caused you to be caught red-handed...literally."

The dancers and band looked on as whispering broke amongst themselves. Malcolm seemed ready to pounce on me, but I didn't give him a second chance.

"Del!" I yelled. The tone of my voice could cut steel.

When she acknowledged me, her eyes widened, surprise etched into them. Her face flushed. I don't care if humans were the last living beings on the planet. I would never entertain or let them touch me like Malcolm did.

"Sorry, your Highness." She stumbled out. Her face was flushed. Since she had finished the Fae wine from earlier, she had been sipping on the weak human drink Yves bought for her from the bar.

The nerve of these humans!

I was about to forsake my parents' rules of no magic in front of these useless bastards when Del mentioned she had to use the bathroom. She was on the verge of having a panic attack from her slip-up. I wanted nothing more than to shake her for calling me that in public.

My magic was at the edge of my fingers, waiting to be let out again to peel the skin off every human in this tiny home.

"So, you think you're a queen, huh?" Yves asked. He had a sarcastic smirk that didn't quite reach his eyes.

"No, I'm not. Del, it's time to go," I said, grabbing her things.

"Wait, Queen KD," Malcom sneered. His injured hand was wrapped in the sleeve of his shirt. "If I catch you in these parts again, I'll make you pay, you fucking whore."

Del looked on the verge of crying. My best friend was not made for confrontations.

"Kaydian will be the greatest queen to live. You asshole," she said as the old Fae wine dwindled into her system. Of course, it sounded more like "you ash'ole" with her heavy, drunken tongue—strike number two. Del meant well, but I'm beyond pissed to see reason.

"We're leaving, Del!" I bellowed forcibly.

"O-Oh, KD. Let me get my things." She hiccuped as she gathered her things, leaving me to eavesdrop.

Malcolm and Yves had slithered away like the snakes they were. Malcolm cursed as they disappeared into the door behind us. While Del gathered her things, I leaned my head toward the bathroom and homed in on their pathetic little voices, using my heightened hearing.

"That bitch did this, Yves. I'm telling you, she did!" Malcolm yelled as the screeching sound of the faucet turned on. The soft slosh of the water hitting the sink muffled the noise a bit.

"I don't know, man. She is just a girl. How could she do that?" Yves questioned. "They're weird girls from out of town, by the way, your girl talked. Didn't you find it weird she called her 'your highness'?"

"Princess! That bitch," Malcom muttered.

They both fell silent as the noise of something ripping filled my ears. Rage was like consumption. The more you sat in it, the more it ate away at you. As I sat here wanting to barge into that bathroom and cut Malcolm's throat open, I wondered if it would drip slowly. If I cut a thin line in his throat, I wondered if it would turn into a torrential storm. Would his blood spurt over the table and chairs as the tiny, coiled muscles fought to burst out of the opening?

Would I get into trouble if I did? The laughter from the two imbeciles dragged me out of my murderous thoughts.

I've had enough, and if we didn't leave now, I wouldn't only be wanted by the human world, but the coven would have my neck. That would surely give the town's witches enough gossip for the next hundred years.

As if I didn't have my own fill of disappointment from my people.

No, of course, the goddess had to stick it to me by allowing the humans to defile me. I'm truly sick of it all. I didn't waste any time as I jumped from the wooden stool, dragging Del by the wrist as she stumbled over her feet to catch up. My anger built with each step as we entered the dark, dead-end street next to the home.

"I think I'm going to be sick," Del said as she hunched over.

But I didn't care at the moment.

"Well, swallow it. You're going to puke once we get back, anyway."

I reached out for her and grabbed her upper arm as the emerald aurora poured out angrily, like my mood. Del jumped when it covered her, but I ignored her as I pulled us through the slit and to the same spot we left.

As soon as our feet hit the thick grass, I turned her away from me as she threw up the old Fae wine. Stroking her back, I held her hair in my hands to prevent her from vomiting in her hair. Her small head popped up after a minute.

"Gosh! I'll never get used to that." She wiped her mouth off with the back of the bottom of her dress. She looked at me and saw the scowl on my face. "KD, what's the matter? You look ready to kill me?"

"It doesn't matter now, does it?" I asked.

I knew I was being irrational, but I had no one else to release my misplaced anger. This night was ruined by not only the infuriating humans, but by my inability to reign in my dark curse.

"Woah! Kaydian, let's talk about it?"

"There's nothing to talk about, Del. Let's just go home and get to bed before we get caught."

I turned to leave, but Del grabbed me by my upper arm.

"I'm sorry. I wish I saw it coming. Listen, KD, I'm a failure at every-thing, but I don't want us to leave mad at each other."

"If you weren't drinking and didn't drag me to that stupid house. I wouldn't have burned that human." The words left a bitter taste in my mouth.

"I did my best to stick up for you. I can't control those dimwits. This is my fault, I guess. I'm always the screw-up," she declared.

She was right, but my pride made me not care. I kept walking, not even checking to see if she was behind me. My mood and magic swirled inside of me like an impending tornado. I wanted to teleport to the party and cut their dicks off and shove it down their throats.

Maybe I didn't have two years like those damn witches thought.

Chapter 6
Kaydian

Turbulent thoughts had meddled my brain, obscuring my surroundings. Tree branches snapped under my short heels as leaves hitched a ride to their next destination. As my heavy eyelids threatened to put an end to my angry pursuit, I remained on my path. My shoes stomped through the plush green forest behind the castle to bring me to my other safe space. The east side of the castle forest is rarely visited. My mother, Ms. Kincaid, and Sir Reid were the only brave witches to visit this side of the castle.

The side facing my wing was left untouched since Sera and Luc decided this would be their new home. Grass and weeds that were as tall as me because the gardeners stopped servicing the area when Seraphina froze the last gardener to enter the dragon's wood. The name stuck with me, and I declared it—my mother allowed it to be renamed. Carefully, I moved the tall grass aside as I continued deeper into the area. My focus was not stepping onto Sera or Luc's colossal size shit, which happened once, but it's something I rather not talk or think about.

Stepping out of the tall grass, past the overgrown trees, was a clearing. That's where the feeding shed I built with my magic for my babies was stored. The tiny brown building was just big enough to hold whatever animal I found dead in the forest for them to eat or for any prisoners my mother may have sentenced to death. I think Sera loves the days she gets to eat a prisoner. The last prisoner here was a witch who mistreated his wife. My mother allowed me to bring Sera to the coliseum so everyone could watch her devour him. Sera, usually the worst of the duo, holds a special place in my mother's heart. She likens Sera to herself sometimes, controlling and loving at the same time. No truer words were spoken.

"Kaydian!" Del shouted as I opened the tiny shed.

The scent of rotten flesh hit my face the moment the door swung open. My eyes watered as I gagged for fresh air. Backing up from the wooden door, I doubled over, wheezing as the clean air filled my lungs. I guess this was payback for the theater incident.

"Are you alright?" Del asked as she reached the shed. Like the other coven, Del only comes here when I'm present.

When the dead carcass smell subsided, I turned to Del. The smell from the cabin caused her mouth to pinch.

"Something smells like death in there!" She fanned her face as she took a step away from the cabin. "I'll clean it up for you."

Del waved her hand, and within an instant, the putrid smell was gone. My face heated. She shouldn't have to clean up my mess. Especially since the coven witches' magic was only strong enough to complete simple tasks around the town like cooking, cleaning, and other useful coven tasks. And although our magic isn't endless, the coven members had to ration their magic more.

"Thank you, Del..." My shoulders slacked.

Del's hand reached out to fix some of the loose hair that escaped my bun. "I'm sorry, truthfully. I ruined everything. When all I wanted was for us to have a good time."

"Del," I exhaled loudly and grabbed her hand. "No, I'm sorry. I was acting like a brat, and it wasn't your fault. I should have demanded we go home, but I didn't."

"Friends." She held out her hand, and I grasped it.

"Best friends to the underworld." I pinched her cheek as we reenacted our old saying. I loved Del, and I couldn't stay mad at the one person who understood me in this coven.

When I pulled away, I saw Del's eyes triple in size. If I hadn't known better, I would have said she's seen a ghost. Del, hell everyone, was afraid of Sera and Luc, but I promised her since day one that they wouldn't hurt her unless she hurt me.

"K—K—" she stumbled out.

"Del...being afraid of—" I said. I turned around to see what made her stop in her tracks.

I could handle Sera and Luc if they saw Del as a threat and aimed to defend me. That was an easy fix. They were obedient to me and would never go against me. But before I came to the little feeding cabin, I saw Sera and Luc asleep amongst the overgrown Elms trees.

Unfortunately, my life wasn't simple or fair.

Ms. Kincaid stood next to the old trees and on the path to the feeding shed. She had on her mud boots and a black trench coat, and her hair was in her brown silk bonnet. She held the one flashlight my father approved, deeming it the only useful thing the humans created.

Ms. Kincaid's eyes shined in the artificial light as they slowly swept over Del and me. Her two plush lips formed a thin line with her free hand on her hip. She tsked like she caught two kids misbehaving out in the woods.

"Did you ladies get dressed up at midnight just to come out here to feed Sera and Luc?" she asked, even though she knew the truth. There was a glint in her knowing eyes that I despised.

"I—" the lie perched on the tip of my tongue. But Ms. Kincaid had other plans.

"Imagine my surprise when I headed down to get something to drink in the kitchen and saw the princess plowing through the woods like she was one of her dragons." She folded her arms. "Then to see her innocent best friend running and yelling behind her."

Del's eyes were rimmed red, as she knew being caught would get her and her family punished by my parents. They would ensure her family's work doubled, which is almost next to impossible since it isn't the hog's mating season yet.

I had to decide between punishing Del and her family or taking the blame. My mind battled with the decision after my terrible night out. It just seemed my luck kept slipping between my fingers.

Shit.

"It wasn't Del's idea, it was mine." I paused as Ms. Kincaid's keen gaze landed on me. "I went to the Pourciau farm and convinced her to go to this new theater in town."

Ms. Kincaid's eyes made a hole in the middle of my face. One of her silver eyebrows arched as if she knew I was lying, which technically I was. She shook her head as she dragged out that awful tsking noise. Ms. Kincaid knew I hated it, and whenever I did something not "Royal" like, as she would call it, and used that sound.

"Say your goodnights, ladies. Delphine, make sure you get home safely. Tell your parents hello and kiss your little brother for me."

Del's red-rimmed eyes swiveled between Ms. Kincaid and me as she was deciding if it was okay to leave me with her. I gave her a quick nod.

"Ms. Kincaid, can I just have a quick word with Del?" I asked.

Ms. Kincaid's eyes narrowed as she thought about my question. The wheels spinning in her head of all the possibilities that could occur. What could I actually come up with—Oh, the perfect solution to this problem. If I could just remember that stupid incantation.

"I'll attend another one of your etiquette classes." Wincing as I made the statement, I realized it was not my best trade-off, but I could live with it.

"Fine. One minute, and you will do two days," Ms. Kincaid said. Biting my tongue, I nod.

You would think she was my mother as she bargained with me.

Ms. Kincaid turned to walk to the small path. Her boots raked in the dirt as she did. I hauled Del a little further than necessary to avoid her overhearing. She didn't have enhanced hearing because she wasn't a royal, but that didn't stop the glare she leveled at us from her makeshift post.

Turning my back to Ms. Kincaid. I hurried quickly and said, "Listen, I will fix this mess, Del. Do you remember the 'forgotten incantation' I told you about? One that can erase a part of someone's memory?"

"Yeah." Del furrowed her eyebrows at me. "Kaydian…"

"I know, I know. Not the right time for my tricks."

"That's dangerous…let me just take the punishment. My family will—"

"No, trust me, Del. I've got this. Ms. Kincaid won't be a problem for us…well, for tonight at least," I said with a yawn.

"I hope you're sure, Kaydian. You look ready to fall asleep right here."

"What?" I asked as I held up my hand. The green aura from my magic flickered a couple of times before it pushed, twisted, and pulled in my hand, forming a white light that floated in the middle of my palm. Holding up the small magic mirror, I choked. It was way past my bedtime. The whites of my eyes were the color of the fall leaves. The dark ring forming under my eyes looked big enough to carry Luc and Sera in.

"I'm not tired..." Another brief yawn slipped through before I could finish my sentence. "I promise I won't fall asleep until I get to that spell."

"Kaydian, I think everything that happened tonight has finally caught up to you."

"Your time's up, young princess," Ms. Kincaid called out. "Wrap it up! You're going to have a brief rest today."

A groan fell from my lips, and Ms. Kincaid tsked again and shook her head. I hugged Del, and we made our way through the small pathway. With each step, a muffled yawn escaped from me. Once we reached the east side of the castle, Del glared at her shoes as she disappeared into the darkness of the night. She won't feel good until she knows I'm okay, which I will be...I hope.

"Let's go, princess," Ms. Kincaid said as I frowned into her back. "I can do without the daggers being lodged at my back as well .... or the eye roll," she commented as I did just that.

She's been here too long. We used the side door by the kitchen to enter the castle. Thankfully, everyone was still locked behind their doors when we walked along the darkened white hallway. We marched in silence, but I swore I could hear the conversation she'd have with my mother play out in her head. If Mother finds out, I'm dead...maybe literally, as I followed her upstairs.

Ms. Kincaid is the only other person who slept upstairs in the room across my parents' wing. She said it was to tend to my mother faster, but I swear it was to keep an eye on me. Not that it benefited her...or me, if we're being honest.

I slipped past her, quickening my pace to get to my room. Passing her brown door, I kept walking to my wing, hoping she would turn into her small room. But no, Ms. Kincaid strolled to my wing and into my room.

"I'll run you a bath. You have twigs and mud on your...dress," she said as she searched me over in the low lights of my room. "Do I even want to ask where you got that dress from?"

I loved Ms. Kincaid, truly, but it was like having two mothers living with me. Youna! This was punishment as I watched her walk into my bathroom, leaving the door open for me. Watching her turn and twist was magic in itself as she got my bath ready for me. Usually, I could shoo the other housekeepers off, but not Ms. Kincaid. Once Her mind was made up, I couldn't change it.

When she's satisfied with her work in the bathroom, she heads to my closet and pulls a clean gown and towel for me. I think she likes to mother me because she had no children of her own, and as I stood there, the seventh hundred yawns fell from my lips. Maybe I will allow it tonight. Climbing into the tepid water made my eyes slip lower. Ms. Kincaid found the almond shampoo I adored and rubbed it into my scalp until the night's events washed away when she rinsed it out with the smaller bucket by the tub. Ms. Kincaid's meaty hand stopped my head from hitting the tub during the yawn.

"All of that yawning makes me think you had a good time."

A smirk unfurled on my lips. My Ms. Kincaid had a sharp tongue one minute and a mother's touch the next. Plus, she was nosy.

"I did, for the most part, I guess." I unfolded every detail of Del's and my night out, minus the touchy asshole, since she won't remember anything soon enough. When she was done, she rinsed and massaged me with lotion until my golden-brown skin shined. She helped dress me as well. My soul might have slipped away if she hadn't said the next words to come out of her mouth. Every muscle in my body stiffened.

"Goodnight, my princess."

In simple terms, I panicked. My heart was lodged in my throat as it pounded against my ribs. My magic, which had been dormant since Del and I got back, shot out before I realized the deep slumber incantation I had drummed up in my mind. Cursing out loud. I couldn't do anything but watch the green aura hit poor Ms. Kincaid square in her back.

"Wha—" Ms. Kincaid said right before I pushed out more magic to catch her before she fell to the floor from the spell. She floated an inch above the gray floors until my magic placed her softly on the floor.

My nails dug into my wrist as I scratched at the imaginary itch. I had to hurry. It's not like Ms. Kincaid will wake up anytime soon, but the risk of me getting caught sent my heart racing as it fought with my gritty eyes. My muscles felt like lead, which made running twice as hard. My bare feet slapped against the cold, hard floors. I dashed down the old stairs, through the adjacent pathway, and into the corridor with my parents' offices.

Opening the brown door to my mother's office. I locked the door behind me, too afraid to even think what would happen if someone caught me. I may be a glutton for punishment. My mother's office was pitch dark except for the soft glow of the moon. It was beautiful, but I had enough work to do as I felt the wall for the light switch. My mother's personality could be summed up by the black and gold office, dark and beautiful. The black walls held floor-to-ceiling gold bookcases. On the other side of the office was a line of windows that ran behind her big gold desk. The small seating area was home to the gold and blue chairs from my sixth great-grandmother. My mother magically treated them weekly as a tradition. Once, I tried to offer to do it, and she said, "No, your time will come, but not today."

The old family book of our history and long-forgotten incantations were normally stored in the bookcases across from the desk. The black and emerald book was as thick as my thighs and weighed a ton. I swept the six-tier bookcases several times before my eyebrows melted together. The book's usual place was empty.

"Hell, where could it be?"

When I searched the other bookcases and found nothing, my heart dropped. My body was teetering past its limit for nothing, and so was my magic as the adrenaline had worn off, just leaving me feeling broken. I was about to call it quits when I went to my mother's desk and pulled out the gold chair. Sitting in the middle of the seat was the family book. The emerald gem embedded into Younas eyes stared back at me. Almost as if she was taunting me.

"Oh Goddess,"

Any other time, the book wouldn't be so bad, but today, it was horrible as it hit the desk with a loud thud. I only had two hours...to go over two thousand pages to find one incantation. Great! Piece of cake. I could beat myself up for not paying attention to where the stupid incantation was when my mother used to teach me from the book, but now, because of my neglectfulness, I'm stuck going through each of the pages that go back to the first of our line.

I just knew she was having a laugh in the underworld with her fated mates.

Page after page, I turned until the soft pull of my magic and my body demanded me to close my eyes. With my hand under my chin, I flipped through my seven grandfathers, Youna mates, and history. The tune that my mother sang as she flipped through the book got stuck in my head. My magic had recoiled deep inside of my chest and wouldn't help, not even to keep my eyelids from shutting, as my head found a home on page one hundred and ninety, a spell on how to make the blood dagger to kill a werewolf. The Thibodeaux family history book soon turned into my pillow for the night as I succumbed to the deep slumber that my body demanded.

Chapter 7

Kaydian

My eyes burned against the warm sun as it beamed in from the window. One by one, I slowly opened my eyes as I lifted my heavy head from my half-asleep arm. My arm shot out, shielding my eyes from the sun's glaring rays. Wiping the sleep out of my eyes, a soft, fulfilling yawn slipped past my mouth as I stretched out the stiff muscles in my back and neck.

"Did you enjoy your sleep, Kaydian?" My father asked. His deep baritone voice sent me leaping from my seat, sending the gold chair tumbling over with a bang.

He continued to speak, "You know it's a little after noon, and your mother came into her office to get work done...only to see you drooling over your family book."

What could I say but look at my father. His brown eyes gave nothing away, but I knew he grew tired of my antics. Heck! I was tired of my antics. And all I wanted was to make my life less grim. But I guess that would never be in the cards for me.

"I'm sorry," I said. I sighed heavily as I slumped back down into the chair after I picked it up. The pathetic apology sounded weak to my ears.

My father was in his informal attire today. The soft black dress shirt he normally wore was pristine as it bunched up against his upper arms as he folded them. His pants and black leather shoes matched the black shirt. My father's morning beard was shaved off, leaving him looking younger than he appeared.

"Ms. Kincaid woke up on the floor with a bad back. She was supposed to be going to Tou-sin today with your mother. But I had to send her to the infirmary," my father said as he shook his head. His frown marred his face as it pierced my heart.

"I will apologize to Ms. Kincaid. I didn't mean for this to happen."

"You wanted to put her to sleep. But for what?"

My shoulders caved in, and my wrist was on fire as I attempted to ignore it. There was no escaping my punishment. One can only hope my father would show me some mercy. I couldn't lean on my mother since she wasn't here. My only guess was she was unaware of my run-in with Ms. Kincaid, or they already spoke about my punishment.

"Your mother and I are deeply disappointed in you, Kaydian. Time after time, we've given you a chance to quit acting like a petulant human, but it seems we're too lenient with you. Your mother always begged me to give you more free time when you were younger, hoping you would finally come into your role. I told your mother too much freedom would hurt you in the long run, and I guess I was right."

The lump in my throat grew painful. With my face to the cold desk, my father raised from the older brown chair opposite mine. His brown eyes held a sadness in them I never experienced before. Shame was something I was used to, sadly. I had an aptitude for being in trouble. But disappointment from my parents burned much longer after they were gone.

"Maybe it will make Ms. Kincaid happy to see you interested in her etiquette classes and some more lessons with Sir Reid. Maybe between the two, you won't find time to mess around with Ms. Pourciau," he suggested with his mouth pursed with disgust.

My father's hand was on the doorknob when he turned to me and said, "It seems like every chance you get, you disappoint. We give you an inch of freedom, and you run too far with it. Betrayal and distrust aren't amusing. It's the reason covens get destroyed."

With his last words, I folded my arms and bit back the sob that threatened to break out of me. Not because I'm mad at getting caught, but because I've dug a hole so deep that I can't seem to get out of it. Everything is my fault. I'll admit to my silly mistakes. What I would give to have a simple life like Del. What I would give to not have the weight of my duties weighing me down. Or not to have to worry about running from a fate I wasn't strong enough to complete.

Running my hand through my dry, limp curls that dried out from the blistering sun. I banged my head on the back of the chair.

What a fucking mess!

UNFORTUNATELY, SIR REID HAD DRAGGED ME OUT OF MY WARM BED TO THE oversized sandy brown concrete coliseum the very next day. The plain stadium was beloved and maintained better than any building in Tousin. Not even a single crack was found on the dusty, hard, sandy-colored floor. The three rows of seating wrapped around the building was just enough for every single member of our coven to be in attendance. During our coven meetings and funerals, the mini stages would be in place to seat either my mother on the emerald throne or the Royal Coven table. Underneath the concrete ground, they were stored until there was a need for them and the Royal burial spot for our family. It was the coven's pride and joy. Rightfully so, as my great-grandfather built it for my great-grandmother as a gift of love since she, like my fore-mother, loved fighting as much as she loved Youna. Must be nice.

"Oof," flew out of my mouth as Sir Reid made my tender ass kiss the floor.

Bastard!

For every dumb decision that I'd partaken in within the past couple of weeks was the amount of times Sir Reid dropped me on my aching ass.

And honestly, I'm sick to death of this. My back ached from the abuse I had been enduring for the past three days now. This was the fourth time Sir Reid effortlessly sent me flying to the ground in the past hour. But I had given up, and I've refused to play this tortuous game anymore. My arms were tender to the touch as I folded them against my sweaty chest and stared up at the gloomy sky. The packed dark clouds billowed and seemed to be at a standstill as if they were watching me getting my ass whooped. It was midday, and the sky was ready to shed its tears on us.

Did it matter? No.

Because I was already saturated in my own tears and salty sweat. My straight hair, a mistake on my part, was now frizzy and kinky at the edges. My high ponytail was gone. The makeup I had put on because I thought today was an off day, since I was on my best behavior, had all but made a home on my silver middy shirt. The white cotton bloomers stuck to my generous thighs like a second skin. Not to mention, I smelled like the gardeners' shed when they changed out of their clothing and left their jumpers in the shed for the day.

Seraphina and Lucifer were perched on the steel-enforced ledge of the coliseum as they watched their mother get battered. Several times, Sera attempted to help me by baring her sharp teeth at him, but Sir Reid turned to Sera and pinned her with his black eyes as he pointed his finger at her, willing her to make a move on him.

The man had balls of steel. I'll give him that.

My knees ached from Sir Reid's blade, that swiped across the soft tissue repeatedly as they healed multiple times just to be reopened again. My arms pulsed and cramped each time I lifted the damned heavy sword. I'm beyond pissed at Sir Reid, my parents, myself, and the stupid coliseum.

The hard clink of Sir Reid's boots ricocheted off the mono colored structure. In the very far background, I could hear the bustling noise from Tou-sin Square.

"So, are you just going to lie down there like a whiny dead fish?" Sir Reid scowled.

I'm not in the mood for his bullshit right now. Clicking my tongue, I refused to acknowledge him treating me like one of those brutish men he trains. Maybe if I just squeezed my eyes shut that maybe this nightmare would be over.

"You have five seconds to get up, or I'll make you." He warned.

I couldn't help but laugh as it bubbled up my throat and leaped out of my mouth. If I had any more tears to shed, I would have, but I settled on gasping for air. My face turned to the angry giant. Sir Reid's opaque serrated scar that ran from his temple across his face down to the cliff of his chin twisted even more harshly as he glowered down at me. He was all dressed up in his armor from the steel half-body plated armor suit cuirass & his gauntlets lined with my family's jewels...

All to fight me...with my children, Seraphina and Lucifer, watching. How lovely!

The thought sent me spiraling again. But how fortunate was I that my captor towered over me, and my father, for that matter, and weighed about six of me and mother put together. Sir Reid hadn't given me my five-second warning before his mammoth-sized hands grabbed my shoulders. It felt as if I was being squeezed for dear life as he hoisted me up from the floor. I'm not a petite woman by any means; I was built like my grandmother, or so my mother always said. She was thick and had curves I inherited, which bypassed my mother, whose muscular, lean body seemed dwarfed next to mine. But none of that mattered, as Sir Reid planted me on my sore feet.

When he let go, my body wobbled before his hand held me while I got accumulated. The damn man got on my last nerve. Luc's tortured cries vibrated throughout the coliseum as if he could feel my pain. Sir Reid let go of me as his narrowed eyes locked onto my family's sword a few feet away from where I had given up on my life. The sword looked miniature in his pale hand. Walking over to me, Sir Reid grabbed my hand and shoved the dark green hilt into my bruised hand. The sword was one of my family's prized possessions. From the grip to the pommel, it was decorated in a dark green leather found in the old country before my family escaped the witch hunters. The blade was made from steel and was dipped into the blood of my ancestor, Youna, and every one of her female descendants, including me, on their eighteenth birthday. I still remember the look of shock as my mother and everyone in town watched my blood sizzle on the silver steel blade. Gasps and shocks echoed throughout the coliseum as we watched the rain guard of the old sword receive my blood, and the emerald in the pommel turned multicolored, then back to the emerald color that stained the gem. While I stood there and beamed, the other royal families exchanged silent glances. Even then, I knew the Royals had the sordid fairytale embedded into their memory.

He will be the death of me! I thought as the old memory faded.

"Surely, I can have a break now, Sir Reid. You have all but sliced and diced me from my arms to my knees!" I exclaimed with a heaviness in my voice.

"But yet, in three days, you have only managed to slice me a handful of times. I taught you better than that. Failure isn't an option, little princess," he said. His deep voice was thick with his English accent today. Sir Reid's accent only became prevalent when he was angered or disappointed.

"Another round!" he announced sternly.

The booming sound of his voice hit me square in the chest. I'm too weak to fight back or to tell him off. Even with the sword point resting on the floor, the muscles in my arm pulsed and throbbed at the thought of having to pick the sword up.

Youna!

Hadn't I been through enough punishment for seven years? **You should just kill him and be done with it!** The voice in my head screamed. Shutting my eyes closed as I muttered a quick prayer. The voice, an impending sign of my demise, was back. It had been several months since the voice appeared, and I decided it was just my mind playing a trick on me. I took a deep breath, and when I opened them back up. I screamed and ducked.

"Are you mad?" I screamed. My voice was hoarse from my itchy throat.

"Less talk, more fighting."

Sir Reid, the bastard, hadn't given me any warning when he swung the magic-forced steel sword toward me for the second time. Lifting my family sword, I met him in the middle, just inches from my face being carved up like a turkey. My upper arm begged for clemency as I pushed his sword toward him until he broke the struggle standoff. *Ha!* We continued to dance with our swords—well, just Sir Reid. I was just trying to stay alive. Not that I thought he would kill me, but seeing the glint in his black pupils, I thought I should reconsider that notion.

The sound of metal rang out as I dodged his attempts. Both of us are not giving up on the one-sided fight. My several attempts to hit him were useless. I almost gave up. Nothing was working as I grunted and puffed out my exhaustion. When I sidestepped, he glided. He jumped, and I staggered back, almost busting my ass again. The sweat beads that had soaked the coliseum floor ran down my back and dripped down the back of my legs, making the damp white bloomers turn see-through. The muscles I had long forgotten were there, throbbed with my heart. Spotting an entrance, I hit him on his right, and he countered me with a sidestep. My body was shutting down as the seconds flew by. My hand wasn't sweaty; it was inundated with my sweat with nowhere to wipe it away. I struggled. I swung my sword halfway into our battle, finding a sweet spot to nick his thunderous thighs. But, of course, Sir Reid beat me to it. As he grabbed the blade's edge, the steel bit into his scarred palm as his blood coated it. He ripped the sword out of my hand, throwing it down beside me as if it were nothing more than a pest.

"Good, but not great," he stated.

"I would be greater if you allowed me to use Sera and Luc," I muttered.

"You have to know how to defend yourself without Sera and Luc. What if your enemy had dragons, and they were occupied? What would you do? Wait for them so you can fight?"

"I would use my magic."

"Of course, you would...but what if you used your magic up, and the enemy had the upper hand? I keep drilling into your thick skull that—"

"You have great powers, but it's not limitless powers." We said in unison.

Sir Reid's frown deepened on his pale, grim face. He humphed, and I rolled my eyes. Our usual tango whenever this topic comes up.

"And if someone found out that emeralds were your weakness. Only Youna will be able to save you."

As a royal, I could bend my magic to my will, and just like my progenitor, I could bring back the dead. A special magic that only the Thibodeaux line could wield. Of course, magic isn't limitless for the witches on earth, along with my family's emerald gem, that will strip me of my powers. If I use my magic frequently, it will give out. And I will be dead to the world until my magic has been to restore.

"You're done for the day. I may be hard on you, but I won't always be by your side. We need to know you can at least survive to escape. Go on, young princess. I will speak with your father," he said, as he almost spat the last words out.

Sir Reid disliked my father...with a passion. His usual frown deepened whenever he was around as he spat out his name like it was acid on his tongue. I turned back to feed Sera and Luc the lamb that Sir Reid killed and brought back for them, but he had beaten me to it.

Sera all but was nuzzling the traitor as she thanked him for the food. Poor Luc laid on the floor waiting for his lamb. One thing I could tell you was that my children were like me, fed me, and I will be content.

Dragging my feet to them, my calves burned a little less with each step as my magic worked on the battered muscles. Using my magic to hoist the extra lamb from the crate over to Luc. My hand ran down his blue scales as he made quick work of the lamb.

"You're not gone yet?" Sir Reid asked.

"No, I wanted to make sure they ate before I left."

"They're good dragons, your Highness," Sir Reid said with a little softness to his voice.

I would have teased him if I wasn't mad. Not that it mattered, since Sir Reid would say, *"I don't need you to like me. I need you to trust me."* You know, the boring stuff.

"You know I'm only hard on you because I believe in you. I know you'll be a great queen when your mother gives you the throne," he said as he continued to stroke Sera, who had now joined Luc as she allowed him to stroke her scales. "My job is to see you through your life and your heir's life as well. When that time comes."

"If it ever happens. What if I'm destined to be alone..." I said, my eyes clamped shut as I realized my mistake. I could hit myself for allowing my intrusive thoughts to spill out.

"I—" Sir Reid said as I watched him fight to find the words to say.

But I didn't stay to hear them, so I turned and walked away to avoid the awkwardness.

I didn't want him to see the foolish tears that gathered in my treacherous eyes. Luckily, the castle was far enough to spill some of the blistering tears and gather my wits. But I couldn't help but hear that little voice in the back of my head. The one that sounded nothing like my voice as it screamed, "mateless psycho." A chill raked through my body, causing me to shiver, folding my arms across my heavy chest. My silver shirt, which was damp from my sweat, was now wet with my tears.

It seems like all I did anymore was cry and curse nowadays. Quite pathetic when you think of it. What Queen will I be if all I do is cause disappointment everywhere I go?

The fifteen-minute walk to the castle was quiet. Most of the coven ran inside when they saw Sera and Luc fly over the village back to their home in the woods. I welcomed the silence from the past two days of training, but now it seems stifling as it mixed in with my feverish sobs. The closer I got to the castle, the more dread seeped into my body. I wondered what my mother and father said behind closed doors about me. If they two called me a failure, psycho, or someone not capable of being loved.

What I would do to switch places with Del, but she already said she would never want to be in my shoes. She prefers to be on her farm with her little brother and parents as they tend to the hogs. I don't blame her one bit as I thought about the weight on my shoulder to fit into my mother's shoes.

As I reached the kitchen side door, I opened it. The cooler air made me grateful for the castle more than ever. My stomach grumbled at me as we got closer to the kitchen with the smell of freshly baked bread that fragrant the air. Maybe I could steal a piece from Chef Dubois before he noticed. I mean, for all of my hard work and all.

Approaching the double doors to the kitchen, I carefully took my time slipping through them. The two older assistant cooks had their backs towards the door. They both were in black skirts and white chef's coats. The older assistant, Mary, plump arms worked feverishly as she washed the dishes in the sink. While the newer assistant, Ruth, dried them and placed them in the cupboard.

"Yes, I used to sneak over to the edge of the perimeter and purchase plants from the trader Fae for my mother's tea. I think he was part of the Edgehaven Faes," Ruth replied. Her loud voice sounded hushed, muffled over the clattering of the plates.

Edgehaven Fae's. What are they doing near our territory? My father had long since dwindled their coven. Only leaving a handful of them alive. In my father's words, *"Even the weakest supernaturals are needed for something."*

"Oh, yes, I forgot he used to sell frequently to us. What a shame. I always got the best tassel berries from him." Mary took the washrag and wiped her wrinkled hand. As I slipped out the door, with the warm bread caressing my hand in doughy love, taking care to prevent the swinging door from creaking when I caught the tail end of the conversation, "Well, supposedly, King Thibodeaux wasn't in South America but right here in Texas running them away. Rumor is..."

"Now why are you always sticking your nose where it doesn't belong?" Del's mother's voice rang in my ears.

My heart thumped erratically against my chest. The warm slice of bread I worked so hard for dropped on the floor as my stomach cried at its loss. Mrs. Pourciau stood before me. Her hand was on her narrow hips. Her red hair was pinned up in a high bun. She had on blue jumpers covered in specks of dirt. Mrs. Pourciau's pink lips were twisted in a frown that resembled my mother's. Mary and Ruth peeped their heads out from the door. Their brown eyes were wide like saucers when they saw Mrs. Pourciau and me standing right outside the door.

"You're Highness, are you okay?" Mary asked. Her weather face told her story of her age. Mary was over three hundred years old and pledged herself to our family fifty years after Chef Dubois.

"Yes, she is," Mrs. Pourciau said as she handed the crate with the meat to Ruth. "Do you ladies mind taking this crate? I don't want the meat to go bad."

Mary opened the door for Ruth, and they walked back into the kitchen.

Mrs. Pourciau had one hand on her waist as her red-painted fingernails tapped against her hip. She looked like Del. Her pale skin glowed as she shook her head at me.

"I'm always finding you or Del or both of you girls doing something you ain't supposed to be doing." She shook her head.

"Well, in all fairness, Mrs. Pourciau, I didn't intend to eavesdrop, but they mentioned my dad and him possibly not visiting the South American Coven, which is ridiculous since they're not a threat to us anymore. I mean, everyone knows all the Fae do is...well..."

"Fuck," she said, with one eyebrow arched. "I have a mate and two children, your highness. No need to act innocent around me."

Well, that made one of us, I wanted to say, but I kept my mouth closed.

"Yeah," I itched the inside of my wrist. "They were about to say something...interesting. Do you know any rumors about my dad's trip?"

Mrs. Pourciau looked ghastly. Her hand raked through her hair as her feet tapped the floor. Her hazel eyes were blank as she stared back at me.

"I should get going. Del and I are going to Tou-sin to shop."

She hadn't stayed long after I said goodbye. Her slender frame almost ran out of the servant's hall without a glance back.

Secrets among secrets are what I believe were in store for me. That's if I make it to the throne.

After I walked out of the hallway, I knew I had to face the cold hard facts. My dad was hiding something. My parents' whispered tone sounded louder the farther I got from the kitchen door. Stopping in front of the powder blue sitting room, I watched as my father and my mother sat down for their afternoon tea. My mother threw back her head as she laughed at something my father whispered in her ear. She looked so content and happy at that moment with him. The toothy smile she gave him made me envious. My father took my mother's dainty hand and kissed it as she told him to stop while playfully slapping him. But in the back of my mind, I couldn't stop wondering about that old saying my mother used to say.

For every rumor, there is an inkling of truth to the matter.

Chapter 8

Kaydian

The coliseum had a vendetta against me.

For the past two weeks, I have trained day in and day out with Sir Reid while my father and mother sat in the Royal seating area, watching. Their observant eyes took in every step and every counterstrike I applied. Each time I struck Sir Reid with my sword, my mother gave a haughty humph that resonated throughout the coliseum.

But today, I was tired—emotionally and physically. There was no other way to put it as the days wore on my fragile mind. This morning, as I approached the brown structure, I hadn't been prepared to enter the bronze double arches. I was disconsolate. The constant throbbing of my brain made me wish I hadn't been so frivolous. I wouldn't be in this position. With each day that passed, I struggled to keep up with training and having a life outside of the castle. There was none since I hadn't seen Del in two weeks, and there was not even a magic message to see how I was doing. My shoulders held their current favorite position, hunching over like the town's spinster. The burden of my responsibilities and the disappointment my parents expressed about me last night during dinner followed me into this balmy August day.

But I guess I'm doing well since I only had my sword knocked out of my hand once in the four-hour training session.

A stellar job...I guess. The foreign voice said.

Try as I might, I couldn't stop the voice from reappearing time and time again. This time, it was right when Sera opened her mouth. The fire she produced made the beads of sweat dried up on my dampened skin. Casting the tip of my steel sword into the widespread fire just when the voice crept inside my head, throwing my concentration off.

I wonder how Sir Reid will look if we cast him into our dragon's fire. Would his ashes fall from the sky? Or will he collect another wound as a triumphant souvenir?

The smothering heat scorched the side of my pointer finger and the back of my thumb as I stuck the sword in too deep. My hand curled into my chest as I dropped the sword and dropped to the floor. Throbbing at the brutal assault from the concrete floor. Pain pinned me to my spot, and all I could do was wait until my magic healed the scorched area and my bruised knees.

Sir Reid's soft clicks from his gear boots drew closer to me. I didn't want to face him and hear him chastise me for not having better control of my sword or pointing out my inability to stay focused. Which, in all fairness, wasn't my fault.

My trail of tears coated the ends of my hair as I stayed in the curled position. Sera's and Luc's low growls rumbled through me as Sera rubbed her head against my side. I knew this was her way of comforting me, but I was drained from this training, my responsibilities, and my mother's persistent notion that I was stalling the inevitable. Without thinking, my injured hand shot out before I could think and push her enormous head away from me.

That was the first time that I had pushed Sera or Luc away from me. Darting pain shot through my hand to my shoulder, causing me to clutch the arm against my chest. A rough, large hand grabbed my fore-arm, and before I could protest, the piercing cold sensation slightly soothed my burnt fingers.

"Shh, little princess," Sir Reid's deep voice washed over me. "Your magic is already working to heal the burned skin."

Sir Reid handed me a handkerchief, and I blew my nose into the white cloth.

"Thank you, Sir Reid," I said, my voice still filled with tears as I trembled out the words. I didn't want to speak, but I felt inclined to thank Sir Reid for his kindness.

Stretching the injured hand, the throbbing slowly subsided with each minute. The green aura engulfed my hand, glowing and rippling between the bright Houston sun and the ice water in the brown bucket.

Folding the handkerchief, I tried to wipe my face, but my tears still fell as the pain crept away. The pain may be gone, but not the memories, I thought as I righted myself. I didn't care if Sir Reid saw them or my parents, which, luckily, were not here today.

As I opened my mouth to lash out at Sir Reid and tell him to leave me alone, he spoke.

"You did amazing today. Just like when you were training with me during our royal lessons. I'm proud of you, little princess," he said tenderly. "What were you thinking about that made you stick your sword that high into the fire?"

Sir Reid held his arm out as he helped me to my feet. The subtle ache in my knees was gone, and the blackened skin had steadily turned back to its once golden-brown hue.

Looking at Sir Reid's stony face, his mouth pressed into a line as he waited for the answer. An answer I couldn't—wouldn't dare say out loud. The thought I may be slipping into the depths of my foreboding curse petrified me. It was then that I noticed my hands shook, causing me to ball them up into a fist, shoving them under my armpits. My tongue glided over my chap lips as I struggled to come up with a lie because I couldn't tell Sir Reid that I may be spiraling down a gloomy hole already.

I would be the second person to fall into that dark, cursed hole like Alice in Wonderland. Will my fate be like my third great-grandaunt? Angela Thibodeaux was a great witch and had ruled over the Northwestern region of America long before my father killed and broke apart the different covens. She was strong-willed, and everyone loved her enough to think she was our ancestor's favorite. Until she turned twenty-five, without her fated mate like me, when everything changed. According to our family's history book and my mother's stories, she spiraled slowly enough that no one caught the change until it was too late. She wreaked havoc on the Northwestern Coven, and they crumbled one by one, taking scores of talented witches. And when my great-grandparents got wind of what was happening, they set out to kill her to save the dwindling coven. One night, when Angela returned from killing over thirty of her own witches, they snuck into her bedroom in the darkness of night and slipped an emerald ring onto her finger—rendering her no better than a human. Angela gave them hell as she fought for her life before they killed her and burned her body, ensuring she would never be reincarnated.

Not that it mattered, since according to my mother's story, Angela thanked her parents from the underworld.

Just the thought sent me spiraling down that pitiful dark hole again. My eyes shut as I screamed until the throb in my throat became unbearable and my voice cracked. My voice bounced and danced off the coliseum walls, and when I opened up my eyes, which were blurred from the tears, saw Sir Reid's black eyes. I faltered as worry replaced the cold, hard glint that normally was placed in them.

I hated it...I hated the pity more than the disappointment. My heart thumped against my tender chest as I let the words slip out of my mouth before I had time to think rationally.

"I wish I had a human life—painting and being buried under piles of books until I'm old and wrinkled. Not having to fight you or take over this coven, not having a ton of children because my ancestor is the goddess of fertility... or waiting for the glut curse to kick in."

The moment those words left my mouth, I knew I made a horrible, embarrassing mistake, but I couldn't walk back from what I said, literally, since I never found the stupid remembrance spell.

The hard, straight line that once decorated Sir Reid's mouth turned down. His black eyes squinted in disbelief that I would say something even remotely of that nature. Sir Reid shook his giant head and sighed.

"You're just saying these crazy things because you haven't found your mate yet. When you do, I promise you, things will fall into place," he said as he shook his head to reassure me or himself. I wasn't sure at this point.

As if that were to soothe over the disgust that clawed inside of my stomach. Just the thought that I was destined to be alone and driven crazy by the curse haunted my very soul daily. The sourness of disgust coated my tongue, causing me to grimace when I swallowed.

"Sir Reid, with all due respect, you wouldn't know anything about mates, or love, for that matter. Your sole purpose is to roll around with your motley crew of witches and get off from knocking each other out. If that's what I wanted to do, then I would have done so. I suggest you take Sera and Luc back to their area and stay out of my royal business. That's an order."

I didn't wait around for his snarky response as I turned on my heels and exited the coliseum. It would be no surprise if my feet left impressions in the grass as I stomped my way back to the castle, face streaked with the salty tears of my ego. The few coven members I passed threw me some odd looks. The hell with them. Calling on my magic with my mind in my little messy enchantment room, I stepped through the white slit to my room. I breathed a deep sigh of relief. The cramped space would have made anyone shudder, but this space felt like heaven. Especially when my emotions were crashing inside of me like a tidal wave, as I hoped the quiet space could take the burden of the day away.

You should have killed him!

The voice was like a cold reminder of my situation, bringing me back into reality. A cold sweat formed on my forehead as I slid down the only sliver of free wall space in the room. Yes, I was mad at myself for letting my temper get the best of me, especially since Sir Reid was only being kind to me—in his own special way. I said to the voice as if it could hear me—or if it even cared to hear my opinion.

Without a window in the enchantment room, I didn't know how long I had stayed in the little room with my eyes closed, hoping that the goddess would give me a little more time to find my mate. A little more time for me to save myself. I'm worth saving, Youna. The salty tears that trek down my cheeks and seeped into my mouth. Pressure built deep within my chest until it broke free from my mouth as I yelled into the room.

"I don't want to end up like Angela," I said out loud, even though no one would hear me or care.

Eight more months until I'm twenty-six. I wondered if history would strike again and if I would be ever so lucky to follow in Angela's footsteps. Would my mother cry for me as my great-grandparents had? They mourned her death for a hundred years, my mother said, until they went to be with her in the underworld.

The better question would be, would anyone care enough to mourn me?

A minor part of me knew that most of the coven probably wouldn't shed a tear except for Merrell.

Getting up from the dusty packed floor, I felt the grit against my palms and resolved to be proactive in my final countdown days to insanity. My green aura swept out, touching every nook and cranny of the room. Books flew up from the floor while they waited for the broken shelves of my bookcase to be repaired. Piles of colorful clothing that I had brought when Del and I sneaked out were placed on hangers and hung themselves onto the string clothing line I assembled against the opposite walls. The six beloved paintings that I kept hidden in the room bumped and clashed against each other as they fought for space on the wall. Finally, my magic reached out and swept the dusty floors and made the small armchair look like new again.

One down...about several more to go. With my mind made up, I went to wash the dirt, tears, and grime that hugged my hair and skin like a protective coating. When I was dressed and ready, I worked up the confidence to go find Sir Reid. I owed him an apology for my actions. He didn't deserve the ire that I gave him.

I made my way down to the dining room to see that my parents weren't there. It was well past six, and that was late for them not to be halfway through dinner already. A male server had passed by in the hallway carrying a silver tray with empty drink ware.

"Hey, sir," I called out. When he turned around, he bowed.

He was cute. A button nose to his round face. He blushed when he noticed me staring at his plump lips for a beat too long. And he smelled like sin.

"Your Highness, do you need anything?" he said as he shifted on his feet.

I blinked several times before I remembered why I stopped him. "Have you seen my parents?"

"Yes, they're in the Queen's office with Sir Reid," he said with a nervous smile on his face. If I was in a better mindset, I probably would have ordered him to allow me to ride his face. I mean, it has been a minute since I tried to scratch my itch. Maybe that's the reason I'm so miserable.

"Your Highness."

I smiled at the young server, "My apologies..."

"Julian, my princess." He bowed again as I rolled my eyes at the gesture.

"Thank you, Julian," I said, as my eyes landed on his lips again. I mean, I could just lean in and sample young Julian. Before I could ask, he turned away and scurried down the hall.

"Damn it!" I said to no one as I counted the days since I last had my Stoneseed root tea. It's time for another dose. I don't need my hormones running wild, along with my emotions, especially about the handsome server and whether his tongue was long enough to scratch my itch as I watched the flex of his muscular ass as he disappeared down the long hallway.

It took me several minutes to unclasp my hand from the white brick wall. Normally, I would never go more than a day without the tea, but I guess with training, I forgot about it. Gathering myself and continuing down the short hallway to my mother's office. I hadn't been in the office since I got caught. It was almost as if I was too scared to face my stupid mistake.

Tapping on the door, the voices went silent behind the closed door. When I stepped through the door, I found them sitting around the desk. My mother was in her regal chair while Sir Reid and my father sat on the other side. From my position, I could see the menacing look Sir Reid was sending, which I chalked up to being stuck in a room with my father. My mother and father both smiled at me.

"Ah, there is the young queen of the hour," my mother said with a warm smile on her face. "Come here, my sweet girl."

Is this a butter-up? I thought as I walked over and stood beside my mother. She had on an orange dress with a short hemline, her hair was in its curly state that stopped in the middle of her back, and she still had on a little makeup.

"Hello, Mother and Father," I blurted out. "I actually came in here to talk with Sir Reid."

"Okay, go ahead then." My father smiled warmly at me.

I tapped my foot, but stopped when I realized that was a sign of weakness. Which I wasn't... well, anymore.

"I wanted to apologize for my behavior this afternoon, Sir Reid. My temper and the stress of the day got to me when you were only being kind to me. I hope you can find it in your heart to forgive me."

Sir Reid's black eyes looked small in the sea of white as he sat back in the seat. Honestly, I don't know why he seemed shocked. I've apologized for things before...I think.

"Young princess, you have nothing to apologize for. I'm here to serve you and your mother," Sir Reid said, with a bit of more emphasis on the last part. "You can speak to me any way you feel is just. I'm your humble servant."

"Be that as it may, you're more than a servant to me, Sir Reid. You're a part of my family, and I trust you as much as I trust my parents. If I hold them to a high standard, then I will hold you to the same."

I looked down at my mother, who still had a warm smile on her face.

"We treat the ones we love and cherish with respect." Her hand reaches out to move some of my hair away from my face. "I'm proud of you, my emerald moon. I hope this will make you think twice before you speak in the future."

Smiling at her, "Yes, mother."

One small burden down, and my shoulders felt lighter. Usually, I wouldn't have cared about one of the staff being mad at me, but I do care about Sir Reid. And I meant every word I said inside of this office.

"You were just talking about me?" I asked, changing the subject.

"Yes." My father jumped up from his seat and clasped his hand behind him. His gray button-down shirt was tucked into his white suit pants. "We're going to have a royal gathering next week. Everyone will be in attendance, and it will be a grand event."

"What's the catch, Father?" I was skeptical. My father loved to host Royal Coven meetings because it was the one time he got to gloat in front of the other royals and drink Fae wine until he passed out. Between the wine or his inflated ego...I couldn't tell you which one was worse.

"There's no catch. We just wanted to host a dinner and maybe..." He rubbed his shaven jaw. "You might find your mate there."

"I've met all the Royals and their children. This will be a waste of time on my part." I crossed my arms.

"Well, this time may be different. We have some Royals who have come of age and some that haven't found their mate yet. I think one of the African Heirs was a late bloomer like yourself. He might be the one," my father said. His promising smile felt more disingenuous than this party.

Another day, another way my father has thought of another way to annoy me to no end. The only good thing about these Royal meetings was the food...and maybe seeing William Cross get flustered by my father's bantering. This was just another "dinner" to parade me off as the unmated Royal—something so unparalleled amongst the Royals. Immediately, my mind thought of the unicorn, but you could probably see one before I would ever find my mate. The muscles constricted, making it hard to swallow. My eyelids blinked rapidly, trying to hold the salty water mix at bay.

Try to pull it together, Kaydian! Which was easier said than done.

My mother stood from her chair, drawing our attention. Even though she was the shortest in the room, you couldn't tell. The authoritative air around her told a different story.

With a soft smile on her lips, my mother said, "Please give Kaydian and me some alone time." Dismissing Sir Reid and my father at once.

When the door closed behind them, she walked over to the small gold cabinet which held some of her wine collection she brought during her trips. The glass clinked as she fumbled around, looking for the bottle she wanted, and poured herself and me a drink.

I wasn't in the mood for drinking since my hormones were already chaotic, but I still took a sip out of respect when she handed me the glass tumbler. The spicy taste of the apple cider hit my tongue. I looked at my mother in surprise since I thought she would have gone for her classic Edgehaven Fae's wine, which was bold and earthy.

"I know your father and I have been putting a lot of pressure on you." She took a seat beside me on her desk. "But that's because we believe in you, Kaydian. The people need you, and I need you."

Taking a sip of the spicy apple cider, she grabbed my free hand, drawing my attention to her once again.

"Will you give this dinner a chance like you promised?" she asked.

My eyebrows clenched together as my mind raced to remember when I promised her to attend a dinner. My mother knew I was notorious for skipping out on the stuffy events. Escaping the event was the highlight of those nights. I would fill my plate with enough food for three people, and if Del wasn't working the event, we would sneak off to my enchantment room to eat and get drunk on Fae wine.

"When did I say that?"

"When I visited you the night you got caught swimming in the Jacinto River."

Oh damn!

"You mean when you use your magic to put me to sleep?"

The corners of her mouth twitch ever so slightly. If she laughed, I swore I knew Qroaris, the Goddess of Vengeance, was having a laugh with her best friend, Youna.

"You know as much as I, well, if you remembered." She leveled me with an arched eyebrow and her lips pursed. "That Mear's magic can't be controlled like our inherited magic. If it wanted to reach out and comfort you, then who could stop it? It sensed you needed it and did what it had to do to protect and care for its kindred spirit."

I opened my mouth, with a tart response on my tongue, but closed it because deep down. She was telling the truth. My mother couldn't control it as I sat there and thought about it. I found I honestly wasn't upset with her. I don't think I could ever be. Especially since I won't be sane soon enough.

"I understand, and I'm nothing but a woman of my word, as my mother would say."

No sooner than I said the words, I was enveloped in her warmth. The soft scent of jasmine and sweet oranges filled my nostrils as I buried my face in her curly hair. I could stay like this forever, but as I sat there with my mother stroking my back. The clock in my mind keeps reminding me that my time was dwindling down. Soon, my days of this would be traded in for shackles that would be placed around me once the curse claimed me.

It took me a moment before I heard my mother's soft voice return.

"Hey," she said as she tried to soothe me. As a tremor raked through me. "It's going to be okay. Everything will work out. Trust in Youna. Our ancestors have never let us down."

I scoffed at her optimism. "Yeah, just like Angela, huh?"

My voice was hoarse from all the crying I've done since this afternoon. Pulling away from my mother, I placed a chaste kiss on her cheek. It was then I noticed she was crying with me. I've only seen my mother cry twice. Her bottom lip quivered, and I could see the wheels in her head turning on what to say to make things better, but she and I both knew that time was of the essence, and I was losing every minute.

"I will attend the dinner and be on my best behavior. I promise you, Mother."

Because it may be the last handful of times, I will have to remember before my, hopefully, quick descent into madness.

My mom used her magic to get us handkerchiefs to clean our faces. When we were done, my mother's makeup was gone. She sat with me barefaced and beautiful as I memorized the freckles on her cheeks that I used to count at night or the way her nose became deep red when she was mad or crying...like now. She still looked regal as I locked her picture away in my memory.

The only good thing to come out of this was having something to take my mind off the downward spiral of my life.

"Of course, I was going to ask Ms. Kincaid to send the invites," my mother said as she shook her head.

"There's no need to call Ms. Kincaid. I'll make the invites. When is the dinner?"

"Next week Saturday. It will be the start of a new month," she said as she sniffled. "New month...new beginnings...renewed hope."

My poor, lovely mother. She could be so optimistic sometimes. Flicking my wrist, I sent my magic out before us, preparing for the message. It blended and twisted in the middle of the room to reveal a transparent emerald and gold-colored box. The messenger was used to send private messages to anyone, not just witches. When the recipient accepted the message, the box disappeared along with the message. Using my finger, which shined brightly with my magic, I wrote the party information, as my mother dictated what needed to be written. When I was done, I used the same finger to touch the bottom of the letter, sending it off to all six Royal Coven leaders. The Royal Coven member will receive a splitting image of the letter.

"All six invites are done."

"Thank you, my Kaydian," she said, placing her empty tumbler beside mine. My mother took my hand in hers, squeezing it slightly.

"Let's eat, Mother. I wouldn't want you to fall over from hunger," I said as my stomach growled. We both giggled as I grabbed my mother's hand and led her to the dining room.

Chapter 9

Kaydian

"Raynaud...YES!" I screamed out by accident as my hand flew to cover my disobedient mouth.

After a day of wallowing around the castle. I decided it was time for me to make better use of what little free time I had. And what better way for me to help the staff? It's my duties to strengthen the relationship between the royals and the coven witches. That's how I found myself in the gardener's office requesting Raynaud's assistance for my private flowers. His father all but shoved him out the door. But he didn't need to because Raynaud's big tooth smile and his glazed-over eyes followed me like a sheep. I could ask him to do anything right now, and he would comply without a complaint.

That's how I could sneak my sometime lover into the dark, smelly garden shed.

With my powder blue skirt bunched at my waist, Raynaud deep slipped inside of me. The earthy scent embedded into the small shed mixed with our sweat that dripped into a wet spot on the floor. My curls clung to my moistened skin. I grasped the edge of the hooks used to hold the gardener's overalls to stabilize me as he pummeled deep into me. His large palms squeezed my heavy breast as his moans came out in a whimpered song made only for me. He fit perfectly inside of me, touching my elusive sensitive spot. With my skin so tender, it ached as he pinched my sore nipples. My voice was scratchy from keeping my moans logged in my throat. It was a shame he couldn't make me cum because if it was one thing Raynaud knew how to do, it was fuck...and garden, I suppose.

Raynaud sputtered to an agonizingly slow pace, leaving the tip of his fat cock to rake over the soft spot that made my magic tuck itself into the depths of my lungs. I only needed a couple more strokes before the throbbing urge would die down. It was then that I realized I was begging my magic not to choke me for having Raynaud fuck me. My magic hated it almost as much as an emerald stone.

"I—I'm... Kaydian," he stuttered.

The slick from his forehead landed on the back of my bare neck. I should be repulsed, but it made me gloat to feel how I affected him. I didn't need to know what he was trying to say to me. He was about to shower my insides with his cum.

Gritting my teeth, "You got this. I believe in you!" My words sounded sporadic as Raynaud sped up, torturing me with the promise of an orgasm. One could only wish. Squeezing my tight cunt around his shaft, red and white stars dot my vision as the throbbing in my greedy pussy intensified.

What a waste of our time...

The darkness said, but I blocked its negativity out and continued to focus on Raynaud and the ache between my legs. No one is going to take this one thing I have left away. Nothing else mattered as I pushed back into Raynaud.

I squeezed my eyes and focused on the throbbing until the ear-splitting crack ricocheted in the shed. The bright light from outside washed over us. Shit was the very thought that came to my mind as I shield my eyes until they adjusted to the light. And I can only imagine how we must look with Raynaud still inside me as he trembled as his warm cum trailed down my thighs.

Well, at least one of us got off.

"Is this how you're spending your free time?" My mother's voice boomed. She stood with her formal coven attire on, with her arms folded across her chest, filling the doorway. The sunlight outlined her like chalk. She had on her long emerald dress with our jewels down at the center of the corset. Her hair, like mine, flowed freely down her back. Her frown made me shiver even from my angle.

My mother continued, "Young man, I suggest you take your cock out of my daughter, or your life will become ten times worse without it."

"I—I'm sorry, your Majesty," was all poor Raynaud could stumble out.

"Oh, shit," were the only words that I could form as I pushed Raynaud out of me. The wet, sickening pop filled my veins with a scorching fire of shame. Even though I knew my mother had spoken to Raynaud. Her hard gaze never left me, and all I could do was look down at the dirt and sweat-encrusted floor while we shuffled to fix ourselves.

Poor Raynaud was the same color as the rust that lined the corners of the shed.

"Mother, I'm sorry. This was all my fault," I replied. "I made Raynaud abandon his duties to..."

I still couldn't look my mother in her eyes. Instead, I counted the ridges in the tin roof while my face was ablaze.

"Kaydian..." my mother retorted. "You were fucking your time away while the coven waited for you to satisfy your needs...well, try to, I guess, will be the better term, right?"

"Mother, I—" I sputtered.

My mother held a hand up. "What's done is done. The coven is waiting. Come on. Raynaud, I hope you can find yourself to Tou-sin without the Princess's guidance."

"Yes, Your Majesty," Raynaud said as he rushed past my mother.

"I hope you had your fill. It seems we need to put you to work more often," she retorted, as the corners of her mouth twitched.

"Mother..."

"I'm not mad at you. Although I wish you chose someone not so inconspicuous," she said as a smile broke out on her face. "It's good that you're exploring now because your fated mate might not be so open about exploring. But a little discretion is needed. You have a wing for something else other than whining in."

Of course, my mother loved to poke fun at me. I nodded, which was enough for her as she turned around with a giggle and opened a portal to Tou-sin. My mother told me to go first, which was a mistake on my part. When I stepped through, she had transported us right into the middle of Tou-sin village with every coven member's judgmental eyes on me. Sucking in the air, I found my spot next to the statue of Youna. My father, who stood on the other side of my mother, turned to me with an eyebrow quirked. I almost rolled my eyes in response, but knew better of it. We must not give the coven members any idea that there was turmoil amongst us or any of the Royal families, which was ingrained into me from a young age. Plus, I get the last laugh since my father wasn't allowed to give any advice to the coven since he wasn't a royal. My magic cheered slightly at the thought. Sir Reid and the golden army lined up around the buildings and the statue of Youna where we stood waiting for my mother's coven announcements.

She opened up her black journal and skimmed over a page of her notes. My mother's explanation of making the coven wait made them more duteous, never quite made sense to me. Yet, I never questioned it because her answer was always, "You'll see when it's your time to rule." Just the thought made me shake my head.

Searching out in the crowd. I found Del, her parents, and her brother off to the side of the crowd. Tucking my hair on the right and watching Del do the same with her left was our signature code. It was the only way we could convey to each other that I'd spotted her in the crowd and that I wasn't staring off into space.

A dull thud sounded in the center as my mother closed her book. "Well, this is an impromptu meeting in lieu of our normal meetings because, as you know, we're getting ready to host the royal coven dinner in two days. As you all may know, our appearance means everything during this time, and we must prepare both the castle and Tou-sin. That means we need everyone to use their magic sparingly and focus on the most important tasks. We don't need anyone passing out from exhaustion like last time."

My mother stopped and look out into the crowd, singling out Mr. Petit. He was easy to spot in his white apron and yellow baker's uniform. No one noticed how he shifted on his feet, but I hadn't missed it.

A small smile touched my mother's face as she continued, "I'm hopeful for this dinner party. I have a feeling it will be the beginning of a newness for our coven. Maybe it will breathe a new sense of life into all of us. With that being said, I need Khan to work the dam that night and into the next day. Hopefully, our guests won't stay forever like the previous party we held. That's it for this week, unless anyone has a problem they would like to bring forth."

The coven members paused and waited for someone to make the first move, but everyone stared back with blank gazes. I thanked Youna for this miracle. Usually, someone was fighting over chickens or who encroached on who's land.

"I have a question, your Majesty," a young witch from the back said.

"Well, don't be shy. Come up front," my mother countered.

As the woman approached us, her auburn hair, which was pulled into an afro puff, greeted us first. She was at least my age or older, with skin the color of topaz. Her clothing was plain and wrinkled at the edges, and one of her toes was almost through the opening of her boots. If I were to guess, she worked in the crops with the Jamisons.

"Your Majesty, my name is Nellie Jamison," she said, bowing slightly. "I won't take up much of your time, but my family and I were wondering if you thought about bringing some of the outcast witches back to help tend to the crops. We are short-staffed since my sisters worked in the castle and in town. It's becoming too much for us. Especially after my father went to the underworld."

My mother's smile never faltered. If there was one thing my mother and I agreed upon, it was about not bringing back the people who lost their magic.

"I'm still looking into it, Ms. Jamison," my mother replied. "Please say hello to your parents for me."

Nellie opened her mouth to protest, but she must have seen the pointed look on my mother's face and closed her mouth quickly.

"Thank you, Your Majesty," Nellie said before hustling back into the crowd.

Poor Nellie. My mother will never entertain that request. It was better to ask if she would allow the ghost to harvest the crops.

My mother turned to me. "Princess Kaydian, do you have anything to share with the coven?"

Once again, all eyes settled on me as I rubbed the thin layer of dirt that still coated my hands. "No, I think that's enough for the day, but I will request that we have extra help at the Inn for the party. And let's remember that everyone will be home early the night before. We don't need to have the coven falling asleep in the kitchen. We don't need another incident where the kitchen almost burned down!"

My mother glanced at me with a soft glint in her eyes. "Duly noted. Now everyone, let's get back to work. We have lots of work to do."

My parents and I walked home for a change. My mother kept teasing me about finding me occupied before the coven meeting.

"And what were you so preoccupied with, my princess?" my father asked.

I opened my mouth to answer, but my mother said, "Oh, she was gardening her rose."

My face warmed as my father looked perplexed.

"Rose? Just one rose? I don't get it," he asked.

"Yes, the most important one of them all," my mother taunted me.

She giggled while I walked beside her, mortified that she was laughing at me. I would rather die than have my mother catch me again. Running my hand over my face, I just hope I could make it to my room.

Youna, please send some good luck.

Chapter 10

Kaydian

Two days later, the Thibodeaux Castle was alive, or that's how the massive home appeared to me. Downstairs, the staff were engrossed with cleaning and cooking to their heart's content while Del and I hid out for as long as we could in my enchantment room. We were camping out until the dinner was ready. According to the clock Del brought for me, it was almost time for the dreaded event. I couldn't bring myself to mention to Del that I had no desire to be around the Royal Families tonight.

My leg bounced along with the soft ticking of the clock. Del finally had enough, placing her hand on my leg, settling the fidgeting limb.

"Will you stop twitching! You're making me nervous, and I'm just a server!"

I threw her a weak smile to reassure her I just wouldn't mention that my inner wrist was bruised from me digging my nails into the soft flesh. The faint churn of my stomach had me sucking down more air than usual.

Clearing my throat, "I'm not nervous. I just want this night to be over, and we can plan to visit Houston tomorrow."

Del was in her white shirt and emerald skirt. The white apron was thrown over her chair, along with the black polished loafers. Her thick white socks were folded down by her ankles. Del's hair was slicked back in a tight bun with no hair out of place, just like my parents liked it.

Del's eyes narrowed at me as she slipped on the apron and shoes.

"Yeah, right, Kaydian. We've known each other for way too long for you to hide your feelings from me." She crossed her arms and fixed an annoyed look at me. "Come off of it, Kaydian. You have been acting strange lately. One minute, you're optimistic, then next, you're a million miles away in your head."

"It's..." *Should I lie and tell her something to gloss over the fact that my extraneous voice has reappeared?* I chewed on my bottom lip and spilled everything to my best friend.

"It's already started, Del. The curse has been slowly beginning to take over." I paused, letting the words sink in. The rocks in my stomach weighed a ton as the silence between us stretched out. "I have been hearing the voice in my head since the new year started, and it's gotten worse these past couple of weeks. I'm losing my strength to fight it, Del, and I fear I will meet the same fate as Angela. Youna has decided to end her line with me."

Del was speechless. So, I continued my one witch tirade with my tears staining my face, "I won't get to see you mated. I won't get to tell my future heir all about our crazy childish adventures or about the competitions we used to have. We won't get to travel the world like we wanted to. And I won't get to do the one thing I was born to do, rule. It's over, Del. If I don't find my mate tonight, it's over for me."

Del's eyes narrowed as her mouth dropped open through my latest confession. *What does she think?* I could only imagine. She was losing me as much as I was losing her. My shoulders unclenched from my ears when I ended with the plans for tonight.

Why do we care what this common witch thinks?

The soft whoosh filled the room as Del flopped down in her chair. Her sniffles followed closely afterward, snuffing out the curse. I would have joined her slight sob party if I had any more tears. But I couldn't because I've cried every night since I started preparing for my curse. I think I've surpassed the witch's tears limit for a lifetime.

"Kaydian," her voice sounded shaky. "We'll figure something out. I mean your mother—"

"Del, this cannot leave this room." My head swiveled toward her with tear-filled eyes pleading with Del. "...I just want to make as many memories as possible before I can't recognize myself anymore."

Del just nodded, her face lined with the salty remains of her tears.

"I'll keep it for now, but you should—need to tell her. Maybe she has some Cliff Fieldcress! That could help until you find someone."

I loved Delphine's enthusiasm, but it was going to waste on me. The tiny sparkling glimmer of hope had long since dried up and died.

Even though my sadness was stabbed at my lonely heart. "It's okay, Del. I think I just need time to adjust to my new life."

I've seen what the severance could do as I remembered my mother missing her weekly cup. It was uncanny seeing my mother once fight the staff until she beheaded all five of them. Her tiny body was lithe as she hammered into the staff with her fist and her magic. Luckily, after an hour of fighting, they got the tea down my mother's throat... and that was three weeks right after my father left for a two-month mission with the European Coven.

I looked at the tiny brown round clock. "It's time to go down."

We left the tiny room with a deep sigh and a feeble promise to fix me. Can I be fixed? Or was this all a punishment for trying to flee the goddess's fate?

Who knows at this point?

What I knew was I was dreading this night, and honestly, I wished I could sneak away with Del so we could stuff our faces with food and cry.

But by the time my heels hit the bottom floor, I knew there would be no escaping. If I didn't know any better, I wouldn't have been able to tell the color of the walls. Since every inch of the white walls had a royal or their family plastered against it as they waited. A sea of each coven's colors and their crest filled the hallway. Some were true royals from our goddess ancestors, and some were made Royal Coven members for their unwavering loyalty.

Straighten your back, Kaydian.

Tugging on my billowy sleeves, I made my way through the sea of gold crowns, necklaces, rings, and, for some, gem-encrusted canes decorated the covens' leaders. The African, European, Oceania, and the Asian royals chattered away. Everyone was in attendance except for the Middle Eastern coven, who preferred the sanctuary of their village. I couldn't blame them either. These parties were more for showcasing their wealth and gossiping.

Smile, but don't smile too much.

My head nodded with my simple greetings to the royals. All fake smiles. I avoided being pulled into a conversation for them to just overwhelm me with their sad-looking heirs that looked too young and uneager to be here. The sentiment was mutual. None of the "Royal" heirs seemed halfway pleasant, and I would rather go back to the old home in Frenchtown than entertain the dour-faced heirs. But as the children of the royals, we were supposed to be present and represent our respective covens with honor.

Too caught up with escaping one heir with a mole the size of Texas on the tip of his cheek with three hairs sticking out of it that made me shudder, I collided with a hard body, causing me to lose my footing. A pair of rough hands reached out, grabbing my arms and saving me from falling to the ground.

"Some things never change, I see," the Stentorian voice said, causing me to flinch from the loud obtrusion. "Still clumsy as shit."

The voice belonged to the last person I wanted to speak with, let alone bump into. Victoria Muller, the third and the weakest descendant of the Royals, stood before me. Her red hair was a disheveled, matted mess and shoved in what one could—would call a bun. She wore a tweed yellow suit of her family's color, with black sandals. Her silver jewelry stuck out against her skin, which always reminded me of the blue jays during the spring. Victoria was someone I stayed far away from because, for one, she was a mixling. An anomaly to our kind, as their genetics were a tossup between being normal or unhinged insanity. It was illegal in our coven but not in the others as they waited to see if the mixling would become trouble or remain normal.

Not for us, though. My father made sure Victoria was someone we kept at arm's length at all costs and was only granted clearance to step inside our territory because of Sir Cross, my father's favorite royal, beside my mother. Our coven couldn't handle being shunned by Sir Cross's coven since they were more powerful than us.

Victoria had always been, how one would say, neurotic, to say the least. I blamed her demon mother.

Sir Henry Muller was the descendant of Juna, goddess of judgment. So much of that judgment superiority, seeing as Victoria's father had fallen in "love" with a blue demon that he followed to the underworld. No one but Sir Muller, and I guess Victoria, knows the all the events of their time in the underworld. Word is he begged Sir Cross to be placed back onto his family's seat in the coven when he returned with, to everyone's surprise, a baby in tow. Sir Cross wasn't a fool; he made him a deal, and he's been stuck to Sir Cross's side ever since. Much to my father's dismay, since he's given himself the title of Sir Cross's best friend and his third in command, which was downright ridiculous.

"Are you alright, Princess Kaydian?" Sir Muller said as he joined us. His British accent billowed over the chatter in the hallway.

He had on a ridiculous loose-fitting yellow suit with the brightest yellow shoes known to witches. His typical brown, stringy hair was pulled tight into a ponytail, which highlighted his thin edges. Sir Muller's pudgy stomach greeted everyone before him. There was a soft, rosy color to his pale cheeks, and if it was possible, his British accent was even thicker than I remembered.

"Good evening, Sir Muller." I threw him and Victoria some pity. "It was a pleasure—"

"I hoped that you and Victoria would spend some time catching up," Sir Muller said as he pushed Victoria's thin frame into mine. As if she hadn't just knocked me down a moment ago. I think that constitutes enough time I've spent with the deranged demon. Looking around the hall, I noticed several royals watching our interaction as they lined up with their heirs for a chance of speaking with me.

"Well, Sir Mueller, as much fun as that sounds like, I think my parents will have me occupied all night."

"It's okay, little dragoness. We'll catch up later," Victoria said with a wide smile. Her crude yellow-blackened molars stole the show as it drew my attention. The hair on my arms rose. I couldn't help but think how her teeth might feel when she ran her tongue against them. That was enough to make me jump.

If I didn't leave this hallway, I feared I would transport everyone to the dark dragon woods and let Sera freeze everyone to death. My lips clamped together to surpass the sigh I wanted to let out. The night hadn't even started, and I was ready to call it quits.

Mr. Muller seemed not happy with the response. He pleaded, "Well, maybe you can escort my lovely Victoria to the dining area."

His stubby hands latched onto Victoria's slender wrist and shoved the blue appendage in front of me. It all clicked into place. Sir Muller wanted me to touch Victoria. Witches believed that touch was our greatest sense since we release energy whenever we do so, and in return, that energy either returns to you or creates a bond. A fated bond.

That's how my mother explained it when she spoke about the first time my father presented as her mate.

I threw Sir Muller a lifeline, even though I had already touched Victoria before. He needed proof, or he wouldn't let me breathe for the rest of the evening. My hand reached out to touch Victoria's hand. Her skin was like the back of an alligator, bumpy and rough. Without a second thought, I tried to snatch my hand away, but Victoria was strong as she gripped mine. She brought the back of my hand to her mouth and kissed it. Petrified, I stood paralyzed until she released my hand. Even though her lips were gone from my skin, I could feel her wet saliva that coated my skin. I looked up to see Sir Muller's thin lips pulled into a straight line as his pale face flushed red with his brown eyes narrowed. He was about to say something, maybe even curse me out, when my father's voice rang out over the noise in the hallway.

"Kaydian!" I turned to see my father call me. "There you are. Your mother and I have been waiting for you."

Saved by my father!

I excused myself from an irate Sir Muller and Victoria, whose creepy smile never left her taunt face. She is the prime example of why my family banned mixing with other supernaturals. The risk of the offspring becoming demented wasn't worth it. Victoria was lucky to still function as some of the offspring in our history went hysterical. I still remember when my father told me about the ones he had to kill. Many of them became demented, often wandering the human streets, usually abandoned by their family, naked and threatening to kill the humans with their unstable magic.

When we entered the dining room, warm cinnamon spice and aroma from the serving tables tugged at my heart. The wooden table was decorated with new red and white table decorations along with the gold plate and drink ware. White food tables lined each side of the room, filled to the brim with tempting food as the off-white tea lights hovered above the dimly lit room, highlighting the fresco ceiling honoring the eight goddesses, with Youna front and center. Each seat had nameplates according to the Royals' coven colors and names.

Ms. Kincaid bustled along the busy room, rounding up the guests as I took my place beside my mother. My father's seat was placed next to hers. But everyone knew who the Royal was as she had on her crown and her chair was lined with the fake emeralds. She had on a long-sleeved emerald velvet dress that fit her trim body. Her inky black curls were straightened and placed into a bun with nothing out of place. I wouldn't expect anything differently. My father matched us as he dawned on his emerald three-piece suit. His hair had been cut this week in another short style, and he wore a smile as wide as the Mississippi River on his slim face. This was his forte. You can tell by the glint in his eyes whenever the flame from the tea lights flickered his way that Father couldn't wait to start his typical cajole.

The soft chatter from the remaining Royals filled the room. The wait staff pulled out their seats. One by one, the colorful nameplates wavered, flickered, and disappeared as their respective individual found their seat.

"Oy, if it isn't my favorite princess," Sir Cross said as he flopped down into the dining chair. The enormous piano that played my mother's favorite piano tunes, a variety of soft, uplifting melodies, covered the high-pitched screech of his chair. "And the most amazing queen this side of the ocean."

"You're in a good mood, Sir Cross." My mother took a sip of her Fae wine.

"You're buttering them up already, my friend." My dad looked like a child whose long-lost friend had returned home. I suppose that would be kind of correct.

"Well, teleporting this far away always swipes some of my power, but looking at your gorgeous face is enough to feel reinvigorated. Being in the queen's presence lifted my magic," Sir Cross teased.

Searching the room, Del stood by the serving table. Her white and emerald-suited staff stood out against the now fully bright red walls. Her face was blank as she peered out the window until the main course was ready to be served to her Royal, who was the African Coven's queen, for the night. Del took a quick glance my way, and I winked at her before she returned to stare longingly out the window. A hint of pink colored her cheeks as she tried her best not to look at me.

My father had long since hijacked the conversation as my mother and I exchanged a glance with each other. For the first time since I stepped on the tile floor, I smiled. *Why?* Each server brought golden plates filled with my weaknesses. My plate was stuffed with a pork chop, collard greens, gumbo on the side in a bowl, and shrimp étouffée with white rice. My mouth watered as the steaming plate of food aroma clouded my brain. I wanted to fit everything onto my fork and funnel the hot food into my mouth, but I thought better of it as I peered at my mother, who joined the conversation about the growing tension between the supernaturals in our area with my father, Sir Cross, Sir Sladen, and Sir Muller.

"Sir Cross, where is Prince Liam? It would have been wonderful to see him again. It's been a couple of years since he showed his face here," my mother asked as Ms. Kincaid refilled my mother's glass with wine.

Liam Cross was Sir Cross's only heir. From what I remembered, he was the polar opposite of his father. He was portly and soft-spoken, unlike his father. His bowl-cut blonde hair framed his chubby face. Liam resembled the Michelin man from the human tire company advertisements I've seen around Houston. He was a strange little boy, that one. Del and I would have to be scarce whenever he visited because he would follow us around like a lost puppy, with his light amber eyes lined with red flecks. That was before Sir Cross's mate died. The pair used to frequent the castle regularly; that all changed once Queen Evelyn was captured and killed by one of Sir Cross's enemies when I was twelve. I still remember the way Sir Cross and Liam cried in front of everyone, which was unheard of in our coven, but the European Coven was very open with their emotions. We never knew to what extent. My parents and I sat there while we squirmed in our seats at Sir Cross's open show of affection.

I always wondered how he managed not to lose himself to the separation period.

"Oh, you know Liam has always been a free spirit like his mother." He closed his bright brown eyes and placed his hand over his heart. If we hadn't known better, I would have said he was having a heart attack.

"Oh, com' off of it, Cross!" Sir Sladen's croaky voice called out. "You're always so dramatic. You definitely have Zadia's spirit in you."

Sir Sladen was a cranky brute. I couldn't even call him a man. His thin hair had streaks of black that clashed with the white. He was diminutive and his black eyes reminded me of Sir Reid's, just like his progenitor, Thetris, Goddess of War. So, I had to give him respect. Plus, he gave Sir Reid a run for his money, which was saying a lot since Sir Reid's family trained with the goddesses, and their technique was passed down the Reid line. Although he could rule his own Royal Coven, he joined the Europe Coven to govern the area.

"You're just cranky because your mate couldn't come." Sir Cross finally opened his brown eyes with unshed tears. Sir Sladen rolled his stormy eyes. The servers had traded the large gold platters for a small red plate with creole bread pudding with bourbon.

Everyone around the Royal's table had grown used to the tears, almost paying Sir Cross no mind when he starts on his emotional trip down memory lane. Deep down, I was jealous of Evelyn. The clock dinging brought me back to the table, which I was lucky to only have caught the tail end of their conversation.

"...Eh, what secrets are you hiding, Sir Sladen?" my father teased as he tried to lighten the mood.

"The same as you, my friend, unless you already told your mate about that trip you took with Sir Muller to the underworld years ago?" Sir Sladen dragged his fork against the empty dessert plate. The sound made the hairs on my arms stand. He was a notorious shit starter, and if anyone was brave enough to go up against Sir Cross, he would surely be the one.

Oh hell! as I watched my father become flustered at the slip. As if I didn't have enough on my plate already. And I definitely didn't want my mother to find out I was dragged there with him.

"What do you mean, Sir Sladen?" My mother's lips thinned out, and I knew she was angry by the arch in her left eyebrow. "My mate has never been to the underworld. I would never approve of that."

Sir Muller and Sir Sladen peered at each other. The room had gone silent as the tension thickened the sweet air. My mother's emerald eyes hadn't left the side of my father's face. The clacking of the gold fork hitting the plate rebounded around the room. My mother's magic was unseen to everyone but could be felt seeing as her emotions were getting the best of her. Glancing around the room, the Royals and their heirs gawked at my mother. This was probably the first time they felt the fervid magic as strong as ours. Our family was the second oldest and strongest under Sir Cross's, much to my father's dismay. Her magic wrapped around the room, hugging and squeezing the room air as it sent chills down my spine.

My mother turned her attention back to the now empty dessert plate. She reeled in the last of her magic and she sat back down. Her strained smile may have fooled the other Royals, but her emerald eyes said she would make sure my father heard her piece when it was all said and done.

If it was one thing my mother hated, it was being the butt of a joke, and he had turned her into one tonight. My father's once gleeful face was ashen as he tried to smile and laugh at the awkward tension in the room.

"It was a quick trip and nothing of importance," he tried to whisper, but my father was the worst at lowering his voice. "Just a minor run to secure something down there."

"I'm sure," my mother replied. Looking at Sir Muller and Sir Sladen. "Did you go with him? It's dangerous for us Royals. Let alone someone who's not of royal blood."

Sir Muller turned the same color as the red ornaments.

"I think—" Sir Muller stuttered. He's always been afraid of my mother ever since they were young children, and my mother set his hair on fire during the winter harvest. He deserved it since he was spying on the event that was meant for the female coven members only.

My father waved the server over to refill the Fae wine. The color returned to his dark skin.

"It was a harmless trip we took, my love," my father said. I don't even think he realized the mistake he made, probably from all the Fae wine. "We were in and out in an hour."

My mother's eyes widened as they pinned me to my chair. What would my mother do in this situation? It seemed like trouble always went out of its way to find and harass me. Her mouth twitched, and I knew she wished everyone would leave so she could tell my father off.

My mouth opened to apologize and to make things right, but she beat me to it.

"I'm just glad you're alive. Most witches, royal or not, don't make it back out alive." She reached out and grabbed my clammy hands under the table, giving it a slight squeeze. Even though her eyes still didn't shine when the smile returned to her face.

And until this very day, I still have no clue why my father went down to the underworld. Every opportunity I had to ask about the spontaneous trip was met with a shrug and smile with a lie on the tip of his tongue that always followed with, "I love you."

Now, I wondered as I watched my mother hold the dessert knife so tight that her palms turned a dark red. If that, too, was a lie.

"Well, who said a royal dinner was boring?" Sir Cross said. His pudgy stomach danced as he chuckled.

The bread pudding tasted heavy in my mouth as everyone went back to their conversation except for my mother and me. Looking over at Del, she gave me a worried glance as I held my hand to stop the tremor that racked my body. The worst part is, I couldn't even tell my mother what my father dragged me to the underworld for since he lied to me. My father promised to spend my fifteenth birthday with me in Paris, but imagine my surprise when he shuttled me to the gates that had been guarded to prevent demons from traveling between the underworld and the human world. The icing on the cake was when he left me in a room that made me shiver for hours while he was shuttled away. When we eventually made it out, he made me seal the portal with blood. My blood. It took weeks for me to get rid of the frigid chill from being watched.

Was it paranoia? Maybe.

Chapter 11

Kaydian

After the tense dinner, we shuffled into the hardly used grand great hall. The space was like night and day from the intimate dining room. Gold ceilings with a strip of skylight that ran vertically from one end of the hall to the next. The light moss-colored room was illuminated with the golden light fixtures that lined the walls while the moonlight bounced off the transparent crystals of the massive chandelier that hung in the center of the room. If you stood at a certain angle, the light would blind you. Maybe if I got everyone in the perfect angle. I could escape being the prize attraction of this circus for tonight.

My hand flew up to cover my mouth, but it wasn't enough to cover the giggle I let out. Kato, one of the African heirs, stopped mid-sentence as soon as the sound fell from my mouth. He was handsome with thick black coily curls, a purple Kitenge, and perfect dimples. He was the only heir that was close to my age, at twenty. The tanzanite in his ring glittered whenever he leaned into me—well, he was until I giggled. He pulled back and glanced at me like I was going mad, which may very well be the case because I couldn't stop giggling. The sound started out muffled until I couldn't suppress it any longer as it turned into a full out hysterical laugh. My mind felt detached from my body as my hand flew to my mouth to stifle it, but nothing worked. I could hear myself shout "Stop" over the demented sound, but I couldn't fulfill the demand.

Someone's firm hand grabbed me by my shoulder, pulling me into the far back corner of the hall. I knew it was my mother's touch before her magic seeped into me like medicinal tea, warming me from the inside out. My magic clawed at hers, fighting against the turbulent surge of my slow descent. I couldn't see my mother's magic, but I could feel it fight off the diseased dark cloud of the curse. Protecting me like she always has ever since I was born.

"Kaydian!" My mother yelled. "I'm right here with you, my emerald moon. Come back to me."

Like seeing for the first time, my mind reconnected with my beloved brain. The inky black fog that muddled my brain was gone. Kato, Del, and the two heirs I have yet to meet stood before me. Disgust and pity marred their handsome faces. Del bit her lip and took a step toward me, but thought better of it, stopping in her tracks. Her wet eyes bounced between the small group that gathered in the back of the room.

Finally, finding my lost voice, I replied, "Del, I'm alright. I promise."

But was I really, though? My mother was next as she wrapped me in her vanilla embrace. I plunged my nose into her neck, wishing I could hide right there forever, but now she knew the secret I had worked diligently to hide since the beginning of the year. My time is most definitely winding down...maybe even shorter than I thought. With my luck, I would slip into the demented curse when I went to sleep tonight. Then I would truly be alone.

"Hey, it's going to be alright. We'll figure this out together. I have a stash of Cliff Fieldcress. We will find a solution."

And how long will that last? I wanted to ask, but I was afraid the ball in my throat would burst through me if I parted my lips.

I could deal with the madness alone, but now I had to live with being my mother's worst potential nightmare. She waited there patiently while I tried several times to swallow my sob.

"I'm okay, Mom..." I looked around the area. We were alone in the back of the great hall. Del mother summoned back to the serving room while the others escaped. Luckily, the dancing royals ignored our situation in the back of the room. Probably too drunk to notice my outburst. Pulling away from my mother, I noticed her eyes were rimmed red as she quickly dabbed at them with her handkerchief. She folded the large cloth and wiped my wet face with the dry side.

"Remember, chin up, and don't let anyone see your crown slip." My mother fixed the crown that was pinned in my hair. "Literally."

She chuckled.

"Why don't you go upstairs..."

"It's okay, Mom." I took her hand and gave it a squeeze. "It's going to be okay. I'm going to mingle with others."

My mother opened her mouth, but I turned on my heels and walked away. With each step, the clawing in my stomach increased as I held my arms stiffly by my side. I walked over to the drink table and downed the pink Fae wine. The bubbles slid down my throat, slowly burning a path down to my turbulent stomach, but it did nothing to settle the nerves as I thought it would.

Kato and the heirs were gathered by the tiered Youna fountain in the nook garden outside of the great hall. The smile plastered on my face should be fake enough to get me through the night. When I pushed through the double white glass doors, the heirs turned toward me. Their eyes shifted as they looked at each other. Nervous twitches replaced the smile they once had. I felt exposed, and I hated the thought they could see the flaws beneath my cracks.

"Are you okay?" Kato asked. His voice seemed different from before.

He couldn't even look me in my eye as he stared over my shoulders. Kato took a huge step back when I tried to get close enough to speak to him without the others listening. I winced at the action, not out of embarrassment, but out of anger. My nails dug into my soft palms. My right eye twitched, which was never a good sign. No one spoke a word. They just stared at the loose cannon that is Kaydian Thibodeaux...the cursed psycho. My fisted hands trembled as I recited my mother's chant in my head.

Never let them see your crown fall.

My heart slowed as the words became easier to form. A hand slipped into mine as I turned to look to see who would have the gall to touch me without my consent. Victoria stood next to me. Her manic smile back on her deeply frostbitten colored skin as she hummed along with the music. She swayed with her hands still intertwined with mine.

"It's okay, Princess Kaydian." Her eyes fluttered close as she inhaled deeply. "When you're deep into your madness, then maybe we can be together. Imagine living in a world all of your own. It's not bad after a while 'cause you make friends with the shadows."

The moment the words left her chapped lips. My hand ripped away from her rough one. I won't become like her, curse be damned! With my head held high. Pivoting on my heels, I hightailed it out of the garden. Not one heir tried to stop me. My legs ached from the way I stomped on the concrete floors.

Once I was back in the hall, the band had died down the music to a slow tempo as the Royals thinned out and go their separate ways. Several of them tried their hardest to gain my attention, but all I wanted was a minute to myself...to think and clear my turbulent thoughts of murder...and desolation.

I spotted my mother and my father behind the closed doors in the dining room. My mother was infamous for being able to cut you with her sharp tongue without blinking an eye, but as I looked through the glass door, the thick vein in her slender throat protruded while her dark red lips were pulled into a deep frown. My father's leg shook as he spoke to my mother. Too bad I couldn't read lips because every two seconds, my mother's small hand closed into a fist, and I didn't have to be in the room to know that her magic probably was stifling my father. He stood there, with his mouth in a thin line, as he rubbed the back of his neck.

"Princess Kaydian," Ms. Kincaid called, breaking my focus from the heated conversation. "I have been looking for you. I was showing the guest rooms to some of the Royals who were staying overnight in the castle. Would you like me to fix your bath and bed for you now?"

Ms. Kincaid had the worst timing.

"No, that's fine, Ms. Kincaid. I will be fine for the night."

The last thing I wanted was for Ms. Kincaid to see me shred my room to pieces to get rid of some of the unwanted emotions brewing inside of me. Her dark brown eyes were drowning in light red, and the bags under her eyes told me today had worn on her more than she would like to let on. We were witches, not machines after all. She nodded and shuffled off to the Royals, who stood by the refreshment table waiting for her to return.

When I turned back to the dining room doors, my parents were gone. Rubbing the thick knot in my neck, I proceeded back to the door.

Every nerve in my body screamed for me to just run into my room and lock out everything until the heaviness in my shoulders was gone.

But I was lucky in bad luck even when I was trying to do the right thing.

Funneling through the dining room, some of the staff were busy cleaning the large room and putting the room back in its normal state. Dishes and decorations were flying through the room, causing me to yelp as one almost collided with my head. The staff all turned and ducked their heads as they muttered, "Sorry, Your Highness," as they redirected their magic. Their words fell on deaf ears though, as I plowed through the room into the dimly lit hallway.

It was all too quiet in the hall except for the one light that flickered and hummed down the hall. Chewing on my bruised bottom lip, I turned to go up the stairs. My feet hit the first step before I heard the muffled sound of a sniffle coming from the office hallway. Without a second thought, my feet moved of their own accord as I rounded the corner.

My mother's office door was slightly ajar, and as I inched closer. My mother's shrill voice could be heard. This beat the time she yelled at me when I broke my leg from showing off my horse riding tricks.

Go back to your room, Kaydian. Haven't you had enough for the night?

But like the old saying goes, "Curiosity is like a drug. Once you start, it's hard to stop," and I was nothing but filled with misplaced curiosity.

Through the slit in the doorway, I could see my mother and father were continuing their heated conversation from the dining room. I pressed my hand against my mouth as I witnessed my mother. Her small hand in a fist, her once slick hairstyle, was now out of her bun, face filled with tears as she paced the sitting area. My father stood with his crystal tumbler in his hand with a hard pressed line on his face. My mother's magic was thick and angry in the air, causing my father to wipe away the beads of sweat that formed on his head. She could have killed him with her magic if he wasn't her mate. This I was sure of.

This had nothing to do with me, and I would rather not have to think about another thing that would cause me to wear a fake smile for the next couple of weeks.

That was easier said than done as I peered closer into the room.

"K-Kaydian will be ready to rule," my mother declared as she blew into the little handkerchief.

My father drained the last of his drink and exhaled. "You just said she was laughing like a maniac in front of everyone."

"I never said maniac! I said she might have lost a bit of control," she said as she collapsed onto her desk chair. She dragged her hands over her tearful face, leaving thick black lines of mascara to paint her face.

"It's the same thing, Cel," my father replied by calling my mother by his nickname for her.

"It's NOT!" My mother jumped up and marched over to my father. Her finger poked into his hard chest.

"It is!" My father spat back. "You're just too blinded by love to see the truth. The faster you see reason, the quicker we can find a solution."

My mother sobbed and turned her back on him. He placed a hand on my mother's shoulder and gave it a squeeze. I was too tired to cry anymore as my body lay limp against the wall next to the door. Many in the coven had most likely given up on me. Casting me aside as if I was an outcast witch, but to hear my father speak as if I were already lost to the curse was more than disheartening. It was as if someone had opened up my veins and poured cold water inside of them. My hand covered my mouth as I whimpered like a child behind them.

"She'll be a great queen...she just needs more time to—"

"You and I know that time is of the essence and although we can control lots of things. Time isn't one of them. Plus, the people will never follow someone who is demented...no matter how many lessons we give her. I love our daughter with all of my heart, but it's time to face the fact that the goddess has chosen for her to be alone. She's a hopeless cause," my father said as he rubbed his jaw. "Let's state the facts, Cel. She will be mateless and follow the same path as your great-grandaunt. What can we do, Cel? She's already gone."

My father shrugged nonchalantly, as if he were speaking about the weather, leaning against my mother's desk.

"I know what you want," my mother's voice dripped with disgust. Her upper lip curled over her teeth. "You just want that bastard to sit on the throne."

Who is the bastard?

My father paused before saying, "Do we have a better option? She is our safer option to guarantee that my...your legacy lives on. Can you imagine if Kaydian took the throne? It would be worse than Angela. It's a pity but Youna has made her choice. Our daughter is cursed to walk this earth alone and mad."

Without warning, my mother summoned her magic, sending the metal vase she loved flying toward my father's head. He ducked just before it could connect with him. They bickered again. I couldn't hear anything over my father's words. My breathing quickened, and my mind no longer wanted to be in my own shoes—or here in the castle anymore.

My face felt scorched, and I couldn't keep control of my hand, let alone my legs. The trek back to my room felt stagnate as I passed the makeshift guest rooms, one by one, filled with Royals being pleasured. Their moans were barely above a whisper, but it was enough for me to hear them. When I reached the old stairs, my knees buckled as I stumbled up the stairs to my wing.

Hopeless cause...Already gone...Cursed to be alone.

I shouldn't have been surprised that my father didn't have faith in me. I'd long since suspected that he knew the little dark secret I tried to keep hidden from everyone, even myself. **We are the helpless cause. It's time to just give in.** My heavy head hung low at my dark voice as I dragged my feet to my bedroom. When I opened my door, Del was perched on the edge of my bed. Her serving clothing was gone in place of her blue nightgown. Del perked up when she saw me, but when I lifted my head, her smile turned into a frown.

I didn't give her a chance to speak as I collapsed on the bed and into Del's arms. The tears I held in since...well, since the strange voice appeared, poured out of me. Del held me, allowing me to wet the cotton gown until it was drenched with my pitiful tears. Tremors rack my body as I open up, leaving me open and vulnerable.

"Hey, it's going to be okay."

Will it be? I thought as my best friend's heart thumped slowly against my pounding one. In the back of my mind, my trip to the three sisters haunted me from behind my darkening vision as hard as I tried to push away the memory. It kept appearing, leaving me more confused than before.

Ten Years Ago

Stepping through the portal, the gust of wind had me tugging at the long black fur-trimmed coat as my teeth clattered, standing in the piercing weather. Looking around the foreign area, there was only one way to proceed to the massive cabin that sat on the rocky hill. The long pathway shrouded in trees as big as the buildings in Houston framed the pathway, making it daunting, especially when some of the pathway was drenched in darkness. Even though the snow was already piled high in the deserted area, the smell of more snow was in the air, which made me scurry down the narrow pathway so I wouldn't get caught in the storm.

Contrary to their given name, the Three Sisters weren't related, but were like Delphine and I. Kindred spirits born on the same day at the same time, destined to be together for all time. They were the wayward children of goddesses. Zadia, Goddess of Life and Death. Thetris, Goddess of War. Milmera, Goddess of the Moon.

My mother said the Three Sisters used their ancient magic to keep the secluded area in the far corner of Antarctica hidden. With the same eerie feeling as the otherworld before they burned it down, leaving only the fiery pits of the underworld for our dead. In fear, the sisters were cast out of the underworld before they were even allowed entrance. Casting them to the only available world left, ours. They decided that a life of seclusion away from humans, witches, and other supernaturals was the only way they could maintain their sanity. That caused their ancestor magic to become one with the land and into the gift of sight.

As I walked the snow-covered brick pathway, I wondered if my mother was right, that I would be okay because by the way my legs shook once I speed walked to the steep steps, I begged to differ. My heart lodged in my throat with each step closer to the old black gates. Why did I have to do this? But I knew the answer already. Every Royal must take this trip to see the Three Sisters. It was our birthright, being the goddesses' descendants, to get a reading for our future—or should I say a brief glimpse.

I needed all the help I could get from the Three Sisters as I watched the few Royals who attended the Thibodeaux Royal Academy find their other half.. As

I watched the few Royals who attended the Thibodeaux Royal Academy find their other half, I quickly realized that I was the only one left without a mate. Soon, I clung onto their stories of their dates like it was my last breath, as I pictured what it would be like to be loved and pinned over until their bonding ceremony at nineteen. My mother's encouraging words of, "It will happen soon" and "Trust me, he or she is out there," turned into just fruitless encouragement—for me...or her, I wasn't so sure. It was pathetic to think about even now as I pictured my mother chewing her bottom lip after saying the same line every time the subject was brought up that something would indeed change.

With my luck, I was probably just meant to be the end of the Youna line, and maybe if I were lucky, I would have at least one good thing on my tombstone.

As I approached the large black door, my hands, despite the frigid weather, were damp. Maybe it was a sign that I should just go home and wait for the curse to set in and pray I can do one good thing for my coven before I go mad. Wiping my hands on my coat, I balled up my fist to knock on the door.

A gust of wind sent the feathers of my coat on a chaotic dance as the door opened before my knuckles had a chance to disturb the peace. There was no one at the door, so I took it as a cue to step inside. Myrrh and peppermint drifted out of the small living room of the home. A large brown wood-burning fireplace, wedged between two bookcases, warmed the home. A brown sofa, a couple of wooden chairs, and a table finished the room. In the middle of the table sat a small bowl with a small candle warming the yellow sap and the green leaves. It was as if the scent had control over my mind, drawing me closer to the bowl.

"If you're not careful, you too will be added to the bowl," the dead voice rang out, causing me to jump back from the bowl, almost knocking over the chair that was behind me.

"I'm sorry!" My voice is unrecognizable to even myself with my hand over my chaotic heart.

The Three Sisters stood before me in all of their dark glory. Long blood-red cloaks that were one size too big hung over their frame, and their hoods draped over their faces. If I hadn't known any better, I would have said they were ghosts. Anaisha, Noor, and Ada—The Three Sisters of the Underworld. My mouth pulled into a nervous smile.

"Three Sisters, forgive me. I hadn't meant to be nosy," I said. My face warmed with shame. "I just got caught up in the fragrance's redolence—"

"You mean you got caught up in the trap we set? If you dip any part of your body in there, you will become numb, losing all of your control over your body." The Sister closest to me said with a voice like syrup. Smooth and alluring.

"Then we can harvest your skin for our offering to the goddess," the Sister, toward the end, spoke, her voice low and scratchy. I wondered if I heard her correctly.

With a shaky smile, I nodded, which was the most I could give them in return. I forgot they finished each other's sentences. My mother had warned me the Three Sisters would scare the living daylights out of me with some of their practices, but that was putting it too nicely. Placing my hands behind my back, I stood tall. My back straightened even though my insides convulsed. Show no fear! Taking a deep breath as I pulled myself together.

"Come, young Princess. Let us not keep you waiting," the middle sister said. The rough edges of her voice caused my eye to twitch.

Not bothering to wait for an answer, they turned and headed down the dim, narrow hallway. The further we went, the myrrh and peppermint faded away, and the more I relaxed. At least they would let me keep my skin. Don't touch the walls! I reminded myself as I almost collided with the white walls from not paying attention. The walls in the sisters' home were enchanted with a delirium spell. One touch, and you'll be lost in the sister's trap for eternity. The soft clacks of their shoes against the wooden floor made the hairs on my arm rise. Turning down the hall, this one equally longer than the last, I followed blindly until they stopped at a red door in the middle of the hallway with a gold metal medallion shaped in all eight goddesses. The tips of their oversized sleeves almost touched the floor as they recited, "Blessed be the goddess," in the old tongue.

The door clicked open, and we funneled into the room as I ducked my head in respect to the goddess. The room was void of warmth or anything that suggested they occupied the quaint room. Nothing but a stand with the oversized book of the sisters, the forbidden book with every detail of the sisters' lives and other secrets. My mother said I shouldn't even think of touching the book or face a fate worse than death. I would be written in the book. My life would be brought to a couple of pages in the book, all for a greedy look.

No, thank you. I already had enough problems on my hands.

Anaisha, Noor, and Ada lined up behind the book's altar. Their faces were shrouded in mystery. I couldn't deny my curiosity to see what was beyond their hoods. I waited patiently as they stood there, and even though I couldn't see their faces. Every sense in my body screamed they were staring at me. Assessing me. Judging me. Taunting me. Just the thought caused me to shift on my feet.

"Well, Princess Kaydian, we await your instructions."

"You have the key to your destiny."

"We are just vessels. Ask your questions, but remember, a riddle comes at no cost. The answer, however, is a different story." The last sister said simultaneously. Their muttered agreements filled the room, causing my stomach to do somersaults.

"Of course! Right," clearing my throat. "Anaisha, Noor, and Ada, the great sisters of the goddess. I would like to know what my future entails for me."

The sisters cocked their heads, causing the acid in my stomach to creep up my throat. Two of the sisters chanted in the old Royal language, "Goddess reveal what's hidden., Reveal what lies before us. Open our eyes to glimpse the future." Gloved hands peeped out of the extra-long sleeves as the sister in the middle carefully removed the red glove from her right hand. The sight made me swallow the scream that bubbled in my throat. Her finger was blackened, pieces of the burnt skin hung off at different angles and places. The pungent stench of old rotten fruits and meat made tears rim my eyes, blinking rapidly as I focused on the middle sister.

Holding the singed hand over the book, the book cover flew open with a thud onto the altar. The sisters' hoods fluttered as the pages flipped like a fan until the sister's desired page was found. With the other two sisters still chanting, the middle sister took a piece of the charred skin that hung off the side of her hand between her two fingers and pulled back the skin until the blood bubbled and pooled out of the exposed flesh. Coloring the page with her blood as an offering, the fresh metallic scent mixed with the room's putrid smell. Have Mercy! I thought I had become accustomed to death and all of the appalling things I've seen in the castle, but watching someone peel back their skin, without a sound, like a banana, was dreadful.

"Ah, yes, I see," the middle sister said, causing my feet to tap the floor. "Patience, Princess, while I read."

How she was bothered by my light tapping, but not by the howling of her sisters, was beyond me.

Signaling to the others, she stepped aside while they each read the bloodied book. Piercing a hole into me as she stood waiting...watching. It was worse than my mother's penetrative glare. A cold pearl of sweat that formed on my neck crept down the curves of my spine, making the blue button-down shirt stick to my skin.

When the other sisters joined, they stood on either side of the middle sister in a uniformed line. Anaisha, Noor, and Ada nodded uniformly. The moment of truth, a quick glance into the future. Something to give me hope I won't become another black sheep of the royals or, worse, a failure to my goddess ancestor. Holding my trembling hands behind me, I knew what to ask next, but would I like the answer? That was a different question.

"Anaisha, Noor, and Ada, will you grace me with a glimpse into my future?"

The middle sister turned to both her sisters and nodded.

"A riddle for your future," one sister started.

"Comes at no charge," another sister continued.

"Do you agree to these terms, young princess?" The last sister asked.

My mouth dried up at their question, and all I could do was nod. My mother had already forewarned me that being greedy would be my downfall. I was anything but greedy, so I would take what was given freely and ask for nothing more, even if a small part of me wanted to disobey that rule. I remembered my mother strictly telling me, "Don't anger the sisters, or they will withhold your future, Kaydian."

"Yes, I'm ready for my riddle."

They clapped their glove cladded hands together, causing the book to shut.

"Princess Kaydian, descendant of our blessed and revered Youna."

"Your future reads as this," one sister started.

"Celestoria has four journeys," another sister continued.

"But only three will survive," the last sister said.

"The forth will meet a death by the sun." The sister who started it finished.

Pausing, they stood watching me. The silence in the room is deafening. I dug my nails into my wrist to keep from screaming. What if this was a setup from the goddesses? A test of some sort to see if I would be loyal to the rules. Even as I stood there with their faceless gazes upon me, I knew I was just being inane. Just as I opened my mouth to ask a question, the middle sister spoke.

"We have a blessed gift from your Youna, young princess. She's gifted you another riddle," the middle sister said, her voice holding a menacing timbre. "Are you ready?"

Without hesitating, I said, "Yes, sisters, reveal my gift."

"Fresh as snow," one sister started.

"Blood will decorate the throne," another sister continued.

"For power is never given but taken," the last sister said.

Silence enveloped the room once more. They were done with the reading, and it was now my move to ask another question if I chose. Maybe I was a special case since I received two readings.

"Anaisha, Noor, and Ada, may I ask another question?"

They once again looked at each other, but this time, there was no nodding.

"Princess Kaydian," one sister started.

"Knowing too much comes with a price," another sister continued.

"Your mother knows all too well," the last sister said.

"Despite your unique circumstances," another sister spoke.

"You're not above the rules," one sister said.

"Would you like to proceed, young Princess of Youna?" They said in unison.

My tongue felt heavy in my mouth as my thoughts fell onto my mother. What had she given up? I wanted to ask a million questions, but what would I be deprived of if I did? My magic? My sanity?

"Anaisha, Noor, and Ada, I think you've given enough of my future. I will figure out the pieces as I go."

With my decision made, the weight of my fate was just a little more bearable. Paying my respects to the Three Sisters by kneeling in submission. I left the tiny home with their words heavy on my mind. What journey lies ahead? I wasn't sure, but there was no turning back now. Just before I closed the door to their home, I heard one sister say, "She's smart...unlike her mother."

When I arrived back home, my mother sat on my bed with her hair in her bonnet and a green cotton robe. We stared at each other until I went over and hugged her. I hated riddles, and this time was no different. A trip that was supposed to give me hope has left me grasping at air. And as for Celestoria's three journeys, whatever that means, I would have to worry about that for another day. No words were needed as she fell asleep in my bed—well, she did, with her arms wrapped around me like a protective blanket. I laid awake pondering my mother's decision, my fate, and what I should do next.

Chapter 12

Kaydian

After the last of my tears dried up, I moved out of Del's comforting embrace. My shoulders hung low as I sat up on the edge of the bed, facing the plain wall. Del's small hand popped into my view as she handed me a tissue to clean my face. Brown and black makeup decorated the tiny white tissue when I was finished.

Del gave a nervous giggle when she saw my face and told me to, "Wait here," as she ran to the bathroom. When she returned, she had the small bucket and a washrag.

"It looks like you painted your face."

She chuckled, and I knew she only meant for it to cheer me up, but I couldn't bring myself to laugh or chuckle at her joke. Not when all I could hear in my head was my father saying I was a helpless cause. When I was done cleaning my face, Del took the items and hurried off to the bathroom again.

The bed dipped slightly when she returned, but I couldn't lift my head up from my chest.

"Do you want to talk about it?" she asked as she wrapped her hand over mine.

The touch was meant to comfort me, but I felt nothing. Just a deep-set sense of emptiness and humiliation.

"I really don't want to, Del."

"Kaydian, we promised each other never to go to sleep angry or to keep anything from each other."

It's easy for her to say that. Her father loved her unconditionally. Mr. Pourciau would never look at Delphine as a failure...a helpless cause. **Stop comparing yourself to a common witch...she doesn't care about you like we do!**

The more I kept repeating that Del was just trying to be a supportive best friend. The more the anger welled in my chest like an overheated kettle. Breathe in. **Ungrateful bitch, let me handle her.** Breathe out. We sat down on my bed for what seemed like hours before I could unglue my mouth and tamper down the voice and my festering anger.

I spilled the entire conversation to Del. My face was blank as I worked my way through the moment I found my parents in my mother's office. The words tumbled out of my mouth as my throat quivered. In my mind, a war brewed. I couldn't be sure if I wanted to cry again or scream at the top of my lungs until I passed out. At this point, I might do both. Not that anyone would care, seeing as everyone now knows I'm slowly approaching my descent into madness, and soon, I will just be another soul placed under the coliseum.

"Kaydian, you don't have to keep repeating 'worthless cause' anymore. I get it," Del sighed deeply.

Her words broke my tirade. I hadn't realized I was repeating the insult until Del mentioned it.

"I'm sorry, Kaydian. I didn't realize..." She paused and squeezed my hand. "Your night would turn out like this...I mean, I knew it wouldn't be fun, but this was a bit much."

Shaking my head, "This wasn't how I wanted to spend my last months of having my sanity before..."

Pausing, the words became stuck as they dried up on my tongue. In my over-optimistic mind, I thought the curse would skip me altogether and that maybe, just maybe, the goddesses would spare me. Yet, tonight showed me I was nothing but a joke to Youna and the other goddesses. A plaything just for torturing. An image of my ancestor with her emerald eyes and picturesque face laughing popped up in my darkened mind.

"My father wants to put me down like my grandparents had to do with my grandaunt."

Del paused, and even though I was still facing the plain wall, I could feel her wide shocked eyes boring a hole into the side of my face.

"I-I'm sorry, Kaydian. I wish I could do something to help you...I wish I could switch places with you and take this curse away from you."

I scoffed and rolled my eyes as the anger seeped out of me like a slow-moving tornado.

"And what would that do for me?" I said as I catapulted from the bed and paced the length of the bed. "I would be without my best friend. I would be alone and cast off to the woods to live by myself as my parents scrambled to find my replacement."

Del stared at me with red-rimmed eyes.

I continued pacing back and forth. "Then I would really be alone. Not even my mother would be able to save me. You and I both know the coven and the royals won't allow me to rule without a mate."

"Maybe..." Del chewed her bottom lip. "Maybe you're not looking hard enough, Kaydian!"

I scoffed and turned to face her. "Del, do you even believe what you just said?"

Turning red, Del opened and closed her mouth. Del and I have never truly had an argument or fought since we were thirteen, and I told her that her crush was a human in his past life...which was worse than any curse word I could have thought of.

"You don't have to be rude, Kaydian! I'm just trying to help," Del said through her clenched teeth.

Before I could help myself, I heard my next words slip out, "Well, help a little less then."

"No, I won't let you push me away," Del countered. Del's icy hand landed on my heated skin. "Let's go to bed and come up with a plan in the morning. We can go to the covens outside ours, and maybe we can start looking outside of the royals. It is a small pool here..."

I needed a break from the coven, from my duties, or myself. Honestly, I wasn't sure. Del wasn't aware that my mind had already left my tiny room as she kept on prattling on. The only thing I knew as of now was that I needed to be far away from the coven. Just me and the darkness that lives inside of me as I prepare myself for the downfall.

My shoulders sagged as I dragged my feet into my closet. My magic, the only thing that was working for me tonight, opened the door to my enchantment room. I marched into the little room and counted the brick from the door entryway. Once I found the unsuspected fifth brick, I dug into my hair, searching for the sharp gold hairpin. As I pulled the tiny pin out of my bun, I heard the maddening voice in my head shout, "No!" I paused and closed my eyes as I willed the voice to leave me alone. I had one too many things going on with me right now.

Opening up my eyes, I quickly prick myself with the pin. The small red dot of my blood bubbled out of the small hole. The metallic mixed with my lavender perfume fragrant the stuffy air. Entering my wet finger in the center of the brick as it mixed with my magic, turning the white brick red. Click. The sound of the brick releasing from the wall rebounded in the room. I dug my hand into the hollowed-out space and grabbed the little scrap of paper I kept hidden there. My hand drifted over the small jewelry box with our true family ring as I wondered maybe I should bring it with me, just in case.

Nope! I thought as I closed the secret hideaway, watching the brick click back into place and turn back to blend in with the other bricks. Grabbing my drawing pad and a new pencil, I headed back into the room. Del had gotten up from the bed. The shoulder on her nightgown had an outline of my face in tears as the realization had set in. She stood there in the middle of the room, playing with her fingers. Her once flushed face was now pale as the white sheets on my bed, and the tears flowed from her red eyes. Del's hair was ruffled in the back, which she made no attempt to fix.

I dropped the items onto my bed and turned to her and said, "Are you coming with me? I'm not sure where I'll land, but anywhere will be better than here right now. Or will you stay here?"

Del just wrapped her arms around her small body and hung her head down. Anger washed over me as I could all but tell Del's decisions.

"Oh, you don't want to be seen with the worthless princess, huh?"

"You know I don't think you're worthless, plus you know I can't leave. I have to help my family for the upcoming harvest. I'm not as important as you, KD."

She paused. Her bottom lip was red and swollen as she continued,

"Please don't leave, Kaydian!" She chased behind me as I escaped to my closet.

"I need to, Del."

Throwing off the green dress and changing into a white button-down shirt and the only pair of blue farm overalls I owned, I ignored Del as she trotted behind me, asking a million questions. In the back of my mind, I knew I owed her an apology for being a bitch to her, but I couldn't fix my twisted mouth, let alone my mind, to say it out loud. Just another indication that maybe my father was right after all.

After I found the pair of white sneakers, I kept them in the back of my closet for a rainy day...like today. I pulled out a small bag and threw in some essential items.

"Kaydian, this is ridiculous!" Del said when we got back to my bed. "What about your parents and the coven?"

"Have you not heard a single thing I've said, Del?" I took my finger and placed it in the middle of her chest. "I can't seem to make things right, and soon, the coven will come knocking on the castle's door asking for me to be chained up or..."

I stopped mid-sentence. There was only one secret I'd ever withheld from Del. That real emerald would strip me of my powers—the only way to kill us. It would leave me vulnerable to being attacked. I'd tried many times to rationalize why telling her would be a good thing, but I always came up short and remembered my mother's promise that I made to never spoken a word to anyone.

One deeply rooted secret between Ms. Kincaid, Sir Reid, my mother, and I. Just another thing that made the weight on my shoulder heavier.

I grabbed the pin and pricked another finger. A curse word fell from my lips as I accidentally hit the wrong side of my finger.

"See! That's a sign, Kaydian. Let's just talk it through."

"Goddesses, mask my magic from my foes," speaking the blood-cloaking incantation in our royal language. I rarely used blood magic since my mother's magic kept our town shielded from the outside world. And the incantations had to be spoken out loud. The only time I've ever used blood magic was to practice with Sir Reid and my mother.

In the back of my mind, I could only hope I was doing the correct thing.

As the red drop of blood mixed with my magic, the colors amalgamated to a muddy brown before leaving a dimmed version of burnt sienna. Against my skin, the thin magic hugged my curves, making me glow. The protection spell will cover me and my magic for a day or two. Afterward, If I don't use my magic, my parents won't know where to find me, but I will be back before that happens.

"Kaydian, I know things aren't going how you want them to, but it will get better," Del pleaded.

"It's whatever, Del. You wouldn't understand, Del. Listen, I need some breathing room from..." I paused, sweeping my hands in front of me. "This. I will be back tomorrow before anyone will notice."

I picked up the small bag, stuffing the drawing pad under my arm.

Turning from Del before the hard throb in my throat slipped out. The green aura flooded the room. The white slit opened in the middle of my room, and I jumped into the white light to my next destination. Where to? I wasn't sure, but I trusted my magic and I knew it would lead me to the right place.

Chapter 13

Kaydian

When I stepped out of the portal, I knew Del had probably jinxed me. That would have been the only way to explain how I, Kaydian Thibodeaux, landed in a dark alleyway. The smell permeating from the area smelled like rotten meat and death. Covering my nose with my free hand only made matters worse as I breathed the rancid air into my mouth.

The blaring sounds from the streets beckoned me toward the bright exit. I emerged from the seedy alleyway, squinting my eyes as they adjusted to the bright lights. People buzzed around the busy street even though it was late at night. With their heads straight, caught up in their own world, not paying attention to anyone but their accompanying party.

"Move!" someone yelled as I moved closer to the curb to avoid being mowed down by an older woman with a steel cart.

I've never been to New York City before. It was the one place Del, and I always wanted to visit. But we were afraid to travel too far, even with using the portal. The surrounding chatter was so palpable I could reach out and touch it. Those mini billboards in Houston were nothing compared to the ones here. Instead of the dull, faded prints, it was vibrant and massive, with a variety of colorful lights that decorated several blocks of the long fork road—walking in a trance, taking in the different stores that lined the streets. As I finally got to the end of the long street, I noticed the long street sign that read Broadway and Times Square.

I thought all the humans would be asleep by now.

Honestly, standing in the corner with my blue overalls and my belongings under my arms, that creeping sensation returned to the pit of my stomach as I watched several people pass. Their faces pinched as if they smelled something bad. Their judgmental eyes did a once over of me. Pulling the book in front of me, shielding the offending clothing, my skin felt tight. Everyone I passed looked put together, and then there was me. I appeared as if I just stepped out of the farm. My face warmed when I saw a couple from across the street point and giggle at me.

Shame propelled me as my legs finally got the message that we needed to move, and quickly. As I ran across the street when the coast was clear, I tried to watch where I was going, but the front of my sneakers caught onto the streetcar tracks, which sent me stumbling over my feet. Pain radiated up and down my arms as my hands broke my fall. The people on the other side of the street stopped and stared at me like I was a complete and utter fool.

A blaring sound pierced my ears as I got up from the wet street and scurried to the other side of the road. I dodged the impatient driver as he drove off, leaving me pondering my life decisions. With me standing there, with the front of my overalls damp, matching my armpits, which made the shirt cling onto me like a second skin, I was truly a fish out of the sea. The only thing I could hope for was that my accident hadn't ruined my drawing pad.

I needed to regroup somewhere as I looked up and saw the Macy's store.

My mother's emerald eyes always glazed over when she spoke about her trip to the store, and I could see why, as the eight-story store was a fashion lover's wet dream. I couldn't help myself as my feet led the way to the sandy-colored store.

Too bad they're closed.

I was about to turn around and leave, but out of the corner of my eyes, a beautiful gold-tiered dress. Which that sat on display in the window beckoned me. It had to be magic. My wide eyes roamed the metallic piece of art...for thirty dollars! Digging into the small bag, I felt around for the human money I normally stored in this purse. Of course, I left home with only five dollars. *Great Kaydian!*

"Move it along! You couldn't afford it, anyway." The police officer said as his hand turned an angry red as he gripped his baton. He waited patiently, staring down his nose at me like I was nothing more than a discarded bottle on the ground.

Disrespectful bastard...let's squeeze his neck till he's dead!

For fuck's sake! I don't need anything else to worry about, and I can't do anything to draw attention to myself. My magic raced through me, waiting at the edge of my fingertips for its chance to strike and kill the imbecile in front of me. The overpowering need to crush him with my magic wouldn't be enough. I feared I would find myself on top of the bastard with my hands wrapped around his fat throat, choking the simple, pathetic human life out of him. So, I tucked my tail in between my legs and speed-walked to the corner and into the nearest alleyway.

New York would have been perfect if Del was here with me. She would thrive in the fast-paced environment. I craved to be somewhere I could just paint and work my demons out without the background noise.

Opening up the portal again. Except for his time, I picked where I wanted to go and did not let my magic drop me anywhere. Maybe in Florida, I always wanted to visit that peculiar state.

The humid air smacked me in my face, and sweat gathered on my upper lip the moment my feet touched the grassy ground. Is this weather even real? I couldn't bear this heat. I can only imagine how humans live in this condition. It's like I had visited the underworld again.

Luckily, no one was around, the lights were too dim. There weren't any benches along the path around the lake. My feet ached and throbbed against my sneakers' hard insole that provided little to no comfort. I took a break by the small lake and laid on the plush lawn.

The night sky reminded me of back home. But tonight, there seemed to be billions of shiny diamonds in the sky. Not even a single cloud dared to disrupt them. Even through the heat, you can smell the grass. Although it was peaceful, all I could wonder was if Del was still in my room in her nightgown or whether my mother checked up on me. A deep sigh left my lips.

"Well, at least it's quiet," I said out loud.

I scoffed. Now I'm talking to myself. Why delay the inevitable? I had already started my demented downfall. I might as well get used to talking to myself until my parents came to off my head and burn my body. *Good riddance!* Maybe I will be reincarnated as a famous singer.

A crawling sensation worked its way across my legs. I thought was just from my bag that I threw down when I found the cleared spot. Unfortunately for me, I should have paid much more attention to my surroundings because a pinching sensation started in my lower leg, causing my head to spin as much as my leg throbbed. When I looked down, the black, red, and yellow snake was poised to strike my injured leg again. Without thinking, I bolted up and ran to the paved pathway. Unfortunately, my sneakers caught onto the edge of the pavement, and I went tumbling face-first into the concrete. My hands barely had enough time to break my fall, leaving me to flop like a fish out of water onto the pathway.

Amazing! Falling twice in one night. Wasn't I so lucky?

If Sir Reid were here, he would definitely just stare at me pathetically with his cold black eyes and shake his head.

Snakes were the second thing I hated more than mermaids.

After what seemed like an eternity, I pulled myself up from the cold floor. When I lifted the overalls leg to examine the aftermath, the small puncture wound had already closed, and all that was left was the brown tint of the snake venom mixed with my dried blood.... and my dignity, which, if we're being honest, was gone.

"Why can't I do anything right?" I said out loud.

This wasn't supposed to be difficult. The familiar lull of sleep tugged from deep within me as I wrapped my arms around myself. Goosebumps formed on my arms as I rubbed away the shiver. It was clear as the midnight sky that I needed to trust my magic because I couldn't find a place to land on my own. Pitiful, if you ask me.

I grabbed the book and my bag after I made sure the snake was gone.

"Please lead me to where I need to be. Somewhere I can find peace," I pleaded to my magic with exhaustion on the tip of my tongue.

My magic flickered and waned as it opened up the white slit, breaking the dark-shrouded greenery. This time, it felt different. My green aura wrapped around me, almost as if my magic were pushing me into the portal. This was a first for me, and I wasn't sure if it was normal for our magic to act in such a way.

When I stepped through the slit, I grunted and cursed. The pad under my arm was ruined as blades of grass were encrusted on the book with muddy dirt. I've ruined the last drawing pad I owned. Stomping the muddy ground did nothing but add more dirt to my clothing.

"My magic is out to drive me insane before my curse hits me," I said out loud.

That had to be the only explanation as I stared at the old wooden sign with the words "Sacramento Woods." The overwhelming cedar scent assaulted my nose. My shoulders slumped. I wanted to curse, scream...to do something, but my body was weak, and I was hungry. Del was right. And now my magic had recoiled to the center of my body in protest. Sleep was inevitable, and if I didn't find somewhere to rest soon, I would find myself face first in the dirt...again.

"Out of all the places my magic could take me. It chooses the woods. Great! Just fucking great." I said out loud.

When I looked around the long stretch of road, I couldn't see a home or store in sight. Just the towering pine trees with the rustling sounds of the many critters in the woods. Which reminded me of Sera and Luc. I missed them as I stood by the old rickety sign. Emptiness greeted me like an old lover. I had no one else to blame but myself.

"I guess I'm sleeping in the woods."

The rustling of leaves intensified the crawling sensation.

"I won't be foolish again."

The throb made me slam my sore eyes shut. I just needed it to sweep the area and maybe clean my dirt-covered overalls. The last thing I needed was for me to be eaten alive by a bear. My magic, which had retreated, fought me tooth and nail until my will to do anything else dwindled along with my confidence.

I stood by the side of the road for ten minutes, shaking my right hand as if that may solve the problem. If someone were to pass by me right now, they would surely think I was insane. A picture of me in a straight white jacket popped into my head. With a half smirk on my face, I decided to just bite the bullet and head into the dense woods.

"Well, if I'm eaten, my mother won't have to behead me. So, I guess that was a plus."

Luckily for me, there wasn't any pathway for me to follow. I bite on my lip, looking at the thick bushes. One can just hope for a clearing. Stepping into the bushes, I asked Juna, the Goddess of judgment, to guide me through the forest. Every snap and crunch of the twigs and branches made me jump out of my skin. The poor overalls I wore had several tears in them as the branches from the overgrown shrubs caught on the fabric. *Perfect!* Not only was I covered in dirt, but now I had added holes to the design.

My sweat dampened the white shirt I had on, and my hair became kinky from the sweat that formed on my head. I could no longer see the dust road from where I started. All I could see were the branches and thick bushes I'd trampled through for the last ten minutes. Off in the far distance, the soft rippling sound of water could be heard.

"Maybe if I find where the water is, I can at least wash the sweat and dirt off of me."

Absorbed in finding the soft sloshing sound, I forgot to pay attention to my surroundings. When I heard a low howl in the distance. My heart pounded erratically. I paused in the middle of my trek to see if my magic would spare me just enough to protect myself. Not even a whisper of magic to help me. "Youna really hates me," I said as I ran. Every tendon and muscle screamed as I pushed them to their limit. My calf muscles squeezed, and my heart was in my mouth. I promised Del I would be back. I can't die in Sacramento. My chest was heavy with exhaustion, causing me to curse my heavy breast. These thick thighs I loved ached and burned, demanding me to rest.

I guess I should have paid more attention to Sir Reid's advice because I stupidly looked back, and the next thing I knew...I was making out with the floor. My stomach burned from the impact. All of the little air in my overworked lungs was gone. The book I bought was ruined as leaves and mud coated the paper. But I couldn't stop, as the last of my adrenaline pushed my heavy body up from the floor as I detached my foot from one of the tree's roots.

I pushed myself up after rubbing my sore ankle when the unmistakable scent hit me square in my tight chest. My teeth chattered as I pleaded with Youna.

"I'm not a bad person, Youna! I did nothing... recently. It was all my father's fault."

My tears were coming down hard and fast as I tried to get away from the dog scent that filled the air. That can only mean one thing. Werewolves were close. I jogged to the water sound as I tried to think clearly. If they caught me, I would surely die, and it won't be from my mother but from shifters. This was the only time I wished my father hadn't allowed some werewolves to remain alive. Now I'll probably be on the receiving end of my father's vengeance.

The sound of the river turned into a loud swooshing sound that carried in the light, clean night breeze. Surely, the old saying that dogs hate water holds some truth. I came to a halt in front of a large tree that split the area. *Right or left, Kaydian!* I chewed on my bottom lip and grimaced. The mineral earthy taste of soil filled my mouth as I spat on the ground. My stomach wanted to throw the contents up, but I swallowed the acid back down.

"Great, what else can go wrong?"

A bright white light lit up the canopy of the trees, causing me to flinch at the cracking sound. The rain didn't start with the warning sprinkle of rain, which normally comes before the downpour. Nope, the sky opened up, and the heavy rain soaked me and—shit, well, my overalls. Since I lost my purse and book somewhere when I kissed the ground. I had nothing to protect me from the rain.

The downpour made my hair heavy as it fell out of the hair tie, and strands of my now kinky hair were plastered to my face. Grasping my tears mixed with the rainwater and holding my arm over my face, I headed left...to where? My death or my salvation. I wasn't sure. At this point, does it matter anymore?

My last question was met with a low bark. I stopped the staggered pace to look back, foolishly, as a scream ripped out of my throat. There was a massive black wolf almost the size of me that stood at the entrance of the fork pathway. Its coat was damp from the onslaught of the rain. Those amber eyes glowed in the night's dark. It did not move, leaving me wondering if it was my imagination playing tricks on me or if it was waiting to pounce on me.

"I fucking hate my father!" I screamed out, and the wolf tilted its enormous head.

Maybe I should feel bad about my words, but it felt good to release my demons after all, since I was facing death. I pulled on my magic once more, but it coiled inside of me and bubbled throughout my body. The feeling was foreign, as I never felt my magic react this way. I guess facing death made my magic happy. That made one of us. The wolf took one step forward, and I took one shaky step back. If I were to die here, then I would die fighting.

I turned and ran as fast as my sore feet would allow me. A loud bark was heard behind me as I made my way into the unknown. As if the weather had a vendetta against me. The rain came down harder. The stinging sensation against my tender skin felt like pellets. I could hear the wolf running behind me, and I picked up my pace.

The roar of the water reached a deafening pitch as I got closer to it, drowning out the wolf's steps behind me. One look back, and it was gone. I was left alone, trapped between the forest and the raging waters of the river.

"Good!" I whispered to myself as I turned back. The heel of my foot slid on the muddy dirt that lined the edge before the water. It wasn't until I tried to stop my descent with my other foot I knew my mistake. There wasn't just water to help save me from my impending death, but also a cliff. As my feet disconnected from the edge, I made one last attempt to call on my magic, which was once bubbling inside of my chest, to help, but I pushed my magic too much already. It dimmed quickly as it became dormant.

I closed my eyes, the soft lull of succumbing to my fate, and prepared for the worst as I gave up the struggle.

Chapter 14

Greyson

"Greyson, you're the Alpha of our pack. Mayor Perrins has allowed them to build their box homes just along our perimeter. Next, they will be well over the property line, and they won't stop there. They will take and take until we are no longer here."

Michel, one of the pack members who wants Oni to rule, said, "Your father would have killed that meddling bastard. You can't be docile about these humans. We were once and look what happened to our brothers and family."

"Paráh, Michel... I understand. I just need some more time to figure it out." I rushed out.

"No, Greyson. Listen to me. The humans are nothing but a fucking pest. If we take out the mayor, then maybe we can stall those builders."

"That's a good idea, Oni. Hit him in the middle of the night," Michel announced.

The small pack group of pack members muttered their agreement as they murmured amongst themselves.

Biting my tongue, the fresh burn of acid seared my throat. Sweat hugged my skin as I turned around and faced the watchful gaze of the pack members who crowded the medium-sized temple. Heated tears hid behind my eyelids. As I made my way out of the temple, I held my head down, shielding myself from their words.

It almost made me regret my past decision.

"Greyson!" My Paráh called from the wooded entrance near our pack's field.

Dusting the caked-on dust from my knees, I turned to my uncle, whose stern face greeted me from above the old weathered brown stalks. Even from position, I could see the deep frown that set upon his tan face. A gust of wind rustled the leaves, sending the ends of Oni's hair dancing around his watchful gaze as I dragged my heavy body across the small field. I dreaded the lashing that was to come.

"Paráh, I'm sorry," I said as I stood before him. My eyes were glued to his brown button-down shirt. "I just needed some time alone."

"How much more time will you need, Greyson? Our Pack needs a leader that will be present and not one that's determined to become one with the dirt," Oni said. His dark brown eyes bore into my forehead.

My cheeks burned as I contemplated shifting and running away from his glare. At eighteen, no one expected Oni to step aside from being the temporary alpha without fighting tooth and nail. Especially since Oni had formed a small alliance inside of the pack that would follow him to the ends of the world and back. I've hidden in the shadows of my Paráh and Elder Alo since my father passed away when I was eleven, and Oni loved it. He reveled in leading the pack.

This was why when Elder Alo approached and reminded me that I was the rightful Alpha for our pack on my eighteenth birthday. That was when I made the only other safe place my recent getaway. Some whispered that maybe I was suffering the same fate my mother had once fallen under before she met my father, but others saw it as a weak trait—a stain on my family's noble name for being only a witch. Something neither my mother nor I could control.

"I'm sorry, Paráh. You're right, as always. I needed a quiet place to clear my mind, but I'm ready now."

Oni snorted, "Are you? You've spent almost every day here in the mud since your birthday." Oni lifted my chin to meet his scrutinizing eyes. "All you have to do is relinquish your position, and I will continue to lead the pack. It will be as if nothing ever happened. The pack will get the leader they need, and I will continue to build back the trust for the Swiftwater name."

Oni paused before he continued, "Listen, I love you like my own child, but you know how some of the pack feels about...your other side. This can work out for the both of us. You won't be saddled with the burden of being unfit to lead. Your father and I both learned when it was beneficial for us to back down from situations that we have no control over. So, this won't be a failure in his, nor my, eyes."

Something about the failure and my close relationship with the word made my stomach lurch. The palm of my hands itched. Even though my time with my father was short, I knew he would never back down from his responsibilities. My father was committed to the pack, but in the end, he was more committed to my mother.

A somberness fell between us as we stood in the forest. Before I could think about my response, I spoke.

"No, Paráh. I have to honor my father and our pack. Even if it takes a hundred years, I will show them I'm worth it. I promise from this day forward, I won't hide from my responsibilities. I'll be the leader that the pack needs."

My tongue became thick as I turned from my uncle and walked away from him with his hawk-like eyes boring a hole into the back of my shirt. Pelts of salty sweat dripped down my forehead until I was out of Oni's view, and all I could think about was if he saw the fear that riddled me. Or how I threw up every night since my mother went to the afterworld. But one thing my father made sure I remembered was that, "Even when you're dying inside, fake it."

And that's all I've been trying to do since we set the ancestral fire to send him off. I was vomiting and crying until I fell asleep in a pool of sweaty mess. Too scared I hadn't divulged to even my best friend, Hawk, that I would never live up to my father's legacy. That I wouldn't be a good leader. I just wanted to find my half and hide away...

"WHAT A WASTE?" MY SHIFTER HEARING PICKED UP FROM ACROSS THE ROOM, bringing me back to my reality.

Those words haunted me all the way to the woods as I stripped down in the middle of the wooded path. Feeling the joints of my bones cracked and twisted. My fiery skin felt taut until every single inch of my skin was covered in the black fur as I gave over the reigns to my wolf, who greedily took the opportunity to stretch our limbs and run until the pack no longer mattered. Until I was truly free and one with the earth. Once my wolf had taken over, something changed. Like a flipped switch, our nose scented the air, and we set off in chase to find the intoxicating essence. Without a doubt, the slight shiver down my spine made the soft patter of my heart go erratic.

"Mine! Mine! Mine!" My wolf's voice boomed from within. Was this my reward for trying to be peaceful? I wasn't sure, but I hadn't cared.

Like a maniac, I followed the lily of the valley, sweet and floral perfume. Their scent traveled through my nose, warming every inch of my skin... and my cock as we rushed to their location. It's been hard since then as my nose and cock led me straight to their location. When I laid eyes on her, I knew she was mine. My Hiema. My sun. The dirty and torn overalls couldn't contain her curves, and if I were impudent, I would have walked over to her and run my hands along them. Exploring every dip and softened edge, I knew what lied underneath the dirty clothing.

I'd finally found my mate... and I almost lost her before I got a chance to hold her.

As the rain tapered off to a light drizzle, pulling one of my hands free, I helped move some of her hair from her face. I hadn't meant to follow her, but I was drawn to her like a moth to a flame. I mean, how could I not? She was too gorgeous to let go.

I almost shifted back to my human form when she tripped over the roots of the foothill pine tree. The Shaman in the village said my mate was a tidbit cloddish.

I froze when she reached the fork in the path. I knew that if she turned left. She was headed straight for death at the edge of a cliff, and I didn't want to scare her in the wrong direction by changing into my human form. When she mentioned her father, I paused. It was such a weird thing to shout out in the middle of the woods. You would think being lost would make you nicer, but to each their own. Ignoring the outburst, we tried to get her to go to the right side, but she chose the wrong way. It was a constant battle with my wolf not to jump on top of her to stop her, and when she was close enough to the cliff, I changed so I could rescue her.

"I—" she said. "Y—yo—"

She was a vision of beauty even with her eyes slam shut. Slowly, she opened one emerald eye at a time. Each was just as wide open as her mouth. Under my palms, her heartbeat was the same pace as the rain, hard and fast. When I pulled her back up from the edge of the cliff, she stumbled into my arms, and I couldn't help myself as I felt the corners of my mouth pulled into a smile.

My Hiema teeth chattered against each other as she tried to form her words. It was then my mind just processed that she might have been cold from the rain.

She shook as she wrapped her arms around herself. That didn't stop me from also wrapping myself around her soft body, using my body heat to help her keep warm. I could have just grabbed her and taken her back to my house, but that was being too forward. Plus, I would have to ease her into our world. I inhaled deeply, trying to gauge what she might be, but I smelled nothing but her mesmerizing scent.

My mate is human...but that doesn't seem right.

My heart sank with disappointment for a moment before I looked back down at the captivating woman who stood trembling in my arms. She had dark circles under her eyes and seemed weak. Right then and there, I decided it didn't matter. We would brace whatever comes our way.

Earth Creator blessed me this early morning and led me to my tethered soul.

When her shivers died down, the rumbling of her stomach rang in my ears. I decided it was best to get her back to the village. She needed to eat and rest. Everything else could wait.

"What's your name?" I asked.

Her startling jewel eyes hadn't left my face since I saved her. She squirmed against me, and I almost cum on myself. For a moment, I almost forgot how being close to our mates affected us.

She cleared her throat and finally spoke, "Your dick is poking a hole into my stomach."

Her voice was soothing, but that didn't stop my face from burning at her words. A timid chuckle bubbled up from my throat. When I pulled away from her, she turned into a whole different person. Her face changed from wide-eyed awe to an adorable frown that slid onto her face.

"I'm sorry, Hiema." Rubbing the back of my neck. "I usually don't—"

Her face pinched like she smelled something unpleasant around us as she laid one of her soft hands on my chest. I sniffed the air once again to see if maybe I'd somehow gotten it wrong, but it remained the same.

"Sorry, I didn't get your name?"

"Kaydian," she said before her small hand covered her mouth. I guess the Earth Creator was blessing me from the afterlife.

Transfixed by her eyes and her body. I'd failed to see that her overalls were shredded on the bottom, and she had scabbed-over cuts on her arms and legs. Her eyes were dipped in red. Which I'd assumed she was crying from being lost in the woods, but maybe she was tired.

"Greyson." I held out my hand to her. "How about we start over? You seem lost here in these woods and being lost out here can get you killed. I know we started off on the wrong foot, but my home is a short walk from here. I can get you something to eat and a bed to sleep in. Maybe I can even get you some dry clothes to wear."

I stopped for a moment. "How does that sound?"

Kaydian's POV

"You're a shifter...aren't you?" I whispered, cutting him off as I watched his handsome face contorted. His mouth twisted as he tried to read me.

Absolutely not!

This couldn't be happening to me. Youna and my magic were conspiring against me to see just how far they could push me. When I touched Greyson, I knew without a doubt that he was the missing link. My fated mate. A werewolf. My magic heated us, casting us in a light green aura as magic reached out to him. The siring electric heat that I'd yearned for so long made my heart leap in my chest as we claimed him as ours. Tears welled in my eyes, but I blinked them away. Holding my heavy body, a shiver ran through me, and the rumbling of my stomach rang in my ears. The lemon scent filled my veins and seeped into me, and there was one thing I knew I wanted more.

Greyson's inquisitive eyes paired at me through his long, dark eyelashes. With nowhere to go and my mind clouded with disbelief and confusion. I was stuck and needed to regroup from my conflicted mind.

He probably thought a human knowing about shifters was unusual.

"I'm half shifter from my father and witch from my mother," he said calmly. "I don't know a lot about any other supernaturals outside of the shifter community. Since I was always taught to stay within my tribe. So, I never had an interest in learning about humans. My mistake, I assume."

He smiled at me, and my heart leaped in my chest, sending an unwanted feeling to my core. He continued, "Yes, and you're a human? Maybe half human."

My frown deepened as my breathing became erratic. A string of curse words sat perched on the tip of my tongue, but I clamped my mouth shut. Luckily, Greyson couldn't help but be drawn to my full breast. Which basically was outlined in my wet clothing, with my brown nipples poking through the saturated garments.

As much as I liked the attention, I covered my breasts with my arms. My face was feverish with humiliation as I pulled away from his scorching glare.

"I'm fully human and..." I tried my best not to look bothered. "Is this how you greet people? By rubbing yourself on them the first time you meet."

He stumbled backward, and I fought the urge to reach out and soothe him. I didn't know him; he was a stranger, but here I was, ready to console him.

"...But you're my mate...I'm sorry, Kaydian. This is a new territory for me," he said, running his hand through his hair. "I'm the Alpha."

Alpha. The word rang through my ears and vibrated in my head. He was the leader of his pack. My eyes felt strained as I stared into his handsome face. At least he was handsome for a werewolf. What the hell was I saying? I wasn't even able to blame my dark voice, as it was nowhere to be found. Squirming against the wetness between my thighs. A flush of heat crossed my face. If I were alone, I would chastise myself for being so damn needy. For a moment, I almost forgot how close Greyson was until I felt his hands rubbing circles on my back gingerly, causing me to clutch my thighs together.

"Listen, I know you've probably had a rough night, but I would never disrespect you. It's just I don't shift with clothes on," he said with his arms up in surrender.

My body was sore, but that didn't stop me from hiding the emotions that were painted on my face. If my hands were free, I would've buried myself behind my hair. A timid giggle bubbled up from my throat. When I stepped away from him, I couldn't help the heaviness in my stomach.

What am I getting myself into?

Chapter 15

Greyson

My father always said humans were temperamental and always used their mouths as weapons since they were powerless. I'd already forgiven her. I just needed to get her to the village. Somewhere warm where she can regroup. Maybe if she thought I was being helpful and not trying to harm her, then she'd give me an inch.

I could woo my mate, but even the words sounded foreign to me.

My father taught me, *"Everything comes to you at the right moment. You just have to be patient."*

Even though her emerald eyes kept slipping to get a view of all of me, I could tell she would not come along easily. At thirty-five, I could be patient. I've waited too long for this moment to mess it up more than I already have. I'll get on my knees and beg just to convince her.

"So, how about you let me help?" I said with a hand open to her as a peace offering.

She looked at my outstretched hand like it was the plague. Her small hand found its way to her wrist as I waited patiently with my hand to her.

"No," she said.

When she passed me, her shoulder bumped into my upper arm as she headed back down the pathway. Her pace was slower than before, allowing me to see her back, which was just as appealing as the front. I had the most stubborn mate on earth. Shaking my head, I picked up the broken, discarded purse and followed her down the path. My long legs ate the short distance between us. The sun peeked out over the horizon, illuminating the dark dirt pathway and showing our shadows.

"Hey, Kaydian," I said the moment I got in front of her. "It's about thirty minutes to town from here even more if you're walking. How about I make you something to eat, and then you can leave? I don't have a car, but I can walk with you there."

That stopped her in her tracks, "Why? Why would you do that for me? I'm just a lowly human that got lost out here."

"Because you're my fated mate, Kaydian." I paused to let my words sink in. "I've been waiting for the person who would complete my life since I turned sixteen and shifted for the first time."

I continued, "I know you're probably wondering what I'm talking about. A fated mate is your eternal twin. Someone that has been chosen by the Earth Creator to be your perfect match."

She wasn't budging.

With her hands on her hips and her plump lips pinched, she looked adorable...tired and beautiful. A moment of silence passed between us until her stomach decided it was fed up. She wrapped her arms around her stomach while the tips of her nose and ears turned a deep red.

I tilted my head, "Can we be honest with each other, Kaydian?"

She nodded. I guess that was good enough for me.

"You're thirty minutes away from town. How did you get here without a car? You don't smell like a shifter or another supernatural? A human walking along these roads is dangerous. A female human...even more dangerous."

I paused and let my eyes roam her body, "I haven't seen anyone human with those colored eyes before, but it's okay. Maybe one day you'll come to trust me. Now let's get you some food and maybe a nap?"

I held out my hand again. If her eyes were any narrower, I would have thought she had fallen asleep on me. After a ten-minute stare off, she took my hand and shook it.

"Fine, but no funny business, and if you attempt to touch me without my permission again, I will cut your cock off and feed it to your people," she said with her shoulder squared and her frown back on her face.

Smiling, "I wouldn't dream of it."

"You lead the way then. Just in case this is a setup."

Turning from Kaydian, I led us down the right path to the village. The smile that was plastered on my face was impenetrable. This small feat was well earned from my Hiema.... my sun.

The path to the village was a ten-minute walk from the cliff. Usually, I wouldn't return home until I couldn't hide my wolf in the shadows anymore. I wouldn't want a human to see me especially since my uncle and I couldn't come to an agreement on anything lately. But none of that mattered now because I knew my path would be clearer with my mate by my side.

The Earth Creator had truly *blessed* me today, and maybe I was losing my wits, but a jubilant sensation, somewhere buried deep in my soul, filled me. From the orange-brown Rufous hummingbirds that flew above, luring me with their sweet melody. To the poppies that opened their petals for the morning sun. The closer we got home, the more the scent of pine and baked food filled my nose, making my stomach rumble. Along with Kaydian's scent that threatened my sanity, I wanted to pull her behind the old wide trees and rut inside of her until I passed away. My face felt flush with the thought. She hated me today, but hopefully, soon, she'll see fighting me wouldn't get us anywhere.

"Wait!"

Kaydian POV

Turning on my tattered shoes, I moved to get away from Greyson, who had practically gained wings and flown in front of me, stopping me in my tracks. I folded my arms, but not before I caught myself digging into my sore wrist.

"I don't believe it's wise for me to return with you," I stated, clearing my throat.

"What? Why? No one will bother you. Especially since you're with me," he pleaded.

"Please don't make this harder than it already is, Greyson. We come from different worlds with different rules."

He took a step toward me, and I took one back. I've waited almost twelve years to meet my mate, just to be rewarded with someone who, by the coven rules, couldn't rule. A deep sigh slipped past my lips, which made Greyson shuffle on his feet, and in those few minutes of silence, regret set in with each blink of my lids.

My parents would kill him before he uttered a word to them. His scent made him easy to detect, and I would have to work hard to keep him alive. I had no other choice but to leave before I fell too hard. I wondered what the backlash would be. It would probably be a thousand years before my mother or the coven entrusted me again. Now I'm wondering if it was such a bad thing to go crazy from the curse of glut.

I've been waiting to cry since I left the castle, but now, I wanted to ever so more. Biting into the bottom lip, my eyes burned as I blinked back the salty, useless tears.

"You wouldn't understand..."

Greyson POV

"Well, make me then," I said. My weaning patience got the best of me, and I couldn't tell who I was more frustrated with, her or myself.

Kaydian stood before me, trembling as she chewed on her plump bottom lip. My heart wanted to grab her and kiss the doubt away. She rolled her shoulders multiple times as her inner thoughts played out on her beautiful face. Even the dirt on her face made her look alluring. Swaying slightly as those hypnotic emerald eyes slipped closed.

"I'm a witch..." Her eyes opened with a hint of fear in them.

She winced and turned her attention to the broken pile of trees that we had chopped down. Hiding her face as she moved the thick pieces of hair in front of her face. It was as if that move would stop me from having a meltdown.

Which was too late...

The pounding of my heart drowned out the voice in my head. Standing there in the small pathway, my mind raced with her words. *She had to be lying!* The creator wouldn't have been so cruel. Not when I've waited this long just to allow my mate to be the one thing I hoped never to cross paths with. The other half of me I refused to acknowledge even till this day.

"A witch!" I said. My eyes burned a hole in her face. "So, did you sense I was your mate?"

"I—Yes,"

Kaydian looked weak as she took a step toward me. Instinctively, I took one back. Her narrow eyes stared back at me, hurt laced throughout those gems. Even though she had extended no sympathy to me when we first met. For the second time this morning, we were at a standstill. Only this time, I was the one with the scrunched nose and an upturned upper lip.

I had long since wiped my mother's side away from my memory, only leaving the moments we had together. My magic, or lack of it, hadn't stirred inside of me until I touched Kaydian. As happy as I am to find my mate, the thought of my mother's gift awakening inside of me petrified me.

"I just can't believe the Earth Creator would do this to me," I whispered what was meant for only myself spilled out into the morning breeze.

"I'll just walk it to town. I don't want to cause any trouble, plus I am going home soon." Kaydian folded her arms around herself and chewed on her bottom lip.

I should have let her leave and forgotten about this encounter. Hoping the Earth Creator will send me another fated mate, even though those chances were slim to none. However, my wolf told me she would be the one to fix our broken pieces...and we wanted her more than the air in our lungs.

Kaydian took one look at my indecisive face and turned to leave... or tried to leave. When she turned halfway, she tripped over her foot and almost went face-first into the dirt for the second time today. Luckily, I saved her—again as I grabbed her upper arm and spun her around.

"T-Thank you," Her eyes were glued to my shirtless chest.

My heart pounded against their cage, and before I knew it, I was forgiving her for being a witch.

"Listen, if we're going to get you into the village, then you're going to be honest with me."

The night's events showed on her as she started trembling in my arms. Warm tears collected in the small gap between her and me, dripping onto my damp skin. My shoulders slumped as I racked my hand down her back. The turbulent thoughts of my new witch problem slipped away with each of her tears. All I wanted to do was to carry her off to my home and hide her away from everyone.

Selfish, yes, I know...

"I'm a..." she paused as a tremor passed through her. "Witch. Are you okay with that? I came out here for peace and quiet. I used a magic spell to hide myself from everyone, but it seems I can't even do that right. Listen, I will be out of your hair tonight. I just need some rest."

She couldn't be serious. As I stood there with her, my heart raced with the thoughts of not being able to inhale her scent that became etched in my soul. I knew she meant the words she had spoken as she leaned her slick forehead onto me.

"How about I get you home, and then we can talk about it after I have fed you and you've rested?"

She tilted her head as her narrowed eyes inched closer together. Kaydian swayed a bit and my hands reached out to steady her. At this rate, she'd pass out before I could get her home. We stood at a standstill. She sucked in her lower lip, trying to suppress her yawn as a subtle throaty sound left her. I held out my hand as a peace offering, and her green orbs stared a hole into it.

And she continued to stare at it until the crooks of my arm ached. My hand slipped just an inch before she grabbed the lonely hand. Placing my arm under the back of her knees and her back, I lifted her into my arms. Kaydian yelped as I adjusted her. Her mouth dropped open to protest, but she closed her mouth, rested her head on my chest, and closed her eyes.

I carried her the rest of the way, with my nose buried into her hair, to the small clearing that was open to our village. Fry bread scent overpowered the fresh rain scent now that I was at home. Each of the wooden home's doors was open, with the children already running around squealing their delight as they played. The elders were already outside in their favorite chairs with their colorful plates in their hands. I'd wanted to avoid their hawk-like stares, so I dipped behind the homes, using the forest behind them as cover. As I got closer to my home, there was an enormous gap between Hawk's home and the other homes. Peeking around the pack members' home, I saw Hawk in the middle of the clearing. He was flipping the fry bread over the smokey wood fire. Like his name, Hawk turned to my spot. His keen eyes spotted me behind the home. Those thick eyebrows scrunched as he tried to call me over.

"Hey, Greyson!" Hawk yelled when I made my way across the wide gap.

I loved Hawk, but I wasn't in the mood to talk right now. I was almost home when I saw the red door of my home.

"Not now, Hawk. I'm busy!" I yelled out.

Not wanting to wait, I picked up speed and pretended I didn't hear Hawk yelling wait again. As I reached the red door, I closed it gently without waking Kaydian. I made my way to the small room and placed my sleeping mate onto the small, unmade bed. I dug my nose into her hair to get another whiff of my newest addiction and covered her with the yellow comforter I received from Hawk's mother, who made it by hand.

Staring at my Hiema, I wondered if the Creator was aware of the mountains I would have to move for her. The Pack would undeniably push back on her, especially since I wasn't fully accepted myself.

Am I strong enough to withstand the rocky currents? I guess only time would tell. I just hoped the Creator knew what he was doing.

Chapter 16

Kaydian

My clammy skin was buried under warmth as my body, and my magic dug deeper to keep me wrapped up in my newfound joy. I stuck my nose under the cover with a deep breath. The powerful scent of earthy soil and lemongrass filled my nose. A sigh of pleasure fell from my chapped lips as the scent swept through my overheated body. Rays from the sun cascaded over my eyes, causing me to wince at the abrasive light as I turned on my other side. *I have to move that window!* I thought as I finally became comfortable, only the sun was still torturing me.

The sound of a creaking door opening caused the groan in my throat to slip out. These new housekeepers were annoying me. I know Ms. Kincaid had drilled into them not to wake me, especially since I could sleep for another eight hours. Their heavily clad shoes thunk as they drew closer to my bed and stopped.

"Leave me alone! And close the shades when you leave." I said, but even to my ears, it sounded muffled with sleep.

A deep chuckle from my unwanted guest made my eyes widen at the disrespect. I shot out of the warm cocoon to lash out at the house-keeper...but stopped. The words died on the tip of my tongue as I stared at Greyson. His scent filled my veins, causing my nipples to tighten. *So, it wasn't a dream!* I really hoped that it was all a sick and twisted dream.

Youna!

At least he had on clothing today.

Greyson filled out the older-looking brown button-down shirt with blue shorts that stopped at his knees. A yellow phoenix pendant stood out against the shirt. Rose beige skin highlighted his soft brown eyes with flecks of yellow, his upturned nose and his full bow-shaped lips. His black hair was in a ponytail that fell halfway down his back. Flexing my hands, I had to fight the urge to reach out, unraveling his silky hair and burying my hands—and face into it. Just the thought made my face flush with embarrassment. I wasn't a mate-crazed fool. Swallowing as my eyes roamed, his corded muscles that strained against the shirt sent me clenching my thighs against the soft throbbing in my pussy.

What would my parents say if they knew I was in a shifter's village, lusting after a wolf? I think my mother would take me to the underworld herself and leave me there.

"If you stare at me any harder, I might have to join you."

Opening my mouth to speak, I was about to give him an earful, but then he went and ruined it for me by smiling. His perfect lopsided smile blinded me, rendering me speechless, and my body hummed in the aftershock. My magic did somersaults in my stomach. For the first time in my life, I had an opportunity to break the dreaded curse that hung over my head and have a mate. To have someone who wants me. To have someone that needs me. I didn't know how I would pull it off, but I knew this was going to be way over my head since having a mate, who was not a witch, was strictly forbidden. How would I get my mother to break a rule our family put forth? My mother would sooner die than to change that rule.

Maybe I can ask Youna to give me another mate before the coven, and royals cast me out. If that happened, I would have to learn to live with Greyson without my magic, which was like stripping your soul from your body.

"Um, right, thank you for everything," I said listlessly as I found a spot on the plain wall that needed my attention. Anywhere besides his gorgeous face. "I think I should get going. My parents would expect me to be back by now."

"You've been out for over a day, Kaydian. You should eat and take a shower."

If I hadn't known better, I would have said he wanted me to stay, but the thought was preposterous since the shifters hated the witches as well, thanks to my father.

Greyson took a step toward the small bed. His upturned nose wrinkled, and his lips twisted.

"Um, I don't mean to offend you, Kaydian, but maybe you would like to bathe first?"

"I don't smell bad. You're rude, asshole!"

The nerve of him! This is who Youna picked out for me. The sultry heat of anger coursed through my body. My magic, the charlatan, was fluttering around my chest, refusing to help me. Raising my arm, I poked my nose into my armpit, inhaled, and pulled my face back to Greyson. The acid in my stomach threatened to decorate the yellow comforter. Tears collected in the corners of my eyes as I tried my best to keep my face void of any emotions. It was then that I noticed the dark outline of what I assume was dried dirt that stained the white sheets, and I was still in my tattered overalls.

"Okay, maybe a bath wouldn't hurt."

Throwing Greyson a shaky smile.

"I left two buckets of water for you." He pointed to the pails that were left in the middle of the room. "One for you to bathe with and the other to use as a toilet."

The smile that once was on my face became stuck. This had to be a sick joke. Not even my father's old ways prevented us from having a toilet.

"Ah, you don't have a bathroom? So how do I empty...it?"

"We just take it out to the woods and throw it out there. Nature knows how to handle waste."

Greyson gave another one of his dazzling smiles again. He hadn't noticed the way mine faltered with the thought of taking out my waste. What century was I teleported to? Sadly, the small calendar on the dresser said it was still 1923. The shifters were always known to prefer the old ways, where they ran through the woods until their human side demanded to be released. I learned that during my Royals classes, but I never thought it was true. Boy, was I wrong.

Standing up, I stretched and twisted my rested body. My muscles contorted, and my joints made those comforting popping sounds when the gas escaped them. Greyson placed a simple black dress and white sandals on the small dresser for me.

Closing the door behind him, I waited until his footsteps were drowned out by my thoughts. Greyson's small room was void of any personal touches besides the yellow comforter with a wolf and phoenix pattern etched into the medium-size squares. The bed had seen better days as I noticed the lumps in the twin-size bed that looked like tiny ant hills. Pressing a hand to my hot cheek, I just shook my head and cursed myself. The small soap Greyson brought me lay on the brown side table. He must love the color yellow.

The putrid smell of the dirt and sweat that clung to my skin sent me toward the buckets. With a grimace on my face, I got to work. The crystal blue water turned a murky mud color when I was finished. Every fiber in my muscles trembled with shame. Lifting the buckets, I prepared for my walk of shame with my bodily fluids in one hand and my bathwater in the other. Both made me cringe that I would have to do such a thing.

Greyson was nowhere to be found as I slipped out of the room. The kitchen, if you could call it that, comprised a wood stove with a stovepipe complete with patches of tape along the body. A thick coating of dust made it look gray. The wooden counter held a small bucket with used dishes and cups stored in it. Next to the kitchen was enough space to hold a small, weathered yellow sofa that looked older than me. The sofa had a noticeable dip in the seats with enough dust on the back to fill the bucket in the kitchen.

Thankfully, I wouldn't have to face Greyson until after I disposed of my buckets. Before slipping out of the miniature home, I checked my hand and noted the red outline of the blood-cloaking incantation. If I were to get caught here, that would just be the nail in my coffin. And I was not sure of my abilities to not use my magic.

Things couldn't get worse.

As soon as the thought passed through my mind, I scolded myself. I was the poster child of the saying, *"Anything that can go wrong will go wrong."* Tiptoeing out of his home, I closed the door and turned around before I came to a full stop.

Squeezing my eyes shut and reopening them didn't make the nightmare disappear.

I would go insane in this village. The homes were a carbon copy of Greyson's, and I could bet that the inside mirrored his home as well. A giant circle in the middle separated the homes, pushing them against the wooded forest. The pack members stood in the middle of the clearing, surrounding a pole that drew my interest. The closer I got to the pole, I realized it wasn't just an ordinary pole. Someone carved a wolf into the statue. Intricate colors shone on the artwork, making the magnificent art the focal point. A black wolf's head with eyes like the summer sun sat right above the pack's head. The crafter showed the wolf baring his teeth, frightening away his enemies, I supposed. The deep black body of the wolf remained the same onyx color as the rest of the pole that was stuck in the dirt. And on top, a yellow phoenix extended its wings. The totem pole reminded me of my drawings. Something attuned to a magnet.

It's breathtaking! No wonder the pack members flocked to it.

The two buckets shook slightly as a couple of kids ran by me, snapping me out of the daze I was in. When I looked up, everyone stared at me as if I was repulsive. My mouth lifted into a nervous smile, backing away from the crowd with my buckets. Before I turned around, I heard one kid ask, "What is she?" *Nosy children.* I went back to Greyson's home and followed a dirt path around to the wooded area, where I discarded the buckets along with my dignity.

"He couldn't even empty the pails for you?"

A low, gravelly voice said from behind me. The buckets dropped to the ground with a soft thud against the dirt. My heart thundered in my chest as I swiveled around to see a man leaning against the back of Greyson's home. Graying roots framed his ochre-colored skin. He was perfectly sculpted, with his muscles glistening in the midmorning sun. He pushed off from the home and my wide eyes roamed his colossal frame. When he stopped in front of me, I had to crane my neck to look up at him. He was gorgeous.

"Are you mute? I know humans are prone to many ailments."

A blazing heat raced through my veins, and my magic skimmed underneath my achy skin. Ready for the command to skin this asshole alive.

"I can speak just fine." My fists dug into the meat of my thighs. Holding back my magic and my temper since I was a stranger in their land. "I just wasn't expecting to see someone stalking me while I empty my buckets."

Ignoring Greyson's pack member. I grabbed the two buckets that I dropped and made my way past the ogre. I had to leave before I ripped his heart out of his chest. His large hand wrapped around the fleshy meat of my upper arm, halting me before I could reach the dirt path back to the house. My arm jerked involuntarily, but the movement was fruitless, since the bastard's hand hadn't even budged.

"I don't know why my nephew thought bringing a human amongst our people would be good...especially now."

His dark brown eyes pierced mine as he looked down at me. With his nose sniffing around me, I tried to pull away again, another failed attempt. What's with these bastards and sniffing?

"There's something about you...and I will figure it out, human..."

A growl pierced the air before Greyson's hand grabbed his wrist.

"Leave her alone, Oni!" Greyson's silvery voice from this morning was gone. The guttural low pitch made Oni release my arm and turn his hard glare on him. "She's innocent and has nothing to do with the humans in town."

"She may have fooled you, but I don't trust *ANY* humans, nor do I trust her. If she even looks at someone wrong, we'll have to deal with it."

Oni didn't stay around to hear Greyson's response as he stormed off, muttering, "Some fucking Alpha you are" under his breath. Greyson's shoulders shook as I stared at his bare back.

"Well, that was a warm welcome from your uncle," I said, as the pain in my arm subsided.

Greyson's muscles tensed as I laid my hand on his back. He didn't know I had become immune to people such as his uncle. To be ridiculed, judged, and picked apart until nothing but a shell remained. One would think I would be familiar with it.

"I'm sorry for my párah.... Sorry for my uncle's behavior. We're all on edge because the humans in town are slowly creeping into our territory."

Greyson grabbed my hand and the moment we touched, fire

coursed through my veins, leaving me feverish. My magic bristled with contentment at the small, intimate gesture. He pulled me, with the buckets in his other hand, along the dirt path to the front of his home. With every step, the blood rushed to my clit, leaving me biting a hole into my bottom lip. Not only was I the unwanted "human", but my body was hyper-conscious of the fact Greyson was within arm's reach. If I didn't continue to repeat, *"He is a shifter,"* I would have pushed him up against the side of his home and had my way with him.

I need to go home.

When we reached the front of his home, Greyson placed the buckets by the door and tugged me along the dirt path to the center of the village. Most of the pack had either dispersed from the area or lounged around the totem pole, making it easier to get to the massive wood pit. Gray smoke from the extinguished fire filled the air the closer we got to the pit.

Greyson let go of my hand, causing my treacherous magic to protest and stretch inside of me as it tried to reconnect with him. A soft whine slipped out of my mouth, causing me to cover my traitorous mouth. Greyson turned back toward me. A coy smirk graced his face. *Smug bastard.* My hands squeezed my hips as the urge to run and bury myself in his side became unbearable.

"I'm going to get us something to eat," he said before he walked to the pit.

An unsettling sensation rippled through me, causing me to unglue my lustful eyes from Greyson's broad back. Looking around the small gathering area, to my dislike, everyone was staring at me. I was well accustomed to the stares because they went hand in hand with my position. But this was entirely different. The pack couldn't hide their obvious disdain for me, as disgust had the corners of their mouths pulling down in a frown. All the while, the children pointed and giggled as they hid their mouths behind their tiny hands. This time, the heat that swept throughout my body caused me to pull my hair over my scorching cheeks as I tried my best to hide from their glares.

When he returned, we shared several medium-sized pieces of bread that were left over. We sat—well, I sat in silence as he finished his bread since I had all but shoved my slice down my throat. Licking the remaining salt off my mouth, I eyed the other half of his bread unashamedly.

"Would you like the other half of my bread?" He smiled, and my favorite temptation beckoned me.

My face warmed again, and I think I might die in this village if I kept embarrassing myself.

"I-It's just—"

"It's okay, Hiema. You haven't eaten in more than a day." He placed the rest of his bread on my small dish. Cupping my cheek with his hand, I melted into it. "We don't have a lot here in the village. Honestly, we're barely making it, but whatever I have is yours."

"Thank you…for saving me again, and I'm sorry. It just seems like no one wants me here. Look at everyone staring at us."

"They're harmless and just afraid that you're a part of the scheme, but you and I both know that you're my mate. They'll come around. My pack has been through a lot and trust is hard to come by, even for me, Hiema."

"But how can you be sure?" I said as doubt filled my words. "Your uncle hates me as well, and he doesn't even know me."

"My uncle is all bark and no bite. He will get to know you, just as I will, and he'll grow to love you. And even though you may not want to hear it, I love you despite everything, my Hiema."

"You keep calling me Hiema. What does it mean?"

"It means sun. You're my mate. My other half. I don't have a lot, but what I have is yours."

My heart soared with his declaration, but something in the back of my dark mind nudged at the endearment.

"What's going on in that head of yours?" he asked, sending the memory back into the corner of my mind. Before I could respond, he continued, "How about you give us one day? If you hate us, then I will pack some of this bread for you and help you home?"

Could I abandon my people? The question ran through my mind as I debated whether to leave or stay for a day or two.

Maybe another day wouldn't hurt.

It's been a week since I arrived here in Swiftwater, which I learned after Greyson gave me the grand tour of the village. The Swiftwater tribe resided in the Sacramento woods since their ancestors moved west two thousand years ago. Before the witch's war, they occupied all the forest areas between the Ordbend and Rancho Llano Seco. My father and the witch's covens killed their tribes, one by one, throughout North and South America, forcing whoever was left to hide. Honestly, I shouldn't feel guilty since the war happened a long time ago, and I had had nothing to do with the massacre. That didn't stop me from shifting when the Pack bought the past up.

One hundred and twenty hours since I had last used my magic, and it pained me.

The only shining light was that I got to spend time with Greyson... not that I would ever admit that to him. He's already walking around the village with his chest puffed out like he claimed me. It was kind of adorable. He even planned a date in his favorite spot by the river. Greyson had been busy helping with the wood pit that day. I should have known something was up, since he had mentioned his cooking skills were almost nonexistent. Imagine my surprise showing up to the small little dugout with a plain white sheet laid out for us, and a wooden vase with flowers he purchased from the town close by. All the while, the reddish yellow from the setting sun glowed. It was gorgeous and, if I was being honest, the best date I've had thus far.

"You did this all by yourself?" I asked incredulously. My brow wrinkled.

His large hand engulfed mine. "Well, I had a little help from Hawk, but this was my plan from the start. I wanted to show you I cared about you."

My mother always said emotions were for humans because they didn't have magic to control themselves, but something in Greyson's words made the hard shell my parents firmly planted splinter at the edges.

"And what if you decided I wasn't worth the trouble? Would you choose your pack over me? I mean, I would understand. They hate me rightfully so."

I was fumbling all over myself. My heart was permanently lodged in my throat as it thumped against the tightened walls. *Youna!* Never in this lifetime would I ever imagine that a shifter could make me forget I was the princess of a powerful witch coven.

"Let's not think of the negative right now," he said, brushing off my worries. "This is about you and me. Plus, they just need more time with you. We worked on some of your favorites."

Biting my lips, I stopped worrying about the what ifs. "I'm sorry, I'm just too worried about the future to see what's right in front of me."

Greyson helped me onto the sheet, keeping the ends of my white dress from getting into the mud.

"That's it, Kay," he said as he sat down beside me. "Nothing good comes from worrying about things we can't control. My mother always harped on that."

"Your mother seems wise."

"She was," Greyson replied with a smile, but I saw the sadness lining his eyes. Greyson may have had the same thought as he changed the subject. "How do you like it here so far?"

I wanted to question him about his parents, but decided against it. "It's...different."

"Different in a good way or bad?"

"It's just a major adjustment from my home," I answered as he turned his attention to the spread before us.

When he lifted the wooden food cover to reveal salmon, succotash, and that amazing fry bread, the aroma plus Greyson's lemon scent filled the little alcove along with our conversation and our laughter. By the end of the meal, we leaned against one rock that lined the beach. Greyson's powerful arm was around me as I leaned into him, watching the last of the sun fade away into the night sky. I was content for the moment in peaceful bliss as the little alcove became a temporary shelter from the pack.

"Why don't you tell me about your parents?"

My smile sagged slightly, but not before I caught myself. "My parents are just typical parents."

If Greyson noticed I was stalling, he didn't show it.

"It's so beautiful out here. I'm jealous that your sunsets beat the ones back in Houston." I said, shifting his attention as I snuggled into his side.

"Houston?" Greyson said, his eyebrows knitted together.

Instead, I hummed my answer as I cleaned the lone string grass that found its way onto my dress.

He leaned over and kissed my forehead. "Don't worry, Kay. You don't have to tell me anything. You'll have plenty of these sunsets to take in once we are mated, my Hiema.'

There was something about him calling me his Hiema that sent the pulsating heat to my throbbing clit. I took a chance and turned to kiss him on his lips, but he turned his head, and my mouth landed on the corner of his mouth. *Pathetic.* Heat blossomed from my chest to my face. Even though I practically threw myself at Greyson, any chance we were alone wasn't enough. Every night, Greyson and I were pushed up together on that old, tottering twin bed. His body causes mines to short circuit during the middle of the night. Especially when he throws his big, warm arms around me and his third leg conveniently finds its current favorite place, wedged between my cheeks. At those times, I couldn't help but move my hips up and down his long length until I heard him let out a small groan.

They led to nothing but me falling asleep, feeling just as bothered as when I first arrived. Even when I tried to be suggestive and drop hints about us taking the next step, unsurprisingly, he would get up and run as if the hounds of the underworld were chasing him.

It was frustrating, and I wondered, for the first time in my life, if I were the problem.

Greyson cleared his throat, dragging me out of my head. "I think we should get going. It's late, and we've both had a long day."

"Of course," I said dishearteningly. Another torturous night for me. "Greyson, thank you. This was the most thoughtful thing anyone has done for me in a while."

"You're welcome, Hiema," he said, landing another kiss on my temple as we started the short trek back home through the quiet woods.

With Greyson's head held high and on cloud nine, and my crumbling heart.

Maybe I was just a silly girl.

Chapter 17

Kaydian

The following day, I was in an unusual mood. I woke up with my mind set on repaying Greyson for our dinner date. He laid on his back with his arm behind his head, snoring away in his sleep. From what I've learned about Greyson, he slept naked because werewolves' blood ran hot. Albeit not hot enough to care about what their mates needed.

I placed kisses along his warm skin as my wondrous hand drifted down the taut, muscular slope of his stomach. The tufts of curly black hair beckoned me. My hand slipped through his soft hair, causing Greyson's breathing to shorten as he sighed. My heart thudded behind its cage as my fingers skimmed over his rigid dick. I was many things, but a liar wasn't one of them. It was beautiful. A shade lighter than his tanned skin and long enough to reach my hidden spot.

And I would be mad If I didn't say my mouth was moist with the thought of tasting him.

Positioning myself close to his cock, I wrapped my mouth around his enormous head, sucking him down to the base. The taste of lemon and salty sweat filled my mouth and made my core pulse. My hand worked in tandem with my mouth, covering the area I couldn't reach. Greyson moaned, making the edges of my lips curl into a smile. I knew he would appreciate my gesture. Closing my eyes, I made my way back to the tip and was about to suck him back down when I was pulled off of him.

Greyson's hands enclosed my face, making it hard to move.

"What do you think you are doing?" he asked, and I thought the question was stupid.

"I—I," I stammered over my words. Even with Greyson's hands on my face, I felt the heat of shame flush across me.

I continued, "I was trying to show you how much I appreciate you...I just thought."

"A simple thank you would have been better," he said, removing his hands from my face. "I'm not comfortable with...doing that..."

With those last words, he turned away from me, pulling the comforter over his body. I was paralyzed with my eyes glued to his back. Was I that bad? My magic coursed through me, ice cold, causing me to shiver. Hot tears collected in the corners of my eyes, but I wiped them away, leaving no trace of the offending liquid.

Slipping out of the bed and pulling on the only other outfit I had left. An oversized white shirt with a heavy green skirt that fell past my ankles. When I looked back at Greyson, he had gone back to sleep. Covering my soft stomach, I couldn't help but wonder if he wasn't attracted to me. Maybe it was my weight that turned him off. Back at home, that never stopped me from men wanting me. But maybe I was delusional, and it was just my royal position that drew them to me. Walking out the door, the open gathering area was filled with elders and children. Some of the shifters on the porch pointed and turned their scowls toward me, but I ignored them as I dragged my heavy body to the wood pit where Hawk was working on lunch for the pack.

"Hey, Shorts," he called out as I stood by the pit. "Did you sleep well last night? You look like a ghost."

I tried to crack a smile, but it felt fake and stretched. "I'm good. It's just, you know, human problems."

"Well, nothing beats cooking to take away your problems," He smiled. As much as I wanted to return the gesture, I couldn't bring myself to do so. It felt as if the thin thread of magic that was holding Greyson and me would snap, and I would hate to give the pack a show.

I nodded, which was enough for Hawk as he took it as a sign to continue with small talk. Since he was nothing but nice to me, I pretended to listen, but my mind was still in the little room with Greyson's back toward me. As we prepared the corn soup, Hawk's mother joined us, taking some of the weight off of me.

Hawk had given me the job of watching the flour they would use as crackers. I hadn't heard when Kathleen stood beside me, bumping her shoulders into mine.

"So, tell me about how your night went. Was it magical? I made sure to beat it into Greyson that he was supposed to be on his best behavior."

I opened my mouth to lie, but I decided to be half truthful. "It was wonderful. The food, the atmosphere, and him. He was a gentleman through and through."

I tried to smile, but it came out as a smirk. Kathleen's eyes bore into me. Her gray orbs made me believe she knew I was gazing over the truth, but luckily, the pack gathered near the pit with their plates for food.

One by one. Children, men, and women came through the line. Greyson had finally appeared as he spoke to some of the pack members on their porch with his back once again to me. I was so preoccupied with watching Greyson with his pack that I didn't notice when a small child, no more than six years old, trudged up to me, almost as if I was a monster, and I missed his plate. We both stood watching the toasted brown chips as they fell to the ground.

The child's eyes filled with tears as he cried. His father, who was next to him, bent down to comfort the child as Kathleen and I stood watching. When he stood up, his harsh glare landed on me.

"Why would you do that?" the man said through clenched teeth.

It wasn't enough that I dropped the poor boy's chips, but now I had to deal with his irate father, who hated me for being myself.

"I'm sorry. My mind was elsewhere," I said to the child, dismissing his father, which I might as well have spoken to the father because the little boy shook as his wide eyes stared at me.

"Mark," Kathleen interjected. "This was an honest mistake. Kota can have more if he likes."

"Kathleen, we already have to stretch our resources for..." Mark paused to cast a hateful glare at me. "Others, and now she's wasting our food."

"She's not wasting food. She belongs here with us and Greyson as much as you and I," Hawk said with his arms crossed over his white shirt.

Even with my snark retort forming in my mind, I couldn't unglue my tongue from the roof of my mouth.

"Mark," Kathleen said, her red lips pushed into a frown.

"Mark, what are you doing?" Greyson said as he joined us finally. He took a clean plate, scooped up some chips, and gave it to Kota. "See, problem solved."

Kota smiled through his wet face and went to hide behind his father's leg as he watched me like a hawk.

Greyson continued, "My mate was just helping Mark. Next time, let's exercise some compassion."

"Learn to control her, or I'll have to speak with Oni about her," Mark spoke through his clenched teeth.

"Her name is Kaydian, and I think you forget I'm the Alpha in the pack. Not my uncle," Greyson said without taking his eyes off Mark. "Unless you would like to challenge me."

Mark frowned as he looked down his nose with his cold eyes fixed on Greyson. He turned away with Kota tailing him, but not before my ears picked up *"filthy human waste."*

Kathleen placed her arm around me and took the spoon from my vise grip. "Mark is a short-tempered fool. Don't mind him."

"It's okay," I said when my tongue finally unglued from the roof of my mouth. "It goes with the territory, I guess."

Greyson came up to me. His blue shirt clung to him like a second skin as he hugged me. Which made my insides scream and quiver. He grabbed my hands and kissed the back of both of them.

"I'm sorry, Kay," he said. Those enormous hazel eyes landed on me, making my knees buckle. "You shouldn't have gone through that...or what I did this morning. It's just—"

"Greyson!" came the deep voice of his uncle from across the clearing. He stood on the porch of his home with one hand on the doorknob and the other on the door frame.

I wish he would tell his uncle to go fuck off, but Greyson turned pale as he kissed me on the cheek and ran off to him.

"Let's finish feeding these children, and then we can take a break.

Maybe I can show you what I've sown for the market tomorrow," Kathleen said with a big smile.

"Okay, that sounds great," I said.

Since I've been here, everyone, except for Joseph Hawk, hawk for short, and Hawk's mother, Kathleen Hawk, were the only two people who didn't act as if I had leprosy. *The nerve of them.* In six days, I had seen more people turn their noses up at me than I have in my lifetime. One of them even mentioned my weight while Greyson's uncle stood far away from me with a sullen stare geared toward me. No one in my coven or the other covens would dare to even blink the wrong way at me, much less blatantly be disrespectful. I'd bitten my tongue so many times I was shocked not to have bitten through it.

A single tear fell from my eyes, and I regretted it the moment it happened. Panic squeezed the air right out of my lungs, leaving me gasping for air. My knees shook, and I almost collapsed if it wasn't for me sitting on the rock. I probably would have landed face-first in the muddy bank.

No, I wanted to say, and if I didn't bond with Greyson soon, I fear the curse will return with revenge.

"Kaydian!" Greyson yelled out. His long legs ate the distance between the river and the massive rock I sat on, leaving Hawk floating in a world of his own. He looked peaceful, at least.

"I can't get wet!" I hissed out, causing Greyson to stop and cocked his head to the side.

"Sorry, I was getting a bit too eager," he said. His dimples deepened when he smiled, causing my core to clench.

Dammit!

Pulling my legs to my chest, "I'm sorry. I was thinking about how jealous I was of you and Hawk. I love swimming. Me and Del..."

"Whose Del?"

"She's my best friend. She's my Hawk," I said, smiling as I thought about the times we ran away to swim for hours on end. "We would spend almost all day swimming until our muscles were sore enough to cramp. She knows all of my secrets...a little too much. She's always been there for me through thick or thin...and she gets on my nerves, but I wouldn't trade her for anyone else."

"We found this spot by the river close to the cas...village and marked it as our hiding spot. We skipped school there." Chuckling, hoping he hadn't heard my slight slip up. "Oh, I had my first kiss there as well. Talk about awkward."

Greyson turned silent as he listened to me babble on about my memories. When I was done, his face had a pinched look as he watched Hawk floating in the water. Shifting on the rock, I wondered if I said something that was off-putting. What the fuck did I do now? My hand molded with his, squeezing it slightly, bringing his attention back to me.

"Are you okay? You went silent on me."

He smiled, but it didn't quite reach his eyes. "Sorry, it's—never mind. I'm jealous of Del. She seems like a great friend."

My mouth opened to respond, but he already jumped off of the rock. He undressed as I sat there and tried not to stare at his hard dick. Not that it mattered, seeing as all he could stomach was a chaste kiss on the cheek. I wanted to ask him what about me repulsed him, but since Hawk was finally stumbling out of his little world on the water, it would have to wait. Hawk walked up behind Greyson, naked as the day he was born with a smile.

"Hawk and I are going for a run. Do you want me to walk you back to the village?"

Did I imagine him being upset? Maybe I was thinking too much about the situation. Greyson would tell me if something was bothering him. It was just my imagination getting the best of me. Without a second thought, I leaped off the massive rock and gave him a kiss on his lips. When I pulled away, his tan skin became the color of the Sacramento sunset, vivid red.

Every day I stay here, I fall deeper...

"The tip of your nose is as red as Grey's, Shorts!" Hawk chuckled.

I hated that nickname at first, but it grew on me...not that I would ever let them know.

A princess must have some secrets.

Hawk, Greyson, and the other shifters were just as looming as the trees at night. Come to think of it, everyone in the village, except for the children, was taller than me. Hawk's large bronze hand landed on Greyson's shoulder with a wet sound. His gray eyes danced in the sun. The stalk difference always made me wonder about Greyson's parents.

The only thing he told me about his parents was that they passed away when he was young. No backstory or his mother's name. And a fat chance of me getting it out of Hawk or his mother. They're just as tight-lipped as Greyson.

"No, I'm fine. You guys go ahead. I'll walk back home."

Greyson slipped his hand into mine. Our fingers intertwined as he stood there, appearing unsure of himself. My magic almost slipped out the way it jumped for joy, but standing here just touching his warm skin was heaven...it felt like home.

"Are you sure? I could take you back home. Do you have enough of the spray on?"

I raised up on my tippy toes before he could pull away and planted a kiss on his cheek this time. Safe and innocent.

"I have enough of that smelly deodorizer," I said.

After I told Greyson a loose lie about losing one on my journey here, he immediately found some among the pack. No one has recognized that I'm a witch so far. Not even Greyson's grumpy old uncle, who would surely snatch me from this realm and deliver me to the underworld.

"I—shit," Greyson replied. "I forgot about the deodorizer."

Hawk, who was watching with a huge grin on his baby face, patted his back.

"Come on, Grey. The sooner we go, the quicker you can get back to being with Shorts," Hawks said with a haughty smile.

Greyson asked one more time before he pulled away. He stood there for a minute before Hawk grabbed his arm and dragged him away.

Not wanting to go back to the village. I returned to my rock and laid down. The slosh of the water and the birds sang a tune I couldn't resist, and I drifted off to the dream world.

A high-pitched squeal woke me out of my nap as I shot up from the awkward position. The sudden movement sent me flying off the rock as the kink in my back throbbed. Note to self: using a rock as a makeshift bed is bad. My body trembled as I focused to get a hold of my emotions and my magic. Luckily, I could rein in my magic before it reached out and killed everyone.

A minute passed by as I sat on the floor with my wrinkled forehead as I tried to figure out where the sound came. The squeal bounced around the woods again. This time, curiosity got the best of me. Or so I told myself. Honestly, I had nothing else to do but go back to that damn village and drum up a smile so fake that even the goddesses would believe me.

Tiptoeing through the woods was not my favorite pastime, as you can tell, but as I crept closer to the sound, it changed. The squealing had disappeared, and in its wake, the sound of multiple people moaning enticed me to move forward. It called me like a siren does its victims, and I desperately wanted to get there to see what the excitement was about.

Everything in me told me to turn around and go home, but if there was one thing I was good at, it was being nosey. The thick wooded bushes gave way to a small clearing by the edge of the water. Hiding behind one of the large trees by the clearing, I peeked out the side to see a couple in the middle of having sex...no this was beyond sex.

My face flushed with want as I watched the little squealer squirm while her lover had their head stuck between her thick blonde thicket of hair that surrounded her pussy. Blondie, as I so affectionately named her, was a woman from the village who wouldn't spare me a glance when I walked by her, but that didn't matter because I was going to take something from her for myself as a little payback for her rudeness.

With her back bowed, Blondie whimpered as her tan hand dug into her lover's inky black curly hair, holding them in place. "Oh god!" she whimpered as I thanked Youna for being close enough to hear every word that fell from her cherry-colored lips. Something about watching the pair embolden me. I'm not a stranger to masturbating by any means, but this would be the first time watching someone have sex while doing it. My hand skimmed down my curves until it slipped under the waistband of my pants, finding my fiery pussy. If Greyson won't kneel, then this will have to do for now. My fingers slowly glided into my pussy until they were coated with my essence. Two fingers into my needy pussy, leaving my thumb to play with my sensitive clit. With my eyes half dimmed, Blondie flipped Curly onto her back. The glint in her eyes told me this wasn't their first go around. Curly chuckled as she grabbed Blondie's muscular thighs and helped position her right above her mouth.

"Quit playing around. We have to get back soon!" Blondie said with a mischievous smile.

"As you wish, my love," the curly feminine voice said right as she placed a kiss on her wet pussy. The sound was sloppy and erotic. As I watched the blonde lover's pussy glisten against the moonlight, it made me bite my bottom lip. As I held back my whimper, speeding up my fingers, pulling and teasing my swollen clit. Her lover wrapped her arms around her thick thighs, controlling Blondie from moving her drenched pussy from her mouth. Curly was out to kill her blonde lover as she inched her down onto her mouth. Curly was faster as she removed her mouth with a pleading whimper from Blondie. She ran her pink tongue along her inner thighs, causing Blondie to pinch her tan nipples and whine her hips to get Curly's mouth back to her aching pussy. The slow, tortuous ascent to her apex made her whine out, "Please Kathleen... Please I—" Curly pink tongue snaked out and licked her soaked slit as Blondie looked ready to crumple in bliss. Her hazel eyes were narrowed to slits, with her mouth agape as curses fell from her plump lips.

Wait...Kathleen...Hawks mother!

This new information should have sent me running, but I was caught up in the lovers' tryst. My fingers trembled as the cooler air caressed my essence soak pussy. The fiery sensation left me feeling warm as more blood pooled my clit. A hazy glaze covered my vision as the heated

Especially as Kathleen glued her mouth to Blondie's pussy as she feasted on the delicate, soaked flesh. Blondie's hand connected with Kathleen's curls as she rode her mouth. Kathleen was out to kill her lover as she slid herself up and down onto her mouth. Chasing her lover's tongue movements with each buck of her hips. It was breathtakingly mesmerizing. Her breath hitched as her eyes shuttered closed. She was almost there as her teeth bit into the soft flesh of her plump bottom lip. I envied her. I thought as my legs shook when I pinch my swollen clit. Kathleen's moans grew hungrier as she gave Blondie free rein of her mouth. A subtle tremor rolled through Blondie, "Yes, I'm about to—"

Her words were cut off as a firm hand wrapped around my mouth and another around my waist, breaking my concentration on Kathleen and Blondie. My body struggled to get the intruder to let me go so I won't miss our—Blondie's final blow.

"Kaydian, stop!" Greyson hissed in my ears.

The pathetic whine that tumbled out of my mouth was muffled by Greyson's powerful hand. My elbow connected with his steel stomach in hopes he would put me down, but all he did was hoist me higher on his chest. Asshole! If he would just touch me...kiss me or something! As I swung my feet in the air, I couldn't feel the ground until he placed me on my two feet in his small brown and yellow room.

"I'm so disappointed in you," he said as he ran his hand through his hair. "Invading Kathleen's and Sidney's privacy...listen, I know it's different here in the village from your home, but some things are sacred."

Reeling from his words, I asked, "What's that supposed to mean?"

Greyson opened his mouth, but the words seemed to have died on the tip of his tongue. His frown returned as he said, "I think I'm going to sleep over at Hawk's house. Hopefully, his mother hadn't noticed."

Panicking, I tried to fix the mess. "Greyson! I'm sorry I—They were having sex in public, Greyson. It can't be that sacred if they're willing to risk getting caught."

Greyson's frown deepened, "And that makes it right? Using their time as your personal entertainment to..."

Greyson shook his head. "It's wrong no matter how you twist it."

"Well, I wouldn't have to watch other people have sex if my mate cared enough to touch me?" I regretted the words the moment they fell from my lips.

"I've always dreamt of how I would meet my mate, and how we would learn about each other together, Kaydian. Just knowing you've been with someone else...I'll see you in the morning." Greyson said before he abruptly turned to leave.

The little voice of reason told me to haul him back to the bedroom and apologize, even if it meant begging, but I couldn't bring myself to do so. Throwing myself onto the bed. The hot tears left a trail of searing regret and embarrassment. At that moment, I missed my Del, my mother, Sera, Luc, Merrell, the coven, and hell, even my father. I missed my little enchantment room... my books and my paintings...my life.

Maybe I made the wrong choice to stay here. In the dark recess of my mind, I can see the three sisters, with their dark hoods risen, shaking their heads at me.

Chapter 18

Kaydian

My mind figured out the perfect word for this place, perdition. That's the one feeling that's bottled up inside of me as Greyson strode back into the home the next morning with an apology as his greeting and a chaste kiss on my cheeks as a gift. I hadn't batted an eye when I accepted it, either. It made me wonder if the curse had set in and if this was just a fever-induced dream. That has to be the explanation because I couldn't even fathom the other opinion.

That I was falling for... a shifter.

A little over a week and I couldn't seem to bring myself to leave this nightmare village. Thinking of how my mother and Del would chastise me made my stomach twist into a knot. It was just another thing that plagued me as I waited for...I'm not sure anymore.

Greyson had been adamant that he would never step foot in the witch's territory. Which I can see why, but it felt like I was missing a piece of the story until we went into town one day.

It was a cold, wet Sunday when Greyson, Hawk, and I went into the nearby town called San Claude to buy food for the pack, or what should be called the underworld on Earth. Everything in the town was dark and dreary. Six medium size stores lined their main street as everyone in town had their tables on the sidewalk lined with their merchandise. Tou-sin was bigger than this town and nicer, if I were being honest. Many of the vendors turned to look at Hawk and Greyson. Their beady eyes roamed over us as the humans shared quick glances at each other. Greyson had mentioned that the people in town had a deep-seated hate toward them because of the land dispute, but I brushed it off as Greyson being too sensitive. I guess I was wrong.

"They've already turned their nose up, Grey. Let's be quick about this and get home," Hawk said hurriedly.

In the short time that I know Hawk, he wasn't someone who was nervous. But today, Hawk's normally wide eyes scanned the area every five seconds as if the boogeyman would jump out at us. It was weird to see shifters being jittery over humans.

"I agree. Kay, please try to stay nearby," Greyson said. I wanted to mention how I could stray when he held my hand captive, but since it was nice to have some form of affection, I kept my mouth shut.

"Um, okay," I replied. "Why are you guys—"

My voice was cut off when a large man walked over. His heavy footsteps reminded me of Sir Reid's when he had on his sparring boots. He had on a bright red shirt that bulged in the middle of his portly belly. The tight blue jeans fit his thin legs like pantyhose. I've never seen a more oddly shaped individual than him before.

"Well, if it isn't my favorite friends from the woods." The man's raucous west accent caused the nearby townsfolk to turn towards us.

Greyson cursed under his breath, and Hawk scowled as he watched the man.

"Hello, Mayor Perrins, we're on a tight schedule. So we can't stop to talk," Greyson said as his hand tightened around mine.

"I won't be long..." Mayor Perrins paused as his inquisitive eyes roamed over my body, leaving me feeling awkward. "Well, hello there. My name is Joe Perrins, and I'm the Mayor of San Claude. What's your name, dear?"

"Her name is Beverly, and she's from Ohio. She doesn't speak much." Greyson said as I contemplated whether he'd lost his mind, but I let him lead the way.

"Ah, the quiet ones are always the best," he said as he winked at

Greyson. Mayor Perrins' eyes fastened on my breast. If we were back in Houston, I would have made him choke on his tongue until he died. "She has the prettiest eyes. Greyson, you're a lucky man. She wouldn't leave my side if I were you."

I threw a cautionary glance at Greyson. He better not respond to that. And he hadn't; instead, he changed the subject.

"We haven't decided to sell Mayor Perrins," Greyson said. "My uncle and I probably won't either way."

"We value OUR land and want to keep it in our community," Hawk followed up.

"Your uncle?" Mayor Perrins asked. "But your father has you as his successor to the land. It's documented at my office. Why would you and your uncle need to think about it when you owned the land?"

Why, indeed, Mr. Perrins. Although the lecherous mayor was off-putting, he had brought up a question that I kept asking myself. Every time Greyson decided, he had to ask his obtuse uncle. I would never question his logic, but it sowed a little seed of doubt in me.

Hawk answered. "Because that's how it goes in our community. Now, I'm so sorry, Mayor Perrins, but we have to go."

All I could do was shake my head and mutter my goodbye to the Mayor. Greyson had turned several shades of red but kept the conversation minimal throughout the rest of our trip.

On our way back home, Hawk had walked ahead of us to give us some space. I couldn't hold the question that was burning on the tip of my tongue anymore.

"Would you ever take a vacation to Houston?"

Greyson paused and turned to me, causing the bags to twist around his fisted hands. "You mean go into the witches' playground? I would rather soon bury myself in wolfsbane than to be around your people, Kay. I'm sorry."

There I stood with the inside of my mouth, turning to a sponge as I watched him. For the first time in my life, I was speechless. My mind told me to run and get away, but the silly little stupid voice inside me said to stay.

"It's just going to be a quick meeting about our upcoming harvest."

"It's about food and decorations. Nothing more."

"The pack has kind of just accepted that you will be here no matter what."

All of those lies slipped off his tongue so easily and I was just as foolish to give in to the inch of hope.

That's how I found my gullible tail marching behind Greyson toward the oversized, stuffy pack house. The massive wood building seemed to have a different wood structure than the tiny homes. If it was daytime, I'm sure this place would be flooded with sunlight from the dozen windows that lined the open room. The rickety old porch groaned as we entered the house. Inside, the wood panels were painted white, with a wood-burning fireplace center and a small stage on the other side of the room. Several rows of small brown chairs filled the middle of the room. Greyson explained that two doors led to a small kitchen and the other was an exit door.

The pack members filled out the several rows of chairs as they waited for Greyson. When they noticed Greyson's tall statue filling out the door frame. They rose and kneeled towards him. Their heads were tucked with one arm folded in the back and the other at their waist. On one knee, they greeted him as Alpha Swiftwater as his long strides ate the distance between the door and the stage. When the pack members rose, they returned to their seats. Some took to turning their upturned nose at me as they sniffed the surrounding air. They kept wasting their time trying to figure me out, but their enhanced smell would always be met with the overwhelming scent of the deodorizer. And maybe it was me, but the tension had me wiping the thin line of sweat from my forehead. I shrank in the back of the room as I searched for a seat. With no such luck, I leaned on the walls. Hawk had offered to find me a chair, but I waved him off.

I stuck out like a sore thumb. My mother would die of embarrassment if she knew I was here playing house with Greyson. If you could call it that.

"We have little for this harvest as the crops were half eaten by the animals, and I doubt we will have enough, since the Blood Moon is tonight. Funds are extremely low. So, buying isn't an option," Oni announced to the pack room. His cold black eyes found mines when he said, "We won't have any room to feed anyone outside of our village."

The oversized white t-shirt became my shield against Oni's

murderous gaze as I gripped the edge of the shirt. My face flushed with blood as everyone turned back to look at me when they realized where Oni's attention had landed. Their pursed lips and raised eyebrows greeted me where I stood in the back of the stale brown room. The muffled snickers of the teens on the other side of the room floated to my scorched ears. I should have stayed at home. I pleaded with Greyson to attend the meeting without me, but he wouldn't take no for an answer. Greyson insisted I was a part of the pack and that "soon" everyone would kneel to my command. When he interlocked my hands, my magic warmed, and soon, my head was nodding before I could realize I was giving in to him.

"My mate can have my share at the harvest. It's not a big deal." Greyson said, breaking me out of my thoughts.

"Well, there wasn't another choice," Oni countered. "And while we're at it, we need to vote on whether she can attend. The Blood Moon Harvest is for shifters only."

"Not always..." He paused and stood in front of his uncle. The top of his bun knot was a hair below his uncle's chin with his arms folded in front of him. All eyes were on Greyson as he challenged his uncle, which, from their gaze, wasn't something that happened often. Oni's eyebrow quirked with a half cocky smirk. Greyson's defiant look softened. "There was a time when other supernaturals attended. A time when we were all at peace. At least for one night."

One of the Pack members closer to me muttered, "What a waste of the Swiftwater blood."

My back ached from the wood panels as the duo went back and forth for ten minutes. Oni and what I've come to know as his supporters pushed Greyson until he folded. Doubt, pride, and pity thickened the pack room as we watched the two Swiftwater's standoff. The pack on Oni's side all wore smug smirks on their faces as they glanced at one another, and with every point Oni made, they nodded, and a resounding yes filled the room. Greyson's supporters' heads shook. A deep frown embedded into their faces every time he said, "I understand, Oni." With every second that went by at this meeting and each "You're right, Paráh," that went by really cemented my inner thought of me being the foolish one.

Was this a sign?

"Let's vote," Oni said. "Who thinks that humans shouldn't be able to attend?"

Everyone of Oni henchmen didn't miss a beat as they raised their grubby hands. Greyson's mouth dropped open slightly. His arms folded tight across his chest. From my standing point, I could see the fist at his side. I've spent enough time around angry men, including Sir Reid and my father, to know he was hurt or mad.

"She shouldn't even be alive. If you asked me!" Mike yelled as I pinned him as Oni's henchman.

"That was uncalled for, Mike," Kathleen stood up and said. "We all know how you feel about Kaydian, but she's here to stay, whether you or Oni likes it."

That sent a tidal wave of mutters amongst the pack.

"I much rather hang myself than take orders from a human," an older white beard shifter said. His frown stretched across his face. "This is embarrassing to your father, our legacy. Your father learned the hard way, and now you will, too."

Before Greyson could respond, the old man continued. "They're taking our land, and now they want to rule us."

"And how do they know we're shifters, Henry?" Kathleen countered. "Did you send a memo about how there is an entire world of supernatural living under their noses?"

"No, but there was a time recently when shifters were hunted by human hunters that knew about us." Henry paused as he cast a sorrowful gaze at Greyson. "You should know better, Greyson. Your father would turn over in his grave."

"Henry!" Greyson yelled. "Whatever my father may have thought about, my decisions are not relevant. He has long since taken his walk to the afterworld to be with the Earth Creator and my mother. Now it's time we welcome Kaydian as my mate and our newest pack member. You're welcome to leave the pack if you please."

Some yelled, "That was uncalled for," and others called for my death. One even said I should be a maid for the pack, cleaning and cooking as punishment for my people's wicked ways. Brazen bastards.

"Now settle down, everyone. No need to act like savages. That's what *her* people are good at," Oni said. His voice was like a soother for his minions.

"That's enough, párah." Greyson finally said. "You're not allowed to treat my mate like that. If you have a problem, then direct it at me."

"…And what will you do about it?" Oni said, standing with his arms across his stomach.

Tension thick in the air between the two Swiftwaters. *So, now he grows some balls.* If the cursed voice was still lurking around, it would have a field day watching me squirm as I waited. Greyson and Oni stood face to face. Both of their fists were balled up at their sides. And I couldn't help myself. I wanted Greyson to stand up to his uncle and for me. The pack stood silent once again, watching the duo in their silent square off.

All he had to do was tell his uncle to kneel and make him apologize to me. I was due for one. *Come on, Greyson! Do it for me.* Oni quirked one of his thick eyebrows. And like a light switch, Greyson folded. Backing away from his uncle, he turned his reddened face toward the crowd.

"Pathetic!" a red-haired teen whispered to his friend who sat beside him. They both fell into a giggle as they looked on.

"His poor father is rolling over in his grave right now," One of the older women from Greyson's side muttered.

A cold lump sat in the pit of my stomach. Just below my skin, my magic tingled and itched to be released, rolling my lips in between my teeth. The soft flesh burned and ached as the metal taste overwhelmed my mouth. I couldn't trust myself to open my mouth or to wiggle my fist. My palms were sweaty as I reeled in my magic. A muffled grunt rumbled in my throat. Snapping my eyes shut, I counted to thirty as my magic raced through me, making my legs quiver. It was the longest five minutes of my entire life. My white t-shirt clung to my skin. The cotton pants felt like weights on my thighs.

It was becoming harder to control my magic each day, and I convinced myself to stay. My once staunch tolerance for these bastards slipped further away from me. My time with them has made me realize that maybe my parents were right about the shifters.

"Are you okay, Kay?" Greyson asked.

Opening up my eyes, cold rivets of sweat dripped down along my face. Using the damp sleeve of his white shirt did nothing to dry my feverish skin. The corners of my mouth lifted as an unconvinced smile broke out on my face.

"I'm okay, Grey. I promise."

I grabbed his hand and laced them together as we walked out of the now-empty pack house with my mind still on Greyson in the pack house. He will never be a good leader if he can't even stick up for what he believes in. Just the thought made me wonder if this was worth it.

Chapter 19

Greyson

I decided we needed a break from the pack for a day. So, we had taken the day off to help support Kathleen at the town's flea market on a chilly Saturday. Kaydian, Hawk, and I helped Kathleen haul almost four boxes of the colorful handwork, a blanket, and a couple of chairs into the small town. Our chatter and loud laughs filled the nearly deserted road with more life than it had in months. Hearing Kaydian's laughter drew me closer to her, and my wolf had no complaints. Seeing Kathleen and Hawk welcome her with open arms without judging her made me thankful. I was glad I could rely on them to watch over her when I wasn't able to be around.

As we entered San Claude, the residents were dressed in their thick sweaters and jeans as they gathered at the entrance of the main street. Food, art, and other vendors lined the street as we walked toward our usual spot, which was in front of the purple-colored bakery shop that Hawk and I usually frequent before we hightail it away to avoid running into Mayor Perrins. The bakery's door was propped open, letting the scent of burnt sugar coat the air as the residents piled into the store for their desserts.

Finding our small spot, we got to work setting up the blanket and chairs to showcase Kathleen's latest work. Once we were done, we waited until someone in this self-absorbed town gave us a chance. Each human that passed our area scoped us out, deciding whether we were worthy of their time and money. No matter how much we tried to fit in. We still stuck out like a fish out of water. It was the same song every other Saturday, but we had no other choice, seeing as the next closest town was about an hour away.

"Here, Kay. Let me show you how I usually fold the items so they won't be too wrinkled." Kathleen said, walking over to her. Her voice drew my attention to the one older lady who was brave enough to stop by our setup.

"I'm sorry, ma'am...Thank you, Kathleen. Can you tell I've done nothing like this before?" Kaydian said as she smiled at Kathleen, who gathered the items for the customer.

The older lady smiled. "There's a first for everything. Hopefully, you sell fast and can get some of the pie at the bakery."

Kaydian nodded as Kathleen handed her the bag. "I sure will. You have a good day, Ma'am."

Kathleen beamed as the woman left. "I'm so glad you're here. It's rough when it's just me with these two hardheads."

"Hey!" Both Hawk and I said simultaneously.

We all dissolved into a fit of laughter, and I may be delusional, but I think it made some residents curious. One by one, they amble up to our poor makeshift table. They picked over Kathleen's items until they were all gone. As Kaydian bagged the last blanket we hauled, I looked into the bakery shop, and the shop owner waved at me through the window. He and his wife were one of the few members of this town that hadn't treated us like we didn't belong.

Kathleen nudged me in the arm with a lazy smile on her face. "Maybe Kaydian would love to meet Mr. and Mrs. Wang rather than you staring a hole into her."

A warm flush crossed my face. "Right."

Grabbing Kaydian's hand, I dropped a kiss on her now reddened cheek. "Let's get something for the road."

"Ok," Kay muttered as she tried to hide her face from me behind her long hair.

"I'll get you guys the usual," I said as we entered the colorful shop.

Mr. and Mrs. Wang's small store was empty as they prepared to close for the day. Brown sugar still drifted in the air. Several empty tables and chairs lined the short wall that wasn't occupied with pictures and gifts from the town residents. Walking into the bakery, the bright purple walls greeted us as we walked up to the counter.

"Nǐ hǎo, Greyson," Mr. Wang greeted me as he bowed slightly.

Mr. Wang's dark brown eyes turned to Kaydian, which sparkled as he bowed to her. Rustling from the kitchen stopped, Mrs. Wang joined us by the counter. They were like night and day. While Mr. Wang wore his unwrinkled uniform, not a hair out of place, and a stern look that would send anyone scrambling, Mrs. Wang was the polar opposite. I've never seen her without a smile, even when some of the residents turn their noses up at the couple. Her bright pink dress that had white flowers printed on it was loud and bright, just like Mrs. Wang. Her brown hair was placed up with a bright pink bow that was bigger than her head.

"Hello, Mr. Wang," I said, returning his bow. I pulled Kaydian beside me, "Mrs. Wang, hello. It's always a pleasure to stop in the best store."

"Hello! Greyson. I've missed you. And who is this beautiful young lady?" Mrs. Wang beamed. Her smile could light up the dark.

"Mr. and Mrs. Wang, this is Kaydian, my fiancé," I said.

I could feel Kaydian's green globes burning a hole in the side of my face.

"Hello," Kaydian said as she greeted the couple, taking their hands in hers. She shook and bowed, following our greeting from earlier.

Mrs. Wang peered at Kaydian. Her head turned slightly as she read Kaydian. "Greyson, you're lucky to find someone as beautiful as Ms. Kaydian. Your aura is the same color as those gem eyes."

"Keep her close and treat her well." Mr. Wang said with a small smile.

The tip of Kaydian's nose turned a deep shade of red as she tried to avert her eyes. "Thank you—"

"I plan to. I can't see myself without her and I can only hope I can keep her happy for the rest of our lives. She's my sun and the reason I wake up, and I will fight for her until my last dying breath," I said truthfully as I took her hand and kissed the back of it.

Kaydian peered at me through her long, dark eyelashes. Her cheeks and nose were the same color as the dragon fruit pastry that sat behind the counter. "I'm lucky as well."

"Well, his father taught him well. He would be so proud of you, Greyson." Mrs. Wang said. Her hazel eyes glittered in the store light. "Look how her eyes light up when she looks at him. It's like magic."

"Thank you, Ms. Wang," Kay said while ducking her head.

"She's my magic," I said.

We stood in the store talking with the Wang's about Mayor Perrins' latest foolish ideas for San Claude and the latest rumors circulating the town. The store's light went from a soft shade of white to brightening up the store before we ended our conversation with the Wang's. When we gathered our things after shoving the pieces of Nian Gao into our mouths and cleaning the brown sugar treat from our fingers. We headed home. This stretch home was shorter this time because we had fewer things to haul after a successful day.

By the time we got home, the sun had settled in for the night. Only a few of the pack were out guarding the area, and the rest were hanging around on their porch. As much as I loved being away from the pack drama, I missed my home. I knew Hawk complained, but he loved a day away from the pit. Kathleen, Hawk, Kaydian, and I stood between our homes as we prepared to go our separate ways.

Kathleen said as she hugged Kaydian, "I'm so glad you came along today. It was really nice having another kindred spirit with me."

"Yes, it was a good day. Though we spent a little longer than I would like because I hate being in town and around all of those humans!"

Hawk's cheek turned a light shade of pink as he realized his mistake. "I'm sorry, Shorts. I forgot."

Kaydian patted his cheeks and said, "I understand, Hawk. I don't enjoy being around them either."

Kathleen and Hawk shared a look. Both of their eyebrows raised as they reflected on Kaydian's truthful words. Thankfully, we didn't have time to go into further explanation because Kaydian yawned loudly. Saying goodnight, we headed in our separate directions.

As we got ready for bed, Kaydian was silent as she got dressed in my oversized dress shirt. I couldn't help taking a peek as she bent over to remove her underwear. A fine line of sweat formed on the top of my upper lip, but I made no attempt to wipe it away. Instead, I turned away from my temptation and cursed as I adjusted my painful dick in my shorts. Each night was becoming harder to not give in.

"Greyson," Kay said from behind me. Her voice was above a whisper. "Thank you. Did you really mean what you said today at the Wang's bakery?"

Turning toward her was a mistake. There Kaydian stood before me. The top buttons on her shirt were open, exposing the soft brown skin of her heavy breasts. Her scent enveloped me, calling out to my wolf. He had been dormant all day, but now he stretched out inside of me, wanting to answer Kaydian's heady call.

I was a strong Alpha, or so I told myself. Kaydian slowly closed the gap between us. Her small hands left a trail of cold heat as she ran them up my naked chest. A low whine slipped from my mouth, and it sounded desperate...borderline needy.

"Greyson," she said breathlessly, as if she had just ran into the room. "Did you really mean—"

My control slipped when her hand landed on the band of my boxers, right above the wet spot my dick created, and my wolf took over. We picked Kay up, throwing her over our shoulder as we took two steps toward the bed and dropped her on to the small mattress. Kaydian's hair sprawled all over the bed like an angel. Our angel. Yes. As my wolf lapped at her soft skin, Kaydian arched, giving us more access. Not that it was needed, as the sound of buttons from my shirt danced against the floor as my wolf ripped it open.

"Mine!" we said. The mix of our voices made Kaydian's chin tremble, and her emerald eyes darkened to black pits. The voice was dark and rough, just like how I felt my wolf inside of me.

"Yes, I'm yours," Kaydian said, her voice thick with lust.

No, No, No...as much as I wanted this moment. This wasn't how I envisioned it. I couldn't. *Coward! She's ours.* I had to fight back. Reaching deep inside of me, I pulled on our thick yellow corded connection that bonded us together as one. Inch by inch, I reeled in my wolf, causing his partially shifted hands to fall from Kaydian. She protested, and a whine fell from her parted lips. This was a mistake. I should have never allowed the slip-up. Now, we played a tug of war as he gripped the last yellow sheets, tearing holes in the weak fabric I could afford. He pushed to stay a front, but he slipped, and I took the moment to shove him into the depths of my chest. A rivulet of sweat dropped onto Kaydian's naked breast as she heaved beneath me. My heartbeat chaotically against its cage, and my lungs burned as I struggled to gain control of my breathing.

Rolling off Kaydian, I closed my eyes as I took several deep breaths. I've lost count of how many times I've lost control of my wolf, but this time hurt the most. If I had given my wolf an inch more, then I would have bitten Kaydian, bonding us together without going through the ceremony. Silence filled the dark space in my mind until Kaydian broke it.

"Did I do something wrong?" She asked, her voice quavering.

Sitting on the side of the bed, I grabbed a clean shirt and wiped the sweat off of my face. My face was warm with regret and shame. Averting the disappointment that most likely painted onto her face.

"I-I'm sorry, Kay," I said truthfully. "I lost control and—let's just go to bed. I'm too tired to talk about this."

"Why don't you want to touch me? You said all of those things back at the bakery, and I just thought... Is it because I'm bigger than the women in your pack?"

I meant every single word I said back at the bakery, but Kaydian would not take a simple 'I'm tired' excuse. She sat in the middle of the bed with my shirt clutch closed. Tears formed pools in her eyes. This was the first time I'd seen her in this state and my heart and wolf cursed me. I'm pathetic.

"What? No, I love you just the way you are, Kay. It's...I don't want to have sex with you because the bonding ceremony is special, and I'm already giving up a lot since you're a witch!" The words slipped out of my mouth before I could process what they meant. "I can't deny that the elephant in the room still scares me, and a part of me can't get over that one detail. I'm sorry, I have to get used to it."

We sat there in silence as if we were daring each other to move. I thought she would have cursed me out, but I received nothing. After a minute or two, the bed dipped, and when I looked back Kaydian had slipped under the covers. With her back to me, I couldn't tell if she was ignoring me. Not that I could blame her. I knew my callous words had hurt her and I would have to make it up to her.

It will have to wait until tomorrow as I laid down with my back to hers, letting the day's event finally pull me to sleep.

Kaydian POV

I woke to the sound of someone pounding on our wooden door as if the hounds of the underworld were on their tail.

If I were back home and someone was banging on the door like a mad person, I would have them placed in the dungeon. My head pounded with each of the mad person banging. Thanks to crying in the middle of the night from Greyson's admission that I turned him off, I had high hopes that I could just sleep in until Greyson had to leave for the day. I guess that was easier said than done.

Whoever was out there was lucky I couldn't use my magic. Losing patience, the person jingled the knob before returning to the tortuous pounding against the door.

Why am I still here? Squeezing my eyes, I shut them against my very own taunting thoughts.

Yes, I knew Greyson would rather watch paint dry than touch me.

Yes, I knew I could just go home and leave everything I learned and experienced here.

After what felt like an eternity, Greyson rolled out of bed. His low grunt shook the tiny bed as he slid on his clothes, cursing along the way to the door. I wish I could joke with him about finally moving his ass, but my tongue sat heavy in my mouth. If I could just have a couple of minutes alone to cry and scream, I think I could manage, but being stuck in this small village made it impossible.

The front door creaked as Greyson opened it before it hit the wall with a loud whack that filled the small home. *Youna!* What the hell is going on?

"Greyson!" Oni's dark voice boomed.

"Paráh Oni, what's going—"

"What the hell did you say to Mayor Perrins?" He asked.

Rolling out of bed, I slipped on the white cotton dress Kathleen had made for me. As I entered the living room, Oni's dark eyes landed on me. Boy, did I want to command my magic to shove his finger into them, but I was trying to be the bigger person.

Oni was all dressed in brown. A perfect choice for the miserable person who he was. His frown deepened as he took in my appearance. I knew my hair looked a matted mess, but I had to work with what I had, and that wasn't a lot these days.

Oni continued, "Come on, Greyson."

The presumptuous asshole didn't even wait for a response. He just walked out of the door, leaving his smokey scent behind. Watching Greyson, I wondered if he would stay behind to spite him and let Oni know he was the Alpha and not him. I prayed he would hear my thoughts and don't be foolish. The dark voice vibrated in my chest as it laughed.

Greyson sighed as he rubbed the back of his neck as he started for the door.

"Greyson!" I called out. He paused to look at me. A ruby-red color graced his face. "You should make him wait. You're the Alpha. Not him. No matter how much he might want to be."

"Kay, I'm sorry about last night. What I said …it wasn't right. You didn't deserve that." He paused. "And I will try to make it up to you, but I have to go out there to fix whatever I did."

My shoulders slumped as I nodded. Greyson stared at me with regret laced in his eyes for a beat too long. The past night's events seemed minuscule. I wanted to help take away his pain and make everything better. Watching Greyson walk through the door and to his uncle was hard. His shoulders sagged with each step he took.

Without a second thought, I walked out of the home and closed the door, following him into the unknown. When I turned around, I noticed every single pack member had gathered around the pit and the open meeting area. Wiping my palms into my dress, I ran to keep up with Greyson. The pack's watchful gaze turned from respectful to scrutiny as they parted for us. Some bowed as we passed, while others clenched their lips together.

As we approached the center, Oni stood erect, with his arms crossed over his chest. His frown was deeper than I'd ever witnessed. The bushy eyebrows he sported became one as he stood in front of his guest, and from what I overheard, an unexpected one at that.

Mayor Perrins stood before the brooding pack, who looked ready to skin him alive. Today, he was dressed in a thick gold coat with the collar of his white shirt folded over. Blue jeans and boots that looked too large for his thin legs. His jet-black hair was slicked back. Mayor Perrins arrived with two other men who kept sizing up Oni as if they had the chance to take him down. I paused next to Greyson.

"Ah, there is the man of the hour." Mayor Perrins said. His face was ruby red as he smiled. Probably from the pack circling him like he was dinner. "Hello Greyson, I was just stopping by to follow up on our last conversation—"

Oni interrupted him, "Which I told him we are not interested in selling to him or anyone."

"But you hadn't heard of our newest offer. I have buyers that are eager to get their hands on some land. Their goal is to make more family-friendly suburbs for San Claude residents and beyond."

"No." Greyson and his uncle both said in unison.

Greyson, for better or worse, stood rooted next to Oni. It was as if he couldn't decide to tell this human off. Silence greeted the crowd, and I couldn't take it anymore. Something inside of me told me to keep quiet, but the other part poked at the question floating in my mind.

"How much?" I asked as the question slipped out of my mouth before I thought about it.

Heat filled my veins and left a trail of thin sweat along its way. Every single eye, human and shifter alike, fell onto me. Some with curiosity and some with a hateful glint. I've overstepped my boundaries. No one wanted the Alpha's "human" mate to speak up.

"See, Greyson, it's always the quiet ones that are the best..." Mayor Perrins gleefully gloated. His eyes roamed my body, and I never wanted to pluck out his brown eyes more than I wanted to right now. "What was your name again, dear?"

Placing a sickly sweet smile on my face, "It's Beverly. "

Somewhere in the crowd. I knew Kathleen was staring at Hawk for answers. Probably like the one Oni was giving as he stared down his nose at me. If I listened closely, I could hear every single harsh word he dreamed up of me.

"You guys will learn one day to trust a woman's intuition...The builder wants the space between your property line up to your crop fields. They're willing to pay one thousand dollars! You will be rich."

"Trust," Oni scoffed. "I trust you as much as I do...Beverly."

Rolling my eyes at the miserable bastard. My magic washed over me, almost pleading with me to torture him in front of the pack. He may be blinded by hate, but one thousand dollars in the human world was a lot of money. Enough to help the pack out with food and to bring more supplies in for their homes. This could be monumental for them. A smile crept up on my gleeful face as I looked to Greyson to tell him, but stopped. Greyson still stood with his arms folded, but this time, his head was bent down, causing his dark hair to hang over his shoulders. If I weren't standing right next to him, I wouldn't have felt how he trembled.

Instantly, regret painted my face.

Mayor Perrins continued, "I mean, Greyson, think about it. New homes, more food, and maybe a new start for your people. Your fiancé agrees, and this is her decision as much as it is yours."

"She can agree with anything you say, but her opinion doesn't matter because, like you, Mayor Perrins. She's an outsider, and outsiders don't have opinions here," Oni stated. "Every year, you make your unwanted trek onto our property to convince us to sell. Do you know how much our property means to us?"

Oni bent down, placing his hand into the brown dirt. "Our family bled here and were buried in these woods. Our traditions and way of life have been well-rooted over the years to this land. And with every..." Oni stopped and gritted his teeth. "The person who gave their life for this piece of land resides here. You may see this as another way to line your pockets with money, but this dirt is worth more than anything money could buy. So, you can take your thousand dollars and roll yourself along with your two pathetic guards out of our lands."

Someone in the crowd yelled out, "Intruding bastards."—no doubt talking about me, Mayor Perrins, and his motley crew. My nails cut into my palms as I held my mouth and magic back. Reminding me once again that no matter how much I try to help, the more I climb on the pack's hate list.

"That's enough, Oni. Kaydian has been nothing but helpful. She doesn't deserve your anger," Greyson said right before I touched his shoulder.

"Mayor Perrins," an elder said. Her gray eyes held nothing but disgust for the mayor, but she managed to keep her face blank. "Why don't we think about it and get back to you?"

Mayor Perrins turned a light shade of dusty rose. Licking his thin lips, his eyes rolled over the pack. He said, "Thank you, Gena. I think that will be a good idea. How about you take a week and think about it?"

"Goodbye," Greyson grunted out, making Mayor Perrins' red color deepen.

Perrins had wasted no time saying his curt goodbye and hightailing it toward the dusty path trail that led to the road near the forest entrance. Slowly, the group dispensed except for a few of Oni's cowardly guard wolves, leaving Greyson, Hawk, Kathleen, and me in his path of rage...or should I leave me in his fiery wrath.

"You need to control your mate," he said, spitting out the last word as if it were poison, before turning his dark, narrow eyes on me. "We have never entertained Perrins when he trespasses on our property, but you just stuck yourself into the pack business. How do we know that you and Perrins aren't working together to steal my land? I don't like it one bit. She lied to him. What makes you think she won't lie to you?"

"She meant no harm, Oni. Kaydian is still learning our ways," Elder Gena replied first.

Oni's tantrum speech drew some of the pack members back to the little gathering. There was definitely a divide, contrary to what Greyson kept telling me. Young, old men, and women lingered around.

"Disrespectful. His father must be turning in his grave," someone muttered.

"Even his mother had more balls than him. He needs to control that thing of his," another pack member taunted.

Whether Greyson heard the inglorious words from his pack or not, he ignored them. Some part of me wanted him to turn around and challenge the pack, but I knew better. Greyson clenched his jaw as rust tinted the surrounding air. When I looked down at his hands, blood dripped into the dusty patch, turning the area dark, but it was those yellow orbs of his that made me want to run far from here. Gone was the hard glint from this morning. In place were fresh tears that threatened to spill.

Shit. I did it again. Putting myself in things that don't involve me.

"Greyson, I'm sorry. I just thought maybe if the offer was good, then we could improve things around here. Sorry for putting my two cents in."

"Well, I'm glad you're finally learning your role. It took you a while, but I guess that's due to you being human."

That cleared any of the tears Greyson had left in his eyes. "Oni, I've told you one too many times that Kaydian is my mate, and she should be respected as such. Yes, she may not understand the situation, but that's my fault in not telling her that selling my land was not up for discussion. No matter how much money Mayor Perrins and those fucking human builders offer."

Straightening up, Greyson stood taller than he had just done a couple of minutes ago and continued, "This is the last time you'll speak to her like that, Oni."

Greyson's voice was lost over the tidal wave of warmness that surged through my body. My magic and I were enjoying this too much as I trembled slightly.

Folding his arm over his chest. Those bushy eyebrows raised, questioning Greyson. "And what will you do if I don't?"

Although Greyson and I hadn't been together for long, I picked up on little clues without him divulging all of his secrets like when he was happy, the corners of his mouth would twitch until I found him smiling to himself. Or when something was bothering him, his forehead would wrinkle as he processed how to fix the situation. Now Greyson stood tall, matching his uncle, as they stared wordlessly at each other. Oni's condescending smirk pulled at the corner of his mouth. It was deathly silent as we sat watching and waiting until Kathleen cleared her throat.

"We will cross that bridge when it happens," Greyson said through his clenched teeth.

Oni threw his head back, laughing, and the remaining pack leaders snickered along with him.

"It seems my nephew is trying to channel his father." Oni shook his head as he turned to leave. He said, "Just make sure all humans know where their place is around here."

When he entered his home, Kathleen came up beside me. "We know you meant well. The Swiftwater men have always been hardheaded. So, hearing anyone's opinion besides the one in their head is their weakness."

While Greyson and Hawk huddled together, I sneaked in a question that had been bugging me, "Has Greyson always been like this with his uncle?"

Kathleen blushed a dewy pink shade. "I—Greyson is still young and has lots of learning to do, especially since his father died when he was very young. He's...just give him some grace."

As if Kathleen willed them over telepathically, Greyson and Hawk ambled over. Greyson sighed. It wasn't noon yet, but dark circles hung around his eyes, and Hawk's charcoal-smudged face was covered in a thin sheen of sweat.

"I'm sorry, Shorts. Oni can be... off-putting, but he means well. We have been going back and forth with Mayor Perrins for years. He just won't take no for an answer," Hawk said.

"He's been more than off-putting lately. I'm sorry for not being direct with you about our problems with Perrins, my Hiema. For the past three years, he's been down our necks. I hope he gets the message once I send him another letter telling him no this time. What's the quote again? The fourth time's a charm, right? How about we get some food and take it back to the house? Maybe we can just stay in for the day."

"Thank you, everyone," I said honestly. "That sounds perfect."

"Enjoy the day off, lovebirds," Kathleen called out.

Greyson smiled as he reached for my free hand, but it didn't quite reach his eyes. This was an excellent lesson for me to never put my nose into this angry pack's business again. If not for my sake, but for Greyson's. Even as we entered our tiny home, I could tell his mind was still back in the small clearing with his uncle. So much for a peaceful day without the miserable bastard. As he climbed back into bed, I changed and got in next to him. Heat enveloped me as he pulled me into his body. Normally, I would enjoy it, but my mind was filled with questions that I knew would push him.

How will he be able to rule two different covens?

Will he always be this passive?

I guess I will just have to wait and take everything one step at a time. *Big mistake.* That was the last thing that filtered into my mind before I hid myself in the pillow and allowed Greyson's heat to put me to sleep.

Chapter 20

Kaydian

Two days later, I realized I still had the same silly sham of a smile plastered on my face even when Greyson spoke about the Harvest with a glint in his eyes.

The Blood Moon Harvest was their sacred time to honor their god, the Earth Creator. Every year during the winter, they gathered to bring in the new moon. When the moon turned red like their blood, they ran and hunted their kill until the sun bled into the midnight moon. Each kill brought them closer to their god. It was more important now since the shifters had forgotten how to wield the magic they once had, even before my father slathered them.

The Blood Moon Harvest started about thirty minutes ago. On the edge of the gathering area, I sat by myself, as usual, at one of the old picnic tables. When I first stepped out of Grey's home, I was puzzled, but he told me the only decorations I would see were the regalia they wore during the harvest and a red awning covering the picnic tables. A variety of meats, bread, and vegetables were surrounded by empty cups that were discarded everywhere as the pack drank their outrageously bitter beer. Ms. Kincaid would surely fall over if I told her their harvest wasn't decorated to an inch of its life.

All the men were dressed in their vivid leather regalia bottoms that broke away at the sides when they went for their midnight moon run. The females had something similar. Their red and yellow regalia dresses snapped along the side streams. Everyone had their hair in a bun with red and yellow feathers tucked into their buns. Fanned out behind their head, it reminded me of the sunset here just before the darkness chased the reddish-yellow sun away.

The elders wouldn't be joining the midnight run, so they dressed differently from the rest of the pack. They donned the same dress and bottom regalia but with long red capes and had the same bright yellow phoenix in their capes. A massive headpiece finished their outfit with the same feathers as the pack, except they were lined up down the middle, splitting their heads in halves, except for the oldest elder, whose headpiece resembled a great white wolf with ears that hung low down to his elbow. He stood strong as he watched the others. It was as if he was a principal watching over his students. I suppose that was accurate since the Pack held their elders in high regard.

Watching the rest of the pack as the thumping beat of the drums uplifted the dancers as their lean bodies became entangled with the music. In the middle of the gathering area, I'd almost lost balance on the old, rickety bench, from swaying to the flute's energetic melody. Children paraded behind the adults with their scrawny arms flaring in the air. Their infectious giggles thundered in my ears. I wanted to join them, but I was already met with the common repulsed look that was reserved especially for me. Greyson, Hawk, and Kathleen were huddled together as the music died down. Sensing my staring, Greyson turned and winked at me, causing my breath to hitch in my throat. Some elders participated in their traditional dance made me miss home.

One of the children stopped in front of the refreshment table, filling their plates with food. She couldn't have been older than nine years old with her small tongue peeking out of the corner of her mouth as she struggled with the plate and juggled her drink. I didn't think twice but to help the small girl as I leaped from the bench and offered help.

"Hey, how about I help you to your seat?"

The young girl stared at me with her gray eyes widened. Her red curly hair was askew as a light breeze sent them scattering. She was on the verge of tears as she stared at me like I was a monster. I never wanted to flee away from somewhere, but I did now.

"Get away from my daughter!" A woman identical to the small girl stomped over and grabbed her daughter's arm, sending some of the juice to decorate the girl's regalia. Opening my mouth, I wanted to apologize or curse her out. I'm not sure, but she didn't wait for me to explain as she dragged the girl away to the other side of the clearing where the pack members sat.

My arms wrapped around my stomach as I returned to my seat, kicking the floor that was littered with cups from the packs of brews. In less than two weeks, I had become more unsure of myself. Was it my fault the pack hated me? What could I do to make this work? Despite everything, I needed him. I racked my brain for the answer, but was it enough? I wasn't sure. The only time I felt like myself was when I was with Greyson or tucked away in the small bedroom of his home. The only good thing that came out of this was that my deranged voice had disappeared.

"Don't mind, cranky Red." Looking up to see the oldest elder with his headpiece gone. The reddish-brown hue of his skin was beautiful against the moonlight. "Do you mind if I keep you company?"

I shook my head. My eyebrow crept up as a smile touched my face. Even though I didn't mind sitting by myself, someone wanting to sit next to me made the hot tears behind my eyes blur my vision. Luckily, when the old, rickety bench groaned and shifted as the elder sat down next to me. I wiped my eyes before he could notice the tears. His warmth, mixed in with his smokey scent, filled my nostrils. He reminded me of Tou-sin Square during our festival when we smoked the meat during the town harvests. It made me long to leave Greyson here and just fall into my madness...well, just a little.

"I'm sorry to be rude, but I forgot your name."

A warm smile engulfed his wrinkled face. "My name is Alo Bird, and excuse my tardiness in meeting you."

Something about the older man reminded me of home. Back when I didn't have to worry about the dreaded curse or filling my mother's shoes. When I could run for hours on end in the wooded areas until the Golden Army caught me and dragged me back to the castle.

"My name is Kaydian. I'm... with Greyson."

"You mean you're his Hiema. His twin soul."

Heat crept up my neck at the term of endearment coming out of

Alo's mouth. I was slightly mortified that he had overheard Greyson's nickname for me.

"Ah, no need to be bashful, young one. Swiftwater already told me all about you."

"Oh," I said, holding my head down to cover my scorched face against my curly hair.

A silence fell amongst us as we watched the pack line up to start their midnight run. Greyson trudged over to us. He looked glorious when he was happy, and I couldn't help but stare at the way every muscle contracted and bounced as he ran over. A lone bead of sweat formed on his skin, beckoning me to lick it off of his chest. My thighs dug into the bench as I clenched my throbbing pussy. I have done many foolish things in my life, but at this very moment, I would definitely throw myself on the table and offer myself up to Greyson...in front of everyone, with no shame or regret at all.

If only I had one of those rubber penises that I read about in the Houston newspaper.

Greyson kissed my cheek. He smelled like grass, beer, and lemon. The scent wasn't supposed to turn me on, but here I sat with my essence wetting my inner thighs. Greyson sniffed the air and paused. A scarlet color painted his cheeks as he shifted uncomfortably. Elder Alo chuckled at Greyson—us. If I could die of embarrassment, I would have done so right now.

"Young love! I remember those days." Alo said as he winked at both of us. "Go ahead, Swiftwater. Your tethered soul will be safe with us. We will be in the temple when you get back."

Kathleen jogged up to our little group, and I couldn't help but flush at the memory of her and Samantha's tryst in the woods.

"Hey, Kaydian. Do you mind if we grab your mate?" Kathleen said as I got up to hug her. The words couldn't form in my mind, so I just nodded instead. She bowed and greeted Elder Alo and grabbed Greyson, who she had to all but drag across the dirt clearing into the forest while he stared mindlessly back at me. Leaving Elder Alo to chuckle at him.

"Shall we?" Elder Alo held out his arm for me, and something deep inside of me didn't want to disappoint him, so I snaked my arm inside the crook of his arm. Just the minor touch sent a surge of warmth through my body, and soon, I wasn't able to feel the chilly air.

We approached the second larger building in the village. Nothing was special about the outside, but my skin puckered as soon as Elder Alo opened the double doors for me. The temple was blocked off to me because I wasn't a shifter, and I respected their rules. I was too nice to tell Greyson that their sacred building held no interest to me, but with Elder Alo by my side, my curiosity peeked.

The inside of the temple was nothing like I'd expected. History packed the walls of the dimly lit room. Wood and citrus filled the room. A lazy smile crept up my face. The scent reminded me of Merrell's book and art store. Paintings filled the walls of lost times with mini statues on several tiered shelves. Someone made four long benches that formed a circle in the middle of the room. Just enough to seat the pack leader and some elders. The mammoth-sized wood fireplace already had the room warm as my body slowly melted into the warmth. I could kick myself for not exploring it before tonight.

One of the powder paintings had a woman with long, curly brown hair that framed her oval face. The woman's face wasn't average by any means, but her honey drew eyes with citrine tugged at my soul. She was dressed in regalia similar to what the female Pack members wore today for the harvest. Her headpiece was the yellow canary that I've seen on the totem pole. Behind her was a striking man who was the carbon copy of Greyson, except his dark eyes were almost black, his skin the color of the sunset during the summer, and his broad upper body filled out his red regalia. His massive hand engulfed the woman's shoulder. You could tell they were mates because their gazes mirrored one another. Both their eyes told a story of passion, love, and possessiveness. A shiver ran through me at the mere thought as I stood wishing that I was the woman in the painting.

"Come sit beside me, and I can tell you about the paintings. Swiftwater mentioned you love art and books. I can see he wasn't lying." He chuckled.

My eyes were glued to the paintings as I studied the other vibrant hues and textures. It wasn't until it turned to find Elder Alo on the bench that I noticed I had all but abandoned him and floated to the painting. I couldn't help it. They were all so captivating as they pulled at my spirit. My hand itched to reach out and touch every brush stroke, but

I knew that would be disrespectful. That was the last thing I wanted to do. Greyson would never forgive me.

"Sorry, the paintings are just so awe-inspiring. If I'd known what laid in here, I might have snuck in to view them," I said honestly.

My hand shot out to cover my mouth. Loose lips strike again! Elder Alo chuckled.

"It's okay! I'll keep your secret. Plus, it's an honor." He bowed his head slightly. When he rose, he had a smile on his thin lips. "I painted many of our artwork here, and I dabbled in sculpture here or there. Most of them were made by Greyson's mother, Mary Ann."

"Shit," I muttered. Just the mere thought of the shifters being able to practice art freely without being judged was unheard of in our coven. I had to bite my tongue to keep my jealous remarks to myself.

He continued, "The Swiftwater's founded this little piece of heaven for us when the shifters split into different tribes five thousand years ago after the first shifter war." He shook his head and sighed. "The Swiftwater's didn't want any part of the brutal war. So, Greyson's first great-grandfather packed up and headed west with about two hundred of his supporters, including my family, and found these woods. At the time, we occupied the entire woods from the edge of the San Claude to the River until the humans built closer to the woods. It was our getaway to keep us out of sight of the witches, but we had forgotten the common enemy we shared, humans. Little by little, our wooded area shrank as bulldozers and humans cut down the trees and claim our area with their box homes."

"It wasn't until Greyson's second grandfather went down to San Claude and purchase the land that the killing of the forest ended...or so we were made to believe. Between the witch's coven killing half of our population and the humans pushing their way onto our lands...This is all that we have left. The witches hunted us down again, and we fought back until we couldn't. The pack became tired of the fight, and King Thibodeaux poisoned the majority of the land with his magic...or should I say, the Queen's magic. How could we compete? I could only salvage these art pieces before we were pushed into this small clearing. Luckily, we can still hunt, and when we make enough money selling at the market, we can buy food from the human stores."

Elder Alo paused and sighed. His wide shoulders shook. "We were once rulers of the woods and had no need to sell because we fed from the land. No one would ever cross the thicket of bushes, but now it seems like no one is afraid anymore. Just the other day, we found a couple of humans in our territory, skinny dipping in the river. I didn't have the strength to chase them away."

My arms hung limp at my sides. Elder Alo had been nothing but nice to me so far. If only he knew my parents ignited the last shifter war.

Would he hate me? Or better yet, would I be surprised?

Elder Alo seemed to sense my wayward thoughts as he placed his weathered, russet hand under my chin and lifted it until I had no choice but to face him. His brown eyes spoke of wisdom that most hadn't obtain.

"We all have a duty to fulfill, whether it's from the gods, goddesses, or the Earth Creator. Although I may have hated the way it happened, I knew there would come a time when the tension between the witches and other supernatural's reached a boiling point. Sadly, we weren't on the winning side. I went away to explore the human world and to learn more about humans and our packs. My time, though short, amongst the humans was knowledgeable. It opened my eyes and heart to something we often overlook, destiny. I realized we all play a part in the future, whether good or bad, and we all must follow what has been put before us. Greyson is a lot like his father. Soft-hearted and sometimes lets his feelings muddle his mind."

My eyes ran as I watched a slow smile appear on Elder Alo's face. He wiped the wayward tear that escaped my eyes. Could he have known my destiny? No, not possible, I thought, shaking my head. He doesn't consort with goddesses, anyway.

"Greyson's dad, Tyee, fell hard for Mary Ann. He went to visit some rogue shifters pack a couple of years after the second war and found her in the town. She was so tiny you could make out the bones in her chest. She barely had a scent to her because she seemed to have almost withered away. Tyee always confided in me, as many others often do, that she walked the streets half naked, muttering that "Henry will pay". When she arrived at the village, it took a month for her to get back to normal.

"Is that her in the picture?"

"Yes, that's Mary Ann Muller. She was the first witch we let into the pack because she was Tyee's fated mate."

I blinked a few tears away.

My mind was slowly processing the story Elder Alo told me. Mary Ann was a Muller. My head shook. There was no way that Henry Muller had a sibling. I would have studied her in my Royal classes like I had our previous royals. Elder Alo cocked his head as I sat there with my mouth agape. He probably thought I was stupid as I sat there, puttering my rejection.

"Your parents and the other witch coven members erased her from everything. She was cast away like she was nothing more than a Mixling...someone expendable. But when she came out of her stupor, she didn't want to talk about the past, deeming it "irrelevant" but I could see in those cat like eyes that it was far from the truth. I guess we all are born with that silly need to hide our ugly past.

Elder Alo finished and hummed. The song was low and peaceful as it floated from his throat to my ears. Even though he wasn't aware of the downward spiral taking place inside of me, my heart raced, and my palms became slippery. Would he turn me in? My magic quaked deep inside of my chest as it prepared itself to fight, transport me, or flee from me. With my luck, the latter would be true.

"I—How did you know?"

"I knew before you arrived here that you would be a witch. The Earth Creator gifted my family with the ability to see glimpses of the future. I never see the entire picture, but just enough to put two and two together. I knew about what lay in front of us when your parents showed up on that bleak rainy march." Elder Alo's smile returned. "Plus, that deodorizer doesn't fool me. I think the magic shield you first arrived with was more effective, but luck is on your side, young queen. Many of the newer pack members are not well-trained to spot witches since most hardly use the magic we can access anymore. Pity! The hate for witches caused most of us to lose our connection to it. I still do a little, but Greyson can do so much but refuse to dishonor his mother."

"Why? How does using his magic dishonor his mother? Wouldn't that be the opposite?"

"No, Mary Ann was strict, and she refused to use her magic. She instilled into Greyson that magic was horrible to have and to never to use it, not even if you were dying. He'd never even cast it before, but his father cemented things by banning him from using magic altogether."

I opened my mouth to speak but was interrupted as Greyson and Hawk opened the door to the Sanctuary. My mind wanted to ask more questions about Greyson's mother and his father, but it seemed this was all I would get for today. I knew I would be back because this was the most I had heard about Greyson or his family.

Just before Greyson and Hawk reached our sitting spot, Elder Alo leaned close to me and whispered, "You look just like your mother, and despite our 'bad blood' I truly admired her. It's time for you to stop hiding and fulfill *your* destinies, no matter what or who may stand in your way. Heed the vision the Three Sisters had given to you. *You're* the sun, Princess Kaydian."

Greyson and Hawk made it over to us. Sweat dripped down their chest and dampened their regalia bottoms.

"Thank you, Elder Alo, for keeping Kaydian company," Greyson said as he bowed.

"It was my honor to be in the presence of greatness."

If I didn't die from shame tonight, I surely would from Elder Alo inflating my ego. My face was feverish as Greyson took my hand, pulling me up to hug me. Which should have repulsed me because he was drenched in sweat, but it only made my magic flutter in my chest. As we said our goodbyes to Elder Alo, I took one last glance at the painting that once pulled me in that left me puzzled, and now...the stunning art left a bitter taste in my mouth. So many secrets laid within the powdered paint. Unease sat heavily on my chest like someone was holding me down in the muddy dirt paths.

Greyson, none the wiser, kissed the back of my hand, drawing my attention back to him. A lazy smile gathered on his face as we headed out to home...his home, not mine. I thought as the pack members that milled around turned their backs, ignoring us as we walked by. I was silent as we walked Hawk to his place, which was next to Greyson's. As we made the short distance to his place, my mind played with the idea of just leaving him here and going home, apologizing to my mother about disappearing and try to fix the broken pieces of the puzzle.

Back to my home.

Back to the ordinary.

Back to being safe and, mostly, respected.

Heed the visions the Three Sisters have given to you.

Fresh as snow. Blood will decorate the throne. For power is never given but taken.

Celestoria has four journeys, but only three will survive. The fourth will meet a death by the sun.

But I couldn't get Elder Alo's words out of my head. How did someone, a shifter, no less, know about the Three Sisters? Which led me to believe that getting Greyson to go home with me would be a thousand times harder. Youna! Haven't I been through enough?

Now I was even more confused as I thought about the neglected riddles.

I sat on the old yellow couch as Greyson washed off the grime that was caked on his skin. Even though I'd seen him naked before, he always asked me to step out of the room. It's gotten to a point where I just sat and waited for him like a fool, as Merrell would have said.

Ten minutes later, Greyson was done getting ready for bed. I played with waiting until we got some rest to ask him, but my mind won the battle. The questions piled up and clawed at my brain to be let out.

"Why didn't you tell me about your mother?"

Greyson stopped at the tiny bed and flopped down, causing the bed to groan under his weight. Gone was his smile from our walk in place, a deep frown.

"Because I'm not ready to talk about her," he said with a shrug. His tall frame filled out the mattress when he laid down. "Let's get some rest. We both had a long night."

My veins were scorching from his flippant attitude as he waved off my concern like it wasn't something of importance.

"No," I said and snatched the pillow from underneath his head. "I won't sleep until I have answers...and I mean it. I can just open up the portal and go home!"

"I promise–" Greyson said, but one look at my twisted face shut him up. I allowed him to skim over the truth ever since I arrived here. Hell, I even let him talk me into staying one more night and then another like the gullible witch that I was. I could understand why he didn't want to talk about it because if I were in his shoes, I think I would do the same.

"You can't be angry with me about not wanting to spill all of my secrets when you yourself won't tell me anything about your family. All I know is you're from the worst coven," he continued.

I guess the pot is calling the kettle black.

Exhaling deeply as I dragged my feet to the other side of the bed, curled up in between Greyson's firm body as his arm held me close to him. My free arm stretched out over his upper body as my head rested on his chest. The lemongrass scent filled my nostrils, clearing my thoughts. Greyson was right.

"Listen, I know…" I didn't know how to find the right words. I'd have years of royal training, but nothing prepared me to deal with my own feelings. "I'm sorry, and if I'm being honest, I feel blindsided."

Minutes ticked by as we laid there together in the dark, staring at the wall. His even breaths matched my beating heart. Everything I dreamt of in a mate…my future…my life, had shifted to a staggering degree.

"My mother was the most beautiful person in the village. Inside and out. We spent every single waking hour together when I wasn't at school, and I loved it. She managed the garden when it was thriving. My mother taught me about nature and how we can all learn to adapt and live together, so there won't be any more ego-driven wars. It wasn't until later in my life that she taught me about the witches history, not a lot, but just enough to keep me in the know. I used to beg her to teach me how to use my magic, but she always turned stony-faced and swept the conversation under the rug and said, *'You don't need magic because you're going to be as stubborn and powerful as your father.'* She evaded the subject so much that I left it alone and replaced it with learning how to sculpt statues, and that became our hobby. It bonded us and made us closer than we already were, much to my dad's disappointment, but I think he was just jealous." Greyson paused. He trembled under my arm, drawing my attention to his face as a lone tear slid down his beautiful face, and I swept it away. "The last summer before she was murdered, my father, mother, and I finally got to get away, for the first time, from the pack. I had been asking my parents forever to see the emporium in New York. I used to spend time reading about it in the human newspaper and hearing them gloat about it. My father, who was a man of few words, was awestruck when we arrived in New York. My mother and I popped in and out of the stores without caring about the stares we were receiving because of our ratty clothing. After a while, my poor father basically pulled us away because "he couldn't take it anymore." It wasn't until we found a spot by our campgrounds that my dad became paranoid. He checked the area three times before we could settle in for the night."

Greyson's arm that was wrapped around me tightened, bringing me closer to him. The skin where his thumb drew circles on my lower back left a trail of heat with each pass.

"Nothing happened that night. My mother begged him to rest, but my father just said, *'You guys sleep while I keep watch.'* We—I thought he was just being too protective of my mother, but I think he sensed something out there. Even though shifters can wield magic as much as a common witch can, we have long forgotten how to use it in fear that the coven members would find us and completely wipe us out. That has been ingrained in my head from a young age. But the way my father was on edge when we left the campsite made me nervous. I begged Mother to use her magic just once to make sure we were okay, but they both shut me down, saying I was just worried because my dad was. The closer we got back to the pack, the more my parents relaxed, and I did the same...of course, that was our downfall. The following day after school, I ran to our garden to search for my mother, only to find her dead with a gaping hole in her chest. Her red essence poured out of the hole was fresh, and her heart was missing. I think that's why our crop can only grow in that little clearing. Her blood offered us a lasting gift. No matter how many times I attended a smudging ritual, our cleansing ritual, I couldn't get the image out of my head."

Greyson sighed as he continued. "My father became lost and became a stranger to me and the other pack members. Until he ended his life by shifting on his tiny boat, capsizing the boat. His soul was lost to the sea. My dad knew our wolves couldn't swim in deep water. Elder Alo said it was meant to be this way. He missed my mother and hated himself for not protecting her enough. That's when I stopped caring to learn about witches, my tainted side. And since we're being honest, that's why I had a hard time when we first met. I should have known because Elder Alo once told me I would know ultimate joy but no peace."

A war between my head and my heart took place inside of me. I didn't want to make Greyson hate me even more than he might do unconsciously, and to be honest, as I laid against his chest listening to the soft thudding of his heart, I wouldn't blame him.

A blanket of quietness engulfs us as I laid on Greyson's chest. His breathing was so slow which brought me some peace to me in the darkness. When I opened my mouth, I knew how I would craft my story.

"My parents are complicated." I chuckled, but it sounded awkward to my ears. "They met young and when they both awakened, it was no surprise to my maternal grandparents or the coven that they were to be tethered soulmates. My mother had me much later than most in my family, but she always told me she knew when it was the right time for me to enter the world. I chalked it up to her being full of herself, but I think deep down I knew she was right. My grandparents died, willingly, when I was six...this may sound callous, but I'm glad they passed on because it made my mother and I closer. We traveled all over the world and saw so many cultures and people that it influenced me to paint as a way to capture my time. That's when I realized I couldn't—didn't want to stop painting. It was a way to escape. But then Roy—classes started, and my mother taught me for half the day. The other half was foundational classes. I had to cut down on my paintings."

"What about your dad?"

"My parents were like night and day. We all used to do everything together. If you saw me, you saw my parents. He's what I would call a semi-traditionalist. It was the old way or the highway, unless it directly affected him. He was a soft marshmallow when he was around me. I could get away with so much stuff when I was younger." I stopped to chuckle. "One time I got caught sneaking a human book out of his library. I was almost in the clear, but when I closed the door to his office, he was standing there with his eyebrow cocked and shaking his head. He made me write an essay on the book as punishment, but he didn't tell my mother. She would have died if she knew I was reading human books back then. Those were good times. Then something changed. It was clear as day. I was so absorbed in him that I couldn't see the cracks in him. I had once chalked it up to my father having no one else after killing his family, but I was wrong. Now, I see all the cracks in his beautiful face."

Greyson stopped drawing circles the moment I said those last words. Did I spill too much?

"Your father killed his parents? That's so—" He hadn't finished his statement, but he shook his head.

"Yeah, I even thought it was excessive, but my father's side hated my mother. So much they denounced my father and went around saying he was an embarrassment for straying from their belief of abolishing the old and outdated ruling system. So, my father had to make a choice, his mate or his family. Needless to say, I'm here, but they're not." I gave a nonchalant shrug. "I only have one living relative, my mother's last living uncle, Uncle Fabien, and my mother goes to see him in the Bayou twice a year. I went once and determined it was not for me. Between the mosquitoes, snakes, and the 'gators. No thank you."

Greyson chuckled. "What did your parents do? From the sounds of it, they were important."

"They worked in the castle." I said hurriedly. Forcing a yawn, I buried my face into Greyson's chest. So, he couldn't see how I squeezed my eyes shut so hard that my eyeballs knocked behind my eyelids. A long stretch of comfortable silence found its way into the small room. Inside, I mentally berated myself, but I knew it was for the best. *Yes, play it safe.*

"Thank you for sharing. I know we're both navigating through this, but at least we have each other."

He kissed the top of my curls.

Only when Greyson's chest slowed down did I take a breath again. There in the dark, I was left with my turbulent thoughts and Elder Alo's words, "*Heed the vision of the three sisters*" rebounding in my head.

Chapter 21
Greyson

In three weeks, Kaydian had crash-landed into my life, and if I was being honest, it terrified me. Elder Alo had warned me that not only will I never know peace until my second time around, but they would be a force to be reckoned with. What did the second time around mean? He wouldn't expound on it. He just stated that nothing ever given comes free. Never wanting to be disrespectful toward any of the elders, much less Elder Alo, who's been like a second father to me, I left it alone. Ever since our conversation a couple of nights ago, I kept thinking back to that conversation that cold February night.

After spending all day fixing the repairs on the elders' homes and dodging the death stares from the pack and Oni, which were becoming unbearable, I laid in the darkness of our tiny haven. One would think she would be tired until a small finger poked me in my side. Kaydian's plush mouth was twisted into an adorable frown.

"That's the second time you zoned out on me. What's bugging you?"

Should I tell her how nervous she makes me? How would someone like me fit into her life? Kaydian had a not-so-subtle way of sneaking in her return to her coven...and that scared me more than using my chaotic magic that had seemed to be permanently embedded in my chest since Kaydian and I touched. The mauling sensation of the one thing I ignored for so many years. Choosing to bury it deep inside me behind the brick wall around my soul. My magic, the little I may have, wanted to reach out and touch Kaydian's even when I was on the other side of the forest, letting my wolf run. It called to both of us, like a siren song, begging to be touched by her magic. My wolf growled from deep inside my body, wanting to mark her as ours and bury ourselves deep inside her soft body.

The thought scared me and excited me.

I had always been attracted to the female pack members in the village, but I never could bring myself to touch them. Their scents made my wolf hide deep in my chest, and no matter how much I tried, I remained unmoved by their advances. But Kaydian's body was made to be loved. To be researched as I found my way around her it. Will she be okay with being patient with me? I knew she had kissed her previous "boyfriends." My stomach churned at the word. I was never brave enough to ask her if she's ever been with someone...sexually. The thought alone sent a throbbing pain in the back of my throat.

Kaydian's finger came out, nudging me again. This time, I plastered on a smirk, doubling over as I clutched my stomach. I guess I wasn't convincing enough, as she gave me a haughty smile that caused my inside to melt and my dick to twitch inside my blue swimming trunks.

"Sorry, Hiema. When I'm with you, I tend to lose time staring at you."

She tucked her head down, causing her wet, long curls to stick against the side of her face. My hand reached out to tuck one side of her hair behind her ear, which was red at the tips. She folded her arms under her plump breast, pushing them up, drawing my attention to the red one-piece bathing suit I brought her when I snuck into town. We had crept down to the shallow spot of the river, deciding we wanted to get away from the prying eyes of the Pack.

"Thank you...you're good for my ego, Grey." I loved when she called me by my nickname. The sound sent a shiver down my spine.

"Maybe we can..." She bit her plump bottom lip. Her soft, small hand glided down my naked chest, leaving me trembling, not from the water but from my magic and my wolf that has become deranged with a single touch. With each painstaking inch she took, my tongue dried up, and the magic in me chased her hand, begging to burst out. Her little tortuous finger plunged under the salty freshwater mix, stopping right by the patch of dark pubic hair. I shuddered as blood rushed to my already straining length.

"We—We should get going. It's late." The words stumbled out. My wolf bark juddered and scraped, begging me to let him out. I turned away from Kaydian, but not before seeing the tears well up in her emerald eyes and her finger dug into the soft flesh of her wrist. Using my speed, I ran ahead of her and gathered the little things we carried with us. I wrapped my towel around myself and handed hers to her when she finally trotted back to the dry area. When she was done deodorizing herself, I handed her the handmade bag Kathleen had made to replace her old one, and I carried our clothing.

Each step back to my home thudded in my brain, and the sound of her swallowing her sobs made me wince. I'm not unfamiliar with this feeling. I knew it all too well. Disappointment hung in the air like my father was right here with us. His deep frown that marred his russet-colored face. The eyes that cut me down to nothing as he railed about being me just as feeble hearted as my mother when I disagreed with storming the coven in Britain. My dad became best friends with homemade beer we made in the village after my mother died. And then he became my biggest tormentor. At every corner, he tore straight into the wall of love and self-confidence my mother helped build.

Some part of me still pined after my dad as if he could love me from the other world. If he could make me the fearless leader that the Swiftwater Pack needed.

Entering my home, I held the door for Kaydian as she breezed past me without a backward glance. She sat down on the yellow battered couch my mother had brought. Her lips folded between her teeth as she stared aimlessly at the blank wooden wall on the other side of the room. I'm almost sure that if I said go, she would prance up like a deer in the woods and leave me here standing like a pitiful dumbass.

"I'm sorry—" I said. But was cut off when the night air rushed into the room, and Hawk's lanky statuette filled the downtrodden room.

"Hey, Grey! What's up, Shorts?" Hawk said. His brown eyes gaze between Kaydian and me. He opened his mouth to speak, but I stopped him before a stupid question fell from his lips.

"Hey, Hawk, yes, let's go!" I blurted out as I grabbed Hawk's bony arm.

Turning to Kaydian, whose eyes looked right through me as if I weren't there. I wanted to run away from her absent stare, but my wolf and my magic wanted to kneel, begging for forgiveness. "I'll be back in fifteen. We're going to run the perimeter."

I didn't stay around to see if she would spare me a second glance without those sorrow-filled gem eyes. *I'm a shitty coward!* As Hawk and I made our way to the edge of the forest behind my home.

"Ah, did I walk into something back there?" Hawk asked. His question was innocent and Hawk, who is my brother in every sense of the word, was the only person who knew I was a virgin. "What happened?"

"It's nothing, Hawk. Let's get this over with so I can sleep early."

"Hey, Grey...don't do that." His large hand cradled my shoulder. "Spill it before we do the perimeter sweep."

My tongue was heavy as it moved around my cottonmouth. Should I tell him how I fumbled? I knew Hawk would never judge me, but the stones in my stomach were weighing me down. A deep sigh from my chest left me as I spilled the events of the two weeks, besides Kaydian being a witch. That was her secret to tell. With every major detail, Hawk's bushy eyebrows furrowed and rolled his lips into his mouth. His head shook rapidly, and I was afraid he may lose it at any given moment.

When I was through with my sordid story, he slapped my back and sighed.

"My friend...I hate to break it to you, but you really fucked this up."

"I—I know." I finally admitted out loud.

"I know you're nervous, and I don't blame you, but being truthful is essential if you want this to work. You already have an enormous battle before you to complete the bonding ritual. Don't make this any harder for yourself. You've made up an unrealistic, perfect mate in your mind and now that you have your mate right in front of you, you keep putting your foot in your mouth. If she's trying to get closer to you, then let it happen. Tell her you're a virgin. I don't think she'll judge you...well, too hard."

"I know, but you know I wanted to wait until..."

"After the bonding ritual." We both said simultaneously.

I chuckled awkwardly, trying to sweep away the embarrassment.

"How long are you going to wait to complete the bonding?" Hawk asked. I had stuck inside of my mind since Kaydian arrived.

"You're right. I'm nervous, and I'm not sure why. I just know that something feels different."

"That's normal, Grey. It's a new experience for you." Hawk squeezed my shoulder. "Just talk with her when we get back."

Throwing him a shaky smile, we headed off to the edge of the woods. Once a week, Hawk and I ran the perimeter to check for any changes. When we got to the area with the old Sacramento Woods sign, I kept watch as Hawk transformed into a goodly brown wolf with deep brown eyes, just like the rest of his family. Hawk trotted close to my thigh and nudged me in my side with his massive head. Biting my lip against the sharp pinch that I'm all too familiar with as I gave my wolf access. A spine-tingling warmth spread throughout my body, dropping me on my knees and hands. Every bone in my body stretched and molded to welcome my wolf. My toes and hands kissed and dug into the soft ground as my wolf's paws clawed at the soft tissue. The dark coat of my wolf's fur replaced my fleshy skin. The pine and earthy smell of the forest dampened and mingled with my scent. I blinked rapidly as my vision adjusted to the dark shadows of the forest. My headache left me weak enough onto the ground as my wolf plunged me to the back of our mind completely. Any other time, the darkness would bring me peace, but not tonight as I let my wolf take reign over our body.

Hawk and I traveled through the thicket of brushes as we scanned the forest and the deserted road. It wasn't long ago we didn't have to worry about patrolling more than once a month. Now that the humans were slowly venturing into our lands, we had to make sure our pack, what little that we had, was protected. Our paws gripped the dirt as we darted around the acre of land. Leaping over the trees that the Earth Creator called back to the earth and running over overgrown beds of weeds that used to be a part of our garden. Even though the old corn husk had all but withered away, the moldy scent that seeped into the ground stayed as a reminder to us of what we lost. My mother loved the multicolored corn she grew as a labor of her love. *Too bad it was all in vain.* Hawk bumped into my side, nodding his head for us to continue. Dragging myself away from the old memory and closer to the edge of the woods just before we entered the town...or what was supposed to be the edge of the woods. The woodland was nearly gone in this area as the scent of sulfur overpowered the air. Bulldozers and wood planks flattened the shrubs that grew here as the humans encroached on our land.

My wolf and I were of the same accord as a growl quivered deeply in our throats. *Just another thing to worry about!*

Hawk had stopped a couple of feet away, whining to get my attention. Something about our human situation held me captive, staring at the stick-built homes. My wolf wanted to find the people responsible and give them back to the earth. A gift for the Earth for their disrespect. I'm never violent, but tonight, I was on edge.

Hawk's heavy paws crunched the brittle foliage as he ambled over to me. He nudged me against my stomach, drawing my attention back to his wolf. After a last glance, we started our trek back into the thicker bushes, away from the human homes. I was almost through the thicket when a loud snap resonated among the fallen trees, followed by a loud howl. My wolf didn't waste any time turning ourselves around and spotting Hawk. His muzzle bit at the brown rusty bear trap that closed in on his front leg.

An ice-cold chill ran through my veins as I hurriedly shifted back into my human form. Luckily, my wolf didn't fight me as I ran toward Hawk. I grabbed the rusty trap without a second thought and pulled at the rusty metal death trap until the screws gave up their hold. Poor Hawk's whimpers rang loud over my heart beating in my ears. "I got you, Hawk!" The metal grazed Hawk's bone, sending the tiny bumps on my body to attention. Rivulets of Hawk's crimson blood flowed from both sides of the pinky-sized wounds that were the length of his long front leg as the sharp metallic scent filled my nose. Another unintended sacrifice to the Earth Creator. The damaged leg hung off the small thread of skin that held the severed leg attached. Hawk was weak. His dark brown eyes stared aimlessly into the dark woods as he whined and begged for relief.

He was already drifting off to sleep, but I had to get him back to the village. Hawk couldn't change back or heal without bandaging the broken limb. *Of course, I had nothing but my hands!* I did the only thing I could think of. My hands held the broken ligaments, holding them tightly together. One would have hoped my magic would have swooped in to help, but nothing. It just curled itself into my chest. *Useless.* Slowly, under my palms, I felt the soft juddering of Hawk's bones as they repaired, causing the hairs on my arm to stand. I've never been as lucky as tonight for our shifter abilities to heal faster, even with our lost magic. The metallic scent that once filled the air was whisked away by the light breeze of the night.

After Hawk's leg was healed, I said thank you to the Earth Creator.

He won't wake until his strength is back to normal. I grabbed the trap and lifted a knocked-out Hawk onto my shoulder as I sent thanks for my shifter strength. My feet hit the ground running as the forest blurred before me. Even if I lost my vision, I could make my way back to the village without my sight.

When I entered the now silent village, I carried Hawk to his home and laid his wolf onto his bed. He will be pissed since his wolf had dirt caked onto his fur that crumbled into the blue sheets, but he will survive, I thought as I locked his home and entered mine.

Kaydian had changed into one of my white shirts. *Damn!* As my eyes landed on her heavy chest. Her nipples strained against my shirt as I wondered if the brown buds would taste as good as they looked. She noticed my wandering eyes and folded her arms under her chest. Hiding away from my newest temptation.

The stones in my stomach threatened to weigh me down until I made it to the afterworld.

"I'm sorry, Kaydian. I'm a coward—"

"You're bleeding!" She exclaimed.

I had long forgotten the old trap. My hands gripped the nonsensical item in my hand until it created cuts in my palm. Kaydian rushed over to me as I dropped the trap with a loud thud on the floor.

"It's okay. I—"

But before I could finish, my body floated like I was transcending into the sky. My mother explained nothing about magic, but if this was what I was missing, I regretted it. A searing heat touched my soul, mind, and body. Her sweet and floral scent mixed with my lemon and filled not only my nose but my soul as it staked a claim to my heart. My long forgotten magic fluttered in joy as it warmed me deep in my chest. It felt like I was home. I'm whole for the first time since my táat, my mother, died. I couldn't see her magic, but I felt it working to accelerate the tender, broken, fleshy skin of my palm.

Kaydian gasped and jumped back in fear. Her eyes were the size of the sand dollars in the San Francisco Bay, but that didn't matter at all.

Not at the very moment of my awakening.

I've kissed no one before tonight, and hopefully, I won't make a fool of myself. My hands captured her soft, warm cheeks as I planted my lips on hers. She tasted like the afterworld, rich and tempting, in the simplest words. My mouth engulfed hers licking and sucking on the plump, soft lips. Her hands barely wrapped around my upper arms as I plunged my tongue into her soft palate as I mimicked the few times I'd seen some of the pack members kissing. The loud whooshing of my heart in my ears made it hard to hear. Kaydian pushed against my arms, but I barely felt it until she dug her short nails into my arms, causing me to pull back immediately.

Kaydian and I both were silent in the dimly lit room as both of us stood rooted to our spot, heaving as we grasped for air.

"I'm sorry."

After a moment, a half-smile graced her face.

"It's okay...I...It just caught me off guard."

Her answer calmed the doubtful voice in my head that told me I wasn't good at this. That I somehow fail at every aspect of life. Lifting her into my arms, I led us to my small room, placing her on my bed. Strings of her dark curls fell loose from her bun. My finger itched as I fought the urge to run my hands through the tight curls. Her dark emerald eyes stared back at me with wonder... or repulse. I wasn't sure, neither did I care as she ran the tip of her pink tongue over her plump bottom lip, causing my breath to hitch in my throat. She shifted to remove the thin white shirt, leaving her naked on my white sheets. A vision of perfection laid before me. Her soft curves looked even more tempting than before. I wanted to trace them as I buried myself deep inside of her thick thighs. I wanted to paint her insides with our future and mark her beautiful skin, letting everyone in my pack know she was mine.

"Are you sure you're ready, Grey?" she asked.

She was simply gorgeous as she bit her lip, waiting patiently for my answer. *Does she know how nervous I am?* My hand shook as I worked up the courage to say something.

"I'm sure," I whispered.

Please let me do this right!

Was my last thought before my mate opened her thick brown thighs. My mind short-circuited. My eyes traced along her soft skin until her damp brown lips turned into her pink fleshy pussy. Hot coals settle in my groin as my dick wept at the sight. With my face flushed as the room perfumed with her sweet floral scent. Kaydian's scent made my mind hazy, blocking my naïve brain. Sensing my hesitation, her small hands snaked out, grabbing hold of my steel-hard dick. My wolf howled, and my magic burned through me the moment her hand connected with us. With my fist balled up and my breathing shortened, a war to take control broke out inside of me. Death would be the outcome, surely, if...

Kaydian's small hand glided up my shaft, making my knees buckle, and the last of my mind turned fuzzy. The small glob of pre-cum hadn't formed fully before her finger swiped over the sensitive head, causing me to moan behind my clenched lips. My balls were tighter than I've ever felt them, and I knew I wouldn't last long. Two weeks of sleeping with her plush ass on my dick made the both of us anxious.

Kaydian stuck her pre-cum covered finger into her mouth, moaning as she lapped at my essence. The hypnotic rhythm made my dick twitch as I grabbed myself. Deep in my chest, my wolf dug into our soft, wet flesh. Begging. Pleading to come out and play. She released her fingers with a wet pop and laid back on her elbow in her original position.

Her thighs slightly parted as she bit her plump bottom lip.

"You can have a taste, Greyson," she said.

Her mouth twitched as it turned into a smirk. Those same small, perfect brown fingers held me hostage as they slithered down her curves until they reached her saturated lips. My mind spun with the idea of lapping the clear juices that dripped from her pussy. *Maybe I'm way over my head.* But I was too far gone to think twice. A groan from the wood floors filled the room as I introduced it to my knees. As I paused, I looked up at my Hiema and saw her sitting there, watching me intently, like a predator stalking its prey. Her eyes were blown as her mischievous hand held her petals open for me.

I can do this!

My insides turned into a liquid pool as I ran my tongue over her wet folds. She tasted forbidden, like decadent chocolate, rich. The favors exploded on my tongue as I licked every inch of her soft pink pussy, her wet, thick brown lips and thighs. Kaydian shook every time my tongue roamed over her warm pink center. The soft moans shot through my veins, causing my groans to mix with my wolves begging pleas. If I could, I'd suck the little wet spot on the sheets dry just to savor the taste.

"Please, Grey!"

Kaydian begged, but my thoughts were frozen as time slowed down. I opened my mouth, but nothing came out for once. As if sensing my hesitation, her hand found her center as she opened her delicate folds to reveal her moist center. Her essence leaked out of her middle. Gingerly, I licked at her weeping pussy. Her wet hand delved into my hair. My magic wolf and I shuddered as her fingers raked my scalp. Slightly pushing my head into her center as she gripped me. Licking and groaning against her sweet hole, she grounded herself into my face, coating me with my new addiction.

A painful groan fell from my lips as a sharp sensation radiated from my scalp. Hissing her small hands were intertwined with my hair, pulling and controlling me. Her breath was uneven as she said breathlessly, "You can suck my clit, fuck me with your fingers or tongue, but please, all of that licking is killing me." Heat blossomed in my face from shame. *I don't remember what a clit is!* As my hand shook against her silky, thick thighs.

I wanted to please her and not disappoint her.

My two shaky fingers slid into her wet pussy. Heat scorched the exposed skin as I slid them deep inside of her. A deep sigh fell from Kaydian's parted lips as a single tear streaked down her face. My mind took over my fingers as I unhurriedly moved my fingers in and out of her wet center. The velvety texture of her canals was foreign to me, and I couldn't wait to feel how she would fit around me. In and out, my fingers plunged into the soft canal as I watched her beautiful face contort. Her scent was potent, causing hot tears to spring in my eyes, with my balls tightened even more with every tortured minute.

"Bend your fingers, baby."

Her silvery voice dropped several octaves as she whimpered her request. The beating organ thumped against my chest. *Does she mean to bend it all the way? Or just partially?* Panic set in as she waited for me to comply. So, I bent my fingers inside of her, and my fingertips caressed the heated, fleshy walls.

Kaydian's hand shot out and grabbed my wrist.

"Straighten your fingers, Greyson..." Her eyes were wide as saucers. "I'm ready," she said softly. Gently, she removed my drenched fingers with a wet pop and brought it to my lips. My tongue snaked out, washing my own fingers clean of her essence. I almost cum on myself, and I shamelessly didn't care. Standing on my shaky feet, I watched my Hiema position herself against the headboard of the rickety bed. Her thick thighs dropped open, welcoming me again to her kingdom. The compliment on my tongue died in my throat.

This was it.

The bed cried and dipped under my weight as I crawled between her long legs, which engulfed me, holding me close to her as my dick pressed flush against her pussy. My wolf whimpered while I growled. The result was something unnatural, causing me to drop my head onto Kaydian's soft chest. Licking and sucking her cinnamon nipples until she arched her back, bringing her heavy breast flat against my inflamed face. If I died tonight, I wouldn't complain. I would gladly welcome death like it was my best friend. A shudder raked through my body as fire lit a trail through my veins. Sweat dripped off my body, coating the bed and Kaydian's slick skin.

It took all of my might to pull myself away from her warm body. After several nights of dreaming of this moment, I was petrified. Kaydian's sweet aftertaste had disappeared, leaving my mouth dry as cotton. My glazed-over vision caught Kaydian's mouth moving, but I couldn't hear anything over the thundering beating of my heart. Her hand wrapped around my stiff dick, lining me up to her center.

"I-I don't think I can last long."

The words fell out of my mouth before I had time to think about it.

A sweet smile graced her slightly dampened face. *How is she not dripping with sweat?* As I nudged my wide head into her pussy. Inch by tortuous inch. It felt like pure agony as I entered her soft, fiery core until I was fully inside of her. Pelvis to pelvis. Nights of dreaming about what she may have felt like wrapped around me couldn't compare to this moment. Kaydian was tight as her soft fleshy walls gripped me, tattooing herself onto my dick, marking me as hers and hers alone. Slowly, as I practiced before with my hand, I moved. Pulling myself out of her until the tip of my head lined up with her opening. The loud bang of the metal headboard hitting the wooden walls filled the room when I entered her once again.

Kaydian's soft hand wrapped around my wrist as she tried to move my hand, causing me to falter slightly. Luckily enough, I caught myself before I lost balance, pausing. I shakily nodded to her.

"I want your hand around my neck, Grey. Don't squeeze me too hard."

My eyebrows drew up as she guided my hand, placing it onto her long neck, causing me to stop my thrusts. Sand filled my mouth as I yanked my hand away. *She wanted me to choke her.* I wouldn't...couldn't be able to fulfill that wish of hers. How would I know if she was okay?

"I'm not comfortable with that...I'm sorry." I choked out.

Kaydian's smile faltered for a split second, but not before I noticed it. The corners of her mouth twitched, but she nodded, patting my heated cheek, and said, "It's okay, Grey."

Sticking my head into the crooks of her neck, my hips moved once again as I continued to fuck her. With each thrust, her scent blossomed and blessed me with her essence that coated my dick. *Agony.* That was the only word that came to mind as a rush of raging heat filled my veins. It was painful and blissful simultaneously. Kaydian sharp nails raked down my back, causing me to softly bite into the tender flesh of her neck. Not hard enough to break skin, but enough to coat my mouth with the salty taste of her sweat, which caused black dots to swirl in my vision. My magic and my wolf wrestled inside my chest, but it was my wolf that dominated my feeble magic. The muscles in my back stiffened as my balls tightened. My mouth fell open as I pushed myself further into her fiery core, and my wolf howled. The joyous sound shook me as my cum emptied into Kaydian. Shaking, I tried to move, but I ended up falling back into her, careful not to push my throbbing knot into her. I'm not sure if she is ready for that yet. My room was a hazy cloud of lemon, sweat, and happiness. The mixture caused my balls to clench one last time as I gave Kaydian the last drop of my cum. When I rose from on top of Kaydian, this time, those gem eyes held curiosity. Giving her a chaste kiss on the lips as I pulled myself from her, limp and satiated. I dragged her close to me in our usual sleeping position, with her nestled by my side, only this time we were naked together.

And I'm not a virgin anymore.

Kaydian, who was silent until now, turned to me. Her face broke out into a smile as she patted my cheek.

"You were amazing, Grey." She paused and bit her lip. "...was this your first time?"

I covered my face with my hand as I stared up at the ceiling. Do I lie? Or tell her the truth? "Yes, this was my first time...was I...I mean. Did you..." I said. The thought I was so nervous about asking was preposterous, but I needed to know.

Kaydian's mouth twitched slightly, and I couldn't make out if that was a good thing or not. "Yes, I came. Maybe I can get on top later."

My hand stifled my yawn. *Later?* I could sleep for about two days. My wolf and my magic had found peace within me.

"You could do whatever you want to me after I get some sleep."

She smiled and turned away from me as I drifted off to sleep.

Kaydian POV

Clamping my eyes shut in the room's darkness. I prayed to Youna that I could keep the acid tears behind my eyelids. I've dreamed of this night for years. Years! Only for this moment to fall flat like Greyson had when he was done from my countless boyfriends to my fingers. Night after night, I wished to experience the longing need for my first orgasm. To the fiery touch, I spent dreaming up on my lonely nights at home. Now I had to sleep with the unforgiven pent-up need from Greyson, taking his fill and leaving me high and dry.

Not that I blame him because it was his first time having sex.

I waited until the soft snoring filled the dark room to let the pent-up tears coat my face and onto my half of the pillow. Plunging my face into the softness as I sobbed, hoping that Greyson wouldn't awake from his sleep to find me suffocating myself. Maybe then I could find some relief. Whimpering, I cursed myself for being so weak.

I should wake him and demand Greyson to take care of me, but I was too much a coward, and that was something else I hate to admit. Every neatly planned idea that I've made for my life has crumpled in front of my eyes. And what can I do to fix it? Cry. Hot shivers racked my body as my fist wadded up the bedsheets to keep from shaking the small bed.

Everything they said about being mated felt like a sordid lie right now. My poor lips ached from gripping the soft structures.

My mother would be so embarrassed if she could see my face right now, all with a snotty nose and red eyes. Greyson exhaled deeply as he turned towards me. My body stiffened as his arms wrapped around my body, pulling into his arms. Engulfing me into his heated body. He placed a kiss into my hair and went back to snoring. Ending all of my late-night breakdowns.

As I gripped the yellow comforter, I wondered if this was worth it.

Chapter 22

Greyson

I wish I could say I stood in that peaceful bliss, but that was asking for too much. My morning started with Kaydian pacing my tiny room. The white shirt she ditched last night strained against her curves. Her hair was in her favorite bun with the tip of her nose and ears red. Although we barely knew each other, I've learned enough of her ticks.

"Shit, Shit, SHIT!" she muttered.

The old bed creaked when I sat on the edge of the bed, causing Kaydian to notice I was awake. Her eyes widened as if the hounds of the afterworld were chasing her. The fragmented magic cruised through my veins, causing my heart to thump against my chest. My wolf was no better, as he sensed our mate's distress. A sickly sweet floral filled the tiny room, a blaring contrast from last night.

"What's wrong, Kay?" I asked. "Would you stop pacing the floor? You're making me nervous!"

"I used my magic to help heal you..."

"Oh, right. I'm sorry. Look, we can't think about that right now. If something happens, it happens." I said, as my shoulder tightened. Even having to think about magic will take years for me to get used to, but now that I could have caused the same witches to find us has my heart sputtering in my chest. *Shit!* What if they come and finish us?

She exhaled heavily as she plopped down onto the bed. Her tiny foot shook the bed until I couldn't take it anymore. I needed air and time to think about what I would tell Oni. Leaping up from the bed, I grabbed the buckets for us. It will give me enough time to think about our situation.

The sun was glaring in the sky as I stepped out of my home and went to the hose. Hawk and I shared, filling up the bucket as I thought about Kaydian. Surely, a common witch wouldn't be in much trouble. If they ban her from the coven, she will be free to live with us. It would be an adjustment since Oni had all but turned everyone against her. I would have to speak with my párah before we complete the ritual. Bad blood always had a way of clinging onto your soul like a demon, and I never wanted that bad omen.

"Swiftwater!"

Elder Alo shouted as I hoisted the four buckets in my hands. His eyes were wide like the phoenix pendant he wore, and his mouth was set in a thin line.

"Ayukîi Elder Alo..." The hello died on the tip of my tongue as Elder Alo grabbed my arm and pulled—dragged me away from the hose to my house.

"Hold on, Elder Alo!" I shouted.

"They're going to be here any minute, Swiftwater."

Why was he so strong?

If this was anyone else, I would have fought them off, but I knew better. Elder Alo was our oldest Pack member, but he was an agile fighter in his younger years, and I doubt he ever forgot those fighting techniques. Once he dragged me in through the doors, Kaydian came rushing out of the tiny bedroom. He slammed the door shut behind me. When he turned back to us, his face relaxed a bit, but worry was still etched in his eyes.

"You need to hide or give yourself up. If I were you, I would not choose the latter."

My head swiveled between Elder Alo's patient face and Kaydian's widened stare.

"How did..." I paused mid-sentence. "I know you already knew about Kaydian. You know everything. But who's coming?"

Elder Alo cast Kaydian a sad look. The white tranquil of hair fell around his face, making him appear older today without his headpiece on.

"It's time to tell the truth. Your time is winding up. What are you going to do, Kaydian?"

My frown pierced my face. A sick flutter in my stomach intensified. I don't think I will be prepared for whatever secret Kaydian had stored away.

"But that will have to be for another time. Get her onto the roof and meet me at the clubhouse. We have less than ten minutes before the Golden Army arrives."

My legs swaggered slightly, but I caught myself before I fell onto the couch. *The Golden Army!* Why would they come here for Kaydian? Those monsters only knew how to seek and kill for those royal bastards. As questions piled up in my head, I knew I would have to wait for those answers, but hell, if I won't stop thinking about them now.

Kaydian stood in the middle room with her hand on her damn wrist, staring off into the distance. Her eyes were lost in her own little world. My feet moved on their own accord as I went before snapping her out of her daze. She looked up at me with unshed tears in her eyes.

"Let's get you to safety. Time is going."

She nodded. Her hand slipped into my waiting one, and I shuffled us out to the back. Under my home housed the ladder that I stored there for repairs. Quickly, I grabbed the ladder and helped Kaydian up to the flat top roof.

"Greyson..." she called right after I shoved the ladder back under the house. "I'm sorry."

My feelings swirled around in my chest at the possibility that she could be the one thing I hated in the world. My head nodded, but I was starting to believe I wasn't in control of my body or my decisions anymore. The walk to the pack house seemed longer than it should be as I watched the small crowd gather near the Great Spirit Temple.

Oni was already there, along with a handful of our best fighters. The lack of men worthy to fight had not gone unnoticed by us. When the witches war was over, we were never able to gather enough shifters that wanted to rebuild, much less fight. Most of the pack would rather play it safe and keep their heads down until we regain our numbers. That was easier said than done.

Tension was thick in the air as I approached the group. Last time the Queen's trolls were here, they took half of our crops away with them. Leaving us in worse shape than during the last witches' war.

The pack was bundled together, hanging onto Oni's words like it was their last lifeline. And by the way, Oni's face was twisted like he ate something sour while his arm flailed as he paced inside the tiny circle. I could see why. Elder Alo had probably warned Oni of our visitors, and that's why he was on edge. The group parted as I walked through them, catching the tail end of the conversation.

"These devils think they can come to our village and scare us! We need to show them we can defend ourselves now." Oni was shouting as I stood next to him. He was being loud and oh so wrong.

"Listen, párah is enthusiastic about our revenge. I can't blame him. The witches have dwindled our numbers and stolen something from all of us. But right now, we have one too many enemies. The humans are encroaching on our property. Hawk and I noticed they're building homes closer than before." I paused, letting the frightened whispering die down. "Let's just give them what they want for now. Live to fight another day."

Elder Alo's somber speech drew agreement from the pack members in the small circle. All of them shook their heads and gave Alo their support as he continued, "I agree with Alpha Swiftwater. We're not strong now, and we can't afford to lose anyone in our villages. Let them search peacefully. This is what the Earth Creator would want. For us to be wise and think before we act."

I nodded to him. A somber silence fell throughout the crowd. Oni's deep growl could be heard through the forest, if I had to guess. His mouth formed a harsh line that made his face look aged. One thing about my párah was that he resented me for stepping up as the next leader of the pack. Everyone knew he wanted—demanded to be the pack leader after my father died, but I beat him out because the pack leader always goes to the first son.

"It's time." Elder Alo said, his voice just above a whisper.

Elder Alo always told me that the person who walks like a ghost is of the afterworld. I never believed him when he said the silly saying. That was until today. Our shifter hearing was sharp, better than any other supernatural, but the Golden Army remained undetected, even in a village filled with shifters.

Golden armor cladded soldiers slid into view as they encircled us. They stood out against the wooden homes like miniature golden statues of death. My eyes sought my roof as I looked just in time to see Kaydian's small face peep over the rim of the roof at us. She took one look at my face and ducked back down. A sharp pain radiated from my upper arm. Hawk pinched me, drawing my wayward attention to the dreaded scene in front of us. Hawk and I both muttered, "Shit!"

In front of us was something out of my nightmare, a witch—giant, stalking toward us. His pale face contorted into a scowl with a jagged scar that ran from one side of his scalp down to his chin. He was dressed in all-black armor that made his skin look deadly pale. There were about forty men surrounding him. That was thirty more than what we had. When they stopped in front of us, my stomach dropped. We were neck and neck. An even match. The scent of fear was thick in the air as the non-fighting pack took a step back, leaving just the ten of us ready to fight if necessary.

I hoped it didn't come to that!

That wasn't what caught my wandering eyes. It was the woman on the chest of armor. She was the spitting image of Kaydian, except for she had a slimmer face as the truth dawned on me. My lungs squeezed, taking the last bit of air from me.

"Are you okay, Grey?" Hawk whispered.

All I could do was nod as my stomach clenched. *She lied to me.*

That didn't matter right now. Pushing the disappointment into the bottom of my stomach. My knees shook ever so slightly. I hoped no one noticed.

"How can I help—"

The giant in black turned to me. "We're here on the Queen's orders. We're to search this place."

"That's fine... sorry I didn't get your name again?"

His jet-black eyes roamed my body, and even though we were the same height, he made me feel five feet.

"Sir Reid...Will there be a problem?" Oni asked, with one of his eyebrows quirked.

"Sir Reid, right hand to the Queen and Youna heirs. It's an honor to meet you again. I had the pleasure, before the war, of meeting you. My name is Elder Alo." He stepped beside me.

Sir Reid, or the giant bastard, as I nicknamed him, bowed slightly. "It's a pleasure to meet you again. We will search the grounds now."

"Of course," Elder Alo replied. "Our homes are open to you. We have nothing to hide."

"R-Right, yes," I stammered.

For reasons beyond me, I didn't know why he made me so nervous. *Was it because he could haul Kaydian away from me?* The thought seemed moot as I remembered the lie that hung between us like stale air. But was I really mad at her? Or just disappointed. The Golden Army separated. Opening the doors to the small homes as they searched them. My palms became slippery with each door they opened. Hawk's foot would make a hole in the dirt, clearing from his pacing before this was over. He leaned over and whispered, "Do you think we could take all of them if we shifted?" My poor friend has the worst timing known to shifters. Sir Reid whipped his massive body around. A frown embedded into his face, making his rose-colored scar stretch as he pinned Hawk with a look that made me shiver.

"He was just joking!" I said hurriedly. When Sir Reid turned back, I dug my elbow into his side.

I whispered. "You're going to get us killed, Hawk!"

Sir Reid had inched closer to my home. My legs decided they were going to take me over there to the giant to stop him, but he stopped dead in his tracks. His sword clanged against his armor as he placed his large hands on the hilt to steady it. We couldn't see the front of the giant when he turned his wide head.

"Swiftwater..." He said, "Who's the pack leader here?"

"It's me," my párah said before I could respond. He stepped in between Sir Reid and me.

My face was flushed as I stepped away from him. With my hands fisted at my side, I fought back the curse I wanted to shout at him. This was going to be another thing the coven and he would hold over my head. They already see me as a weak leader. A disgrace to shifters. This will surely be the nail in my coffin.

Sir Reid nodded and turned his attention back to the homes near mine. My shoulders relaxed the moment he did.

"Chin up. Your uncle is making sure you live to see another day." Elder Alo said, as his hand rested on my shoulder. "He would kill you right here before the pack if he had an inkling that you were a mixling."

I nodded, too mortified to say anything else. Slipping back in the crowd of our pack. Their sideways glances made my throat throb as I held back the sob that was buried in my throat. Their eyes were painted with exhaustion and shame for me...and that word that always haunted me ricocheted in my head. *Mixling.*

Like a tarnish stain on my soul, the little doubt that was held over my head since I was born began to fester and grow. And now, I'm wondering if my pack and my uncle will ever truly let me lead.

Kaydian POV

Sir Reid planted his large boots flat on the dirt with his massive legs lined with his shoulders. Those haunted onyx eyes roamed our tiny home. Deep down in my chest, I knew he knew I was here. The wild thrashing of my heart was definitely from the thought of being caught on the roof of a shifter rather than the sun that was doing its best to melt the skin off my body. My heart thudded against my ribcage as I laid flush against the metal roof after Greyson had caught me looking at the crowd.

Every quick glance over the metal roof I took made the sweat trickle down my back. The repercussions of my actions weighed me down. Was this the most foolish thing I've ever gotten myself into? Yes. I think this topped it. Unfortunately, I couldn't help that out of all the places in America I ended up here in this camp, finding my mate. With fear of madness preventing me from listening to reason and Greyson, along with my magic, made it harder for me to leave. Each time the rogue thought of leaving him sprouted in my mind, my magic squeezed my chest, driving the thought away. Even though I miss my home, my parents, and Del, it wasn't enough for me to draw myself away from his tiny room and back to my wing in my home. Back to the smell of Chef Dubois making his signature crawfish étouffée, or gumbo. Back to my life.

"Princess Kaydian!" Sir Reid called out, speaking in our royal language. His thundering voice did nothing to calm the tidal wave in my stomach. "Your parents are worried about you. Your mother has been beside herself. Delphine is worried about you as well. Your mother assumes she had a hand in helping you escape, but I had to remind her what a persuasive witch you can be at times. I don't know where the hell you are, but I know you're nearby. You think you're going to run away from your responsibilities to live in this dog kennel, then you made a sad mistake. If you're not back home within the next two days, I will come back and burn every one of these dog houses. And don't you think for one minute that your mother wouldn't give me her blessings to do so...I can only hope you've bumped that thick skull of yours and forgotten that you're a Royal of one of the strongest covens and not a dog whisperer."

Sir Reid stopped mid-speech. His noisy breathing could be heard without me peeking over the roof. I've never been so grateful that Greyson didn't know the old royal language.

My mind was too preoccupied with watching the tension filled visit. IT had failed to see that Bernadette, one of the castle's ghosts, materialized into the space beside me. Her hand propped up on her head as she smiled with a glint in her eyes.

"You know he's serious about it too! I heard him on the portal over saying, 'If she's laying down willingly with dogs, may Youna have mercy on her because I'll drag her back to the castle.' I've only seen Big Daddy this mad once, and that was when you almost got run over by a horse in the human town." Bernadette babbled, without giving me a chance to process her appearance.

I sucked in my lips, biting down on the meaty flesh as my hand tried to suppress the scream that bubbled up my throat. My ghostly friend held her chopped finger to her mouth to silence me. She didn't need to worry since my throat was too sore to speak at the moment.

"Oh yeah, they got one on both sides, too, Kay! But they're not moving, so you're safe.... with me, of course."

My eyes rolled so hard at her corny joke that my heart slowed its pace. Bernadette was one of the humorless comedians to haunt the castle. She was the last person I wanted to see in my current condition.

"Bernadette! How did you get here?" I hissed between my clenched teeth.

"I hitched a ride through the portal with Sir Reid."

I opened my mouth to respond, but it was hard to stop Bernadette when she was worked up.

"Man, oh man, Kaydian, you've done it now. Oowii! I don't think I've ever seen your mother so mad and sad at the same time in my life," she said. Her Mississippi accent was just as thick as ever as she shook her head. Between the soft tissue from her brain jiggling and half of the minced stringy black hair that hung on for dear life, had me fighting the urge to jump off the roof.

"Well! Go on, tell me then," I said, trying to keep my voice low.

Sir Reid paused as he continued to walk back to the pack gathering.

Bernadette's little body started to shake as globs of red coagulated blood splattered the metal roof and disappeared. The rotten smell of eggs permeated the air between us. The older the ghost, the stronger their sulfur scent gave off. As of right now, I would give my left leg to send her to the underworld as her scent drifted to my nose, causing a slight tickle in my throat.

"Sorry, you know that hefa stuck that knife inside of my throat before I died," she said, wiping her mouth. I didn't have the energy to tell her that she was a ghost, and it wasn't physical blood. "Your mother has cried enough to fill the castle with her tears. Every night she paces that room of hers, worried sick about you, with that basta..."

Bernadette paused and shifted her eyes when I glanced at her.

Clearing her throat, she continued, "That lovely father of yours, I meant. A true visionary king of the ages... I know you think I'm lying, but you know, since you guys won't help us, we just sit around and watch the madness unfold."

Bernadette smiled, showing off her missing front teeth. My mother crying was uncanny. The only time she cried that much was when I fell from a tree and shattered my forearm.

The plunging sensation from my stomach had nothing to do with my current situation. But that everything, once again, was falling onto me. However, this time, who could I blame other than myself? I'd known better that Greyson's soft eyes and demeanor would turn me into someone who would have killed everyone in California if I needed to be with him. "I hate my life." Now, I can see how some of the common witches rather give up their magic than be tied to someone.

"Looks like Big Daddy Reid is retreating with the A team. Two days, Princess? What are you going to do? And why are you here? You know our enemies are shifters, right? Your...gracious father made sure of that."

"Bernadette, you should really get going. You wouldn't want to miss your ride back home," I said, pointing to where Sir Reid's enormous frame opened the portal, and one by one, the equally tall shoulders disappeared into the white light.

"Eh, I think I'll stay and watch. It's not like I have anything better to do." She sighed deeply with her hand strumming the roof. "So, answer my question. Why are you here?"

One thing about ghosts. They were persistent.

My eyes shuttered as my shoulder relaxed. A slight weight had been lifted from my overflowing basket of problems.

Watching the small group clustered around Oni and Greyson, their pursed lips and doubtful eyes watched the two as Oni's grumpy face contorted. The vein in his neck jumped as I heard him cut down Greyson in front of the pack. Greyson, always wanting to be the bigger person, stood there with his tail tucked between his legs. Some things weren't acceptable. Between my stomach rumbling and Bernadette's humming the old song she created in my ear, I couldn't concentrate on what was being said.

"Fine," was the last word I said before opening up my mouth and spilling out everything. I sat, still watching Greyson's somber face while Bernadette's little "Oohs" filled in the gaps. It wasn't until the small group dispersed and Greyson walked back over to our home that I stopped speaking. The only sound between us was Greyson rattling with the ladder and my stomach protesting against me.

"Sheesh! I thought my life was sucky, but yours take the cake, my princess! You had to wait until you're almost insane to find out that your mate is a..." she shuddered. Her red translucent body shimmered against the gray tin roof. "Shifter...and a virgin at that. At the very least, one would think Youna would have picked out someone with a bit of practice...as yourself."

I narrowed my eyes at her the moment Greyson finally got the ladder in place.

"Stay hidden...you're already working my nerves for that joke," I said through my clenched teeth.

"Well, I mean, you're the only one who can see me..." she muttered, but stopped speaking once she saw my eyes narrowed at her. Bernadette's red body shimmered, and this time, she disappeared, leaving me to scoot the rest of the way off of the roof. Each step down the dilapidated ladder caused my anxiety to peek. It's time to face the music. The time for the truth was long overdue.

"Why didn't you tell me?" Greyson asked through his clenched teeth the moment my feet touched the ground.

My fingernails itched my favorite spot on my wrist. The lie was at the tip of my tongue, but the heaviness in my heart won. Would he ever forgive me? Tired of being somewhere I knew I wasn't meant to be, but most importantly, I missed my mother and Del.

I couldn't negate the fact that I was in love with Greyson and that was a major problem. A problem that my coven would never agree on. My mother's bulging eyes as I told her that Youna, the goddess, fated me to a shifter. I would surely send her into an early grave.

"Sir Reid said the Princess was missing..." He paused as he shifted his feet. His brown eyes were glassy, as if his tears would fall at any minute. With a frown on his face, he continued, "Then I realized I was the one being strung along. You lied to me, Kay. You're not only a witch, but you're the Princess of the North American Coven, aren't you?"

Hugging myself tightly, my body burned with shame as I shifted my gaze away from Greyson. I had to tell him the truth because time was running out, and like Elder Alo had told me, "I couldn't delay the inevitable."

"He was speaking to me. It's an ancient language that only the Royals and their loyalists use." I swallowed the lump in my throat. "And you're right, Grey. I—I'm the Princess of the North American Coven. They're looking for me."

"Why?"

It was a one word question. It shouldn't make my palms sweaty, and my magic wanted to curl up and hide.

"I knew you would hate me, and by the time you told me about your parents. I—I'm scared to lose you...us. For so long, I waited for my mate to find me. Days turned into months. Months turned into years. Almost all the royal descendants found their mates early. Even my parents found each other earlier on. Everyone besides me."

I cleared my throat. "I was falling into a curse called Greyson and I couldn't escape. I knew it, my magic knew it, and most recently, most of the coven. The voice in my head appeared more frequently, and I had a breakdown in front of all the coven heirs. My mother and my father... they thought I wouldn't make it. I just wanted to get away from everything, and I wasn't expecting to meet you. Honestly, I'm falling for you. I can't deny it, and maybe I'm being too eager. That's the truth, but love can only take us so far."

Greyson's unshed tears broke free, staining his reddened face. Without a second thought, my hand swiped away the warm tears from his cheeks. He captured my hand, holding it close to him. My magic warmed my fingers. Although I couldn't see it, I felt the energy from his sporadic magic.

Greyson closed those sad brown eyes and muttered, "I love you, too. I'm just not sure what to do next."

My hand slipped from his hold. Sucking my lip into my mouth, I released a deep sigh.

"Greyson, maybe you can come home with me and we can go from there."

His brown eyes widened as he struggled to make sense of what I just said.

"You want me to go into the lion's den?" I could see the wheels turning in his red eyes. Rubbing the bridge of his nose, he said, "Let's just talk about this later. The pack is already...never mind."

Greyson grabbed my hand and led me to the house.

"Well, he may be nothing to write home about, but at least he's something to look at," Bernadette said as she appeared next to me. Right before I threw her the evil eye, she said right before she disappeared, "Too bad he's a shifter...and alive."

Youna help me.

Chapter 23
Greyson

The best way to ignore my angry pack that was chomping at my neck from yesterday's fiasco was to ignore everything. Ignored my duties. Ignored my párah, who was beyond pissed about the invasion that occurred. Ignored the pack's heated gazes as they watched me walk back to my home to help get Kaydian down from the roof. Their stares were worse than bullets that were lodged in my back. On that trek back home, my father's last words rang out clear as day in my head, "You're not meant to lead." It followed me to bed and all the way into my sleepless night as I stared up at the tin roof, praying for some answers. Sooner rather than later.

When I could finally pull myself from the bed, I noticed I was alone in my room. Kaydian's voice could be heard from the next room, whispering in a hushed tone. Maybe she's going crazy. My body protested as I dragged my heavy body out of the comforter. If that wasn't any indication, today was going to be taxing on me, then I didn't know what was. Throwing on some clothes that Kaydian had cleaned the other day, I exited my room to find her back toward me. Her arms flared in the air as she spoke to the empty room. My wolf growled inside my chest as the tiny hairs on my body stood up.

"God dammit, Bernadette! I told you to stay hidden and quit with your shit!" Kaydian whispered, her pointer finger aimed at whoever she was speaking to. "Why were you trying to peep in those people's bedrooms..."

Kaydian stopped mid-sentence. The floor bed creaked under her feet as she turned toward me with an overeager smile on her face. I shuddered, wiping the thin sheet of moisture on my upper lip.

"Oh, Greyson! You're up early."

Judging from the sun shining in the only window in the living room, I would say it was late in the morning. My eyebrow arched at her statement.

"Are you okay? Who were you talking to? I swear there are only two things that set my wolf on edge, ghosts and witches...well, that aren't my mate."

"Oh...Well...you remember when I told you about having necromancy abilities?" She paused as she shifted on her feet. Her hand found her wrist as usual. "Well, we have a visitor. Bernadette hitched a ride with Sir Reid and stayed."

"...like forever?"

"Please," she begged through her clenched teeth to the empty area beside her. "And no, she wanted to stay until we went home."

Home. There was that dreaded word that I've been avoiding for a while now. Home for who, though? Coals as heavy as steel settled in my stomach. My hands shook as I grabbed my wrist to steady them. Kaydian's inquisitive emerald eyes, and possibly her ghost friends, stared back at me. I wondered if she knew her scent grew stronger when she was puzzled. She waved her hand in front of my face.

"Let's go get some food."

"So, we will not talk about last night, then?"

"After breakfast... I promise. I have to feed you first."

"You mean lunch? Since it's almost noon."

She gave me a haughty smile. One thing about my Hiema is she loves to win. Right now, I would let her, because only her happiness matters right now. Threading our hands together, we headed toward the wood pit. Corn and spices drifted throughout the air the closer we got to where Hawk and his mother were making food for the pack. Little kids lined up as Kathleen held out the long ladle to deliver the steaming soup into their bowls. Hawk was the first person to spot us behind the eager kids. His gray eyes bulged out of his head, dropping the bread he held with the tongs. A curse slipped from his mouth, sending the kids giggling as they walked away with their food.

"Maybe you should go back home, and I will bring you guys some of everything."

Hawk's eyes shifted between Kaydian and me. His plastered fake smile made me pause. It wasn't until I noticed some of the packs were posted on their porch. Even from here, I can see the curl in their upper lip and the way their eyes roamed over us. When our eyes met, they just shook their heads. My face felt like charcoal ignited as embarrassment raked through my body. Kaydian's hand squeezed mine ever so lightly. At least I have three people on my side.

"Everyone is staring holes into us, Grey," Kaydian stated the obvious.

"...And it's about to get worse," Kathleen warned with her arms crossed. Her gray eyes narrowed at Oni.

My párah exited the Great Spirit Temple. His face twisted into a scowl as his dark brown eyes landed on me and then Kaydian. He found his target and was barreling toward us. Hate was written in those dark eyes, and all I wanted was one peaceful day without any trouble. Like birds, some of the pack flocked toward their small porches. The little kids that sat with their soup at the empty picnic table turned around with their spoons hung halfway out of their mouths.

"Greyson, Hawk, Kathleen, and...Kaydian," Oni said. Practically spitting out our Kaydian's name in spite.

"Please, Oni, can we not do this out here in front?" Kathleen spanned out her arm to show the small crowd that was gathered by their home. "We have too many eyes around and the tension is high already since our brief visit."

"They're as much a part of the conversation as we are," Oni stated blankly. "I find it hard to believe that the moment your... 'mate' came to the village, we get a visit from those fucking revolting bastards. I don't believe in coincidence and them searching for their missing princess."

Párah spat the words out like they were acid. He looked primed to jump at anyone who even breathes in his sight. Slipping my hand from Kaydian's, I moved to stand between them, taking the attention off of her to me, but her hand stopped me.

"Don't! Let your uncle speak. Since he's in such a chatty mood today." I turned to her with my mouth agape. She was definitely fed up with my uncle's behavior, which I couldn't blame her for. A wide smile took over her face. "Uncle Oni, why don't you say what's really on your mind?"

Hawk and Kathleen glanced at each other before their gaze landed on me. I shrugged with my eyebrows stretched to my hairline. I've never heard Kaydian raise her voice at my temperamental uncle.

"I think you're mixed up with that princess, and they traced her here because you helped her escape. Even though I don't know why a Thibodeaux princess would need a human to help her escape, I never question those monsters."

My partially shifted nails dug into the meaty flesh of my palm. The pain eased my anger a bit as I tried to reel in my wolf. I didn't want to disrespect my uncle in front of the whole pack. They already thought I was unfit, since I was only half a shifter.

Kaydian moved close to Oni before I could stop her.

"You know what they say about assuming, don't you, Oni?" She paused as she came within an inch of Oni. She wasn't as tall as a shifter, but you couldn't tell that from her position. Her shoulders squared with her hands on her wide hips. She faced him with not a trace of fear in her emerald, stormy eyes. Only a condescending smirk settled on her perfect face. "When you assume, you're making an ass out of yourself."

Oni's eyebrows touched his hairline as he tilted his head. Folding his arms across his wide chest, his eyes narrowed into Kaydian. My first thought was to grab her and pull her back to our home. The little ball of magic flickered and weaned, but my wolf wanted to rip my uncle's throat out of his neck, using his blood to soak the earth.

"That's not how the saying goes."

Kaydian finally smiled at him. "No, that's exactly how it goes. Now I'm going to eat. So, you can leave my presence now."

Some of the chatter from the nosey pack could be heard. Their ohs and the brief intake when Kaydian shooed him away.

She turned from him. Her stride was long and purposeful. Kaydian meant to piss off my uncle, and she succeeded. No one in this pack dared to piss Oni off. She grabbed the bowls filled with soup from Kathleen, whose mouth was agape, and her gray eyes filled with shock. Hawk whistled when he passed us the soft baked bread for the soup.

"Greyson! I think it's time you and your 'mate' find somewhere else to live. The pack no longer wants her here. She poses a risk to not only you but the pack."

The chatter died instantly. Hawk's eyes whizzed between my uncle and I. Kathleen slightly shook her head, that old sign she used to give me when I was younger getting into trouble. Cold sweat dripped down the small of my back. My uncle stood there waiting for an answer. When my eyes sought Kaydian's for comfort, I didn't find any. It was something else in those gem eyes that were hidden. My uncle's charcoal scent overpowered the food in the area, causing my nose to burn and my wolf to bury itself in the middle of my chest. The magic that was normally joyous to be close to Kaydian abandoned me. There wasn't any tingling. There wasn't any warmth. I was just left to deal with the aftermath.

The deep, commanding growl from Oni's wolf shook not only him, but me as well. Oni wanted me to kneel in front of the entire pack. He wanted me to show him obedience, but my wolf trembled inside of me as it fought back. Kathleen begged him to stop in the background, but I couldn't hear anything over the pounding of my heart. Cooper scent assaulted my nose as my wounds from nails fragrant the air. Oni let out another growl, and I lost the battle. Shame filled my body as I dropped to my knees. Exhaustion won—and maybe I was just tired.

"I'll think about our next course of action," I declared. My voice sounded weak in my ears.

Was that a good enough answer?

Oni stood there a beat too long. His face remained passive as his dark eyes sparkled with victory. Strings from his long black hair whisked in the light breeze. His mouth twitched as if the words he wanted to say were stuck on the tip of his tongue. Oni's fist opened and closed, but he turned and walked towards his home, which was close to the Great Spirit Temple.

Dragging myself and my pride, I got from the dusty ground. Wiping off my dusty knees, I heard the soft snickers from the prying pack members around the center. Regret stabbed at my chest. Maybe my uncle was right. I wasn't made for leading. My father was probably somewhere in the afterworld, looking on, shaking his head in disgust. If

I were a human, I think I would have died from the blood that rushed to my face, when I turned back to my friends to get my food and ran away. I was greeted with sympathetic, quick glances from Hawk and Kathleen, which made me take a step back, but it was Kaydian's look that made me want to run and hide under a rock for the rest of my life. Nothing. Her face unreadable, blank eyes stared right through me. After a moment, she snapped out of whatever trance she was in as her nonchalant smile returned.

"Are you okay, Gray?" Hawk asked. His hand rubbed the back of his neck. Even now, my friend couldn't look me in the eye.

"Yeah, I'm okay, Hawk, annoyed, but I will live," I admitted. "Was it that embarrassing?"

"It's…I'll talk with your uncle, Gray. He was wrong about that," Kathleen voiced.

"It's okay, Kathleen. It's over now." I countered, but Kathleen was headed to the Great Spirit Temple before I could finish, leaving Kaydian, Hawk, and me alone.

"How about we grab a seat at the picnic table? Hawk can join us when he's finished cleaning up." Kaydian asserted. Her voice was stern as she commanded us.

My shoulders sagged a bit as I nodded. The only thing I wanted to do was to go back to my tiny room and hide away. I've said before, but I wished we could afford indoor kitchens as we sat and ate the lukewarm soup in silence. Every so often, Kaydian would whisper something to Bernadette, but I was too caught up in replaying the event in my head. My dad had been long gone, but I could still see his haunted expression as he shook his head, looking down his nose at me with contempt.

"…you should have fought back against kneeling, but it's okay, Gray. The pack will forget about it." Kaydian whispered, trying to keep our conversation to ourselves.

How long had Kaydian been talking? The last of the cold soup sat on my tongue before I swallowed down the last of it. She was very optimistic about the pack. I couldn't blame her, but I knew my people, and forgetting was something foreign to them. Kaydian picked up where she had stopped.

"So, since you and your uncle are at an impasse. Why don't we take some time away from the pack and go to Houston?"

There was that impending question, to stay or go? Something deep within my soul told me this was the last time she would ask. How could I leave the only home I've known? The last place where I could sense my mother's spirit. Hawk, Elder Alo, and Kathleen were my family. And I've only ever been away from them for a couple of days before I would get homesick. Was it that simple to give it up? My father's family legacy for me had always been to rule the Swiftwater Pack, no matter what.

Hawk finally joined us after he was done. The smudges of black soot from the pit mixed with the thin sheet of sweat that covered his body. His small plate was filled with leftover bread he shared with my Hiema, who all but snatched the three pieces of bread out of his hands as soon as Hawk settled down on the bench. A deathly silence enveloped us. Everyone ate with their eyes glued to their plates and their mouths filled with food. Which made a part of me happy because I wasn't in the mood to make small talk.

"I suggested maybe we should go away for a bit," Kaydian spoke, breaking the awkward silence while her attention never left her plate.

"Thank you, Shorts and Gray, for waiting for me." Hawk paused. Clearing his throat, "Are you sure that's a good plan? You have to make sure the pack remembers who the leader is."

"Greyson will have plenty of time to make it up to the pack once we get back," Kaydian announced as she turned to Hawk. "It's just like a brief vacation...to the coven in Houston."

Hawk's tanned skin turned a deep shade of red as the small bread logged in his throat. Kaydian knocked on his back, and I flew up from the bench, almost causing it to flip over. Hawk needed some water before he choked to death. When I returned, Kaydian had returned to her bread. My shoulders slumped before I could stop myself.

Hawk polished off the water. His face was a slight hue of pink as he breathed properly. Those small gray eyes bore a hole into me. I could almost hear his mind screaming, "What the hell?" at me.

Didn't he know I knew this was a crazy idea?

I looked around the tiny village that I grew up in and what my being away would mean. This urge to step away from it, from everything, was stronger than anything I've experienced. Would anyone miss me?

"I said a trip somewhere...not a trip to the center of hell," Hawk replied. "Why would you go there? Do you have a death wish? And who do you know there?"

A deafening pause fell between us, causing me to shift in my seat. My tongue felt heavy in my mouth. Kaydian's narrowed eyes focused on Hawk, and I felt pity for my friend.

"He knows me…" Kaydian's eyes relaxed a bit, but I still could sense her being perturbed by his blatant disrespect for her coven. "I'm the Princess of the North American Witch Coven."

The words clanged against my skull. My heart squeezed at the thought someone else knew about our little secret now. Hawk's mouth formed an O as his widened gray eyes gawked at me. He scooted away from Kaydian, drawing an annoyed deep sigh to fill the surrounding area. She crossed her arms. The corners of her mouth twitched as rapidly as my heart pounded in my chest.

Hawk could very much shout our secret or, worse, run straight into the Great Spirit's temple and confess to Oni. Even though we were thick as thieves, his pause had concerned me.

"You're a witch…and you're Greyson's mate." His noisy swallow filled our table. "Well, I guess it was always a possibility seeing Gray is half a witch. I—"

He stopped mid-sentence to shake his head, sending his black locks tumbling over his shoulders.

"This is crazy. I'm assuming Oni doesn't know," he presumed, even though we both knew the answer to that foolish assumption.

"No, and I'm hoping you will keep this between us for now," I requested.

"Yes, since I will help Gray find his mother's murderer." Kaydian declared with triumph in her voice.

Hawk's eyes grew wider, if that was possible, as Kaydian's words tumbled out of her mouth and hit Hawk. A small part of me screamed cowardly because I should have been the one to tell my brother, but I couldn't do anything but apologize for now. If I could just get this one thing right, maybe the pack won't look at me as a half-bred that doesn't deserve to be their Alpha, and someone who would risk their lives for their pack members.

The thought of redeeming myself to the pack sent my heavy head nodding.

"Yes, I'm going to find my mother's killer and come back. You and I both know that the pack and even my párah loved my mother dearly. What do you think, Hawk?" I asked.

I needed him to say it wasn't a stupid idea and that I should do it.

"This is so dangerous, Gray. I would never be okay with this. You're my brother, and that would be like sending you off to your death!" Hawk warned. His worried expression made me pause and think for a minute, but I had already decided.

"We're going," I said.

"Wait, what?" Hawk replied.

"Oh, that would be the best way to give me enough time to figure out a plan," Kaydian said, ignoring the puzzlement in Hawks' question. Her voice perked up. If I wasn't mistaken, this has been the first time today that I heard her sound so elated.

Glad that makes one of us.

Kaydian stood from the little picnic table, and we followed suit. She dusted off the bottom of her skirt and her hands before coming over to me.

"We should tell your uncle now and leave soon. You can just grab some of your clothing, and then we can leave." She stopped getting a good whiff of her armpits. "And I need to clean up a bit."

"I think I need to clean up as well...I think my mom and I should be there just in case Oni tears your head off." Hawk chuckled nervously. I knew he was putting on a brave face for the both of us because I, for one, was scared to death.

As we approached our homes, we split up with me going to sit on the little yellow couch while Kaydian cleaned up in the room. My foot tapped the creaky floor until the living area was filled with her floral scent. When she was done, she came out in a blue wrap-up shirt paired with a white shirt. Her black shoes held scruffs from the previous owner that, no matter how much I scrubbed, I couldn't get them out.

Kaydian was brimming with happiness. Her smile stretched across her face and was nothing short of pure joy. The floral scent that I came to love intensified, making the room smell like we were in the woods by our favorite alcove.

"I'm ready."

I paused. "What happened to your deodorizer?"

"You were supposed to buy me another one today. Remember?" she said, shaking the empty small bottle in her hand.

"Right...I forgot," running my hand over my face. "Well, I guess it doesn't matter anymore."

Walking into my room for the last time of the day, Kaydian had placed the old, tattered brown suitcase my mother bought me on my bed. I packed a couple of shirts and bottoms. My old pair of low, muddy black boots that had seen better days would have to do until I got back home. Maybe Kaydian can conjure up a new pair of boots for me. I sat on my tiny bed for what seemed like hours, fiddling with the ends of the sheets. I knew I couldn't stay here forever. That would be too easy. After I finally talked myself into getting up, I walked out of the bedroom with the luggage, my clammy hands gripping the handle as if it were my last lifeline. I wondered if I was making a good decision.

I guess it was too late to back down. *Earth Creator, please protect me.*

"Everything will be alright, Grey. I will keep you safe," Kaydian suggested as we walked hand in hand to the temple as a united front. Pulling her closer, I kissed the top of her head and allowed her to lead us until we reached the brown double doors of the temple.

After a minute of giving the door a death stare, I opened it. This was it. No more hiding. If they hadn't scented Kaydian as a witch before we entered the temple, then the discombobulate looks upon the faces of Oni, the few elders, and some of the pack members, including Kathleen, confirmed it. Nothing about this situation was funny, but Oni's black eyes appeared on the verge of falling out of his eye socket as he registered who Kaydian was. Even though the room was mixed with scents from the small wood fire and the other pack's scents, it was Oni's that stood out the most. It was as if I was six again and almost drowned when we went swimming in San Francisco. When Oni saved me. My nose burned as my hand tried to rub the offending scent away.

Oni caught himself as his shocked face returned to his normal grimace.

"Therein lies the truth," Oni said, standing with his arms folded and if I weren't looking at my uncle, I would've never have never thought he would be this calm. One thing I can always say about my párah was that he loved our family, pack, and loved my father. He would lie down in his life to preserve our family's name.

"You brought shame to your family, Greyson. Aligning yourself with the same people who killed our pack, your people, and your mother. What would your father say if he saw you shacking up with a fucking witch.... a royal witch at that. The same royal witch family that probably had your mother killed. What a waste of the Swiftwater name. My father would disown you if he knew you would sully our family name."

Oni's words were like a hot branding iron piercing my mind and my soul. My wolf cowardly recoiled in my chest. The pack members in the room all hummed their approval toward Oni and twisted their faces at us. Over the years, my uncle has lashed out at me, but this was worse. It was as if he took my thoughts and laid them out for everyone to see that I was a failure. I wasn't meant to lead. That I was just a black sheep in wolf's clothing, like I heard several of the pack members mutter when they thought I wasn't listening.

Kaydian's small hands slipped into mine and lightly squeezed, drawing my attention to her. Her emerald eyes pleaded for me to say something, but what could I say when Oni said was the ugly, unspoken truth.

"That's enough, Oni." Elder Alo warned, walking in from the back of the temple. He had his old hand-carved cane today, meaning he wasn't feeling well enough to be up today. "Greyson is only doing what any Swiftwater or shifter would have done."

Elder Alo started a maelstrom in the small temple. The pack member's growls filled the room as they shouted, "Abomination" and "What did we expect from a half breed?" All the while, my uncle stood in the middle of the temple, his arm still folded with his black eyes locked onto Kaydian. One look at her told me she didn't fear my uncle as she returned his glare back to him.

"Everyone be quiet," Elder Alo said as the chatter died down. "Greyson doesn't need your approval, Oni. The only approval he needs is from the Earth Creator and the ancestors which they must have given their blessings, or we would be paying. Greyson has to think about his future mate and keeping her safe, even though Princess Kaydian is more than capable of handling herself. I give the two my full blessings."

Mutters started up around the heated room again.

"Thank you, Elder Alo." I got out. "We're going away for a while, and when I get back, I'll make everything up to everyone."

Elder Alo paused.

His somber brown eyes peered at me as a smile that didn't reach his eyes planted on his face. He nodded. It reminded me of the time Elder Alo gave my future in a quote, *"You will never know peace until your second time around."* Never expounding on the meaning because telling me anymore would change my destiny. Just the same grim stare as he had at this moment, which made the stones in my stomach increase twofold.

"Greyson, time to go. You've given my hand a bath." Kaydian said, pulling on my dampened hand.

"I will see you soon, Oni. We'll talk about this later. Thank you and bye, Elder Alo."

"Don't bother coming back, Greyson. We will manage just fine without," Oni said. Elder Alo turned his gaze on him and said something, but I hadn't stayed around to hear what he said.

Kaydian ended up tugging me outside, away from the glares of the angry pack.

"Are you okay, Greyson?" she asked the moment she found a place to open the portal to go to Houston. "Listen, it's going to be alright. We will be back in no time."

"We will be back in no time" felt distant and vague. How can she be sure of that? My mind questioned as my wolf tried to break free from the surface. My elongated nails cut into the softness of my palms. He shook and trembled inside of my chest, which made the soup from earlier curdled in my stomach. I wanted to shout, scream, or cry. I wasn't sure if I was being honest with myself. Kaydian turned to me. Her smile, one that I've only seen in private, shined and glowed in the nightlight.

What would my father do? He would grin and bear it. For my mother. For the pack. And that's what I will do. Grin and pray that it will be over soon.

A wide smile stretched across my face. It seemed unnatural and stiff. Even when I continued to keep it on as I stepped through the blinding white light of Kaydian's portal. I smiled. Even when my muddy boots hit the soft brown dirt of Houston, and I threw up the lunch I had eaten, I smiled.

Chapter 24

Kaydian

"So, that was an interesting send-off?" Bernadette said, dusting off the invisible dust off her bloody clothing. "You sure you want to keep this one? I mean, he needs a lot of work...a lot of time...and a **whole** lot of patience."

I squeezed my eyes, rubbing the bridge of my nose. Bernadette had been whispering in my ears since we left Greyson's home for breakfast. How could I have forgotten that she loved gossip and talking? Two of the worst traits a ghost could have since I could never get rid of her unless I sent her to the underworld That would be a huge burden for me because if you send one off, then a line of ghosts would want me to do the same for them.

Fat chance!

My magic brought us right outside the village perimeter. The red tint of my mother's protection spell shimmered in the late afternoon sun. My plan to bring us directly inside the village would have been ludicrous. At least bringing us outside of the perimeter would buy us— me some time to think about where to hide Greyson. Should I place a cloaking spell on him? No, that won't do at all. Despite everything, Greyson smells like a shifter, and I could only cloak his appearance with magic. I would definitely have to go to Merrell's shop. They normally kept deodorizers in their store to cancel out the distinct scents from the witches that frequent the store. Yes, that was it!

My head swiveled to where I left Greyson. He was finally standing upright with that ridiculous sham of a smile. *It will get better!* As I stared at my mate, the corners of my mouth twitched, and now I was the one with the ridiculous fake smile. Now, if my stomach could stop churning, then everything would be okay.

"It's not too late, you know?" Bernadette said, leaning on the tree trunk next to Greyson. "We can just chuck him back into the portal, and I'll help you through your curse."

Bernadette's arms flew up in surrender when she saw the pointed look on my face.

"Youna! You're no fun anymore," Bernadette said with her lips pursed.

"Bernadette!" I said through my clenched teeth. Flicking my wrist, I vanquished her to Tou-sin village for the time being.

"Let me guess, our friend has been bothering you?" Greyson said. His voice sounded small, almost nonexistent. His skin was pale as the white snakeroot that surrounded the wooded area.

I turned that smile onto Greyson. "Yes, she's gone now."

He nodded.

"Listen, I think I'm going to take you to my Dragon's feeding house. It should be safe there. No one besides me goes there frequently..."

"Dragons!" He took a step back as his eyes widened as big as saucers. "You're going to feed me to your dragons?"

"No, Grey," I said, stopping myself from rolling my eyes. "It's the safest place to be right now. Until I can get things sorted out."

"O-okay, I trust you, my Hiema," he said, but his voice shook, letting me know he thought otherwise.

I would just have to make him believe me then.

My arms wrapped around his long neck and kissed his sunken cheek. That was the wrong move, since he smelled like acid and the old soup he ate. It took everything in my power to prevent myself from throwing up.

We tugged through the bushes and the old trees, breaking the twigs of dead branches that had recently fallen as nature prepared for winter. No longer confined, my magic vibrated and pulsed just below my skin. It knew we were back home, and that meant I could finally be myself again. The light orange shimmered in the patchy sunlight that broke through the tree canopy. The crisp fall air kissed my skin, welcoming me back home. Greedily, my nose inhaled. Someone had to be making peach cobbler. Just the very thought made my stomach lurch.

As much as I complained, I was overjoyed to be home. Not being able to use my magic caused me to reevaluate some of my pessimistic thoughts. Hell! Call me crazy, but I would take my village over the Swiftwater's any day of the year. Just the mere thought of being raised in that village alone causes a slight tremor to run through me, causing me to fold my arms around my body. Greyson asked if I was cold. I shook him off and chalked it up to being home.

We stepped out into the small clearing that housed the feeding shed. Without thinking about Greyson, I called for Sera and Luc. This has been the longest time I've spent away from them. Luc's big blue head was the first to appear in the small clearing, followed by Sera. Both crawled straight toward me. Their massive heads rubbed against me as they scented me.

"I've missed you both," I said, stroking them lightly as I placed a kiss on each of their scaly heads.

Sera, never one to miss anything, turned her attention to Greyson. A deep grumble from deep in Sera's massive chest made the ground tremble. As she rose onto her hind legs, her red translucent wings expanded, sending branches and reddish leaves tumbling from the tree canopies. The sun burst through the broken trees, highlighting Sera's thick phalanges in her wings. Sera pulled back her thick mouth to bare her teeth to our new guest, which wasn't unusual for Sera since she hated everyone except anyone I'd deemed worthy.

Any other day, I would let Sera continue to taunt, but she would most definitely cause Sir Reid or someone brave enough to venture here to see what the problem was. Poor Greyson. He was stuck to the dusty brown shed door. His skin was the color of my white shirt. I guess that was a better look than the sickly green he had turned after we teleported here. Sera's snout inched closer to Greyson, sending him scrambling against the shed. Let me put a stop to this as I placed myself between Sera and Greyson, reaching out to wrap myself around her mouth.

"Sera, be nice," I said, scolding the dragon that could easily fry or freeze me if she wanted to.

"K-K-Kaydian," Greyson stammered, causing me to turn around. Luc had slipped past me. His long naris grazed Greyson from his feet to his head, causing him to tremble. Luc moved back, bowing his head to him. As mates, Sera sensed Luc surrendering to Greyson, turning her head when I let her out of my embrace.

"Greyson, come over here so she can scent you," I said, without turning to look at the outrageous look he was probably throwing at me. I continued, "If you want to live through the night, then come on, or Sera will surely eat you when I'm gone."

Greyson or his wolf, I couldn't tell at the moment, whimpered slowly. He took his merry, sweet time getting to me, standing just a hair behind me in case Sera decided to make him a mid-afternoon snack. My hand wrapped around his thick arm and pulled him closer to Sera.

"Kaydian, I don't..."

His words died in his throat when she turned her head sideways to peer at him. Those red, fiery eyes surrounded by fire roamed over Greyson. Sera cocked her head as if deeming Greyson was unworthy of her time, lowered her scaly head slightly, and turned her wide body, making her way back to the broken tree path. Strange. I've never seen Sera treat anyone like that before, not Sir Reid or anyone else. My mind was flooded with hundreds of scenarios.

If Sera and Luc didn't fully accept Greyson. What did that mean? My dragons were a gift from the goddesses themselves. I'd like to think their standoff position was normal for dragons, but as I stood there with my nails digging into my wrist, I wasn't sure. Am I going to have to hide him from them, too? It was too late to doubt myself as the heaviness sat in my chest. I already had to hide Greyson from my parents and the coven. Now I had to hide him from my children.

And I hate to even mention it out loud for fear it may come true, but I was scared.

"Shit!" I whispered.

"W—What was that, Kay?" Greyson stammered.

"Nothing, Greyson," I said, shaking off the voice. Once Luc followed Sera back to their spot. "See, it wasn't bad."

"Yeah...for you! I wish you would have reminded me of your pet dragons. Shifters and dragons have never played well together. Remember the emergence war."

Oh, right!

How did I forget that minor war that happened almost a million years ago? I suppressed the urge to roll my eyes. Honestly, that war shouldn't even be called a war. It technically started when the dragons finally came out of their caves and made the shifters their target. It lasted two weeks, and the dragons won as they destroyed the packs.

"Well, Greyson. I hope you take Sera and Luc's peace offering. They've done worse things to Sir Reid." I said, remembering the first week they met Sir Reid. Both of my hooligans lit his black cape on fire. It was amusing watching him stomp out the flames until he ripped it off. Poor Sir Reid never wore capes around them after that.

"Listen, I have to run to the bookstore in town before I can use the cloaking spell," I said, opening the small shed door. The old rotten smell had long since gone. "It's small, but it will work. I'll clean up."

An image of the small yellow room in Greyson's home was the first thing that came to my mind, and with a flip of my wrist. My magic took hold of the small shed. It circled the room as I walked into the middle of the magic storm. The floors were cleaned of the hay, a single window replaced the open hole in the wall, and a small bed fit the small area. A small bathroom was squeezed into the back.

"I-I hope it isn't too much to ask, but what about food?"

"Oh! Right, well, I will bring you food from the kitchen." I said, heading to the door. "Greyson, please stay inside until I get back. I can't save you from my mother if she finds out you're here."

Greyson, still slightly peaked from his near-death experience, crossed his long fingers. *What a waste of fingers,* I thought, squeezing my eyes shut at my lascivious thoughts. There wasn't any time for that. Greyson just needed a bit of work. Nothing I wasn't used to. Maybe I could teach him to be a better leader while he was here, right?

As I stepped outside of the shed, my heart leaped into my mouth as a squirrel the size of a cat barreled past me and into the bushes. Yes, I was improvising with a little faith in Youna to see me through this time, for once. Locking the door with my magic, I opened a portal and the thought of being in Merrell's shop popped up in my head as I stepped through the portal. I knew I had at least one more chance to use the portal before I became too exhausted to do anything but fall asleep in my bed.... my warm, soft bed.

"Oh, fuck, let's get this over with," I muttered.

The portal teleported me right behind Merrell's store in front of the older brown wooden door that led to the back door. When I entered the back door, a loud crack ricocheted in the store as everyone turned to look toward where the ruckus was coming from. Several eyes, from young to old, gawked at me as I stood frozen like a deer in headlights. Show no fear! At least, that's what was ingrained in me. With my head high, I moved through the small crowd, trying to avoid their stares and the whispers, which was harder than it looked, seeing as they weren't exactly good at whispering.

"The princess is back!"

"What is she wearing? She looks worse than the humans in Houston!"

"I heard she was locked up in preparation for her going mad."

"...you know... maybe Jaqueline is a better choice."

Some new, some old rumors mixed amongst the gossiping coven. If I were on the throne, I would cut every one of their tongues out and when it grew back. I would cut it over again.

Bastards!

It took me five minutes of maneuvering between the coven members before I realized the bookstore. Something was off...way off. The familiar turpentine and citrus scent hadn't greeted me. Soft music from the magic cast instruments wasn't playing as usual. No one occupied the big fluffy couches by the front of the store, not even the chatty children from town. In all of my twenty-five years of living, I've never seen Merrell's bookstore like it was now. If something happened to Merrell while I was gone, I would never forgive myself. They were my little sanctuary from the craziness.

"Merrell!" Looking around the tiny store.

Merrell popped their head around the corner. Dark rings circle their blue eyes. They're dressed in dull, muted black. Merrell was dressed for a funeral.

"Kaydian...I meant Princess Kaydian," Merrell said, as they lunged for me, wrapping their arms around me. "Where in the seventh hell did you go? Your mother was a one-woman army. I've heard about momma bears, but she takes the cake."

"My mother was here?"

Merrell's blue eyes squeezed shut. "Kaydian, you know your mother would burn down this world for you." They paused.

Merrell all but dragged me into the back room, shutting the door with a click.

"She found out about the canvas, and she came here with the Golden Army. They took it all and destroyed them in the middle of the town. She 'allowed' me to keep the books because it was an essential hobby for the children. I should be mad, but if I had a runaway child, I would kill anyone that stood or helped them," Merrell continued.

My face heated, and not because of my mother's overprotective antics.

"I'm sorry, Merrell. I was only supposed to be gone for a day at the most, but..." I paused, debating whether I should tell them the truth or just a half-truth. "I—If I tell you, then you can't say a word, Merrell. Promise me?"

Merrell cocked an eyebrow at me.

"Okay," Merrell said, painstakingly slowly.

"Listen, Merrell, I, um, I found my mate, and he's a shifter." They placed a hand over their mouth as they muttered, "fuck." Using my hair to hide my heated face, I continued. "I need to borrow a bottle or two of deodorizer, please? I need a backup. Since I won't be able to be with him every day."

"Kaydian—what do you mean... never mind, I'll get you it. The less you tell me, the better. Hold on a minute, and don't move from this room," they urged.

Merrell's curls dropped from the hair tie as they shook their head. They went around the counter and produced five small bottles with the translucent purple solution filled to the brim. I didn't have enough time, but I thanked them profusely. Merrell finally let me go after repeating that they were sorry for the hundredth time and giving me some food for Greyson. When I slipped out the back door, I heard Merrell whisper low enough for only me to hear, "And please, for the love of us all, take a shower before you go back home. You smell like you were playing with a pack of dogs!" I cringed.

Using the portal again to get back to Greyson was more taxing than it should have been. The sun's bright orange glow almost disappeared in the sky. When I opened the door and handed the bottles and the food to Greyson, he looked relieved. He had changed out of his clothes and was in bed.

"Sorry, I had nothing else to do, and I didn't know how long you were going to be gone," he said, dropping his colossal frame onto the small bed. He wasted no time digging into the food. "Thank you for the food."

I hadn't had the heart to tell him my stomach had been growling for the past hour.

"You're welcome, Grey." Clearing my throat. "I think it's time for me to face the music. I probably won't be back until the morning...and yes, I will bring you extra food—"

"And maybe something to read or whatever."

"Yes, of course."

My foot tapped the creaky floor, rolling my neck. I placed a chaste kiss on his lips and told him goodnight. Right before I exited the shed. I made sure he knew not to step outside. And for extra measure, I locked the door again with my magic. I couldn't have Greyson wander around. Especially at night, Seraphina might mistake him for a midnight snack.

I thought about my emerald jumpsuit and my magic wrapped around me, cleaning me and removing the old clothing. My green aura swiped around me, washing off Greyson's scent.

My heavy body padded through the pathway. I can only hope it's almost over. Just the thought sent a small bolt of energy through me. I have my speech and my apology recited and ready to regurgitate. By the time I approached the kitchen door, a warm sensation filled me, pushing through the warm, decadent smell of the peach cobbler and gumbo filled the large kitchen. Closing my eyes, I inhaled the familiar rich scents. Pots and pans had stopped rattling as the staff in the kitchen became quiet. My eyes opened, and all seven of the staff were staring at me like I was hallucinating. I felt like I was an alien that just landed on Earth.

I cleared my throat, causing the staff to fumble and avert their eyes.

"Hello, why is everyone so shocked to see me?" I said joyously.

Chef Dubois was the first to answer.

"We didn't know that you were coming back home…We—"

"We never expected you to come back, Your Highness. But we will work on a plate for you." Mary said, cutting off Chef Dubois, jumping as she started fixing me a plate. "You should go to your room, and I'll bring your food up."

"Go to my room…and eat…Do you want my mother to have my head?" I said, astounded that Mary, of all people, would suggest that idea.

What is wrong with them?

The one time I tried to eat in my room, my mother placed a spell that made anything perishable that entered my room rotten in mere seconds. I learned my lesson that day and never repeated it again.

"Just bring the food to the dining room. I know my mother is still eating."

Not waiting to hear another preposterous word from the staff, I bolted from the kitchen and sped walked to the dining room. If I hurried up, I could eat and finally get a good night's rest in an actual bed. I missed my bed and my bathroom, silly, but just the thought of taking a bath in a real bathtub had me weeping for joy.

I stopped mid-stride when I entered the dining room. Everything was the same as I left the grand room. The walls were the same colors. The dining table was the same. My parents were seated in their typical seats, except for my mother's lasered eyes that bore a hole in my face. Her arms crossed with a frown the size of Texas on her face that became even more prominent when I walked into the room. The brown hue of her skin turned a deep shade of red. If I knew anything about my mother, she was beyond furious. And by the way her dimples deepened when she clenched her teeth, she was going to kill me. My father just stared at me. His brown eyes bounced between the strange woman at the table and me until they finally landed on me. With a nervous smirk on his face, he tucked his hands underneath the table even though we could all hear his hands rubbing together.

But it was the girl who was sitting in my seat that was out of place. Her deep brown skin glowed. She had a short straight bob and a pink kaftan dress, and she was beautiful. My feet shuffled, adjusting to their stares.

"Mother...Father," I said, slightly bowing, and headed to my seat. "We should talk."

"About what?" My father said, swirling the ice and, what I assume, Fae wine.

Right.

I stood at my seat where the strange lady sat. Unmoved. Clearing my throat, I hoped she would take the hint to get out of my seat. But her brown eyes just stared up at me from her seated position like I was a stranger. The nerve of this girl.

"Excuse me, but this is my seat, the Royal princess," I said in my most pleasant voice. I was not the one to force my title down people's throats, but this seemed to be the time to do so.

"Jaqueline can stay seated. She's been in your spot for a week now. So, she shouldn't change because you came back." My father coolly said, but the words left my cheeks burning as if my father had slapped me. My mother stayed silent. Her head was still glued straight, as if I hadn't walked into the room. My chin trembled as I made my way to the seat next to Jaqueline and sat down.

Pathetic! I must admit. But what was I supposed to expect? My mother trusted me to take the throne, and I've ruined it.

Mary hurried in with my plate. She looked around the tension-filled room and fled. Most likely formulating the gossip she will spread amongst the staff already. And I would be damned if I hadn't wanted to run behind her.

I wished I had taken her advice.

We sat in total silence as I picked around the plate. Not hungry as I was before I walked in. The soft rhythm of the instruments mimics my breathing. No one uttered a word while I ate the now lukewarm food. Everyone's faces were glued to their plates as they ate. Ignoring the big intruder to their dinner. *Me.* I guess I should count on my blessings. Maybe I could stay silent until she leaves, and then I can try to make this situation right. A win for me. That was until my mother's fists pounded on the table, sending the other side of the large table and some of the table decorations into the air. Lights flickered with my mother's magic right before the heavy wooden table landed on the floor with a loud boom that ricocheted throughout the large room. Dishes clattered to the floor, leaving food scattered everywhere. Her magic stifled the air, causing Jaqueline to choke on the thickened aura.

"For over three weeks, you've been gone! And you waltz right in here like everything is okay. Not an apology or an explanation," my mother yelled. The vein in her neck extended, and her tiny hands gripped the edge of the table for dear life. I've never seen my mother this mad enough to yell at me in front of a guest. The poor dinner staff who stood off into the corner shook as he remained in his position against the wall.

"I'm disappointed, Kaydian. I've raised you better than this..." my mother said, pointing a long finger at me as she rebuked me in our royal language.

She didn't need to use magic. Her words cut me deep, dragging the air from my lungs. Biting into my lip was all I could do from sobbing in front of everyone in the room.

"I'm truly sorry, Mother. It was only meant to be for a day or two." Easing the pain in my throat, my hand found my comfort spot on my wrist. It's a miracle I don't have scarring from it. "Do you mind if we talked in private?"

"You can speak in front of your sister," my father said as he blotted the wine with his napkin.

"Excuse me. I don't think I heard you correctly, Father," I repeated, shocked.

"I'm Jaqueline. Your sister," she said in a silvery tone, bravely holding out a hand for me to shake. My eyes ogled it as if she just told me she was from a different planet, which could very much be true.

This situation was a conundrum, and I couldn't decide if I was going mad or if this was a sick joke. My chest trembled as it worked its way up to my mouth. And I couldn't help but throw my head back and laugh. Guffawing, the sound bounced around the room, holding my sides as a stitch sent my arms, hugging my stomach soft.

"Is she mad?" I asked, wiping the tears from my glassy eyes. Jaqueline's hand faltered as her mouth twisted into a frown.

"Your sister was brought here to fill in your role since we thought you had fallen deep into the curse and ran away," my father said, avoiding my mother's murderous stare. Her hands never unwrapped from the edge of the table.

Rage filled me. The small salad fork, the only thing that survived the crash, cut into my fleshy palms. The corner of my mouth twitched. Never show your anger, Kaydian! As the hair on my arms stood, my magic skimmed the surface, waiting.

Taking several deep breaths, talking myself down from the ledge. I turned to my mother to follow up, but she beat me before I could speak.

"Jaqueline, please see yourself out." My mother finally returned to herself. Her face washed off the tight expression, and in return was my mother's typical unreadable gaze as she picked at the imaginary dust on her coral-colored dress.

"But—" The daft imbecile stuttered. Her angry gaze landed on our father. "You said I could rule. You said she's mad with the curse."

My father averted his eyes, staring at the silver watch I brought him. Rocks formed in the pit of my stomach just knowing he spoke so lowly of me. He didn't even have the decency to look at me as I stared with contempt at his blurry image. Flexing my hand around the fork, which had bent under my manipulation. My magic spilled slightly into the stuffy room, causing my father to choke. The man I called my father, who I once looked up to, could give a rat's ass about me. All the times I defended his name because he was my father, which was a waste.

"That's enough, Kaydian," my mother said, causing me to break away from my intrusive thoughts. My father's wheezes greeted my ears. His eyes were the color of strawberries and the size of saucers. Jaqueline had slipped away from the room. I hadn't realized my mother had moved from her spot until her hand squeezed my shoulder. Rose and cinnamon mingled in the air.

"I'm sorry... Father." I said, which I think I meant. "I lost control of my magic."

My father took a deep, haggard breath, rubbing his throat, "I—It's okay. I think we've both got up on the wrong foot today."

He threw me a shaky smile as his hand slightly trembled. Maybe I was supposed to feel bad for him, but in the dark recess of my mind, it gave me a little thrill knowing I paid him back for humiliating my mother and me. The unmitigated gall of my father to pin his indiscretion on me. Dark, reddened shade lingered on the tips of his short, pinned ears.

"So, enough procrastinating, spit it out," my mother demanded, waving her hand in the air, forgetting about her choking mate. "And tell me everything because for the life of me, I couldn't imagine *you* would leave for weeks without a guard or a word to anyone. Not even Delphine! I was worried sick about you."

Tucking my hands underneath the table, holding them, so no one could see how they trembled. Stretching inside my chest, my magic felt content with what little freedom it had. It took me a moment to tell my mother about my time in California and Greyson while omitting the shifter part and his name. Of course, I didn't need her to figure out what happened on her own.

My mother, who was the principal of indecipherable, looked dumb-founded. Her red cherry lips hung open as she sat wide-eyed, hanging onto each word that spilled from my mouth. She probably thinks I'm a completely manic person. My father's shoulders slumped as he tugged on the white sleeves of his shirt. This might have been the longest I've seen him this quiet. Ten minutes later, my mouth dried out from speaking for so long that a comfortable silence fell upon us.

"You found your mate?" My mother was the first one to break the silence. Her arms wrapped around me, enveloping me in her warmth. "I'm so happy for you, my moon. I guess you needed the time away."

All I could do was smile. My poor mother would never think that if she knew the truth about Greyson.

"Of course, mother. Everything is falling into place." My voice strained as I tried to keep up my imposter smile.

"Well, I guess better late than never," my father said, getting up from his seat. He was standing next to my mother. "Kaydian, I'm sorry for jumping the gun. I was thinking about you and your mother's legacy—"

"You never had faith in me before. So, I wasn't holding my breath on you, father," I said.

"Kaydian..." My mother's voice was soft-spoken as she pleaded.

"Mother, he didn't even care enough to wait until I got back before he dragged his bastard here to take my spot," I choked out. Turning to my father, I continued, "We may be witches, but we have feelings. And I'm tired of not being protected. I would expect that from a common witch, but from my father—"

Shaking my head, "I know that everything has been about the curse lately, but you've written me off without even trying. I think that's what hurts the most. That I'm just another expendable person on your power trip."

"I never meant to hurt you, my little princess," my father sighed heavily. Dark circles decorated his eyes. "We all make mistakes, and I'm sorry you felt that I abandoned you for Jaqueline. My intentions were never to hurt you but to give us another option. I hope you can see that I was just thinking about the coven."

His words went down hard as I tried to digest them. "Mother, why would you even entertain this plan?"

My mother's mouth opened before she closed them shut. Her emerald eyes scanned the room before they landed on me. Sadness dripped from those gems when she said, "In my moment of doubt, I thought you left us. Jaqueline was presented to me, and she had no one. So, she would be easy to bend without there being anyone to influence her besides us. It was a foolish mistake on my part. I wasn't thinking when I agreed to it. For that, I apologize because I would never hurt you, my emerald moon. I love you."

And maybe I was foolish as well, because I forgave my mother at that very moment. "I want her gone, though. As soon as possible."

My father, who had poured himself another glass of Fae wine, said, "Kaydian, your...Jaqueline has no family left. Evie and Urick need more help at the Inn. Why don't you allow her to work so you can keep a close tab on her?"

I do like the sound of having to watch her clean puke off of the floor. Something about Jaqueline on her knees scrubbing the putrid puke and piss from the drunks off the floor warmed the cockles of my heart.

"Fine. She can work in the Inn as that's it, Father."

My father nodded. His presence used to bring me joy, but now all I can see are the fine cracks in his charm. It was a damn shame, was all I could say.

My mother, who was rubbing my back. Sniffling, she said, "I think we've all had a long day. And I, for one, am just happy you're alright and that you could make your way back home to me in one piece."

"It's okay, you're right...we've both had an extremely long day," I said, dodging my father's attempt to hug me, to pacify me. Leaving his arms splayed out in the air, hurt had the nerve to show up in his large brown eyes. He really thought his excuse was acceptable. It was as if I was viewing my father for the first time—only this time, I could see through the cloud of bullshit and empty words that surrounded him.

"But I wanted to let you know. I'm back, and although you may not believe 'I'm ready,' I will earn your trust again. I've tried to hold off the inevitable, but this trip was exactly what I needed to see that I was stupidly ignoring my destiny. Our beloved Youna has never steered us wrong, and it's time for me to put my full support into leading our people." Stopping, I laid a hand on my mother's cheek, swiping the tears that soaked her skin. Those gems swam in a red sea as she gazed back at me. "I'm ready, and there's no turning back now."

The warmth from my mother's arms, coupled with her scent, greeted me like a warm welcome home. Stuffing my face into her curls reminded me I was where I belonged, and the only thing that mattered was to make everything right. My mother broke our embrace, planting kisses around my face, which made me want to complain, but I let her have this moment. Plus, her toothy smile had me mirroring hers. I missed her. Even when she was a thorn in my side, I would take that over anything any day.

"I'm going to bed now," I announced when she finally let me go. Turning on my flat, I was prepared to leave when my mother's question stopped me in my tracks.

"So, when are we going to meet your mate?"

"Oh, I'll have to coordinate a time for you to meet?" I replied hurriedly.

"Okay," she said, watching me with her keen eyes. "What's his name?"

"And what does he look like? Maybe I know his family?" My father picked up from my mother's last question.

Lies, lies, lies...

And ones I didn't quite think of until this very moment. Shuffling on my feet, I did the only thing that came to mind.

"Tomorrow, I'm longing for a hot bath and to sleep in. Goodnight, Mother...Goodnight, Father." I yelled as I turned on my heels and fled the dining room with my mother calling after me.

All the way to my room, I couldn't stop thinking about how I would make this lie work.

Chapter 25

Kaydian

"Rise and shine, Princess Kaydian!"

Moaning, I turned onto my stomach, covering my head with my pillow and my comforter thrown over me, locking out the intruder. The scent of fresh lavender that Ms. Kincaid normally sprayed onto my pillows and sheets filled my nose—hoping whoever would get the point and leave before I turned them into horse manure. Silence greeted me as my eyes drifted closed, snuggling into the warmth of my very much missed bed.

Peace!

...And quiet until the pillow was forcibly removed from my head, taking my headscarf with it. My black curls framed my face like the polka dots on my sheet set. The comforter was next to go, leaving me shivering against the cool room temperature as the metal clanking sound of my curtain made the hair on my arms stand. Streams of the bright sunlight burst through my window, causing me to wince against the abrasive light.

"You've been gone for over two weeks. You had enough sleeping in for the next six hundred years." Ms. Kincaid said, buzzing around the room and pulling out clothing for me to wear. "I have a lot to catch up with you. So, I hope you enjoyed that brief vacation."

Vacation? I wish. If being in the middle of nowhere with a pack that hated you was a vacation, then I would rather have stayed home.

"Good morning, Ms. Kincaid." I stood and wrapped my arms around her thick frame. "I've missed you, too. What things do I need to complete today?"

"Well, for one, it's not mornin'. It's actually afternoon since it's a little after twelve!" She bustled me along into the bathroom, where her magic had already started my morning bath.

Oh Youna!

"What do you mean, noon?" I asked. My stomach churned faster than Ms. Kincaid as she flew around my room, gathering clothes for the day. All while I sat on the edge of my bed with a handful of my nightgown stuck in between my hands, I worried about Greyson. He must be starving.

"Come on, Princess. Let's get to it." Ms. Kincaid shooed me off into the bathroom across the hall.

Bathed and dressed for the day, we made our way down the staff stairs to the kitchen, causing Chef DuBois and Clarissa to go scurrying around the kitchen like mice. There must be something in their bloodline that makes them skittish. When they both finally got a hold of themselves, they warmed up my favorite blueberry oatmeal and a plain scone. The scent caused my stomach to yell bloody murder until Clarissa sat the food in front of me. Shamefully, I inhaled the food into my mouth, thanking Youna I was in the kitchen so my parents and the other staff couldn't see me. They will surely say I've lost my mind.

When I was done, I waited until Clarissa and the Chef were gone to gather a bunch of food from the pantry, dumping them into a bag. With the bag in hand, I cracked open the door, noting Ms. Kincaid was nowhere to be found. Thank you, Youna! As I slipped out the back of the kitchen with about two days of food...well, hopefully, because Greyson eats like he's never seen food a day in his life.

Sprinting through the small path, I reached the small shed in no time. Absentmindedly, I opened the door without knocking to see Greyson naked as the day he was born with his hand wrapped tightly around his hard dick. I dropped the bag on the floor. Try as I might, it was a beautiful specimen, as my rapacious eyes took it all in. The stuffy air mixed with Greyson's heady scent made me wet my bottom lip. The throbbing in my slick folds made me clasp my thighs together as I fought the urge to jam my hand down my pants.

Greyson cleared his throat. "I-I'm sorry I dreamt about our night together and...woke up...needing some help." His voice strained as he flushed red.

He's so adorable when he blushes.

My mouth dampens as I amble over to him. I was only supposed to drop the food and books off for him, but I would be a bad mate if I didn't lend him a hand... or mouth. I think so as I used two fingers to push him onto the queen-sized bed.

"That's okay, my sweet Greyson. I'm going to help you with your problem." My voice sounded thick as I hiked up the bottom of my red dress and straddled his sculpted frame. His steel rod nestled against my soft stomach. "If you want me to, that is?"

Greyson's Adam's apple bobbed, and my mouth watered at the thought of running my tongue along the protruded bump. A finger trailed down his bare chest, stopping an inch before his thicket of curly black hair. A thin sheen already coated his length as more of the clear goodness bubbled at his bulbous tip. Greyson shuddered as I wrapped my hand around the thick base of his dick.

"Yes or no, Greyson?" I asked, my free hand twirling some of the hair near the base of his cock. Greyson's hip bucked as a moan slipped from his lips.

Greyson's breath came out as shaky as he did when we first had sex, "Y-Yes."

Not wasting another second, I shifted my drenched panties, exposing my dripping folds. My finger swiped the small pool of cum from Greyson's shaft, sticking it into my mouth. A soft moan seeped out of me when his sweet, tangy taste exploded on my tongue. He tasted better than the peach cobbler I had last night—actually ever, if I could think straight. But the horny haze fogged my brain. The warm air licked at my dampened pussy, causing a slight shiver to rake through my body.

"Do you want me to—"

"No, let me," I demanded. "Play with my breast until I've soaked your dick."

Greyson's black pupils consumed his amber iris, leaving it pure black. He placed his large hands over my tender, heavy breast, palming the sensitive tissue with his warm flesh. My eyes shuddered close as my hand traced the tightly corded muscles in his arms until my small hands covered his large ones. Molding mine to his as I showed him how to please me. How to tease the tender breast to make me creamier. Greyson and I pinched and kneaded the sore nubs, pulling small moans caught in my throat. His whimpering moans were my guide as I ground my swollen clit against his leaking dick. A picture of us danced across my black lids of how I envisioned our first time together would have been. Each stroke of my clit on his shaft caused a tiny lightning sensation to shoot down my spine and into my dripping pussy. As I imagine him holding me down to the bed, his hand firmly latched onto the tender muscles of my neck. A stuttered moan escaped my lips, causing my hips to buck against his hardened flesh. My punished neck screamed for mercy as Greyson's heavyweight sunk us deeper into the bed. If only he could...

"Kaydian! Please!" Greyson begged, knocking me out of my dream Greyson.

A hazy gaze greeted me once I opened my eyes. My breath grew ragged, and my heart pounded in my chest. All I could do was nod as my hand found his now reddened hard cock covered in my juices. We were both a wet, sweaty mess. Gripping him wasn't easy as my small hand couldn't fit around him. Dammit! I thought.

"Grey, take even deep breaths and push yourself not to cum until I do. You think you can do that for me, baby?"

Greyson nodded. A lazy smile stretched across my relaxed face as I positioned him at my entrance. After everything I've gone through, I needed this like I needed air. A trail of fire laced my veins as my magic tore through me, stopping in my weeping pussy. Greyson lacked length but more than made up for it with the width. Inch by glorious inch, I dragged myself down his thick cock, stretching the tender flesh of my walls until our heated flesh touched. Greedily, my magic slipped out, encasing Greyson in my green hue. A light shudder rambled through my body as the ache between my legs pushed me to move.

In the back of my mind, I knew I had no time for this. I had a mission. I had duties, but I didn't care as I raised myself all the way to the tip of his cock and plunged myself to the base. A jolt of pleasure pooled in my lower stomach, making me itch to get him deeper inside me. Greyson's rugged moans sent a silver of painful pleasure to my engorged clit. His thick length glided and hit the soft, sensitive spots that made me grind myself against him, yelling out words I would be ashamed of saying out loud.

Manic would be the word I would describe how I must look as I rode him like one of my stable horses, fast and hard, like it was my last day on earth. The control of my magic slipped as it leaked out, coating the room and shaking the shed when I moaned. Quicken breaths filled the room as some of my magic fulfilled my needs, wrapping around my delicate neck. Squeezing to my longing. My heart hammered to the beat of our wet bodies connecting. Sweat dripped onto him, creating little pools on his stomach and cooling his burning body. My back arched as I sped up my pace, chasing the hot, piercing sensation. Leaning forward, I dug my nails into Greyson's wide chest, dragging them down his chest, leaving my mark on him. My knees wobbled as black spots decorated his beautiful face, as my needy pussy clenched down onto him. "Shit," I yelled as I felt a smile decorate my face. Falling on top of Greyson, his hips bucked up.

"Good boy," I muttered. My voice was thick with content.

As I rolled off of Greyson, I pushed my long, heavy curls that were glued to my face with sweat away. My straggled breathing came out in quick puffs, but the smile on my face couldn't contain the glorious sweet rush throughout my body. After what seemed like five hundred years, I couldn't help the silly smile on my face.

When I turned to Greyson to continue thanking him for giving me my first orgasm—he, for better or worse, clung to the sheets for dear life. My stomach dropped at the thought I might have hurt him.

"Greyson, are you okay?" I asked, worrying my bottom lip.

He took a minute. His eyes were glued to the ceiling.

"I-I'm okay," he said, getting up and going to the closed-off bathroom to get the buckets. "Do you mind filling these up? You forgot some of us can't use our magic."

Greyson chuckled, but it sounded strained and strange. Red lines from my nails stood out against his reddened skin as he looked everywhere but at me. Setting the empty buckets down, my magic filled them up to the brim. He placed them back into the small room while I sat on the now cold bed with my legs drawn to my chest. The warm euphoria of my post-orgasm quickly turned into hot coals of shame. I was supposed to be reveling in my first orgasm, but something didn't quite feel right.

How could I celebrate when Grey seemed so disgusted by me?

Greyson held a handout for me, and I took it. He might have been fooling himself if he didn't think I felt the slight tremble of his hand. After we washed up and doused ourselves with the deodorizer, changing out of our sweaty clothing, I magically repaired my messed-up outfit. Since I knew Ms. Kincaid would wear me out if I came home with different clothing.

"...Have I hurt you?" I asked. The question had been nagging me since our first night together.

Greyson shuffled his feet. "Was I that obvious?"

Should I bite my tongue and lie? Or be truthful?

"You won't even look at me," I said, thinking it was better to tell the truth.

"I...just," The bed creaked under Greyson's weight as he sat down on the edge. "Please don't hate me, but I always wanted my mate to be a virgin so we can go down this path together...you like things that make me uncomfortable...I don't want to put my hands around your neck, and if I'm being honest, I didn't like how aggressive you were."

That sinking familiar feeling reared its ugly head. What does that make it three times in a month that Greyson has judged me? My cheeks burned as my magic course through my veins like wildfire. Never once had I been ashamed of exploring my sexual needs until I was standing in the middle of this room with Greyson's eyeballs glued to the floor. The new clothing became heavy, weighing down my soul. I wanted to crawl out of my skin and my magic.... I wanted to skin him alive for disrespecting me.

Royals were always taught that our magic could never hurt their kindred spirit, but as I stood by the bathroom door, my magic clawed in my veins, waiting to pick him apart. None of this made any sense to me as a fated mate. We couldn't kill each other directly. My mouth opened to say something...anything when I heard my name being called from outside of the shed.

"Princess Kaydian!" Ms. Kincaid's voice boomed throughout the wooded area.

Her voice was like cold water being thrown over a fire. I should be upset by the intrusion, but right now, I welcomed it. My body gladly pushed itself into overdrive as I sprayed another layer of the deodorizer and scurried out of the tension-filled shed, making sure to magically lock the door, plastering on a bright smile even though my insides were filled with jelly.

Ms. Kincaid's heavy footsteps were coming from the cleared pathway.

"I'm coming!" I yelled out, not wanting her to make it to the shed, meeting her halfway down the pathway.

She placed her hands on her hips, a frown placed on her face. "There you are...you're as slippery as a fox. I left you for two seconds, and you were gone."

"Sorry, Ms. Kincaid. I was feeding Sera and Luc. I've missed them."

Ms. Kincaid's brown eyes narrowed as they roamed over my face, hoping to catch me in my lie. Which, to be fair, was only a partial lie. Honestly, she was being too strict with me. I came back willingly.

I continued, "...but now that I'm done, I will head to my enchantment room for the day."

"I will check on you throughout the day then—" she said as I cut her off.

"No need!" I said before she could finish. "I have to catch up on some old royal readings."

I didn't give her a chance to respond as I jetted out of the pathway. When I turned back, she stood with her hands on her wide hips and her lips pursed. Slipping into the kitchen, which was empty for once, I hid in the pantry as Ms. Kincaid came waltzing into the kitchen as Clarissa entered from the staff hallway.

"Did you see the Princess?" Ms. Kincaid asked her. Clarissa flushed a deep red as she shook her head no. "That girl will be the death of me!"

Ms. Kincaid left Clarissa in the kitchen to tend to the dishes. With her back turned towards the pantry, I slipped out of the large storage and out the door. I craved to see my best friend and if I knew my mother, she'd probably have to work overtime just to meet my mother's demands.

I voicelessly spoke the transformation spell.

Impatiently, I hadn't waited until the green aura of my magic wrapped around me, warming me, breaking the structure that made me who I was. The glint from the light hinting at a window drew my attention as I peeped at my reflection. Pale blonde curls, big blue eyes, and an even paler skin to match. Shit! I was Del's twin. I can already hear her high-pitched laugh from here.

I definitely will change back when I get to her house.

Walking through Tou-sin square, it took me longer than expected as I stopped to buy Del's favorite, Creole Pralines. My mother kidnapped — borrowed the only human in the world to make them, casting an incantation to rid him of his human memories except on how to make these delicious candies. Poor fellow doesn't even remember how to talk. He just nods with a smile plastered on his face.

Fifteen minutes and a half bag of my Pralines later, I stepped foot into the dirt path that broke off into two sections. Right side to the barn and the left to Del's home. The farmhouse was an old, weathered gray-colored barn with enough stalls for over two dozen animals. Someone had to be attending to the animals since they were all out in the pen that covered almost an acre of land. But no one was around, and I honestly didn't want to run into Del's parents right now. They would probably tell my mother, and that would be another thing she would harp on. Besides, I'm dying to see my best friend so I can spill everything to her and not Bernadette.

The Pourciau home was a small blue house that Del, her parents, and her kid brother lived in since we settled here in Houston. Del's mother loved to collect items from the human world and showcase them on their porch for everyone to see. You could find everything from string lights to a wooden pergola. Their home was far enough not to hear the commotion at Tou-sin, but close enough to be caught coming out this way. But they liked it that way.

Heading to the side of the home, away from the barn, I changed back to myself. No need to scare Del any more than I would since I was ducking and peeping into her window, which was towards the back of the house. Thankfully, I was tall enough to see that Del was lying down on her blue bed. Her long blonde lashes fluttered as she slept. Knocking on the window only made my sleeping best friend turn her cheek the other way. Shit, I guess I'll just have to go through the front door.

Rolling my eyes, I turned to leave when I ran into a soft wall with a soft humph.

"Ah, so the rumors are tru'. The princess is back in town...but for how long? That's the question."

Mr. Pourciau stood before me in his farming overalls that were only buttoned up on the side. His pale skin in which Del inherited, was sunburnt with freckles all over his portly body. Hazel eyes, bald, and barefoot, which was normal for him because, *"he felt more connected to the earth, I reckoned."* He would say in his thick country accent.

"Mr. Pourciau, I'm happy to see you. Glad you still look only a hundred." I said, knowing good an' well that'll get him on my good side. "I was just stopping in to see Del, but she's asleep."

"Huh...Why didn't you just go through the front door?"

Pushing my curls over my cheeks to hide my embarrassment.

"Well, old habits d—"

"Aht! Aht! I was over at the castle this mornin' when your mother mentioned to keep an eye out for you."

Of course, my mother would get to the Pourciau's first.

"Right." Clearing my throat. "Can I see Delphine since I'm already here?"

Mr. Pourciau folded his thin arms, resting them on top of his potbelly while cocking his head.

"I will promise...one of my father's Fae wines. If you kept this between us?" I said with my hand held out to seal the deal.

Mr. Pourciau's pensive golden eyes stared at me. It felt like he was waiting for me to say, "Gotcha!"

"Deal!" He pushed his calloused hand into mine, sealing the deal. "I can't turn down an entire bottle of Fae wine. Bless'd be Youna! I can't wait."

His wide body all but gloated to the front door as I followed behind him with a smirk on my face. Mr. Pourciau was just like Del, sweet but a little too free. As soon as he opened the door, I flew past him, down the narrow hallway with their wall of black and white photographs. Bursting through the door, I leaped onto her bed. Del moved, but not fast enough. So, I placed my hand beside her small body and shook the bed until she rolled over rubbing the sleep out of her eyes.

"What in tarnation..."

When she opened those blue eyes, she broke out into a smile as she threw her arms around me. Burying herself deep inside my curls.

"I hate you so much!" She said, sniffling into my hair. "You left me…"

"I know, and I'm sorry," I said. Soothing her by stroking her back. "I'm a terrible friend for leaving the way I did. I can't take it back, but I can promise you I won't ever leave you again."

Pulling away with a chaste kiss to my cheek, Del's blue eyes were red-rimmed from her tears. My hands held hers in mine as a lazy smile graced my face. It seemed like an eternity since I last saw her.

"I'm glad you're slacking off during the day now."

Del snorted and smiled. "The Queen showed us mercy after she realized I wasn't in on your plan. Kaydian…I've never seen your mother like that before. The whole town went into 'high alert'. Every corner of Tou-sin village said you had fallen early into that dreaded curse and had gone mad. That's why you never came back."

Del paused, shifting her eyes before bringing them back to me, "Some of the Royals kids visited Tou-sin and told people about…the events of the party."

"I guess they had their full of gossip for the rest of the year, huh?"

Del responded with a weak half-smile.

"So…" she said, raising her blonde eyebrows. "Are you going to keep me waiting? I want every detail and it better be a good enough reason for keeping yourself away from me for so long."

A bitter acid filled my throat before I swallowed it down. It's hard to say it out loud. That shame and disappointment were my new bedfellows.

"I found my mate…in the woods of California," I said, letting the news sink in. Del blinked twice before her blue pools settled on pinning them on me. The weight of her stare made me shift on the small bed.

"You found your what?" Del repeated as she fidgeted with the ends of her sleeves.

"My mate. His name is Greyson, and he's a…" I replied. "Different. I'm not sure If I'm ready for someone like him, but I guess I have no choice. The goddesses had finally answered my pleas. So, I shouldn't complain, right?"

Del's sad eyes found mine and said, "You don't sound so happy about your mate."

"It's complicated, Del."

"So un-complicate it, Kay," she demanded.

The words tumbled out of my mouth as I spilled out everything from the past three weeks, except for the mixling secret. The shock of my mate. The disappointment. The humiliation and now shame. Halfway through my ordeal, my shoulders sagged with relief, and my cheeks burned, but I knew better than to hide it from Del. She would be offended if I tried to, and I didn't want to disappoint her again.

"So, this Greyson isn't what you asked Youna and the goddesses for," Del said as she tried to smooth over my bleak disposition. "The more important thing is, how was your...time together?"

Del asked as she turned. A rosy blush crept up her cheeks.

"Parts of me disgust him, Del. At first, I thought I could overlook it or compromise. But it seems the goddesses won't have it that way. I feel ashamed...It almost feels as if I did something dirty."

We sat in a deafening silence, letting the words sink in between us. Drawing my watery eyes to Del, her face flushed pink with her mouth agape. Did she find me off-putting as Greyson does? A slight chill swept through my body, causing me to shiver. Del's hand squeezed the one that was still in hers.

"I'm sorry..." she said, casting her eyes downward to our entangled hands. "I-I couldn't even imagine how it must feel to find your mate and..."

Del paused, biting into her thin bottom lip. Never in our twenty years of friendship had I ever seen Del advert her gaze. Almost as if she couldn't look at me. It was as if I swallowed my sword whole as the heavy weight sank into my stomach.

"...and for him to be a worthless bag of pig shit. How dare he rob you of your first orgasm! *The fucking leech!* He doesn't have a clue on how to please someone like you. For over twelve years, I watched you wait and begged Youna for your mate to come. All of those nights, you've cried until you couldn't do anything but fall asleep. Listening to some of those gossiping witches who had nothing better to do with their worthless, pathetic lives. They have it WAY to good if you ask me. I wish I could set them all on fire and burn them." Del paused, looking at my bulging eyes. I could only guess she knew how shocked I was. "Kaydian, you deserve better. You deserve someone who's going to make sure your needs are met and not shame you for being you. No one should have that power, not even you."

I loved my best friend to the underworld and back.

Finally, Del returned her attention back to me, and my body relaxed, knowing she wouldn't see me as repulsive and paraphiliac. Something lay in those robins blue eyes as I tried to decipher it, but I hadn't needed to because one minute Del was staring at me, and the next, her lips were on mine. Her small, soft lips touched mine, and I allowed her to kiss me. Opening my mouth to her, she lapped, nipped, and tasted every part of my palate. My Del has never been shy about being bisexual, and I knew she was lonely, having not found her mate or aligned herself with a common witch. So, I would let her have some intimacy, and if I was being honest, she was a better kisser than Greyson. I've always had a feeling she wanted me to commit to her, but she never pushed it.

Del wrapped her arms around me, pulling me flush against her small chest. Her nipples rubbed against my large breast. Del moaned before pulling back, nipping at my bottom lip as she went.

We sat in a comfortable silence. I had a feeling Del had been waiting a long time to kiss me. If only it were that easy.

"Nothing, huh?" she asked, even though she knew the answer to that. Her face matched the color of her red shirt.

"You and I both know the answer to that...but thank you for giving me one of the best kisses I've ever had since...heck ever." I fixed my frizzy curls that fell loose. "Life would be oh so easy if it was."

Sucking in my lip, "I'm sorry for not stopping you. It was wrong of me to lead you on. I—I just wanted you to have this moment."

Del's small hand landed on mine. "Oh, thank you, my generous queen," she said, bowing slightly.

We both dissolved into a fit of giggles, and for the first time in three weeks, I felt free. If I could bottle this moment up, Del falling onto the oversized bed clutching her stomach and me stifling my laughs, I would. When our laughter finally died down, I squeezed her hand.

"You're going to make one amazing mate for someone one day."

"I know...too bad it couldn't be you. I've always foolishly hoped that maybe if I kissed you, that maybe it would spark something."

"Aht! Aht! We are meant to be...just not in that capacity, which is sad because we would be amazing together. I wouldn't have bothered with Raynaud and Cary."

A deep sigh left me as I shoved my hand under my chin.

"Ah, I'm so sorry, really...but if I had a mate like what's his name... Greyson. I would kill him...start anew or go mad."

Her words made me pause. Del, seemingly not aware of the magnitude of her words, went to use the bathroom. Leaving me in my little tortured world of what ifs.

Quickly, I remembered to ask her about digging up information about Greyson's since her mother knew lots of the Royal Coven secrets.

"Before I forget...would you ask around about Mary Ann Muller? She's a part of the reason I stayed gone."

"Of course, I'll ask around."

Mr. Pourciau had called Del to tend to the animals. Walking outside to the little porch, I watched as Del and her dad trekked across the large farmhouse, smiling and laughing on their way. A wide smile stretched across my face, watching them as they disappeared, but as I made my way home, my mind drifted into a world of what-ifs.

Chapter 26

Kaydian

In the last two days, the castle was in bedlam, and trying to sneak away to Greyson was harder than expected. Especially when my newfound twin, Sir Reid, had all but attached himself to my hip. The brute reappeared after being gone on a personal trip for my mother, only to gloat about his new role, being my extra shadow. Every step I took, he was there. Whenever I wanted to be alone in my room or my enchantment room, I had to get permission from my appointed twin.

It was even more infuriating that he hadn't broached the subject of me being in the Swiftwater camp. Although, when I found him staring at me, I knew he wanted to ask me. It seemed to be on the tip of his tongue, but Sir Reid knew better than to question Royals about personal affairs in front of the staff, let alone me...Even though some stupid part of me, deep inside the dark recess of my mind, wanted him to ask me about it.

Silly, yes, I know.

To top it all off, Greyson was still upset with me. Even though he tried to play it off, his face showed it all. Every hello was met with a tight smile that made those gorgeous brown ones that I love seem distant and tired. Every chaste kiss was met with a slight nod. Not wanting to leave him alone, I bought him books I held dear to me, only to find it cast to the side. But that only seems to make him even sadder than before we arrived. Somewhere inside of me, I knew he probably felt like I was the source of all of his problems. And now I have to add not doing enough to find out more about his mother's death to the list. I have searched through almost every journal from my family and risk asking people who knew the Mueller's about his mother. Some of the older housekeepers I asked would shrug me off with a "She was so smart and too independent." While others pinned me with a confused look upon their deeply wrinkled faces, asking, "Why do you want to know about her?" Every corner I searched, I came up short, which had me questioning if Mary Ann really existed.

I guess tonight, when I finally question my parents, I will get some answers.

Staring at the stark white ceiling as the afternoon sun sank behind the horizon, I heard the frantic shuffling of shoes against my hall's floor. The sound drew a curse from me as I opened my eyes just wide enough to see the person who barged into my room through the slits of my eyes. Instead of Ms. Kincaid bustling into my room, disturbing my little peace, a newly meek housekeeper almost tripped over herself into my room. The housekeeper's black and white uniform was a crumpled mess. I knew she was running behind because if Ms. Kincaid had seen her like this, she would have had a stroke. Her pale skin was beet red as her small hand shook me awake. She didn't need to try hard because my sleepless nap had me tossing and turning, leaving me barely functioning.

Forcibly, I said, "I'm up!" causing the housekeeper to leap back from my bed, stumbling over the edge of my rug before she caught herself.

"I'm s—sorry, Princess Kaydian, forgive me. Ms. Kincaid is attending to the Queen...I mean your mother...A—I was so busy I forgot to wake you up."

A smile graced my face. With my hands up in surrender, I tried to calm her nervousness. "It's okay, no harm done, and it's my fault. I'm sorry. We still have thirty whole minutes before this place is overrun with stuffy old men...what's your name?"

The lady paused. Her eyes shifted between the space over my shoulder as she fidgeted with her fingers with a nervous giggle. Clearing my throat, her brown eyes landed on my face. My eyebrow raised, asking her the question again.

"Oh, sorry, it's Ann, my Princess. Ann Petit, my family, runs the bakery in town."

"Oh, I know your parents very well. I used to sneak into the bakery and steal some of those amazing chocolate beignets." A deep sigh fell from my lips. I could almost taste the creamy chocolate. "I could go for five of them right now."

Ann offered me a bright smile. Her shoulder dropped from their hunch position.

"Yes, my mother always gloated when you came into the shop. I'm glad they were to your liking, Princess Kaydian." She paused. "I'm not as fond as my family about baking. So, it was my decision to work in the castle."

Luckily, the Petit had four other children who were eager to run the shop.

Ann got to work, taking over Ms. Kincaid's job, running my bath, and picking out my green wool dress that fell to my calves. With my hair washed and magically straightened into a low bun, we headed downstairs, following the typical royal event turmoil. Chef Dubois' high-pitched voice carried over the ear-splitting noises of the pots and pans as the staff hustled to prepare the food for the Royal meeting tonight. Clarissa almost collided with me as she shuffled out the kitchen door with the food in serving ware trailing behind her.

How wonderful!

When I got word, the royals, Sir Muller and Sir Cross, wanted to stop by for dinner. The rocks on my shoulder became boulders. My mind raced with foreboding thoughts as I imagined the worst likely outcome. Why in the hell would they want to come and visit out of the blue? I thought about when my mother told me two nights ago. I'd only imagine my father told them I found my mate. They'd probably have taken bets on me if I went crazy and ran off. Didn't they know I was too busy flipping through old books and journals of past Royals, seeing if I could find anything about Greyson's mother?

Why do men like to put their noses in others' business?

Since I avoided going to the shed all day, finding anything to take my mind off of the current state of my "love" life. Just the thought alone made my magic bristle inside my chest. Even now, alone in my sitting room, I wanted to go out to Greyson, and…the cup of Fae wine I poured for myself paused in the air. The dreadful thought crossed my mind every so often after my last visit with Del. She had opened up Pandora's box and didn't even know it.

Not to mention, Red had made a reappearance again, this time speaking his disappointment from between my thighs as he tsk and shook his slightly long red hair, muttering.

"A damn shame," his husky voice said before his sinful tongue slipped inside of me.

My mouth parted as a soft sigh drifted from my lips right before he pulled away, leaving me chasing his mouth with my pussy. He chuckled lightly and continued, "He's wasting my favorite treat. This pussy is made for worshiping. For savoring."

"It—He's not used to being with someone." I panted out, hoping he would return his tongue into my heated core.

"Bullshit. He's all wrong for you," he said from between my legs. The wisp of his breath tickled my drenched pussy as goosebumps appeared over my body. "He made your first orgasm about himself. Greedy bastard. When I find you, there will be no more guessing whether you're satisfied."

I opened my mouth to respond but quickly forgot the words that I was about to form when my brain short-circuited as he replaced his tongue back into my waiting cunt.

The damn bastard. If I hadn't known any better, I would have suspected Red knew everything that was going on.

Imagine going from being without a mate for so long just to having one that couldn't stand you even when you're trying your best. It would be just my luck. Turning the small crystal tumbler to my mouth, draining the purple contents. Ann scurried in with her head bowed, like she couldn't look me in my eyes. I never liked that Ms. Kincaid scared the newer housekeepers so badly that they were afraid to death of me. It ostracized me, making me feel lonelier than I already am.

When she nearly ran out of the room, my intrusive thoughts tried to return as I glanced at the brown grandfather clock that ticked down my freedom. Greyson needed to be deodorized and ready since my mother all but ordered me to invite him to dinner. She couldn't wait to meet the witch that I was fated to. "If only she knew," I said out loud in the empty room.

A deep sigh left me as I maneuvered my tired body from the castle to the tiny shed with my hand clutching the skirt of my dress so that none of the branches and dirt stained the dress. Curse words slipped from my mouth as I sped walked down the path. A sigh of relief left me when I finally made it to the tiny shed with only a small leaf stuck to my dress. Sera and Luc were moved to the coliseum to avoid them making the Royals snacks. I could only imagine Sir Muller willowy, and Sir Cross' portly bodies running to escape, most likely, Sera. I couldn't help but laugh.

"What's so funny?" Greyson asked, causing my laughter to die in my throat.

I hadn't even noticed when I opened the door to the shed.

"Nothing," I replied with a smile. "You cleaned up nicely."

Before my last visit, I stocked the tiny shed with everything he might need. Something to shave his scruffy beard, books, writing tools, and his outfit for tonight. Which was made for him. The brown three-piece suit molded his tall, muscular frame, which was paired with brown penny loafers shoes. His long hair was pulled back into a pony-tail, and his shaky smile adorned his beautiful face. My tongue was thick in my mouth as heat pooled in my stomach. He looks so hand-some. It almost made me forget he made me feel guilty about my sexual needs.

His smile seemed genuine this time. "Thank you, Kay. You look amazing as well."

And now I was smiling like a fool. "Listen, tonight is really impor-tant, Greyson. We could finally get an answer about your mother's death. I know we've talked about this before, but please remember less is more and to stick to our story. You're Morgan James, a lost baron from England. Let me lead—"

"Yes, I know. Let you lead the story because you know how to navi-gate these events," he said dismissively, waving a hand in the air.

"Greyson..." Trying my best to keep the irritation out of my voice. Greyson held his hands up in surrender. His face melted into a smirk as his eyes softened. It will be alright... if not, I don't know what I would do. "Come on, everyone should be already here. Let's change your appearance. We don't need to have any slip-ups tonight. Hopefully, this night can go by quickly."

The corner of Greyson's mouth twitched, but he nodded. Placing a hand on his dimpled cheek, calling and picturing what I wanted to change. My magic curled and...fought against my demand. I could hear Greyson asking if something was wrong, as a fine mist of sweat prickled my forehead. But I ignored it, putting all of my focus on my insubordinate magic until it gave in, curling angrily around his face like it wanted to strangle him but changing his appearance. His narrow brown eyes turned to the color of fog in the morning here in Houston, gray. The shape of his nose and lips changed, making them thinner than before. Last, he and I were able to see eye to eye as I shrunk his size.

Everything will be okay.

We will find something out.

Everything will work out for the best.

I thought to myself as we trekked down the small path with our hands filled with our garments. There will only be six people we have to entertain for an hour or two.

The closer we got to the castle. A frown etched onto Greyson's shell shock disguised face. His head shook, side to side, almost a hundred times, and we hadn't even made it to the entrance yet. My mind wanted to comfort him before we got to the castle, but silence filled the gap in our walk instead. I had to remind myself and my fickle magic that everything would be all right. Before we turned the corner of the castle, my magic washed the dirt off our shoes and straightened our clothing from the wrinkles made by our hands. Grabbing Greyson's hand, giving him a tug along the brick path towards the front door. When we entered the castle, Greyson muttered, "Assholes." Pausing, I wanted to make him take that back, but I decided against it. I'll just have to watch him closer than I thought.

"Ah, Princess Kaydian! There you are. I'm going to have to put a tracking spell on you one of these days." Ms. Kincaid called out, stopping in front of me and Greyson. Her eyes bobbled back and forth between Greyson and me. "Oh, this must be your mysterious mate?"

"Yes, Ms. Kincaid. This is Morgan James." The lie we've practiced rolled off my tongue like it was second nature. As they introduced themselves, I continued, "His father was an old baron from England. Poor

Morgan was living amongst the humans and close to a shifter camp when I found him."

Ms. Kincaid gasped as rings of her white curls danced as she shook her head, "You poor child, Baron James. Don't you worry. You've found your mate, and luckily, she's a royal. So, no more living alone and near those dogs."

Greyson's grip on my hand tightened and trembled as I thanked Youna that he couldn't break my hand. His skin was almost the color of the bright red painting in the hallway. Maybe I was a little optimistic about things going smoothly tonight. Did I jinx this whole night? Hopefully not. All we had to do was last one hour.

"Oh, yes...very dreadful," I said quickly, pulling Greyson along. "See you inside, Ms. Kincaid."

Dragging Greyson down the foyer to the dining room. As we approached the double door arch, I turned to him.

"Listen, I'm sorry for Ms. Kincaid." Seeing him blink back tears made me pause. "It's going to get worse like we prepared the other day, and for that, I apologize to them in advance."

Greyson nodded, which wasn't enough for me.

"Grey—" I said, but he cut me off before I could finish.

"I know, Kaydian." Holding up his hands in surrender. I guess it was too late to question him. The thought of trusting Greyson when he could barely stomach being around me made my hands slick.

I did what I knew best, shrugged it off, and grasped his heated hand. Here goes nothing. Holding my breath while we walked into the all-white lion's den. Everything seemed perfect and spotless. White candles floated just a couple of inches above the Royals' heads, and white décor graced the table, which offset the gold dinnerware. The white walls were trimmed with gold borders, which made the staff's white uniform blouses blend into the walls. There was a mint fragment that permeated throughout the room tonight. A stark difference from the usual citrus notes. If Bernadette were here, she would definitely show up to poke fun at Mother for going all out just for some stick-in-the-mud folks.

"Shit," Greyson mumbled so low, I would have missed it if I weren't standing in front of him.

My mother and the other guests, which included several other coven members, had already been seated. Great! Chatter buzzed around the room while my mother's green eyes sort out mines. She took me in with a wide, toothy grin on her face, then she turned them onto Greyson. With an eyebrow arched, she combed over him, inspecting every detail of him. Those hawk-like eyes settled back on me, with her cheerful smile placed back on her face. I sighed heavily at the fact that I could pass my mother's test.

Standing from the table, everyone quieted down. Her brown skin laminated under her silk green dress. My mother's curls framed her pointy face, making her appear younger than her age.

"Ah, there is the young princess," she paused, the high-pitched of my mother tapping her wine glass with her knife filled the room. Everyone Royal and Royal loyalists turned to us.

"And this must be the next King of Youna, Morgan James, isn't it?"

Greyson, thankfully, played his part perfectly, mostly. His face was unreadable, thanks to the disfiguration incantation. He bowed slightly. "Yes, Your Majesty. It's a pleasure to meet you," he said with his jaw clenched so hard I thought it might shatter.

My father's three-piece suit matched my mother's green dress. The scruffy beard was back as he ran his long fingers through it. Looking around the room, I noticed his "daughter" sitting on the other side of Greyson and I's seats. Her short, dark hair was pulled back into a low bun. The long-sleeved silver dress made her dark skin shine in the dim lights of the dining room. Even though she wasn't royal, there were several men who attended whose eyes never strayed too far from her. Biting my tongue, I chastised myself for giving her a single moment of my time.

Jacqueline turned those hazel eyes toward me and Greyson. Her eyes swept over him just a beat too long for my liking. Her smile made my magic burn under my skin. "Hello, my dear sister. You look lovely tonight. Thank you for inviting me to dinner."

I nodded at Jacqueline before I sat in my seat. If my father wanted me and his bastard to play nice, then he was doing a horrible job at it. She should work at the inn or bar cleaning the puke that lined the floors daily. Not here with the royal coven members in attendance, and surely not close enough to make the hairs on my arms stand.

"Morgan James, our daughter, has spoken highly of you." My father started smiling, even though I wanted nothing but to shove that smile down his throat. Greyson greeted my mother, stiffly bowing to kiss her ring while doing the same to my father.

I'd guess he was paler than a ghost under this mask.

"Princess Kaydian, we all knew you just needed to leave the village to find your mate." Sir Cross said, chuckling. Against the white chairs, he was so bright it strained my eyes. His red trousers with suspenders covered his white button shirt. Sir Cross's hat, tie, and shoes are equally loud as himself. His ring finger was almost the same color as his family's ruby ring. Poor ring!

Was it too early to start grinding my teeth? Probably.

"Yes, even though he's just a baron, your mother, and I thought it would be another Royal...pity." Sir Muller scoffed.

The corners of my mouth twitched slightly. He was a dreadful idiot on the best of days, but today, I wanted to choke him with the canary yellow tie he wore around his neck. It took all of my strength to place the wide, fake smile.

"Well, Sir Muller, it's a pleasure to see you as well. I wonder what happened to Victoria. It's a shame your half-demon daughter couldn't attend." I said sweetly with my smile directed at him. Sir Muller almost matched the white tablecloth. Greyson lightly squeezed my knee.

Some of the coven members humphed their distaste for my joke.

My mother cleared her throat, drawing my attention. Seeing her mouth twitch with just a twinge made my smile more triumphant. Sir Muller's face became as crumpled as his bright yellow suit. I always pegged him as a leech, but I couldn't help but stare at the large golden phoenix pendant that stood out against his suit. Has he always worn it? It was almost as large as his head.

"So, tell us about your family and journey to America, Morgan?" My mother asked. Her soft smile made Greyson strangle my knee. I would lose circulation to my lower leg if he squeezed again.

Greyson gulped. With a shaky smile, he said, "Well, from what I remember of my family. They were the last ones left in the small town of Fordwich. They passed away in our home, and a neighbor, a common witch who just so was moving to America, found me. I didn't have any other family members, so I didn't have any other choices. The gentleman took me with him, and I stayed with him until he went to the underworld. I had been alone for a long time until I went in search for more people like me. That's when I took a trip to Sacramento and found Princess Kaydian in town. She was like a beacon of light that drew me to her and when we touched, I knew we were fated."

My hands were a slippery mess as Greyson told the story we practiced to a tee. Coq au Vin, chicken stew, red Fae wine, and bread were served while Greyson spoke. Turning to him with a smile, I noticed his attention was stuck on the plate of food the staff had served while he spoke. Even though I could mask his appearance, I couldn't mask his feelings.

Hopefully, he knows I've tried my best.

"I'm truly sorry for your loss, Morgan," my mother said. "Hopefully, you guys can make new memories now."

Greyson nodded as he excused himself from the table and made his way out of the dining room to find the restroom.

Jacqueline's lowly snickered as she leaned over Greyson's empty chair. She whispered, "That's some farfetched bullshit if I ever heard."

"Come again? I don't know what you mean." I whispered back.

Jacqueline's smirk deepened, "Oh, my dear sister. You can fool your mother, but I see right through your half-baked lie. What are you hiding, Princess Kaydian?"

Turning to the bastard, she had the nerve to tsk me like a child. Shoving my fist under the table as I gritted my teeth. Greyson stalked back into his seat before I could curse Jaqueline out. The only thing I was thankful for was that no one seemed to have heard her, thanks to Sir Cross.

"James from Fordwich..." Sir Cross said, greedily chewing the stew while he spoke. Little red spots of sauce decorated his side of the table. "I've passed through the town before, but I never knew of any witches, much less a baron that lived there...surely my guards didn't miss your family."

"That's unlike you, Sir Cross. You're always thorough—" my father said, with his thick eyebrows melded together.

"Well, they were shunned by the other families and lived like the outcast witches. They tended to themselves to make sure they didn't draw any attention to their family." Hurriedly, I said, cutting off my father. I could throw this bread at him right now. Greyson muttered, "Right," weakly, vouching for me.

"But that's impossible!" One of the English Coven members gasped. He was almost the color of Sir Cross's ring.

"I agree, father." Jacqueline chimed in as she took a sip of the Fae wine. "Something seems a bit off. Don't you think so?"

My mother and the inquisitive coven member's gazes landed on me…well, Greyson. *For Youna's sake!* I'm going to skin her alive and feed her to Sera and Luc.

Yes, then we can worship in her blood.

Maybe my dark voice wasn't the only one with a murderous strike. Especially when Jacqueline's repulsive soft hand reached around Greyson to pat me on the shoulder as her leech like smile appeared on her face. I swatted her hand away. I'm truly going to enjoy her downfall.

"Alright everyone, no need to cry over bruised egos," my mother said, waving a hand in the air, coming to Jacqueline's rescue. "We don't need to show Morgan the ugly side of the Royals before he gets to the throne."

With that, the conversation turned light around the dinner table. My mother and I spoke about the latest messy gossip from the last weekly town meeting. And I wanted to be interested, but I was too busy kicking Greyson so he could pay attention while keeping my eyes on Jacqueline. Dessert was served, Crème Brûlée, between Sir Cross and Sir Muller, fought over Victoria and Liam about who is better than the next, as they typically do when they are around one another. Of course, my father gloated about my return home. Liam was now attending Grand Central School of Art in New York. I definitely bit a hole in my tongue as the very thought made my teeth grind. He probably doesn't even know the nuance of art. My father caught my sulking face and turned his unwanted attention towards me. Almost coddling me like a child. Since I've been back, he has avoided speaking with me. It was as if I had leprosy. But here he sat, his smile as wide as the Pacific Ocean, telling me to cheer up. It almost made me want not to finish the Crème Brûlée —almost.

Turning to the sulking giant next to me, Greyson had redirected his attention from the plate of food, which was empty, to staring a hole into Sir Muller's narrow head. My mother had been eerily quiet this evening as she sat back with her keen eyes taking us in. I had to nudge him to get him to act accordingly. The staff refilled the wine glasses with the sweet

Fae wine as, one by one, the coven filtered out of the dining room and into our sitting room. The Fae wine mixed with the rocks in my stomach made me nauseous.

I couldn't wait for this night to end.

Greyson's POV

My mood hung over me like a heavy cloud, ready to open up and soak all of us who remained in the dining room. Since I've stepped foot inside of this grotesque castle, my wolf jolted and tugged, begging me to shift. And he almost won when he caught wind of Muller's scent. It reminded me of the rotten food behind the stores of San Claude. When his snake-like eyes connected with mine, mask or not, it was as if he could see beneath the magical veil. Even when the grand witch and her puppet kept speaking to me, I had to remind myself that Kaydian wouldn't approve of me jumping up onto their finely decorated table and coating it with their blood for my mother and my pack. I may not gut all of them, but I will suffice by getting Kaydian's parents and my so-called uncle, who did nothing to help avenge my mother's death.

I should feel bad because, despite everything, they were still her parents. But something deep inside of me made my stomach reel from the knowledge. Of course, I won't utter a word to Kaydian about it. It's just something I will have to take to the grave.

Kaydian grabbed my hand, pulling me up from the stiff seat. We trailed along with her coven members, putting a few members between her murderous parents and us. The goal, as we rehearsed, was to find Sir Muller to ask him about my mother without her parents hanging over our shoulders.

She hoped things would be peaceful while I had my doubts even now, as I pulled at the tight neck of the uncomfortable white shirt. My mind warred with the idea of abandoning the plan. *Coward!* The wolf wanted blood just as much as I.

Luckily, I was the only one thinking, since he would get us killed.

"If you pull me any harder, you're going to rip my arm out of my socket." I hissed into Kaydian's ears as we entered a blue sitting room. It reeked of wealth and dread. And all I wanted to do was to run far away from this castle and these people. One of their staff had lit the wood fireplace, amplifying the orange scent with lavender, which made Kaydian relax as her shoulders, which were pinned to her ears all night, slumped down to their rightful place. She loosened her hand from my arm. Shifting on my feet, I peered around the crowded room where everyone was mingling. When it dawned on me, my mother used to be one of them. Royals, as Kaydian called herself, dancing and grinning in each other's faces while contemplating on whose life they could ruin next. And from my standpoint, I couldn't view Muller.

"Do you see him?" I asked.

On her tippy toe, she whispered into my ear, "Okay, remember our plan, Greyson? We corner and ask him without causing too much attention, okay?"

"Yes, Chief," I replied, saluting her, even with my nefarious thoughts.

I ended up closing my eyes so she wouldn't see me rolling them as a curse word caught on the tip of my tongue. When I opened them back up, I gave Kaydian the biggest fraudulent smile I could muster and nodded. She opened her mouth to most likely give me a piece of her mind, but paused when she spotted Muller, who left the small group and headed out of the sitting room. I could hear her mother calling her from across the room, but she ignored her as she hightailed it out of the room, leaving me in the middle of the killers.

"Greyson, I think he's going to the bathroom or to harass the kitchen staff," she said hurriedly, pulling me with my hand in hers. "He has a thing for Mary, the assistant cook. He's always trying to siphon her away from us."

I grunted in response, slipping out the door as her mother still called us from the back of the sitting room. We rushed down the stretch of hallway, passing the guest bathroom along the way to the kitchen. When we entered, Mary and Ruth, two staff Kaydian pointed out, greeted us, and busted our bubbles. Sir Muller wasn't here. That only meant he was in the bathroom that we passed. I huffed, my new favorite thing to do, as we charged to the bathroom. Only to find it empty.

We missed our chance. I thought as I ran my hand over my face. The sharp points of my nails skimmed over my cheeks. Kaydian sighed deeply. When I noticed we were heading back to the sitting room. My breathing deepened as I tugged at the dampened neck of my dress shirt. My wolf, the other half of my soul, was trying to kill me.

"Are you okay?" Kaydian asked.

"I'm fine!" I snapped back.

My teeth were sore from clenching them, and before I could stop myself, "That was a stupid plan." Tumbled out of my mouth. Which made her pause right before the double door as she turned toward me. Kaydian green eyes turned into slits as she tried to hide the way her balled-up fist by digging them into her thighs. I guess we were both fed up. For better or worse, she was giving her all to help me find answers about my mother's death. I couldn't care enough to say anything. She could do better. And between sitting with devils for dinner and being packed into a room with them, my patience was as thin as Muller's hair-line. With my hands balled up in fists, we entered the room with my fake smile plastered. I started a backward countdown from ten to stop myself from lashing out at him.

I knew I was really taking her kindness for granted, but my mind was filled with nothing but revenge.

When we entered back into the crowded room, Kaydian grabbed a glass of Fae wine for me. Sweat beads formed on my forehead when I pushed back at the pointed tips of my canines. Not that Kaydian cared because she kept moving without me. I swallowed the strain of my problems and caught up to her.

We walked over to Sir Muller, huddled in the corner with his wine glass filled with Fae wine, speaking with two of the English Coven. But between my sulking, miserable mood and my wolf being in a frenzied state, my patience was hanging on by a clear, thin thread. Which snapped, leaving my wolf and me to succumb to our anger.

"Sir Muller," Kaydian said loudly enough for the two coven members to acknowledge me. "Can we speak with you?"

"Of course, Princess Kaydian," Muller responded, excusing the two coven members. I watched them bow to her and excuse themselves to the other side of the room. "I'm all ears. What would you and the future king like to talk about?"

His accent dripped with honey.

Biting her lip, Kaydian was trying to keep her voice low. And it pissed me off to see her make the situation comfortable for him. *Kill him!* My wolf called out from within as he tried to take over.

"Well, Sir Muller, I would like to know about your sister, Mary Ann Muller?" Kaydian asked.

A little too nicely. If you ask me.

Sir Muller turned the color of paper, his mouth agape with his hands balled up in a fist. If this was any other time, I would have some sympathy. His hazel eyes widened to a painful point, and he stuck his trembling hands behind his back.

Sir Muller swallowed, "Oh—" he averted his eye to land in between Kaydian and me. "Right, my sister died tragically at a young age...I think she was like one year old. Our family thought it was best not to even mention her in our family book. It's old news."

Something deep within me snapped. The harsh thud of my heart pierced my ears as my body became hot with rage. The lines between maintaining this "perfectly" planned setup blurred, and I could no longer hear my thoughts. Just the deep ache that had festered even before I met Kaydian. When I found my mother in the crop fields.

"Lies!" my wolf and I shouted. The glass in my hand shattered as the pieces embedded into the soft flesh.

That's all I remembered before I slipped.

Chapter 27

Kaydian

Eyes from across the room made the hair on my neck stand. I placed a hand on Greyson's arm to calm him. Which was a big mistake. He felt hot enough to burn himself alive.

"WHAT DID YOU DO—" Greyson said, but I jumped in front of him, covering his mouth with my hand, muffling the words.

"Grey—control yourself!" I hissed out, trying my best to keep the watching crowd from finding out.

Greyson ripped my hand from his mouth and said, "Kaydian, move or I'll move you myself." Greyson's voice was deep gravelly, which meant he was probably going to shift right here and kill Sir Muller or die right here.

"What in the bloody hell is wrong with that lad?" Sir Cross asked loudly from across the room.

Greyson placed his hand against my arm and pushed me to the side, but I'm nothing if not clumsy by nature as I stumbled. The loud tear filled my ears as the heel tugged at my train until the thin fabric gave up the fight. My skin felt tight, trembling as I found my footing. No words could form in my head at the sheer audacity that just took place, just utter disbelief. Even my feet wouldn't move as I watched Sir Muller, the third powerful coven member, glued himself against the wall while he looked on as Greyson grabbed the lapel of his suit. He sputtered and kicked. Greyson trembled before a strangled cough crept out of his mouth as I figured Muller's magic was finally kicking in after the shock. The illusion incantation flickered for a moment, revealing the golden hue of his eyes as Greyson was close to shifting. Muller whimpered, "Please, your—you're."

Snapping out of my stupor, I called onto my magic to open a portal in the middle of the room. I needed to get Greyson away as the white light brightened the dim room. Before Stepping over to them, I untangled my shoes from my dress, tearing the skirt until the end of the dress looked like a jagged mess. I said, "Please Muller...you're both drunk and confused. Let him go!"

Greyson had a slight blue tint around his lips. And despite everything, I couldn't—wouldn't lose him like this. I begged Muller again. This time he stood taller with death written in those syrup eyes. As he dropped his magic, Greyson fell onto the floor with a thump, causing the group of coven members to gasp.

"Princess Kaydian, I don't know what you're up to, but I never would have thought you would have turned on your own people. I had to bury her and preserve Thetris name. We all have to sacrifice for our coven and family. You, princess, should know more than he does about that. To go against our goddess fate and to..." Sir Muller paused, his pale hand waving the words away. "Don't you know that if you lay with dogs, you will get fleas? I'll keep this mishap between us, but remember this...what's done in the past should stay in the past."

My parents ran over to me with the house guards in tow, closing into our fiasco. The guards pulled Greyson up. His legs buckled and swayed. *Just fucking great!* My heart logged in my throat as my mother's gaze landed on me.

"Are you okay?" my mother asked. Worry coated her voice and her eyes as she hugged me.

"Are you hurt, Kaydian?" my father asked.

Shakily, I nodded. "Yes, I'm okay...I'm fine. We just had a misunderstanding. Right, Muller?"

Sir Muller, who still looked worse for wear, being one of the right-hand man of the strongest coven. His hand dusted off the atrocious yellow coat as if he wasn't shaking just a moment ago. When he looked at us with a twitchy condescending smirk, "Yes, like the Princess said, it was all a little misunderstanding. It seems someone can't handle their wine."

"This is unacceptable behavior of the next King—" my father said, but I cut him off before he could finish. My father threw me a pinched mouth look. One thing my father hated was to be cut off.

"I will take care of Morgan," I said, walking over to him, relieving the guards from holding him up. "He's not used to Fae wine. This was his first time drinking it. I think we can all remember the first time we drank Fae wine."

Some of the coven members chuckled at my words. Probably remembering their drunken first time. Even though I knew Greyson had taken a sip of the wine during dinner and cast it aside without a second glance.

"You're draining your magic, Kaydian. Why don't you take Morgan home?" my mother said, in a whispered tone, with a finely plucked eyebrow raised. My knees buckled as I trembled. If it wasn't for my magic holding me up, both Greyson and I would have fallen on the floor. I opened my mouth to refute her claim, but she beat me to it, holding up a finger to her lips, telling me to be quiet. Her small hand cupped my cheek, warming my already heated body as some of her mear magic poured into me, giving my own a boost from holding the portal open for this long. I wasn't about to complain about it either. Turning with Greyson in my hand and all the coven members watching me as they shook their heads. We entered the portal and landed right inside the cold shed.

And like a flip switch, my mood went from panic to absolute alarm. How embarrassing for us! What if Sir Muller changes his mind? My mother would murder him.

As she should...

Greyson wouldn't even look at me. He just went to the little bathroom and threw up what little dinner he had eaten. Leaving me with the only source of comfort, the light pattering of the rain hitting the metal roof, as I wished it could wash away my burdens. When he returned, he didn't have the decency to even look at me or apologize for pushing me. Even when the illusion incantation dropped, his eyes were still yellow. Greyson undressed as if I weren't in the room. As if I was nothing but a fly on the wall. As if I hadn't just burned a bridge with one of the Royals in the strongest coven.

I was just as stupid as him because there Greyson stood naked...and hard. Those yellow eyes piercing into my soul with not love or desire but with hate. Nonetheless, it made my thighs clench as the seat of my panties became doused with my essence. My heart logged in my throat as he stalked towards me. The only thing I could do was step back until I was flushed against the wall. Something deep inside my love-deprived chest screamed I should leave him and go back to my room, but the need to help soothe him was stronger than my will. I heard him stumble, and the sound of the springs popping in the mattress filled the room. Once upon a time, Greyson smelled like lemons, but now only a rancid smell overwhelmed the room as it singed my nose hairs.

Pulling myself off the icy wall, I ran my hand over my sweat-soaked face. My hand was clammy as my magic tried to calm my chaotic heart. It took five minutes for me to gather myself, fixing the holes my shoes made in the green dress I used to love that now felt like a starch reminder of tonight. Walking into the bathroom, I washed him off of me the best that I could, making sure not to look into the small mirror above the buckets. Not because I wasn't mad at what happened, but because I wanted nothing other than to run back into the room and figure out how to make it right. To make him love me as I did him. I wanted to hug him and kiss the pain away until he looked at me like he did when we first met.

Youna must be having the greatest joke right now.

After I gathered myself, with what little dignity I had left, I fixed my hair and swept my magic down the mangled dress—drying my eyes with the sleeves of my dress. I walked back out there with my head held high and a slight tremble in my chin. Greyson was still lying on the bed, staring up at the ceiling. Still in his semi-shifted form with his blue checkered pajama pants, I had brought for him.

"Greyson..."

"You're just like them, aren't you?" he asked without looking at me. His wolf's voice was rough with disappointment. "We could have killed him! But you stood there. Remove your magic, witch."

Ignoring his dig at me, "Listen, Greyson, I have been trying to learn more about your mother since we got here. I've been asking people and reading the Royal journals. I keep coming up at a dead end." I paused as the pain in my throat became unbearable. "I'm trying to help...but killing Muller wouldn't be in our favor, and I'm really trying my best—"

"You're not trying hard enough then." He paused, folding his arm beneath him like a petulant child. The bite in his voice made me step back. "We could go back and let me shift...put an end to him for once and for all...You're just another fucking witch."

Greyson's wolf was inconsolable, and nothing I could say or do would make him see reason. His words were sharpened by his wolf's hatred for me, a change I hadn't anticipated coming. My stomach turned sour as the rancid lemon scent exuded from his pores. Greyson was a blur as he got up. His long legs connected with the small trash can, sending it across the shed, causing it to ricochet off the wall and sputter until it stopped. Watching him act out caused me to shake my head. Is this how it's going to be from now on? I can't live like this. Something has to change. A wolf with an erratic temperate spelled disaster in the making. I guess that's why the coven made the mixling rule.

Would I have to keep watch of him every time something doesn't go his way?

That made me pause as Greyson flopped back down onto the poor mattress and closed his golden eyes. When he opened them back up, it was back to the soft brown eyes that I loved. "I'm sorry...my wolf... It's becoming harder to control him since we got here. Are you okay?"

The question was harmless, but I still played it safe. "You could never hurt me, Greyson, but you and your wolf had taken more than enough from me tonight. You think this is easy for me? I've spent my whole life waiting for Youna to show me my mate. Only for him to be my people's enemy. I've bent my back for you twice now. You're disappointed in me for keeping you alive another night. Well, fine, so be it. Next time, I will let Sir Muller have his way with you."

My body moved on its own accord as my magic swept out, removing the "offending" magic and opening the door, leaving before the tears I've placed on hold fell. Greyson's heavy footsteps were heard as he repeated, "I'm sorry," chasing after me. But like my heart and magic wanted, I slam the door, hopefully, in his face. Pulling my arms around me, I wondered if this was how my mother felt when my father roamed the world, sleeping with every living thing that walked. To give your all to someone who is clearly not fit to be beside you. My mind drifted to Del, and I wished I could tell her how lucky she was to have the option of picking her mate. She's so lucky.

"Kaydian! Wait." Greyson called from the entrance of the small pathway.

My eyes widened. "Greyson, get back into the shed! You're not covered by my spell anymore, and you've washed off the deodorizer."

"I know, I know…I'm sorry! I just can't let you leave mad at my wolf."

For fuck's sake, "Fine, let's go back inside and talk then," I said, clenching my jaw for dear life. He's lucky it's almost midnight, and everyone has probably gone home. Grabbing his wrist, I moved around him to walk us back to the shed…well that was the plan, but when I turned around, Sir Reid was there standing at the entrance of the clearing. His bulky body leaned onto the massive tree trunk that was almost the same size as him, covered in the darkness from shadows. The only way I knew it was him was that his pale skin stood out against the darkness.

"Princess," Sir Reid's booming voice echoed throughout the wooded pathway. "What's done in the dark always comes to light."

Should I have been surprised that he caught us? No.

Sir Reid was the best of the best. Not even Sir Cross, a secondhand man, could take on Reid. Blinking away the puddles in my eyes, I lifted my teary face to meet Sir Reid's stony one. I tried to keep them at bay, but they got the best of me. His bleak black eyes morphed into something I wasn't accustomed to seeing with him, sorrow. I guess there really was a first for everything as he laid one of his rough hands against my cheek, his hand engulfing my face in warmth while wiping away the tears that fell. Never would I have thought to see the enormous giant be anything but a brute…well, except with Ms. Kincaid. She was his weakness.

"Let go of her!" Greyson said, wrapping a hand around Sir Reid's thick wrist.

"If you don't want your hand to be embedded into your anus, then I suggest you take your fucking paws off of me," Sir Reid spoke lowly, his steel-like voice dropping an octave deeper than normal.

"Sir Reid," my voice was higher than normal. Clearing my throat, "Please, he meant no harm. Greyson is just really overwhelmed right now."

"He should be, Your Highness. This entire area smells like a kennel. I'm surprised Sera and Luc hadn't eaten your mixling." Sir Reid said through his clenched teeth. "What would possess you to even think this would have been a good idea?"

Sir Reid stared at me like I had the answers. Hell, I can't even be sure keeping Greyson as a mate was a good thing. There goes that little stupid thought again. I just want to run away to my room for the night.

"Greyson, please—just stop. I'm tired, and you are as well," I said, placing my hand on his arm. He dropped his hand from Sir Reid's wrist. "Let's go...I'll walk you back to the shed. Just give me a few seconds to talk to Sir Reid, please."

Turning back to Sir Reid, "I understand this isn't appropriate for me as the future queen, Sir Reid. I want this to work...because I...I love him, and I think I can save him—"

Sir Reid shook his head and sighed, "Your Highness. Love isn't about saving someone or trying to mold them into the perfect mixling. I know you were scared shitless from the Royal Party, but that doesn't equate to forgetting your role in your coven and as a descendant of Youna. In case I have to remind you, the Thibodeaux family is the second powerful family of the six covens." Sir Reid paused, folding his arms across his chest. "Listen, I know nothing about love, just war and protection as my father did and his father, and so forth. And I don't claim to have the answers to fix whatever is going on inside of you. But is this d...excuse me, your Highness shifter worth losing your family's legacy? Is he worth giving up the Thibodeaux throne? Does he love you enough to abandon his pack? Or did he want you to leave your people to live with his?"

Closing my eyes shut to calm my nerves for a moment. I thought about the questions, and no, that was the simple truth. A truth I seem to keep forgetting because I wanted to hold on to some glimmer of hope that Youna and the goddesses would fix my gloomy reality. Was I asking for too much? I deserved a life of peace and happiness, whether the goddesses deemed it. And standing here in the night's darkness with Sir Reid made me suddenly realize how Mary Ann may have felt.

"Sir Reid, can you wait—" Cutting myself off after I opened my eyes again, but he had already slipped away into the shadows of the night.

Shit! My only thought was to chase after him and beg him not to tell my mother that he was a mixling, but Greyson wrapped his hand around my arm and begged us to go.

I bit back the curse, waiting on the tip of my tongue as I gave up, walking back to the shed.

It wasn't until Greyson had fallen asleep, after he spent an hour apologizing, that I snuck out and found my way back to my bed where my hot, angry tears damped the pillow until I fell into a sleepless rest.

Chapter 28

Kaydian

The next morning, I decided to admit the whole truth. Surely, Sir Reid had already gone to Mother with the information and told her I was consorting with a mixling. I could see her widened eyes and her eyebrows connecting with her hair. That would do it for my mother. No spells. No swords. Just a quick mention to send her overboard. Shaking my head, I wrapped my arms around my body as the caramelized, nutty aroma of my mother's coffee tickled my nose. Beyond the door, my mother was either reading or talking with someone. Maybe Bernadette found a way back into the castle. The sinking pit feeling in my stomach hit me hard as I remembered the annoying ghost I summoned away. She has spilled my business to my mother one too many times.

Even though she was a pain to deal with, I missed her and the latest gossip in the castle. And right now, I could use all the distractions I can get.

Knocking on the wooden door, I waited with my hand on the cold knob until I heard my mother's voice ring out, telling me to come in. My brief prayer to Youna, I hoped she would untie my tongue and give me the ability to say the right things. Exhaling, I turned the heavy knob and opened the door.

My mother had been seated behind the seat. Her curls were neatly piled on top of her head. She had on a white sleeveless dress with a pin of Youna over her heart. My mother's green eyes found mine, and a smile graced her face, melting the stones in my stomach.

Well, some of them.

"Good Morning, my emerald moon. How did you sleep last night?"

Her eyes twinkled as she watched me closely. I knew she meant it jokingly, but the question sent my heart into a panic.

"...I slept well," I said, smiling feebly. "I actually wanted to see if Sir Reid spoke with you recently?"

My mother nodded her head toward the chairs across from her. When I was seated, I tried to fold my hands together, but my hands had a mind of their own, as they found my wrist itching until I felt I could speak. My mother sensed my hesitation, which was my mistake.

"No, I haven't seen him since yesterday," she said, leaning back into her chair with her hands folded in front of her. "So you want to tell me the truth about Greyson before you've come up with a different story?"

The sound of my mother's light chuckle helped quell my nerves. Sir Reid hadn't made his way to Mother after all. I could hug him.

"How do you know his name?" I asked as the hair on my neck stood up.

If she had figured out Greyson's identity, then she was doing a great job of hiding it because she sat unmoved with a smile on her face.

"Kaydian, you have the memory of a thousand-year-old witch. You slipped up last night and called Morgan... Greyson."

Pieces of my hair fell when I shook my head. Another foolish mistake I've made.

"Well, everything was true except for his name. He doesn't like his name. It reminds him of his past life," I admitted.

My mother just watched me under her green gaze. If I hadn't known better, I would have said she could see straight inside of my soul. She and I both knew that half-lie was weaker than a human. My mother's sigh filled the quiet void. When she opened her mouth, the door opened, causing us to follow the sound. My father came ambling in with his jeans and black button-up shirt on. His face had that typical smug smile that I knew would ruin my day.

"Good Morning, my loves!" My father's boisterous voice filled the room. "How are my two favorite girls doing?"

Using all of my willpower, I repressed the urge to roll my eyes at him. Instead, I turned back to my mother, who rolled hers before she noticed me staring at her. My mother averted her eyes. She almost looked frightened that she got caught, but she recovered quickly as she placed her smile back on her face. Interesting.

"We're just talking about the Winter Harvest plans." Smiling sweetly. "Is there something you need?"

My father kissed my head as he passed me to sit in the seat beside me. The petrichor clouded our small area, washing away the coffee aroma. My mother muttered, "Fix your face," as I folded my arms against my chest.

"Last night was a madhouse. You've gotten yourself a handful to take care of Kaydian...Morgan James is such a strange person," my father said, rubbing the short beard on his face. "Sir Cross and I spoke after that fiasco, and he's going to do some digging into Mr. James. We have to be sure he's fit to lead with you."

The breakfast I ate this morning churned in my stomach as I turned my attention to my father. His brown eyes pinned me to my seat. My father and Sir Cross were nothing but persistent when they fixed their mind to something. I could only hope that Sir Reid took his time.

"Braxton, why don't you leave Morgan alone? You remember your first time drinking Fae wine? You almost got killed by my father for taunting him," my mother said, drawing our attention. "Your father had to be placed in the dungeon until he was sober again."

My father chuckled at the memory before he saw the look on my face. He immediately coughed, covering himself, fixing the cuffs on his sleeve, avoiding my questioning gaze.

"Oh, right...yeah, old times," he said, squirming in his seat. I wanted to laugh at him, but I knew better. "I was looking for you, Kaydian. I went to your room to check in on you and you were already gone. I went to the Dragon's wood, but I hadn't seen you."

My mouth twitched as I exhaled. If I didn't know my father, I would have been scared for Greyson, but my father always forgets I know his little secret. He feared Sera and Luc. When I brought them home from the Pourciau's farm, he nearly passed out. His skin turned ashen, and his wide tooth smile he had on his face wiped away. I never saw my father run so fast as he did that day. Ever since then, the furthest he would go was the entrance of the pathway.

"...come to think of it. Have you noticed anything weird over there? It smells like a shifter is nearby."

Licking my dry lips, I smiled nervously, "Come on, Father. A shifter near our coven is just preposterous." I dismissed him with a flippant wave of my hand.

"Anyway, shouldn't you be busy with your daughter?" I spat the words out like venom. Childish. Yes, I know, but I preened from the fact my father averted his eyes. But not before I've seen the look of shame seated deeply in them. This made me feel a little sorry for the question... just a tab bit.

My father turned back to me, his eyes bright and not murky for once. "I'm truly sorry for not having enough faith in you. Yes, I jumped the gun, and let's be honest, we've had many times you have given us enough reasons to worry. However, that doesn't excuse my behavior. I love you, Kaydian. Ma petite étoile, my little star. Ever since I held you in my arms when you arrived in this world, I knew you would be a force to be reckoned with. Remember that no one can take what was meant for you."

Turning to my mother, who sat at the edge of her chair, her green eyes sat in a pool of tears As one escaped down her reddened cheek and landed on the soft white fabric of her dress, she whispered my father's name as if he just entered the room. "This is how it ends," she muttered afterward. The room was more silent than a graveyard, but my mind couldn't get the words my mother had spoken out of my head. Why would she say something ominous like that? My puzzled gaze landed on my mother as I sought the answers from her face. Her face went back to staring into the void. When my father turned back, his eyes were back to the same murky brown eyes that I'd known him for. He blinked rapidly, almost as if he was in a daze.

"Jaqueline doesn't have any other place to go. So, I've asked Evie and Urick at the Inn if she can stay permanently with them," he continued, and I had to wonder if I had imagined the whole thing.

My mother was still silent, staring off at our ancestor chair in the distance, waving my hand in front of her face instead of wearing out her name. She turned to me, her eyes still glossy and a small smile on her face.

"What's more important is who will perform at this year's Harvest? Right, Mother?" I asked, trying to make the room less awkward.

"Yes...yes indeed. Sorry, my mind was elsewhere," she said, but I couldn't be sure she was talking to me or to herself.

Biting my bottom lip, I guess it was time to break the awkward silence in the stuffy office. Clearing my throat and sitting up a little straighter than before.

"I want to know what happened to Mary Ann Muller...and I want to know the whole truth."

"Oh Gosh, why do you want to bring—?" My father's boisterous, dismissive voice returned. His head tipped with his eyebrows scrunched together. It wasn't a lot of times I caught my father off guard, but this time was one of them.

"Mary Ann has always had a way of getting in trouble, even from death, it seems," my mother said, cutting off my father. Her smile dimmed, but she continued, "I will tell you, but in return, tell me about Greyson."

"Who's—" Father asked.

"Deal," I answered, ignoring my father.

"Mary was... an unsuspected surprise, as your grandmother once said. The late Ms. Muller had trouble conceiving, a rare problem for Royals, after having Sir Muller Jr. They repeatedly tried to have another child, but every other time afterward either died before their due date or before they drew their first breath. Until forty years later, when Mary arrived. Your grandmother was there for the birth and said Mary came out hollerin' like we were tryin' to kill her." She chuckled at the memory. "She was brilliant and everyone that graced her presence fell in love with her. The Mullers didn't need to worry about Mary until she decided she was going to take fate into her own hands. Mary had set her eyes out on Layla, your father's last female cousin. Layla had been guarded tightly since your father's family was the last of the barons, but they underestimated Mary, or any royal, for that matter. One night, when your grandparents were gone, Mary kidnapped her and kept her in one tower that had no protection against the English winter."

My mother swiped her hand, sending the small tumbler with Fae wine and ice to her. While my mother drank, my father picked up where she left off. "I got word that Layla was missing. Your aunt was screaming from the rooftop that the Royals finally got their revenge on us. I hadn't taken it too seriously at first because Layla had a tendency to sneak out for some much-needed time away from the house. I mean, could anyone imagine being a young adult and only being allowed to stand by the doorway once a week? We would go crazy. When she didn't return the next morning, I became worried and panicked. Layla was the last family member to actually care about me after I left to be with your mother. So, I was disappointed in myself for not finding her quick enough. It took a month before we found Layla frozen to that mattress. We were the same skin color, but she looked as pale as Sir Reid when we found her. After failing Layla, your aunt cut me out of her life for good, which I understood, even if it felt like I lost a piece of myself."

My father shook his head and continued, "No one knew why Mary Ann did it. The curse had long since set in before I arrived."

I nodded along to their recount of Mary's life, which made me think about her ancestor, Juna, the god of judgment. Before she started her bloodline, she killed many to find her perfect match. I guess the apple didn't fall too far from the tree. To turn your back on your ancestor as a royal was unheard of but I guess Mary Ann really wanted to follow in her foremother's footsteps.

"Mary was cast out of the coven a year later, after her parents died. That's when she became senile from being truly alone. No family or mate. Somehow, she found herself in California, near Sacramento, with a bunch of shifters. Sir Muller asked us permission to kill a cast-out witch on our land, and we granted it. However, later on, we found out it was Mary Ann. He said she was in too deep in her glut curse and needed to be handled. He never returned with her body. His excuse was that he transported her to their family's burial ground."

Oh, damn!

How can I tell Greyson this? If I thought he was unhinged before, I would hate to see what would happen afterward. My teeth dug into the fleshy part of my lip. A big part of me understood Mary and her desire to find her own mate on her own terms. But was it worth it? Because in the end, she ended up paying the ultimate price. Death. If I were being honest with myself, this was becoming more than I wanted to take on.

Ice filled my veins as I watched my parents move on to the next topic as if I weren't crumbling inside. As if Greyson wouldn't hate me even more than he already did, whether he wanted to admit it out loud.

Excusing myself from the office, I headed straight to my enchantment room to clear my thoughts. The tiny room has been abandoned by me since I returned home. When I walked into the room, thick grayish dust that lined the small items took flight and disseminated throughout the room. After coughing up a lung, I willed my magic to dust the room. The green aura wrapped around the walls of the room as it faded away, taking everything that didn't belong with it. Nothing in the room held my attention. Not even the very last canvas that sat in the corner. Not the two books I hadn't finished reading. Definitely not the peg board game Del had brought a couple of months ago for my birthday. Throwing my body onto the plush brown chair in the corner, covering my face with my hands in frustration, I screamed. The harsh pressure strained my vocal cords, making my throat scratchy and dry. Despite that, no tears formed. I needed Del and I couldn't wait for her to travel to the castle. With my mind made up, I used the magic spell that I promised Del I would never use unless I was in dire need—the manifest incantation spell.

Using the manifest incantation spell wasn't often used because it was one of the few magic spells, whether royal or not, that can't be ignored. I've only used it twice, and both times were traumatic. Those two times were enough for me to realize it was one too many times.

"Delphine Pourciau!" I whispered.

"Delphine Pourciau!" I said again, she's a stubborn headed woman sometimes.

"Delphine Pourciau!" I said, clenching my teeth. If I had to find her and drag her back here, I would.

The air in the room became thin, causing my lungs to gasp for air as sweat coated my forehead. A gust of green and white finely misted mixture swirled before me, causing my hair and the end of my dress to flutter in the magic storm. I watched as the colors shaped and molded themselves until I saw a pale arm formed from the mist. Clutching the arm of my chair, Del morphed and appeared in front of me as the magic storm died down. Half-naked and barefooted. The pink dress she had tried to put on was hanging off her waist, leaving her small breasts exposed. Del fell to the floor, screaming. The blood-curdling sound that formed out of Del sent my hands to my ears to prevent them from bursting. I had to get up and help her. Every step toward Del made my covered ears ring against my palms.

When I finally reached her side, the screams had stopped, but she had her arms wrapped around her so tight that her chest and stomach were the same shade of the orchid-colored dress. Not wanting her to suffer, I wrapped my arms around her. My green aura engulfed her pale, trembling skin. We stayed in our position until I no longer felt her tiny body shivering, and she picked up her head that was tucked against her chest and leaned against me. The pine-scented soap tickled my nose.

After two minutes, Del muttered, "Shit," and we both chuckled.

"I really hate you right now, KD," she said, leaning off of me. "Why couldn't you have sent me a message and then I can walk here like a normal witch?"

Pulling my lips between my teeth, I fought the giggle that threatened to come out. Del knew I would never laugh at her pain, but it's rare to see Del being mad and bratty.

"I'm sorry, Del. I—I needed you. I needed my best friend."

Del, who was fixing her dress, peered at me. Those robins egg blue eyes turned from murderous to worry. Her small hand cupped mine. Lowering my head in complete and utter shame, I stared at our entwined hands, both different as night and day, but perfect in their own way.

"What the hell is going on, KD?"

She squeezed my hand after a moment of realizing I was stuck inside of my head.

"Greyson is a shifter...well, half shifter and half witch." I paused, letting everything sink in. When I looked at my best friend's face, all of her blood rushed to her face. Before she could make sense of my revelation, I continued, "His mother was a Royal, Muller's youngest sister...I'm mated to a mixling."

"A fucking shifter!"

The weight of the secret finally lightened, even if it was a little. A deep sigh left me as I watched Del's face morph again for the second time. This time to pure disgust.

"So, you lied to me then? Or should I say again?" Her voice dripped with resentment. Del folded her arms across her chest, this time not in pain but in disappointment.

"I hadn't lied about anything else. I'm sorry. I should have told you, but I—I really thought I had a handle on things and Greyson, but..." biting into my fleshy bottom lip. "I can't stop thinking about what you said the other day."

Poor Delphine she had a look of utter confusion on her face. Her thin upper lip twitched up, and her eyes bunched as she tried to remember what I was talking about.

"Okay, now you've lost me. What are you talking about... I mean, we've talked about—" Del paused, and I saw those globes widen as big as her mouth. "Wait! You're serious, aren't you? I didn't mean to actually kill him!"

As I turned to my friend's stunned face, I really thought about her question. Did I really want to kill Greyson? No, but something kept bringing me back to The Three Sisters and my prophecies. I had pushed the confusing riddles aside, hoping I could turn a blind eye to it. Not wanting to deal with finding out what they may have meant for my future. I guess Elder Alo was right.

"Celestoria has four journeys, but only three will survive. The third will be met with a death by the sun." Aimlessly, I spoke the riddle out loud. "Maybe I'm supposed to go on three journeys to find Celestoria? Or maybe...I'm not sure."

Del worried her bottom lip. "Listen, I hardly should be the voice of reason when it comes to these things, seeing as I will probably never find my better half. My Youna! How will you sit on the throne with a shifter? And what is Celestoria?"

Del's questions rebounded in my head, leaving me with thoughts of my future and what lay ahead of me to take my rightful position, the position that was mine from birth. The one thing, other than Del, I would kill for and make sure everyone knew that Youna's name would live on. No matter how nutty I became.

"I don't know what or who Celestoria is, my sweet Del, but I know I want what's mine, which is my time on the throne. I know you said I should keep what the Three Sisters said, but I have to tell you, Del. I have to hide Greyson until the bonding ceremony. My mother would kill Greyson if she found out he was a mixling...I just need more time."

Del blanched, which I knew she would. She sat pale-faced, squirming in her seat. I knew she believed the words that came from my lips. If I can just get Greyson to see reason and work with me, then we can both win, but with each visit, the idea of us ruling dwindled into the dust. I could see the doubt in his brown eyes.

Looking at Del's pale face. She seemed ready to pass out at any given moment. Walking over to the small makeshift bookshelf, I searched for one of the family's journals I had taken from my mother's office and forgot to return it. My shaky hand hovered over the pages until it stopped in the section about the Muller family. Shifting through the different family members' questionable handwriting, I landed on the sentence that I needed.

July 20, 1750: Silver defeats the Mullers, not their beloved golden beryl, the jewel of their family. After years of searching and observing, they finally made a slight mistake and gave themselves away. When I handed them the silver necklace, I purchased for Sir Joseph Muller, his brown eyes widened as the metal siphoned off his magic...

Closing the book mid-sentence and placing it back onto the shelf along with my other books. My hands became damp with my sweat as I stared idly at the bookcase.

"...what's the plan, then?" Del's voice was unmistakably so low I almost thought I was hallucinating.

That was the million-dollar question, as I couldn't directly kill Greyson. Because I was a coward, and I wanted us to work. But second, it was physically possible for fated mates to kill each other. If I were to drive a knife into Greyson's chest with a silver knife, the Muller's stone, he would just pull the knife out and heal. The pit in my stomach became heavy with the thought. Then, like a switch, it hit me.

"I have the perfect plan until I can figure out my next steps."

I turned to Del, scratching my wrist as she threw herself into the chair.

"Oh shit, I don't like that look...at all."

"Del, I promise it's not bad. We have to lock Greyson up. It's the only way. He's a liability. His wolf has become unstable. What if he leaves the cabin? I can't have him attacking anyone else," I said as I delved into the story of last night's events. By the time I was finished, Del looked ready to pummel Greyson—or me, for that matter.

Running her hand down her face, she said, "Kaydian, you know my family and I can't get into any more trouble with your mother. I'm only lucky your mother likes mine or else we would have been Sera's lunch a long time ago."

Getting up from the floor, I walked over to my best friend. "Listen, Del. I understand, but we won't get caught. I'll carry him with my magic. I just need you to watch my back. So, no one won't catch us. This will only be temporary until Greyson and I figure out our next step."

Del sat, rubbing her hands together as if the small space was cold. Pacing back and forth as my mind racks through How I can get Del to help me. If push comes to shove, I could order Sir Reid to help me, but I would rather walk on nails. He probably would just laugh at me and proceed to hack Greyson into pieces. He would love that since he had been ever so eager to offer his help to me. Leaning against the wall, Del still hadn't uttered a word to me. She just sat with her head bent to the ceiling and her eyes closed. If she doesn't say something soon, I will throw up every bit of my breakfast. Back and forth, I paced the small room until I marched over to the chair, grabbed her by the shoulder, and opened my mouth to plead with her. Hell, I'll beg her at this point, but she beat me to it.

"Fine, but I hope when the time comes, I will get a favor out of this... if I survive, that is."

Biting my tongue, I fought to say she was overreacting, but I couldn't fault her for wanting to be cautious. Instead, I dragged her out of the chair and hugged her tightly. Del dug her face into my hair and sighed. I had almost forgotten about the kiss with Del until now. Standing here with Del's nipples, threatening to poke a hole through me. She pulled away abruptly. Her face was blazed.

"It's okay, Del. Thank you for helping me and just trust me. I don't have all the details planned, but know that I will always protect you. So, let's do it tonight. Sir Reid has gone on a secret trip for my mother."

Del rolled her eyes with a pinched look on her face, "Of course, it would be last minute."

Hopefully, she'll still feel that way when it's all said and done. Del had returned to the farm to finish her chores before tonight as I got ready for the plan.

Chapter 29

Kaydian

Fifteen minutes before our meet up, I entered my mother's office. I made it with no signs of my parents. My mother had placed our family book back on the white pedestal next to my grandmother's chair. When I stood in front of my nemesis this time, I pulled back the small hidden wedge in the cover that revealed a small needle with emerald dust in order to prick my finger, deactivating the slumber incantation. After ten minutes of flipping through the off-yellow pages, I found the insensate incantation buried behind notes from my second great-grandmother.

A loud thud resonated in the office as the book slammed shut. "Damn it," I muttered. When I heard the clock chimed at the top of the hour and went late as usual, I all but ran to get out of the office. Almost scared someone might walk inside and catch me again. Each step toward the kitchen backdoor made my teeth clench as what I was about to do sunk in. My stomach churned worse than the summer night storms in Houston, but I kept my head up as I almost reached the kitchen door. Just before I heard my mother's voice call my name. Snapping my eyes closed and reopening them, I turned around to face my mother. She was dressed for bed, and Ms. Kincaid was nowhere in sight, meaning she was purposely looking for me.

"Now what could my mischievous daughter be up to this late at night?" My mother folded her arms, tapping her slipper cladded foot, all the while the corner of her mouth twitched.

"Well, I have to feed Sera and Luc. It's been a long day, and I forgot they need food to survive, or they will find some of the coven to munch on."

My mother tsked as she stepped down the stairs to stand in front of me. In my mind, I prepared for her to chastise me with her words, but all that came was the light touch of her hand as it caressed my cheek, throwing me off my tracks.

"You have a situation on your hands with Greyson." she paused, smiling up at me as I bent my neck down to look at her. "If I could do it all over again, I wouldn't have changed anything because I got to see how powerful you'll become. Every trial and tribulation I've endured was to bring you to this point in your life, and I support you no matter the outcome."

Heaviness filled my belly as I looked at my mother. She never confirmed whether she asked to see her future. I only learned that secret from the three sisters. My hand reached up to cup hers as her mear magic slipped through my veins, warming and mingling with mine. Her crooked smile I looked forward to when times were too tumultuous. Now only made me realize how lonely it can be, having the weight of your fate on your shoulders. Was it always going to be this way?

My mother slipped her hand from my face, retreating up the stairs. Once she was halfway up the stairs, she stopped and pivoted toward me.

"Greyson... might be impulsive, don't you think? If you want to rule, then you will have to make some changes or, at the very most, get him on the same page.... If not, then produce an heir. The people and the coven love new blood. It will give them something to look forward to. Something to give our people hope in you and our family leadership... and quickly. Have you drank your Stoneseed root yet? You were due two days ago. It's perfect timing."

My face had turned cold as I laid a hand on my cheek.

My mother's eyes narrowed, and she chuckled, "Youna! You look like Bernadette on a bad day! Kaydian, having children is not a bad thing.

We're the descendants of the goddess of fertility for a reason. You will know joy when you have yours. Just as I knew it when I held your tiny body to my chest." She turned back to continue up the stairs right before I left the hallways. I heard her mumble, "I can't wait for all of this to end."

An Heir? A child? A Mixling? I think my mother bumped her head. Yes, like everyone in my family, I felt the powerful urge to get pregnant almost every month. Even with the Stoneseed root, it just made it easier to manage. Placing my hand on my soft stomach, I thought I was too young to have kids, even though my mother and almost everyone in the village said otherwise. With so much change going on, that would be an awful situation, but what other shitty option do I have? My mother was right, as I wrapped my arms around my body, guarding me from the cold Houston night air. Luckily, I could bear it for the five months until our child got here. Youna! I would have to give a sacrifice to the goddesses every day and night to make sure he or she doesn't come out like Victoria Muller. What a catastrophe that would be. That would be just the tip of the iceberg. To imagine having to explain my baby to the Royals would be a nightmare in itself, especially since I would have to beg Sir Cross for acceptance since they were the first of the goddess descents.

"Kaydian!"

Del yelled my name, snapping me out of my turbulent thoughts. It took me a minute to realize I was standing in the small clearing entrance with my fist balled up and digging into my soft thighs. My lips felt sore as I loosened them from pressing them together. Del massaged my shoulders, loosening up my tightened muscles.

"I'm sorry," I said, finally getting my lips to work with my brain. "Thank you for coming. Let's get this over with. We won't have any problems. I will tell you everything along the way."

Del just nodded as I walked over to the shed to remove my magic from the lock I placed on the shed before I left the last time.

"A magic lock?" Del asked, whistling afterward. "He's that bad?"

This time, I just nodded and told her to wait outside.

When I entered, Greyson was sitting on the side with small size holes decorating the soft mattress. He had repeatedly used the bed as an outlet for his misplaced anger. The act was innocent, but it made me angry. He turned to acknowledge me. His eyes were golden, but as he blinked, they turned back to brown.

"I'm sorry, Kaydian...I—I never meant to hurt you. Last night...my wolf—"

I wanted to protest and ignore his apology, but even now, those thoughts felt forced. I played with the idea of keeping his mother's last moments on earth a little longer. That was until I looked into those wide, pleading eyes and crumbled.

"It's okay, Greyson. Do you mind putting on a shirt? We should talk about your mother."

Greyson paused, his face broadcasting the emotions that he kept hidden before his eyes became a watery grave. "It's not good, is it?"

Forcing the corner of my mouth into a straight line. He knew the answer to that already. "No, Greyson. It's not good at all, and I just hope you can at least hear the entire story."

My hands felt foreign to me as I tucked them into the crook of my arms. The words started, but I couldn't tell if it was me or the dark voice speaking. Word after word, I watched as Greyson's handsome face morphed into sadness as he alternated from hanging his head down, letting his hair cover his face. When he looked back up, peeping at me through the openings of his inky black hair, I saw it—no, felt it before I could understand it. Hate thick as the humid Houston air filled the tiny cabin, but he didn't move an inch. Just the wisp of his hair fluttering as he exhaled through his nose.

I've never felt uncomfortable as I do now and though I understood why. It still made a cold tingle creep down my spine.

When I was done, we sat in uncomfortable silence. After a moment, Greyson's wolf's yellow eyes landed on me, causing me to shiver. The muscles in his tightly corded arms flexed as a barely audible growl filled my ears, and it made me take a small, shaky step backward.

"Your parents helped kill my mother..."

Swallowing, "I can't take back what was done. Your uncle killed your mother without giving her a second chance. My parents gave him permission to capture someone, but they didn't know it was your mother, Greyson. I'm so—"

If there was one thing. I underestimated was Greyson's wolf.

Greyson jumped up from the bed, causing me to almost trip over my shoes. A mistake on my part as he took the foot of the bed into his hand and flipped it over with ease, which caused a loud banging noise to fill the small shed. The yellow light flickered and buzzed from the impact.

"Greyson, please! Control your wolf. He's making too much noise. I understand you're angry at me and my parents, but we can work it out."

"You're no better than your parents. Oni was right!" he said as he gathered the remainder of the food and clothing. I brought him and hurdled them across the room. Bread, fruits, and jugs of water colored the items that were flung to the ground.

Greyson's wolf wasn't done with its fit of rage. His glowing eyes narrowed in on me. "I'll promise you this, Kaydian. Once we're bonded, I will burn everyone in this murderous compound, including my mother's brother."

"Listen, right now, you're not thinking straight." Shuffling on my feet as his wolf watched me. A bead of sweat trailed down my forehead. "Let's try this again tomorrow. I can bring you more food and books."

That's when I made my next mistake. I let my emotions get the best of me, and tears formed in my eyes, blurring Greyson and his wolf as I tried to blink them away. All of the bravo I once had sailed out of the tiny window of the dim light shed.

Sharp pain fleeted down my head to my toes as my back hit the wall. The pleading words I had in my head dissipated, leaving me dumbfounded. Greyson's wolf partially shifted, hand wrapped around the delicate skin of my neck, cutting into my flesh. Metallic mingled with the tension in the air. Grabbing at the hand around my neck, I tried to get him to let go, which only made him slam me into the wall again. Black dots danced in my vision, and this time, the air had been knocked out of me, leaving me panting against his enclosed hand. I watched as Greyson's eyes turned back to brown and then back to yellow again as he fought for control. But his wolf was winning the battle.

"Greyson! Please." I said, despair coated my breath.

"We can work..." I gasped for the little air I could. "I promise..."

With a last attempt, I squeezed out, "I love you, Greyson. Please."

The words only held so much truth as I spoke them into existence. I loved him in a sort of twisted way, but there was no hope as the weight of the moment sat on my soul. Greyson's wolf, none the wiser, tightened its hold on me as Del slipped into the room. Her blue eyes locked onto us.

"Oh, shit!" Del yelled loud enough to wake the coven up.

Greyson's wolf turned his sight on Delphine as she glued herself to the wall. Without a second thought, it determined that Del was the bigger threat to him. A quick sigh of relief escaped my parted lips as his hand abandoned my neck. As he ate away at the distance between him and Del.

"NO! NO! NO!" I yelled as he reached out to grab Del with his sharp talons that would shred her apart.

I couldn't let anything happen to Del. She was innocent, and I couldn't live with myself if she got hurt because of me.

My magic bubbled, a hot scorching sensation raged just underneath my skin, and the insensate incantation in the old language.

I watched the green light of my magic wrapped around Greyson's head, positioning itself to perform my want. Greyson's wolf turned around and an ominous smile graced his face as he realized Del was someone important to me. Looking at those yellow eyes of hate, I knew that this was it. There was no taking back my plan or changing my mind. "Go," the royal language echoed in my mind as I watched the end of my magic drive into Greyson's skull. His eyes widened as he fell with the smile wiped off his face. My heart thudded in my chest as he almost hit the ground, face first, before my magic caught him just in the nick of time.

Grabbing onto the wall, I waited until I gained control of my adrenaline-induced body. Greyson dipped and raised as my labored breath caused my magic to ween. This time the rancid air in the shed burned in my lungs as I bit back tears.

"Are you okay?" I asked. Her pale body was still stuck to the wall, trembling. A small 'yes' left her mouth. I had to be strong for the both of us even if my legs felt like they were about to give out.

"Your throat, Kaydian."

My hand flew to the tender skin. The moment the pads of my fingers touched the spot, I winced. "Well, he can't kill me, but I think this was close enough."

I joked, but something inside of me died when he hurt me. My knees buckled as Del's hand reached out to steady me. "Let me," she said as her reddened hands found my neck. Using her magic, she calmed the sore muscles in my throat. My cheeks scorched as I thought she had used up too much of her magic to heal me, especially when she knew my magic could do it. I truly didn't deserve her.

"Thank you, Del—"

Del grabbed my trembling hand. Her rosy color had finally returned, "Don't even say it. You're my best friend. I would do anything for you. Let's get this over and done with."

All I could do was nod feebly as my magic did the heavy work. As we walked through the dark path and into the dank, empty escape tunnels and down the stairs to the dungeon, I relayed everything my mother had said to Del. Her ohs and ahs filled the tunnel's dark space. Del had offered no advice after I was done speaking. She just muttered, "Shit," and went back to watching out for any of the guards.

When we made it to the bottom floor after our long trek. The scent of death that clung to the red brick walls for dear life made our eyes watered. I almost forgot how many witches and supernatural's died down here. Poor Del coughed until the whites of her eyes turned a faint pinkish hue. Folding my arms against my body to prevent me from mistakenly touching the walls, we ventured left to the deserted hall that hadn't been used since the last war. Two hundred years ago, my family built this section just for the shifters, and the long-deserted hallway now served as a monument to our victory. The red brick wall morphed into walls that were as dark as the midnight sky from the amount of blood that saturated the halls. My mind couldn't think which was worse, the bloody walls or the sterile scent that meant someone tried to scrub the history of these dark halls away.

"Let's use the very last room," I said out loud.

Ten rooms of torture later, I shuddered as my hand pulled the ice-cold bar handle of the silver metal door. The cleaning agent the staff used for their monthly cleaning clung to the room. I guess it was better than the putrid smell from the halls. Del beat me to using her magic to sweep the area of the harsh scent and turned on the fluorescent string light. The room was small with gray walls with no window, a small table, and a sink. A lone silver table that was reinforced with wolfbane lay in the middle of the room. My magic gently laid Greyson on the table while Del strapped him in, enforcing it with her magic.

"He's going to need some heat, Kaydian. He may be a shifter, but he will be a frozen one if you leave him like this."

Delphine was right. Greyson would freeze before the morning sun rises, but as I looked around the room, my mind drew blank. We didn't have a furnace to place down here—I think, to be honest, it's been a long time since I ventured down here. The last time was to confirm which room I wanted to live in once I lost myself to the curse.

Del grunted, drawing me out of my thoughts, carrying an old, small, black kerosene heater. She looked small, hauling the cylinder heater. Setting it down, she said, "I knew they kept a small kerosene heater for the guards. I think I underestimated the size of this thing."

"Oh, that will work. We will just take turns coming down to fill up."

Del paused with her mouth slightly opened, "Take turns? How long do you plan on keeping him here?"

Opening my mouth, I told Del the truth. "Honestly, I'm not sure, but what I know is that I need an heir to rule if Greyson isn't by my side because of that archaic rule made by some old bastard."

"Wasn't it your great time a million family member that made the rule?"

Crossing my arms, I met Del's questioning face as she turned to me with her mouth open to make some other smart-ass comment, but she took one look at my face and closed her mouth shut.

"Never mind," she muttered, averting her eyes.

That's right!

Chapter 30

Greyson

ot

That's how I awoke. Sweltering as if I were placed in an oven that's been set too high. Rivulets of salty sweat ran down my forehead. Some of it caught in my eyes, causing me to squint and curse as it burned its way into my eye. Raising my arm to clean my eyes was a grisly mistake as pain swept through my arms. He's beyond pissed. It clawed inside me against my ribs as I fought for control. Which hadn't been easy since the moment I got to this hell compound. Never in my life would I have thought my wolf would work against me in the time I needed him the most.

Where the hell am I?

The fresh scent of metallic filled the small room, and I could only guess from a quick glance down at my wrist that I was the cause of the scent. Lifting my head just enough to view my new "room." The dim light from the furnace provided just enough light to see my body and the room, but that hadn't drawn my attention. It was the red welts that festered around my wrist. Sticky clear fluid pooled underneath my raw flesh. Repressing my shiver, I worked around the wolfbane metal cuffs.

Whoever placed me here would die a slow death while I fed them piece by piece to my wolf. My heart became erratic the more my wolf fought for control.

Slamming my eyes shut, I counted until I reached ten, trying to refocus my attention on my safe place.

Back in the garden with my mother before it was reduced to nothing. When my father watched us with love in his eyes. Back to when she guided me in controlling the seeds that would nourish the pack. My mother held my hand at every step, which made my father resent me even more. Not that it matters because when she turned to me, I couldn't hear anyone. The sun created a halo around her sunhat that she wore to prevent her face from burning. She looked so majestic as I remembered her bright smile that had canceled out the sun's rays. If I tried hard enough, I could still smell the light rose scent she loved so much as she held the dying corn stalk in her small hands and said, "What's meant to be, will be, my love." It was the only peace I sought these past couple of days. I knew she was keeping me from turning into the beast my wolf wanted me to become, but each day away from my pack was becoming more difficult as the line blurred between my wolf and me.

I won't cry...I won't give in to whoever has kidnapped me.

My canine bit into my bottom lip, causing me to open my eyes. To face my reality, I had to wait until Kaydian found me. To rescue me like a worthless child, but how does that make me feel? Like horse crap. Ever since I all but barked at her, I've been feeling indifferent. And I couldn't distinguish if it was my intrusive thoughts that had become ingrained in me since my mother's death or if it was my wolf taking over. At this point, all I can do is pray that the Earth Creator guides me to get out of this situation and back to Kaydian to make it right because she's all that matters.

It would be just my luck if Muller found me and decided to kill me before I had a chance to get my revenge for my mother. I don't have anyone to blame but myself. I hadn't meant to confront him at the dinner. It was my goal to be seen but not heard. Before I entered that castle, my wolf and I fought for control right before Kaydian came to take me to the castle, and seeing my uncle, who shared features I'd only noticed on my mother and me, made me slip. Rejection was similar to getting ran over by a train, brutal and painful. One would think I was used to it by now, but I guess I was only fooling myself. My magic had briefly reappeared as it helped push my wolf back into my chest. But it was fleeting as I felt it leave my presence within seconds later leaving me cold and confused. The jarring feeling had been foreign to me since I'd lived my life without using it, and that was when I knew I should have returned home and forgotten about finding out the truth. However, it was too late as my wolf sensed my weak moment and ruined the one time for me to find out any answers.

A screeching sound deafened my inner thoughts, drawing my attention to the metal door. Watching the person struggle to open the heavy door gave me some hope. If they were struggling with a door, then I had a chance. All I would have to do was get them to open these cuffs. The door finally opened fully as a girl walked into the tiny room. She rested on the open door as she wiped the strands of hair out of her face. Her blue dress stood out against her pale skin. She landed her blue eyes on me, which grew wider than saucers as she noticed me. A red flush decorated her face that traveled down her chest. Yes, she was nervous. I could see it in the way her hand trembled as she picked the tray off the floor, flinching when the metal door slammed shut with a loud bang. The silverware clattered against the tray so loudly that I was tempted to break out and just take the tray from her.

Finally, after painstakingly slow moving like a snail, she placed the tray on the small silver table. Rubbing her hands together while she stared at the wall as if I weren't in the room, she muttered softly, "You can do this." *Was this the best my uncle could get?* I thought. Kaydian would just have to get me to England, and I would take care of everyone.

Turning her face toward me with her eyes planted on the wall behind me.

"Good, you're awake. I brought you whatever I could find in the kitchen." Her voice was clipped, but she caught herself and continued. "I—"

"I need to use the bathroom." Cutting her off, hoping that it will work in my favor. "I need my hands to use the bathroom. Unless you're going to help me use it...what's your name?"

My capture turned another shade of red than before. She took a step back, colliding with the sink.

"I—I'm... My name is...it's Tiffany. Yes, Tiffany," she replied, shaking her head like both she and I didn't know that was a lie.

"Ok...Tiffany." I paused, drawing out the name. Watching her flinch was mildly enjoyable. "Can I please go to the bathroom? Maybe you can release one of the cuffs? I promise I'm too weak to take you on right now. Plus, look at my wrist. I'm damaged."

Tiffany just stared at me. Her blue eyes were swimming with tears. Her scent was as bitter as coffee. She walked over to where the wolfbane cuff kept me imprisoned and glanced down. That's when I wished I hadn't had heightened hearing because her mouth opened, and an ear-throbbing scream drowned my senses. My initial instinct was to cover my ears, but all I was met with was the searing pain from the wolfbane. And though I wasn't a child, I wept as I placed my hands back in the safe position. When the pain died down, I looked over at Tiffany, who had her head in the sink, throwing up as the acidic smell mixed with my newly burnt scent.

I almost felt sorry for the girl. She lived in this murderous compound and was scared of blood? Or my wounds? Or both? I wasn't sure. The way she gripped the edge of the sink made me sigh in frustration. She could hardly get close enough to let me out. Banging the back of my head against the table. I prayed to the Earth Creator that if—when I get free, I will visit the Elder temple more frequently.

The heavy door opened and closed with ease this time. Craning my neck up to see my new guest, I couldn't believe my luck. A shaky laughter poured out of me. Kaydian walked in like a vision straight out of my dreams. She had on a black silk dress with her long curls tied to the top of her head. Something was way off. Her floral scent that I loved and committed to memory smelled foul, almost as if she was withering away like a rose. Kaydian crossed the room with her mouth twisted in a grimace, staring at Tiffany, who had taken up to gripping the wall.

"Kaydian, thank the Creator! Finally, just take care of Tiffany and free me from this table."

The minutes ticked by as Kaydian stood by the closed door. With her hand itching her damn wrist. She stared at me with those haunting, emerald eyes. Watching me. Assessing me like I wasn't shackled to the table. I wanted to reach out and shake her. It wasn't time for her to get lost in that head of hers. She was more powerful than Tiffany and could have us out of this place before my uncle knew we were gone.

"Tiffany?" she asked calmly. The puzzled look on her face made my stomach tighten. "Delphine, did you tell him your name is Tiffany?"

"I got nervous, and it was the only thing I could think of," Delphine said, waving her hand through the air. "This is too much for me, Kaydian. His..." She paused to point at me with her head turned away from my wounds.

"Y-You did this?" Asking the most ridiculous question.

Everything in me wanted to believe this was all a horrible dream. Even though I lay here trapped on this table with my mate right in front of me, I didn't want to believe it. Was this punishment for when I lost control of my wolf? A single tear rolled down my face as my wolf tried to push me to the back. Running through apologies in my mind, I realized I couldn't get my mouth to form the words that I needed to say, and the only thing in my mind was thoughts of rage. My wolf coiled in the middle of my chest as the wolfbane worked its magic. I knew then that I was all alone.

Kaydian ignored my question as she waved a flippant hand, turning the light on in the tiny room. While my eyes adjusted to the light, she said, "It's okay, Del. Thank you for helping out. I'll take it from here."

Delphine all but ran out of the room after Kaydian sent her off with a hug. Kaydian walked over to the small table, retrieving the tray. She lifted my head with her free hand. *I wasn't hungry*! Just the smell of the food when it was finally uncovered made my stomach churn. It was soup—chicken soup, by the smell of it. Thyme, chicken, and regret seeped through the room. She spooned some of the liquid and brought it to my mouth, but I kept my mouth clamped shut tight, pushing against her hand.

She sighed. The corners of her mouth pulled down into a frown. "Greyson, you have to eat something. You've been asleep for a whole day! I left you to rest after the spell had long worn off."

That only made my lips pressed together even further. At this point, they will probably blend into my face, disappearing. Kaydian pushed the spoon back into my mouth. The end of the spoon wedged between the tight spaces as she fought to get the spoon in. Small streaks of the mouthwatering aroma dribbled down my chin and onto my chest. My stomach sang a song against my protest. I didn't dare look up at Kaydian. Every fiber in my being didn't want her to feel vindicated, but I had no other choice in my weakened state. Defeat was my only option, and I could only hope for a reasonable explanation. Stupid of me, yes, I know. But like my father once said, I was a silly boy.

Opening my mouth, Kaydian fed me the warm soup. The soft wisp of her breath tickled my cheek as she cooled down the liquid, causing me to shift on the cold table. With my entire being, I wanted to hate the food and hate her, but the small voice in the back of my head said not to. I would be lying to myself if I didn't say that the soup wasn't good. When she was finished feeding me the toast and water, she laid one of her soft traitorous hands on my cheek, rubbing it until my dick twitched in my pajamas. *Truly, how pathetic!* My mind struggled to focus on how I could get her to release me and how I would escape this dungeon. Even though she would probably send that big bastard to hunt me down.

Kaydian helped me to use the bathroom in a bucket she retrieved from outside of the room. When she came back, she had that fucking smile on her face. The one that made my heart twitch along with my dick. The smile that used to follow her sweet floral scent now left a bitter taste in my mouth. Goosebumps littered my body as my wolf bristled inside. It made me wonder if I—we had it wrong all along.

"We need to talk," she said, hopping onto the small edge of the table. "I'm sorry I had to do this to you, but your actions...your actions were nothing but impulsive. I can keep you out of sight from everyone and save myself from being hurt again by your wolf...or you, for that matter."

Kaydian paused, wiping her face with the end of her skirt. "I've waited a very long time for you, and I won't let you be foolish. Sir Muller —sorry, your uncle and you come from the goddess Juna, Goddess of Judgment. Your family is the fourth strongest of the goddess descent behind the Crosses and mines. If you had killed your uncle in our coven, every last member of each witches' coven would have your head on a golden platter. Luckily, you seemed to have frightened him off...Don't think I won't forget how you hurt me, Greyson. Your hands left my neck bruised and bloodied."

Jumping off the table, she came back to my side. Laying her hand on my chest, she continued, "I know you don't want to hear this, but you and I know your mother wasn't innocent, and she took an innocent life herself. The goddess looks down on those things and they often seek revenge for their disobedient descendants. No matter how powerful your family line is, you're not more powerful than the fate the goddesses have laid out for you. Your mother knew that and still proceeded."

My gut told me years ago that there was a bigger story at play, but now that I knew the truth, I found myself unsure of how to proceed. My wolf won our internal battle. His painful growl shook every fiber of my muscles. The pressure built in my chest with his claws latching onto the soft flesh until my mouth opened. A torturous, animalistic sound from the depths of my chest escaped me. My eyes, wrists, and ankles burned, but none of that was worse than my heart, which felt shattered. It was like hearing the news for the first time. The raw pain in my throat was only minor, as my mother suffered worse than anything I could imagine. To be killed by your family was worse than any sin. I cried until nothing was left but a shell of myself and Kaydian's soft hand on my chest. Her tears mixed with mine as she shared my pain.

At this very moment, I wanted to kill my mother's killer. No family member of mine would ever kill one of their own. And deep down, I wanted to kill Kaydian's parents even if they were blinded by my mother's iniquitous brother.

Kaydian's soft, low voice broke my thoughts, "I want to let you out, but not only am I scared you might hurt me again, Greyson, but you will do something rash like kill your uncle. He would—"

"I have no uncle other than my párah, Oni," I said, my voice breaking from my raw throat.

"I understand, Greyson. I do, but will you promise not to do anything rash? We need the coven on our side to rule, and then we can go from there. Killing Muller now will only make matters worse! And I can't help you if the royal coven wants your head."

"No," I said without looking at her, because it pained me to do so. "I'm sorry for hurting you. I've never lost control of my wolf before. The only thing I can promise right now is to fight the wolf into the corner before we can hurt you again."

That was the first and only thing that ran through my wolf and my mangled mind. I can't undo what my wolf and I did to her, and I never will let that happen again, but Kaydian's audacity to ask me to be docile while my mother's killer went free was galling. There was nothing I wanted more than to seek my revenge. That was the main reason I came to this fucking hellhole. Struggling against the cuffs, I ignored the pain until the flesh on my ankles and wrist became too much. Sinking down in surrender, I breathed deeply in order to get myself and my wolf back under control. The sickening throb eased against my burnt skin.

When I opened my eyes, Kaydian stood there, the front of her dress drenched with her tears as she wrapped her arms around herself. Her skin was ashen. It warmed my wolf's and my heart to see the tears she cried for me because she was able to feel the pain I had bottled up inside of me, even if it was temporary. Nothing hurts more than knowing I would have to be tied to someone's family who had a part in killing the one other person I needed.

Kaydian stood between the table and the door, shifting on her feet with her green eyes averted from mine. This was one of the few times I've ever seen her this nervous. Sensing my gaze, she fixed her posture and placed it back on her straight face.

"I want an heir, Greyson. It's what I will need in order to rule once my parents step down...first an heir, and then we can work out a plan after I ensure my place on the throne." She paused to clear her throat. Watching her fold and unfold her arms as she nervously shifted on her feet.

Was this a joke?

It had to be because she couldn't be serious right now. My mind was blank as her gaze.

"...You want me to give you an heir so that you can rule?" I asked, with confusion riddled in my voice.

"I promise afterward we can make a plan to keep your people safe and watch over them—"

"Kaydian or Your Highness... Are you serious? You have me chained to a table, and you want me to give you an heir. So that *you* can rule. My answer is no, not now and no tomorrow."

For what it was worth, Kaydian looked sick to her stomach, standing there bobbing her head up and down. Rightfully so, and maybe I was being crass, but at this very moment, I didn't fucking care. The main reason I came here was for revenge and for our future, but it was clear those plans had changed. Kaydian took my silence as a sign to leave, slipping out the door with nothing but a mumbled, "Sorry, I'll be back."

But did I want her to come back? That was the real question.

Chapter 31

Kaydian

There's an old saying that goes, 'Time waits for no one,' but I wasn't just anyone and I'm over Greyson's antics. For the past two days, we've followed the same mundane routine that involves me stealing food from the kitchen while sneaking it downstairs into the dark, damp corner of the abandoned cells. Each time, I would stop by that stupid metal door and gather my thoughts, praying that we didn't fight again. Greyson has taken pure joy in pushing my buttons, which made me hate the male species even a little more. Did I have a right to be mad? I guess not since I had him locked up, but it didn't give him the right to dismiss my requests with a shrug. It was the least he could do since he lost control of himself. Condescending Bastard! The dark voice shouted from within almost every day since he's been locked up. If he would just work with me, we could figure out our next move but that was easier said than done.

Delphine kept harping that I was leading with my heart despite everything. I did want to dispute that claim, but somewhere in me knew she was right. The wolfbane-laced knife I found, thanks to my family's book, in our chest that was filled with old memories crossed my mind. I had picked up the silver gem-encrusted knife one too many times. Every time I held it, my stupid heart squeezed, begging me to give him another chance.

And I was starting to hate love.

Here I stood in front of Greyson with my hand digging into the flesh of my wrist and my teeth clenching together for dare life. As he lay on the table, handcuffed, his brown eyes held humor in them. Our back and forth had become a joke to him. There was nothing more I wanted than to wipe the smirk off his face, and today made no difference.

Smiling sweetly, I said, "Greyson, listen. I'm tired of coming down here and I know you're tired of being down here. Just give me what I want, and then I can work out a feasible plan for us."

Greyson closed his eyes and a deep sigh left his mouth. The silence stretched between us as he disregarded, which only caused my blood to simmer. My nail dug deeper into my wrist as I fought back my temperamental magic.

He hummed and hawed, knowing he was driving me crazy. "What did I say yesterday again?"

With my teeth clenched, "You said 'not in this or the next lifetime.'"

"Oh, that was a great one...how about this one then 'over my dead body.'"

Childish bastard!

"I've given you one too many chances to realize this is the best option for the both of us. I will get the approval of my people once I produce an heir, then I will work on getting your mother justice. I give you my word, Greyson." I yelled, echoing the plan for the twentieth time.

Minutes ticked by as Greyson lay flat on the table with his eyes shut. Without thinking, I placed my hand on his arm. He was lost in his own little world as he ignored me like I was a nobody. My face became hot with shame but my magic that was burning its way through my body, itching to wreak havoc on Greyson.

"Princess Kaydian," he spat out with enough venom laced in his words. "With all due respect, I would rather die than be cast away into the dark while you get to reign supreme. No, I don't want you or any other witches watching over my pack or my child. Now, please unglue your hand from my arm, please. You're just like them."

"Like whom, Greyson?" I asked, even though I very well know who he was referring to since he's mumbled it quite a few times since he awoke.

"Like your murderous parents and that weak bastard that killed my mother. I don't even trust you to lead your murderous coven, much less my pack. When I get free, I will kill my uncle and your parents, with or without your help."

Snatching my hand from his leg, "Fuck you, Greyson," I said before I stormed out of the tiny room. The door slammed shut just before I heard the light sound of his manic, half animalistic chuckle. Sighing, I shook the callous voice from my head. I needed Greyson for now. The deep throbbing pain made it hard for me to swallow. With my eyes closed blocking, out the situation that lay before me, I stood there until those damn tears found their way to my tear ducts.

What a mess Youna had gotten me into.

Escaping the dark dungeon using the staff stairs, I dodged the staff that were working. I entered my small yellow sitting room, throwing myself, face first, onto the white chaise chair close to the window. Inhaling deeply, the citrus spray, or the magic spray I called it, that Ms. Kincaid purchased in town. It was laced with a hint of magic to help relieve stress. The tight muscles in my shoulders were uncoiled as I sunk deeper into the sofa, inhaling the fragrance. My skin warmed from the winter sun that filtered into the room. I could stay here forever, basking in the sun...

"Princess Kaydian," Ms. Kincaid's warm voice called out.

Luckily, I was facing the window. So, she hadn't seen the way I slowly rolled my eyes. There wasn't any time for rest.

Ms. Kincaid cleared her throat. "I know you're probably very tired from running back and forth from the kitchen to the cell that you and Ms. Pourciau have been sneaking off to. The staff and I never venture down that hall unless it's time for the yearly deep cleaning, but imagine my surprise to find the future queen and her partner in crime running back and forth to that unoccupied area. You would think Del would have had a little sense to use her magic to remove the scent of that dog you have in there."

Of course, I wasn't even mad at Del or myself. I knew I should've been more upset with the revelation, but watching the trees sway outside my window and the spray made me not care. All that preoccupied my mind was the nonsense of Greyson and my mother's wishes. The slow, soft tap from Ms. Kincaid's flat turned into a harsh beat as she quickened her assault on the floor. She was losing patience. When I faced her, I couldn't help but place my fake smile on as I sat up on the chaise. It was becoming second nature by now.

With my hands in my lap, I shrugged, "Ms. Kincaid...yes, I have stored someone that is important to me, ruling in the abandoned hall. I thought I was being careful, but I guess I wasn't careful enough to escape you. I guess I forgot who I was up against."

"Your Highness, I can't tell if you're being sarcastic or not," she said, folding her plump arms together with a pointed look that I returned. The muscles in Ms. Kincaid's jaw ticked as she waited for my response. Quite frankly, I wish I told my mother about Greyson. Ducking and dodging from everyone from my parents to the house staff was becoming tedious. And Del and I both sported matching dark circles around our eyes like twins.

"Ms. Kincaid, there are a lot of things I'm regretful of, and this..." I paused to look her in her eyes. "Greyson's situation is something that's on top of my list. Greyson, or Morgan James, is a mixling, half shifter, half royal witch. I'm embarrassed because, quite frankly, he's incompetent Alpha and hates us...me. Rightfully so since his uncle, Muller, killed his mother."

For once in my twenty-five years of life, Ms. Kincaid was speechless. The offending foot stopped mid-tap with her eyes bulging from the sockets. Her mouth kept opening and closing, but no words formed from them. For a whole minute, she stood there and watched me as if I just told her the world was about to end. I had to pull my bottom lip in between my teeth in order to stop me from laughing. Finally realizing I was still in the room with her. She walked over to me, still in a daze, dropping into the empty space beside me, leaving me in a cloud of citrus and cinnamon. Not a bad smell, seeing as I've been spending most of my days in the cell with Greyson.

"Youna! There were some whispers about it, but I never thought they were true. It sounded so unbelievable at the time that we just stopped talking about it. I mean, the Muller's loved their children, especially Mary Ann. She was so sure of herself." Ms. Kincaid paused, shaking her head. "Greyson is her son? I guess that would explain his outburst. Those mixlings are a peculiar bunch. You sure he isn't a bit touched?"

My mouth twitches ever so slightly. These past couple of days were no laughing matter, and I knew Ms. Kincaid would not enjoy me laughing, even if I were laughing at the events of my day so far. So, I swallowed down the chuckle and positioned myself to face her. For the next five minutes, I told her everything, with nothing missing. The tip of her nose was the same color as the cardinals around the woods. Her mouth stayed agape until she noticed I was done rehashing my tortured couple of weeks.

Jumping up from the chaise, she stood in front of me with her hands behind her back.

"We have to tell your mother, Princess Kaydian. She should know that Greyson is a mixling. Even if you produce a child for the throne, what will you do if it turns unstable like Victoria? She was really blessed by the goddesses. You think the coven members will be okay with a mixling child?"

No, I already knew that answer. Just the thought made my stomach churn as I blinked back tears. I've been dreading it since I learned my fate was tied to Greyson. Many could call me a lot of things, but a child killer was not one of them.

Kids...

Yes, they would, but would that be such a bad thing? If I could just manage to have one... I think I would be happy with that. Just one to tell my stories to and bicker at, like my mother did. Even though I would always see the small smile, she would hide when she thought I wasn't watching. My shoulders slumped as I realized my anomalous circumstance.

"Princess Kay—"

"I'm sorry, Ms. Kincaid," I said, coming back to the dreary conversation. "I guess just keep trying until one is almost normal..."

"Are you suggesting—"

She started to say, but I couldn't stand it anymore, "Ms. Kincaid! This was definitely not my idea and nor was the fact that my mate would be a mixling. If you had told me this would happen to me five years ago, I would have laughed. So, my plan until I figure out this mess is to keep him locked up until further notice. I don't know what else to do anymore! I'm out of options and grasping at straws."

Ms. Kincaid's eyebrows furrowed as she took in my words. "Okay, Your Highness. I have no problem with you keeping…Greyson locked up. My concern is in regard to telling your parents."

Of course, I thought as I got up from the chaise, no longer a source of comfort for me. Standing in front of Ms. Kincaid, I said, "Ms. Kincaid, please give me time to tell my parents. You and I know they have way too much on their plate already, with the harvest planning. Please give me a week, and I promise you I'll fix it."

As I stood in front of her, waiting for an answer, I wondered if I did the right thing by telling Ms. Kincaid. However, she was entrusted to our family. She was loyal to the sitting queen without a question, just as she would be to me once I reign supreme. Finally, after she worked out the problem in her head, she nodded and quickly departed to take care of the staff downstairs.

A single tear escaped from my watery eyes, dripping onto my clothes. At least I could scratch off one small victory. I guess Youna wanted her bloodline to end with me. Now, as I headed into the lion's den, the little trickle of doubt nudged at the back of my head like a bad memory. No matter how much I tried to act calm, it still festered inside of me, causing my magic to rip through my very being. On most occasions, I would never seek out Sir Reid, but this couldn't wait until later. We hadn't finished our conversation from the previous night and knowing him. He would have a lot to say. Downstairs the house bustled with the staff zipping in and out of the doors, cleaning and prepping the home for the harvest in two months.

"Early beats being late" is Ms. Kincaid's famous line to live by.

After stopping a staff to get Sir Reid's whereabouts, which was harder said than done since the majority of the staff basically blushed and stumbled all over their words. Five minutes later, I was headed to Sir Reid's room. He chooses to be on the first floor, close to the offices and the foyer. Right before the short hallway to my parent's office, I turned down the hall, viewing the blue door that Sir Reid had painted when he first got here. Face neutral, back straight, no sweat. I got this, and if I don't, I will just command him.

And as I stood at his door, I snickered slightly because Sir Reid was like moving a boulder if he didn't agree with you. My hand curled into a fist as I brought it up to the door to knock, when it suddenly swung open. Loose curls that fell from my bun danced in the gust of air. Sir Reid stood before me. His face was straight, with no glint in his eyes today. He was in his training gear, meaning he was headed out to the coliseum soon. Youna! That means he's in a prissy mood already.

"Your Highness...it's about time for us to talk about your dog," he said as he turned away, leaving me standing in the doorway with my hand suspended in midair. He fixed a chair for me to sit on. "Are you going to stand in the doorway? Or will you come sit?"

Sir Reid's room was just like him, dark. He left the dull gray color that was used in the house. A big bed, a small desk with a notebook, and a lamp without a shade that sat on the small desk. Inching closer to the notebook when he turned around, I squinted to make out the miniature cursive letters on the page. All I was able to make out was Ms. Kincaid's name right before Sir Reid's oversized hand landed flat on top of the notebook, closing it shut from my prying eyes. His smoky scent reminded me of the wood stove back at the pack village. As I took a step back, he leveled me with one of his annoyed glares. I just smiled sweetly into his sulking face, which made the corners of his pink mouth sag even further.

"Sit down, please," was all he said through his clenched teeth, and in a trance-like state, I fell into the wooden chair. "You finally made your way down here...but for what, Princess?"

Pulling at my fingers, "Well, as you know, Greyson is a shifter and can't very well rule beside me without changing the rules. So, I plan to have an heir until I can change the law my family created."

Sir Reid raised an eyebrow and just stared at me with his hands planted on his knees. His intense, unwavering glare made me squirm in my seat. Was it that bad of a plan? It was the only one I got, and it would have to do for now.

Finally, when I was just about to pass out from embarrassment, "Did you learn anything in your royal class?" The poor springs in the large bed let out a long and tortuous creak as he leaned back, folding his arms together.

My mouth opened up, but nothing came out. Sir Reid took the moment to continue, "The people in town are presentiment about you ruling the coven. If they even got wind of Greyson, it would leave us with an ugly case of mistrust. Not to mention if your child is a mixling, how will you explain that to the coven leaders and the rest of the coven, if the child becomes mentally unstable...like his father? What — are you living on a hope and a prayer?"

Well, yes. I wanted to throw back at him, but Sir Reid's incredulous look made my mouth feel like cotton. "Well..."

"Where did you get the idea of having an heir?"

Fidgeting with the end of my sleeves. "My mother kind of suggested it and... It's the only solution I can come up with right now."

Sir Reid chuckled, but it didn't sound lighthearted. It sounded dark. "I'm almost certain she doesn't know he's a shifter. Does she?"

I shook my head. I didn't need to reply to his question because what could I have said? He continued, "I know for certain your mother... neither your father knows about this, or my sword would be lodged in his skull by now...or maybe I could send his head to that cocky bastard of an uncle from his pack."

As I sat in the wooden chair, the permanent stones in my stomach became boulders. Staring at Sir Reid until his pale skin turned blurry against the dark gray walls of the room. Gripping the edge of the chair, I promised not to cry in front of him. But damn, it was becoming harder to banish them from falling. In the back of my tired mind, I wanted to keep Greyson alive because despite everything. I loved him as much as I loved my sanity, but as fate would have it. I had already prepared myself to consider this outcome because Sir Reid was right. Neither my mother nor any of the covens would ever entertain a mixling, much less the Royal. Uncurling my fingers from the seat, I wiped my eyes with the end of my stretch-out sleeves.

Sir Reid sighed deeply, "I—"

"I understand, Sir Reid. I wanted Greyson and me to work...because I...I loved him, and I just thought being fated mates would be enough, but again, foolishly, I was wrong. As Royals, we were supposed to trust our ancestor's path for us and I guess I've drifted off that path one too many times."

That was the truth of the matter. Greyson would never be okay with leading my people. He would never be okay with living here in the "murderous compound" I called home. We both would be unhappy and trying to save ourselves from murdering each other. Would any sane person accept those terms? No answering my own question. Everything I've done in the past couple of weeks after leaving home was to make him happy. But what about my needs? My hopes and dreams.

My mother always said, "You can lead a horse to the water, but you can't force it to drink." The first time she mentioned this saying, I was completely confused by her words. They were like another puzzle from the three sisters that I needed to decipher. Until today, I never gave the saying the time of day, but now those words rang truer than when I first heard them. I nodded at Sir Reid and with my head held higher than it's been, I left the room without a glance back.

Deep down in my heart, I knew without a doubt I would choose my family and my coven over Greyson. Walking into my room, I retrieved the silver knife from the emerald chest. The heaviness I felt before when I first found the knife was gone. My fingers glided over the harsh cut gems until they landed on the button that would release the wolfsbane elixir stored in the hilt.

"It's time to skin a dog," I muttered to myself.

I was surer of myself when I made my way down to the dark cell. My magic plunged through my veins and swept just beneath my skin, prickling my senses and making the hairs on my body stand up. With each step, the fight between my magic and the part of me that wanted to keep Greyson clashed as they have countless times before, but this time, my magic was winning. With the knife in my pocket, I entered the room. Delphine had been feeding Greyson a sandwich. As she turned to me, I could see the relief in her blue eyes. She didn't like coming down here, but she put up with it because I was too afraid. Simply put. And for that, I could never thank her enough. If it's one thing Youna and the goddesses got right, it was giving me a sister. Absentmindedly, I placed a hand on Greyson's thigh, causing him to flinch, muffling his pain as he chewed his food. If this was two days ago, I would have at least tried to use my magic to help his wound heal faster. Looking down at him, I felt nothing. Just the small twinge of our connection that wanted to make this work. That wanted me to allow Greyson to roam free and do what he pleased. I wanted to curl up under him and forget about my family and our differences.

Which was more than a daunting thing to even think about.

Del's face flushed, "Thank Youna! I can leave this dungeon. It smells like old wounds and shit."

"Not so fast, Del...I appreciate everything you've done. I know how you feel about wounds and blood from anything other than an animal. This wasn't easy for you...I trust you with my life and my secrets. I'm going to ask you another favor once more. Only this one will be taxing on you." Pausing to hug her tightly, I retrieved with my shaky hand, the knife in my pocket grabbed her hand, placing the knife, with the silver hilt facing Del, in her dominant hand. "I know I've asked a lot of you lately, but I promise it will be for the best for us and our future. I'm going to take the throne, and there can't be any deterrents in the way."

Poor Del, her face turned ruby red. Liquid pooled in her eyes as she stood frozen. This might have been too much for her right now, especially since I've asked to hide this secret from everyone, including her parents.

I sighed, "It's okay, Del. I can get Sir Reid to do it. I just didn't want him to be around when I breakdown from the separation—"

Hot air pummeled out of Del. "I—It's okay, Kaydian...Your Highness. I will do it for you. You trust me and...I love you. If you trust me with your life and this...then I will do it."

Squeezing her hand one last time before removing them, leaving her with the knife. As I approached, Greyson, who had been quietly peering at our interaction, humphed.

"So, have you finally come to do what you always wanted to do?"

Was he serious? "Greyson, I really did try to help you." Shaking my head at the lost cause of this conversation, my heart throbbed in my throat, but I continued on. "From the moment you saved me, I knew you would be the death of me. But just not how. I stayed with you, despite my better judgment. You wouldn't even entertain trying to work with me to get answers. I should have paid more attention to the signs. Greyson, and this is no fault of yours, but you don't know how to lead your own people, much less one of the biggest and strongest coven. If you would have just trusted my plan and let me lead, we wouldn't be here. It finally dawned on me. I don't need you or any man to rule with me."

Greyson's eyes were closed and when he opened them, they were those golden orbs that I've come to detest, but I knew better than before.

His wolf represented something Greyson couldn't be because it wasn't in his nature. "You're nothing but a fucking piece of filthy shit. Just like your people and just like your bastard mother." His voice was rough from the transition.

All I could do was chuckle. "I will take my rightful throne and carry my coven into the future, and out of mercy for Hawk, Elder Alo, and Kathleen. I will show mercy to your people. This I promise you as.... "filthy shit" you so claim me to be, but at least I will be alive."

"Wait," I said, as I watched Greyson and his wolf power struggle commenced. Yellow and brown eyes warred in his pupils for dominance. That didn't get my attention. It was something that finally clicked in the dark corner of my mind.

I said out loud, "Celestoria has four journeys, but only three will survive. The third will meet a death by the sun."

A giggle bubbled out of my mouth as the truth dawned on me. "My Hiema. My sun."

Looking over to Del, anger and confusion etched in her blue eyes, which made me smile. "Everything makes sense now...Del, I have no further use for this waste of royal blood. Push the button in the middle of the hilt."

With each slight click of the button, my skin became dampened with sweat as I started to tremble in my spot. *Sweet revenge.* As the thick purple liquid slowly coated the silver sharp edges of the knife. Lines of sweat streaked down my back. Although I couldn't smell anything but the rotten smell of fruit, it seemed Greyson could as he turned pale against the table.

"Wait, Kaydian!" Greyson called out, making me turn from Del. "Just please tell Elder Alo, Kathleen, and Hawk that I love them."

Shrugging, I'm not making any more promises. "Del, we're wasting our time with him. So—"

Pain hurled through my veins before I could finish the sentence. The invisible tethered string that roped us together forcibly snapped, leaving me clutching my chest for dear life. Dropping to the floor, I struggled to breathe as the air had been knocked out of me. My knees throbbed and ached as I used my hands to balance myself. Pain racked my body to the point that even my magic couldn't heal them. I had prepared to feel this once a long time ago during my lectures, but nothing prepared me for the real thing. Drops of my salty river tapped against the back of my hand, pooling onto the floor and mixing with my snot. Warm vanilla shrouded me as Del wrapped her trembling arms around me, pulling me into her warmth as I cried into her chest. Rocking me back and forth, the only sounds in the tiny room were my nasal cries and Del's soothing song laced with her magic.

A part of me wanted to tell her I needed some time alone, but my brain couldn't quite get my mouth to do anything but sob. I need this. Need to feel the comfort of someone who still loves me. Who still believed in me. Del's heart became my new favorite song as she held me to her chest. It was like time had stood still, and we were locked in a continuous cycle of my desperate cries and Del's gentle swaying. The tears came in and out in droves. One minute I would be soaking my clothing, then the next my eyes would be dry. My body hummed like it was an open spark. Silence finally greeted us, but neither of us moved as our actions finally caught up with us.

Once my nose finally dried up, I smelt it. Death clung to the tiny room like soot. The rotting, foul smell of decaying flesh filled my lungs, causing me to hack and gulp down more of the horrible air. Del got up, and I followed suit as we stood in front of Greyson's gray skin. His hazel eyes were glazed milky white as they lay in their sunken sockets. My teeth sunk into my bottom lip until the metallic liquid peppered my mouth. Loneliness tugged at my soul even with Del's arms wrapped around me. We stood rooted in front of Greyson's body until the cacophonous of our coughs overtook us, and Del dragged us out the door. Once in the hall, we leaned on each other until we were able to breathe normally.

Del wiped her forehead before wiping my face off. "Are you okay?"

"Yes...I-I'm just really tired...weak. This was worse than what they taught in royal school." My voice was cracked, and my throat was sore from crying. "I just want to curl up and sleep for the next two months."

"How about this? I'll ask Sir Reid to help me with...the body, and you take care of you, go rest. I'll meet you in your room, and I'll stay with you. Deal?"

I paused. Del looked worse for wear. Her blue eyes were surrounded in red, and her face was whiter than the walls in the cells. All of her clothing was a crumple mess. No other word except "thank you, Del" came to mind. Right before she ran off to find Sir Reid leaving me watching her until I realized I was staring down the empty hall with the haunting reminder that Greyson's fate may also end up being mine. Loneliness was now my new friend, and I wondered how long they'll be here to stay.

Lonely? How can that be when we are meant to be?

Chapter 32

Kaydian

You're going to break our poor mother's heart...

My shoulders slumped as the return of the ominous voice shook my core. This time, it seemed more dominant. And just like the two days before, my breath hitched at the booming voice. Before, the voice was a daunting reminder of my slow descent into madness, but now it added to my nerves.

I've been locked in my room, barely able to keep my eyes open. Even though I've stayed asleep almost all day, it felt as if I hadn't slept. My eyes still were rimmed with black circles and my arms gave out twice, trying to push my body out of the bed. The little spikes of terror had long since riddled me as I stood in my mother's office.

That's why it's better to off their pretty little heads...like this.

My arm went numb as the unfamiliar sensation of lead filled my right arm. My magic rushed through me in disarray. A cold, slick sheen decorated my skin as I stood before my parents. It was the one scenario I was hoping to avoid. But that was like finding gold in the cold. My hands trembled slightly as my balled-up fist dug into my sides. I will not let the darkness win, and not in front of my parents.

"Kaydian, are you okay?" My father asked as he sat next to Mother with his book in his hand.

"I'm okay. I'm just thinking!" I replied, my voice rose an octave.

One of my father's eyebrows rose higher than my voice. And I couldn't help but seek out my mother for backup, but she was too busy with her mind in some faraway realm. Her eyes were pinned to her little black book as she scribbled away, ignoring both my father and me. It was then that I wished I could drag my heavy body back to my bed, where I could cry and wither away in silence.

"Mother," I said as I tapped her on her shoulder. Her head bounced up, and her emerald eyes landed on me. Light, dark circles framed her eyes. And it made me wonder what was going on. Knowing my mother, she won't reveal anything until she's ready.

"I'm sorry my attention has been dismal as of late," she said, smiling as her eyes landed on me.

"I have something to say, and I want you to listen to what I have to say before you respond," I said.

A curious glance passed between my parents.

"Well, we're listening then," my father said.

Licking my lips, I took a seat next to my father at my mother's desk. "When I went to California, I met my mate."

"Yes, we know. Morgan. We're not that old, Kaydian," my father interrupted.

Wrapping my hands around the skinny arms of my chair, I fought the urge to wring my father's neck. The man can never just stay quiet for more than two seconds. I wanted to tell my story and move on with my life. Even if it meant walking myself to the cells and bunkering down. My mother pursed her lips and gave him a look that made the hairs on my arms stand. And my father's open mouth shut with a clamp. I promised to make sure my mother received a box of macaroons.

"Anyway...He helped save me from falling over a cliff. I convinced myself that I only needed a night's rest to restore my powers, and I will be able to come back home. I guess the goddess had other plans for me. I met Greyson there in the woods. He was... unexpected. Greyson is Morgan James, and he wasn't a baron."

I paused to think how I could best tell them that Greyson was a mixling without my mother killing me before I had a chance to explain my actions. My parents sat in their seats with their eyes glued to me, as if they needed to hear the next part of my story immediately. Squirming in my seat with my heart lodged in my throat, I continued my one-woman army suicide mission.

"Greyson Swiftwater...he—"

My mother cut me off before I could finish, "Did you say Swiftwater... Kaydian..."

My mother's green eyes turned dark as she rode from her seat, tipping the golden chair onto the floor with a thud. Her upper lip twitched, and this time, it wasn't from hiding her laughter. It was because, in her eyes, I failed her once again, and this time, it wasn't something I could sweep under the rug. Like a clock, seconds ticked by, and I watched her eyes change to disgust as the connections became clear without me revealing them.

"Come here." She gritted out through her clenched teeth.

Every single fiber in my muscles strained as my magic tried to fight back against its familiar pull toward my mother. I had never pushed back against my mother's magic. And that was evident as I felt her magic dwindle to a soft pull. My mother stood before me with her head tilted and a bewildered look on her face. Disrespectful child. I could almost hear her thoughts as she opened her mouth. But I had to finish before she made up the rest of the story in her mind.

"Okay, everyone, just calm down," my father said as he stood from his seat to join my mother. "Let's hear what Kaydian has to say. She did say to hear her out."

My mother turned those angry eyes to my father as she opened her mouth to say something. But she closed it shut as she swallowed and nodded for me to continue.

Not wanting to be the only one sitting, I stood up. "He...He was a mixling."

"I think we've figured as much, Kaydian," my father said, "And I think you should be careful with your next words."

Pulling at my fingers, "I killed him. He would have never fit in here with the coven and—"

"Instead of putting down that dog the moment you met him, you laid down with him, didn't you?" my mother said curtly. "What did you think would happen after you paraded him around here? That we would fall over ourselves with glee that you killed that mixling after you lied to us."

"Ladies," my father said, coming to my rescue for once. He stood beside us with a hand on our shoulder. "Kaydian, I'm deeply ashamed of your actions. You don't need me to tell you that. Do you know what his mother did to your father's family? They've taken Layla from us, and now it seems they've taken you from us."

My father's words settled inside of my chest as it dawned on me that his silence was probably due to Greyson's family's proximity to Layla's untimely death. Shoving his hand into his black tweed pants, his sad brown eyes glazed over. I knew my father was close to Layla, but seeing him stand there made me realize just how much he lost as well.

"Youna must be ashamed. You're willing to disgrace our family name for a...I can't even say it." My mother said as her narrowed eyes cut me into pieces.

Heat blossomed in my chest. My thoroughly thought-out apology has gone to the wind. My mother shook her head at me, causing ringlets of curls to drop from her bun. Her face deepened to the color of Fae wine.

"No, what I did was foolish, and for that, I have no one else to blame but myself. This is me owning up to the mess that I've made. It took me a while to realize that my love for my coven ran deeper than a curse-fated mate. You nor Youna may not forgive me today or tomorrow. But I promise I will make it up to you. One way or another. Before you relinquish the throne to me and retire."

For what it was worth, my mother let the seconds of silence fill the tension-filled room until a chuckle escaped her parted lips. My father shifted on his feet as I folded my arms across my body. We both watched silently while my mother's laugh transformed into a bellow. With her head thrown back, she proceeded to guffaw down air as her small body shook.

My father and I shared a glance as she threw herself down into the open chair.

"Kaydian, my sweet emerald moon," she said, wiping the tears that trickled down her face. "You really think I will just hand over the throne to you? After this foolishness, you've pulled. You're not ready and from the looks of it. You have a long way to go."

Opening my mouth to say something, anything, but I realized that would be as useless as me coming here to make amends. Swallowing the bitter acid that rose in my throat. My parents both stared at me, frustration dripping from their gazes. It would have been better if I stayed in my wing, buried under the pile of books. Goosebumps lined my arms as my magic abandoned me as it retreated to the depths of my chest.

Rubbing my arms, I said, "Right, I'm going to check on Ms. Kincaid."

Which was a lie, but I had to get out of the office before I had a chance to embarrass myself further. On the way back to my room, my dark voice reappeared, snickering into the dark recess of my mind. I guess I'm glad that I entertained someone.

I'VE SPENT THE PAST TWO DAYS CAMPED OUT IN MY ROOM, HIDING FROM MY parents as they went about their day. Shame kept me glued underneath my comforter on my bed. Ms. Kincaid tried to get me out, but for once, I've beaten her. "Bratty witch," she muttered at the end of the day and huffed out of the room. The following day, she all but gave up on me as I wallowed. Good!

I deserved to be able to hide in my bed until the embarrassment from two days ago had gone away. Here in the hole that I've made in the past two days, is where I found comfort. Not even Del could make me move from this spot. My mind was filled with ways on how I would make it up to my mother, how I was going to show her that she was wrong about not stepping down from the throne so I could rule. But try as I might, I couldn't find a good solution to my situation. So, the only reasonable answer was to stay here until I figured out a way or until the dark voice had taken me over.

We are one, and we need to take the throne. Once we do, we can paint the coven red.

Like clockwork, the voice once sent shivers down my spine, but now I've accepted it as my new way of life.

A knock at the door broke my thoughts as Del stampeded her way into my room. Her ruby-colored face was turned into the widest smile. She was dressed in her work overalls with grass and dirt on the blue garment. The white short-sleeved shirt was damp with sweat. Her blonde hair was pulled tight into a bun. I've told her time and time again that the little hairs around the edges will break off. But again, it was another thing no one listened to me about.

"I GOT IT!" Del screamed as she stopped right next to my bed. "Fresh as snow, blood will decorate the throne, for power is never given but taken."

Tiredness got the best of me as I forced myself to turn to the other side of my bed. I was in no mood for Del's shenanigans. Didn't she see I was trying to avoid my life?

"Go away, Del."

Seconds ticked by as I lay listening to her tap those hard boots on my floor. "No, and it's time to stop moping around. I figured out your riddle...well, my father did. You know he loves puzzles and riddles."

Hot waves of my magic coursed through my veins. I told Del in private about my visit to the three sisters. Snapping around to face her. My feet touched the cold ground as I sat on the side of my bed.

Del continued, "Listen, please don't be mad at me, but I've been trying to figure out the riddle for you since you've told me. And I've tried, Kay. I really had. Until my father overheard me repeating it when I was in the barn this morning, I told him it was a riddle that the kids in town were trying to solve but couldn't."

Del stopped to beam as if she won a prize. Could she not see the way I gripped the mattress for dear life?

"Del...spit it out," I gritted out.

"Oh, now you want to be impatient," she said as she used her magic to clean off her soiled clothing before throwing herself into the seat across from me. "My father broke it down into three parts, Kay...And you might not like how he interpreted it."

"What do you mean?" I asked, my eyebrows furrowed together.

"Hear me out, okay." She paused and continued, "Fresh as snow means something pure or something that doesn't have experience like a virgin. Blood will decorate the throne, for power is not given. It's taken... I mean, the only person that's standing in your way is your mother. And there can only be one queen of the coven."

Maybe this one is useful after all.... we can keep her.

Holding up my hand, stopping that thought right in their tracks. Jumping up from the bed, I ran to my bathroom across the hall from my room. The hanging mirror swayed as the door slammed closed before I locked it with a click. My hand found the edge of the sink and gripped it for dear life as a wave of nausea forced my body to heave and shake. Using my magic to provide water, I washed my face over and over again until I thought I had got the riddle out of my mind. I was many things but to...Just the mere thought made the bile rise from my stomach again. But this time, I lost the oatmeal I had eaten for breakfast.

Del opened the lock and entered my bathroom without knocking. Her face had lost the redden tint to it and in place was the pale aftermath. She came up to me, rubbing my back as she sang a calming incantation to help soothe the frayed ends of my nerves.

There's only so much one could take.

"I'm sorry, Kaydian. This journey the goddesses have given you seems to be daunting."

Del paused as the silence stretched between us. During our friendship, there were only a handful of times Del has left me speechless. And this was working its way to the top of the list. When I turned to face her, she threw her arms around me, and we stood there crying. My body shook while the tears drenched her shoulders.

"I can't, Del..."

"I'm sorry, Kay. I wish I knew what to say."

"To kill my mother? Del, I can't. I'm barely alive. I can't eat. I can't sleep. And I'm not motivated to do anything—"

I tried to finish, but my tongue became stuck to the roof of my mouth. Pulling from her embrace, I dried my tears with the back of my sleeve. I'm not sure of anything anymore. Not sure of my pathway. Not sure if this was a dream made by the dark curse in my soul. There was no way Del could help me with this one. My throat burned with regret.

It will have to wait until later as the soft clicks of my mother's shoes echoed against the walls of my wing until they stopped. The door to my bathroom swung open, and my mother stood in the doorway, peering at our tear-streaked face.

"What in the world is going on in here?" she asked with an eyebrow raised.

Del and I shared a look. Her mouth parted with her blue eyes bouncing between us two. I could only imagine how my own face appeared to her. But I didn't have time to think because I turned around and hurled once again.

"Are you okay?" my mother asked after I cleaned my mouth for the second time. Her hands landed on my shoulders as I leaned against the sink.

Throwing on a shaky smile, I said, "I'm okay, mother. I just ate something that didn't agree with me."

My mother's watchful gaze roamed over me, causing my magic to turn cold in my veins. The air became thick in the small bathroom, and I tried my best not to stagger as I pushed off the sink. Ducking away from her gaze and touch, I speeded and walked to my room, but not before my mother asked Del, "Did I do something wrong?"

Unable to face my parents, I snuck out of the castle the following morning. **Coward!** The dark curse nicknamed me for the day. Looking for the easy way out, but all I was faced with was pig shit, literally, as Mrs. and Mr. Pourciau made good use of me by putting me to work on the pig farm. Del was hauling the three-wheel barrow loaded with shit, as if it weighed no more than an ounce. We had been working for five hours, with Del moving at the speed of light as her magic worked in tandem to clean the barn, while I stood out like a sore thumb. The shovel I was using weighed down my heavy body. Every time I shoveled, I had to lean on the shovel to rest.

When I closed my eyes, my mind or the curse recreated Greyson's wolf eyes, which shined out against his beautiful face. It plagued me when I was awake and when I was asleep. There really was no rest for the wicked. Familiar tears blurred my eyes until the entry of the barn became a watery haze.

The loud clicks of Del's boots filled the barn as I quickly moved to wipe my face clean of the tears. I was too ashamed to allow her to see the tears, and my need to run to my enchantment room intensified.

"So, have you thought about what you're going to do about..." Del said as she shifted on her feet.

Yes, I had, in fact, been thinking about the fate Youna had chosen me to complete. It's the only other thing I could think about ever since Mr. Pourciau solved my riddle.

"Uh, I understand my fate, Del. Does it make it easy knowing what I have to do? No." I paused, turning toward her. The move drew a deep sigh from me. "I just don't know how I will be able to live with myself."

Del's smirk sat sadly on her face. "I know how much your mother… and sometimes your father means to you, but might I suggest something?"

Del's face reddened. I nodded, giving her the right of way.

"Remember the time my mother brought white odollam from the Fae's for Tyan, the old seamstress in town? My mother finally gave in when Tyan refused to live anymore. She drank the tea, and she died peacefully within seconds with just a quick goodbye."

Before our coven relocated from New Orleans to Houston, and before our coven shifted the power to the witches. The mermaids gifted the little pale white flower to my grandmother and the coven as a peace offering. During the harvest moon, the Oceania royal's heir went snooping into the garden behind the castle. The young heir decided to eat several pink stamens, and, in the morning, they found him as pale as the petals of the white odollam. His small fingers were buried into the ground as his magic seeped into the ground, feeding the greedy flowers.

Ms. Tyan, the poor lady, had to turn two thousand years old and became tired of "stalling around," as she put it. Everyone knew Tyan longed to be with her beloved, but stuck it out for our family. My mother loved her creations, even putting it above Ms. Kincaid's. The coven mourned her as if she was a royal.

Del hadn't said a word, but I knew that this was the only way to do it. I just needed to secure the white odollam by finding the Fae. As I leaned against the old shovel handle, I couldn't help the panic that swept through me, causing my heart to beat in my ears. I turned away from Del before she could see the tremble in my hands. I couldn't face her without the guilt that was riddled me.

It's well past her time to go. Don't you think?

What do I think? As I stared out the small windows in the stall. I can't imagine why Youna thought I would be the best for this position. As I stood around the small piles of hay and waste, I wondered if I could survive what was to come. A cold shiver ran through me as a slight wind slipped into the stable. I didn't have a choice anymore, and it seemed that would be the extent of my future—just the painful reminder of the sacrifice that I had to make.

THE NEXT DAY, I FOUND MYSELF OUTSIDE THE PROTECTIVE SPELL ABOUT A MILE away from the coven. My hand joined to each side of my hips as I tapped my foot. According to Del, her mother confided in her that the Fae trader came between three P.M. and five P.M. to the wooded area where Galveston Bay begins. A place where my mother or Sir Reid ventured to unless warranted.

And there I waited like a lurking predator behind the wider elm trees that lined the area—tapping my foot and cursing. **This is a waste of our time.** The dark voice stated as I shoved it to the back of my mind. The hairs on my arms stood as magic reached out, sensing the stranger before he made his presence known. Oddly, every hair on my body stood, and I could only hope that the goddess hadn't planned to kill me in these woods. I turned and squinted against the shadows of the trees.

"You must be waiting for me," a voice said from behind one of the older trees.

"Are you the Fae trader?"

"Yes, and you're the Princess of the Youna Coven. Has your mother sent you to kill me? We have paid our dues, and she has given me permission to sell, albeit not close to your sacred ground, but this is the only way I can make enough for us."

He was scared of me, and I understood why. The Fae's probably had a worse hand in the last war than the shifters. My father's tirade didn't stop at the Edgehaven Kingdom. He managed to wipe them clean off the slate; it seemed. Not even the magic they possessed could be felt anymore. I've managed to see the area where the Edgehaven Fae's now reside, and to say even a mouse would be claustrophobic, there was an understatement.

Swallowing, "I understand your trepidation, but I can assure you. I've come on my own accord. I'll make it quick because this is a timely manner. Do you have some white odollam?"

The trader stepped out from behind the tree's shadow. He had hair the color of dandelions that littered the wooded areas. Huge pools of silver framed his pupils. He wasn't handsome, but he was homely, and couldn't dress a lick. A crushed pink coat was thrown over his oversized orange pants. In short, he looked like a mess.

Crossing his skinny arms, he said, "How can I trust you?"

I wanted to tell him off. Curse him and send him back home, but I bit my tongue.

"Listen...what may I call you?" I asked.

"T is fine with me."

T? What kind of name was that?

"Ah ok...T, listen, I know you have no reason to trust me—"

"None whatsoever," he retorted.

Holding my hands up as I surrendered. "Listen, T, both you and I know that I'm being cordial. If I wanted to harm you, I could have easily used my magic to summon you and let my magic have its way with you. I'm coming to you like every single one of your customers does."

T paused as he contemplated my words. Those metal eyes pinned me to my spot. It was as if he thought I was going to pounce on him at any minute. The rustling of the surrounding trees picked up as the afternoon storms drew closer to us. Before I could open my mouth, he beat me to it.

"Fine. I hope this will earn my people and me some leeway, if possible. Maybe we can get a chance to visit our old land."

"Fine, but only this once. Do we have a deal?"

T held out his willowy hand, and I shook it. "It's four hundred for white odollam."

"Four Hundred!" I paused to stare at the yellow-haired fool. "You—"

"It's expensive because I have to go out of the country to secure it. Usually, I would get a huge batch from the demons in the underworld, but your parents sealed the portals to them."

Smart bastard.

Of course, he spoke nothing but the honest truth. After our trip to the underworld, my father, with my blood, sealed every underworld port, barring demons from entering the American region. I never questioned it because, quite frankly, I'm glad they couldn't enter this land.

Sir Cross and the other covens have opened their arms wide open to them. Good for them.

"You're right, T," I said, admitting defeat. "We have a deal."

T nodded as he dug into his leather satchel. Patiently, I waited until he pulled out a small blue drawstring bag. I took a step toward him, and he stepped back. "Money first," he said as I rooted around in my pockets for the money I left home with. Luckily, I had enough to give him.

Playing with the soft velvet bag, my mind a tumultuous storm as I replayed this plan over again. What if I had gotten it wrong? What if the message the three sisters gave me was wrong?

Don't be foolish! We're meant to sit on the throne.

And for what seemed like the hundredth time since my darkness presented. I agreed with it.

"Are we done here?" T asked as his metal eyes started to roam the area. "I don't think anyone else is coming, and I would rather not get caught by your guards. Last time I did, I thought they would keep me in your prison forever."

"Right, yes. Thank you, T," I said sincerely.

Saying goodbye to T, I watched as the Fae slipped into the wooded forest, back to the other side of Houston that my mother had carved out for them. And even though he was gone, I still wondered how the once powerful Edgehaven Fae's were fairing until I reached back into the safety of my castle.

Del was on her way out of the castle when she spotted me.

"KD, how did it go? Was he as nice as my mother said? You look exhausted! Are you sure you're okay?" Del hugged me and gave me a chaste kiss on the cheek. Her questions came out as one big sentence.

"Del..." I paused. "Everything went as planned. I got the tea. And yes, my sweet Del. I'm tired, and I just want this..."

Before I knew it, the scorching tears fell from my face. One by one, they splashed onto the concrete floor. A soft hand touched my cheek and wiped the stream away. I never thought I would have to say goodbye to my mother so soon. There wasn't a future that I hadn't envisioned my mother being a part of, but I guess I was naïve. Wrapping my arms around Del, I stuffed my face into her neck, washing her with my tears. From behind my hiding space, I heard a hard thud before whoever went back into the same door. It was unheard of to see a royal or any coven leader crying in front of the staff. But I didn't care. I was too preoccupied with coming to terms with losing my first best friend, even if she wouldn't admit it.

Del rubbed my back until she pulled away. Leaving me cold and alone. Which I should be used to soon.

"Your parents will be getting ready for bed soon. If I remember correctly," she whispered.

I nodded, "I know... Del, will you stay with me after it's done?"

"Yes, of course. You think I will leave you?"

I paused to think about the question. Del cleared her throat, "Sorry, Del. No, you would never leave me."

She chuckled, "Good, I was starting to worry."

Del and I stood in the hallway as she wiped my face clean of tears and sent me on my way with a kiss on the cheek. Her promise that she would be there afterward stayed glued to my mind.

Let the fun begin

The four words my dark voice said echoed inside of me until I made it to the kitchen. The big clock over the door read nine-thirty P.M. Let this be easy. Scrambling in the kitchen, I used my magic to save time. It swept out, the green hue mixing with the dim lights, finding the kettle and drink ware. When the tray was set, I opened the pouch and laced the teas with the white odollam. For my mother's cup, I dropped the last of our emerald dust that I had lying around my library, blending them together until nothing was left.

Taking several deep breaths, I left the safety of the kitchen and up the backstairs to my mother's wing. The moment I turned down the tan hall, my hands started to tremble so badly that I almost dropped the tray. My parents' room was on the right towards the end, knocking on the door with the tip of my shoe. My mother opened the door with a smile on her face, and her cinnamon scent flooded through my nose. I took in her scent for what would be the last time. I don't think I will get over not having her with me. Not anytime soon. Her emerald eyes sparkled with pure joy. There wasn't any other word to describe it, and my tongue became heavy in my mouth.

"Kaydian, it's late. Your father and I were just getting ready for bed."

"I know. I just wanted to talk with you and Father." Lifting up the tray with the cups. "I come bearing tea."

My mother just smiled and nodded her head for me to come in. She walked over to the seating area, where a small brown table and three dark wooden chairs occupied the comfy space. Nothing fancy, like the one downstairs. The bulge in my throat throbbed as I swallowed. Tears sprung in my eyes, but I quickly wiped them away before she could see. My father walked into the room with his brown robe on.

"Oh, Kaydian. I didn't hear you come in. I just got out of the bathroom," my father said before ducking into their closet.

My mother sat down in front of me, and when my father, dressed, returned from the closet. He sat beside her with one eyebrow cocked. Puzzlement etched on his face, a stalk comparison to the euphoric look my mother had painted on hers since I knocked on the door.

Pushing back those doubtful thoughts, I said, "I made you tea. Here, let me serve you." Handing them the lace tea, I made sure my hand didn't tremble as much as my insides shook.

"Either you've done something bad, or you're about to...what have you gotten yourself into now, Kaydian?" my father said after he sipped the tea.

I knew he meant it as a joke, but for once, I just smiled back at him. "I'm not up to anything, Father, but I do want to say thank you." My father started coughing as he took another sip of the tea.

"T-Thank you?" He managed to get out.

"Thank you for showing me what not to look for in a mate...If I ever decide to give one another chance." I grabbed his clammy hand. Those brown eyes I once loved were dripped in red as the white odollam worked quickly through him. His hands dug into his neck as he fought for air. A rusty odor of blood hit me first before I saw the cuprous thick liquid stream from his ears and nose. Since he wasn't Royal, it would kill him faster than my mother. "Thank you for the few amazing times we had together. I just wish they weren't washed away by how you treated my mother. Nonetheless, I wish you nothing but safe travels to the underworld, Father. We will meet again one day when it's my turn to go."

I paused as a thought crossed my mind. "Why did you cheat on my mother?"

Leaning over the small table in the middle of the sitting area. I kissed my father on his cold cheek right before his wet cough sent blood splattering across the table. He said in a hoarse voice, "I'm sorry".

My father's murky brown eyes brightened, even in its own Red Sea. "I never got to be the father you needed or the mate that your mother needed. I'm only fortunate that your mother was at least able to give you more love. All I could do was watch from inside of me how I single-handedly destroyed your mother's trust in me. No matter the circumstances. I guess now that I'm going to the underworld, the goddesses decided to free me from my curse."

He paused, wiping the bloody tears that trailed his brown skin as he leaned back in his chair and exhaled. His skin had already turned a gray shade, and the outline of his lips reminded me of the blue ink my mother used.

He tried to raise his arms but failed after the second time. It made me wonder what was behind his story. Tears sprung from my eyes and fell for him. Because despite everything, I still loved him. Staring at his ashen face, I thought about the last time we truly enjoyed each other's company. I drew a blank as I racked my memory. This would be the last good memory of him. Me with his limp hand in one hand and the other, preventing his head from jouncing.

Good riddance...one down.

I ignored the cold, dead voice from within me.

"Well, that was fast. I always imagine that if non-royals drank white odollam that they would at least have a little more time," my mother said.

I had almost forgotten about her. She placed her now empty cup down on the tray, leaving a trail of wine-colored blood that trickled from her eyes, nose, and ears. "I was hoping for a quick death, but I guess beggars can't be choosers, huh, my emerald moon?"

Her smile softened. "I don't have much time, but I want you to honor your father as you would do me. It was my fault your father was occupied often. That was my price for asking more questions...taking more than I should have from the three sisters. 'Love is blind, and you will be the blindest.' I didn't fully understand those words until I went back home, and your father had changed right before my very own eyes. There was something amiss. His eyes didn't quite touch his soul as it once had. Even at fifteen, I could tell that knowing my future was my downfall. The only time I've seen your father… completely whole again was when you were born and the other night when he apologized to you. He held you in his arms and wept for a week. Call me crazy, but even though I had to live through the lies, mess, and cheating, I still wouldn't have changed the outcome. I still love your father."

Pausing, she leaned over to hold one of my hands, and another graced my heated, wet cheek. Droplets of her warm, thick blood dripped onto our joined hands and the floor, creating a serosanguineous painting. I thought I didn't have any more tears to shed, but I was wrong as the warm liquid saturated my face and mixed with hers in our entwined hands. I didn't dare move it though. This would be the very last time I would enjoy feeling the soft hands that cared for me.

"Celestoria is going to be astounding. I wish I could be here to see it, but I can't. Your father and I will be watching over you from the underworld, as your grandmother once did for me." The sound of her wet cough rebounded in the room. She abandoned my cheek and hand, leaning back into the chair for support. "I love you, my little emerald moon. Even in death, I know that will ring true. I'm so proud of you."

Shaking her hand lightly, I asked, "What is Celestoria?"

Her eyes had closed shut as a weak half-smile touched her lips, "It's Peace. You—"

My mother stopped mid-sentence, and I wanted to beg her to keep going. To stay with me some more. To guide me for just a bit more, but I knew that was foolish. Blood arose out of her mouth like a river, and she coughed again, sending spittle of blood flying all over the tray, the table, and me. Nonetheless, I didn't dare move. I stayed right there, perched at the edge of the chair. Reaching over, I grabbed her hand with my bloody one, not caring about it, and pressed my lips to her now cold skin. When she stopped coughing, her body went limp. The hand that I held was like rubber, and I became too much of a coward to look up at her face right away.

So, I stayed in this position with her rigid cold hand against my cheek until the all too familiar scent of rotting flesh intensified. The magic my parents welded was decomposing their body, and by tomorrow night, they'll be nothing more than skeletal bones. My body was tense and pushed beyond its breaking point. Tightness in my chest made it hard to take deep breaths. Acid bubbles formed in my throat, but I swallowed down, leaving my throat aching.

I had to complete the last part, transferring my mother's magic to me, before her magic perished along with her. Saying an invocation for safe travels for my parents. The cold metal of the emerald pocketknife slid across my blood-soaked palm and did the same to my mother's cold hand. Placing our hands together, the warmth of her magic flowed into mine, combining and intensifying my own. My body vibrated and stretched in its confinement. Eager and hungry for the increase in power.

The connection I felt to my family matriarch multiplied and intensified.

When the transfer of magic was done, I spotted the clock. It was two A.M. I was long past due to meet Del in my room, but as much as I tried to will myself, I couldn't move. Dragging myself to my mother's drawer, I picked out the gold-colored robe she loved and wrapped it around me. Shoving my face into the garment filled me with her rose and cinnamon clove scent. At least I had one thing left with her scent. I thought as I crawled onto her side of the bed.

My damp eyes shuddered closed as a knock at the door drew my attention. Del poked her head in and hurriedly entered the room, opening up the windows to let in the fresh air. Watching her through my blurry eyes, she entered the bed with not a single word and wrapped herself around me until I fell asleep in Del's tear-soaked dress, with her arms around me and our coven song on her lips.

Chapter 33

Kaydian

My teeth chattered against each other as I let out a muffled curse. That's how I awoke in my parents' room with their pillows shoved around me with my mother's robe and comforter wrapped around me, securing me and keeping me whole for the moment. A deep shiver ran through me as I remembered the window Del had opened last night, which allowed the cold winter wind to flow into the large room. Pulling the comforter down to sit up, I had to close the window. Then I opened my sleep-filled eyes to the ugly nightmare from last night. White sheets were thrown over my parents' bodies, but they couldn't cover the blood that seeped from them. The bitter acid in my stomach threatened to make its way up my throat.

Luckily, you have me, and we will never be alone.

Of course, how could I ever forget the impending unfortunate fate that I've acquired?

Swallowing, I counted to ten and got up from the bed as soon as my feet hit the ice-cold ground. The door to the room opened and closed. Del rushed in with Ms. Kincaid's spray in her hands. Her hair was in a ponytail and she wore the same red dress from the night before. She smiled, but it seemed off, not like her typical wide-toothed smile that I adored.

"I placed the tray down in your parents' sitting room," Del said quietly. "You should go eat it before it gets cold."

Opening my mouth, I wanted to protest that I didn't want to leave. In the corner of my eye, I caught the edge of my mother's ashen toes, and it was enough to send me rushing into the next room before I threw up. I sat in front of the tray until the acid settled in my stomach and uncovered the food. Eating the oatmeal with my head down, Del got to work with Ms. Kincaid's citrus spray, trying to diffuse happiness into my parents' dark-shrouded room. A faint whisk of the magic-induced scent drifted into the sitting room, and I felt myself breathe a sigh of relief. Even if it was temporary, but try as she might, Del couldn't take away the memories of last night. Only time and the goddesses can save me from the picture burned in my memory.

Del's soft footsteps resounded in the hallway as she appeared and sat on the edge of one of the empty chairs. "Hey, how are you doing?"

Picking up my head, trying to avoid the pictures of my dead parents. "I'm fine...I have to be fine. T—This is just the beginning of taking the throne."

"I understand, and you're not doing this alone, KD. I'm here with you and Sir Reid...who almost gloated down the dungeon when he found out about Greyson. We took him to the old burial site in Louisiana. No one goes there anymore."

Nodding my head, "Thank you, I know I'm not alone, and I love you, Del. I think the hard part is over, but..." Holding my head up to look at her. "I have to make my mother proud. I have to make my ancestors proud. They wouldn't have wallowed in their misery. They would have gotten up today and went about their day as if nothing happened. So, we won't stay in this room and be unproductive. We're going to plan a Royal funeral for both my parents."

Delphine stopped as she rose from the bed with her blonde eyebrows pointed to the sky, "Your father...as well?"

I nodded and sighed as I told her my mother's last parting words about her trip to the three sisters. Even though I wasn't surprised by the revelation, it was the knowledge that my mother loved my father despite the cheating and lies. All the rumors the coven pinned onto my father made me regret not believing them about his behavior. Then again, I was in denial about most things and wanted to live my life in blindness. Although I couldn't dwell on the past, I had to fulfill my mother's wishes for a Royal funeral. When I was done updating Del, a somber look fell over her. Her mouth opened, and she sighed.

"We're all just a pawn to the goddesses, huh. Your mother suffered enough during her time on earth. Let's not let her suffer anymore. I told Ms. Kincaid I would help you and your mother this morning. So, she's still downstairs with the staff giving them hell." Del smiled, squeezing my hand with hers. "Do you want me to take your parents down to the burial room?"

Although I planned for my parents' death, I hadn't planned on what to do afterward. One step at a time, which I thought at the time was a good plan but now that the time has come, I'm flying by the seat of my pants. How would I stop the rumors from spreading? Because once Ms. Kincaid finds out, the entire staff will follow suit. Word around the coven was fickle. Once one person finds out, the story will take shape and turn into a full-length novel. That was the last thing I needed. Even though killing was as normal as using our magic, some of the coven would be hellbent on the reason and revenge. Commanding my magic to close the window, slipping my hand from Del's, I heaved my heavy body from the chair. My body and my mind protested, but I had no other choice.

"No, let's leave them here until I speak with Ms. Kincaid. It's important I speak with my mother's—my entrusted coven members first, and then we can have a quick funeral."

Del humphed, "I would hate to be in your shoes."

Me too. I didn't have another choice though. Del slipped off to find Ms. Kincaid as I walked through the castle to my mother's office. And I couldn't help but think about the drastic change that occurred from last night. The castle was uncannily quiet this morning. It was as if every staff member already knew that my parents lay in their rooms cold and stiff. The cold air got worse on the bottom ground causing goosebumps to form over my body for a moment before my magic hurled through me, knocking the wind out of my lungs. A hand grabbed my arm before I fell to the floor. "Are you alright, your Highness? Should I send for the healer?"

I looked up at the foreign voice. It was a young woman I had never seen before. Her brown eyes stared worriedly down at me.

My face felt flushed, "Thank you, there's no need to worry the healer."

The young housemaid looked unconvinced but nodded and headed off in the other direction. My magic alone was a force to be reckoned with, but combined with my mother's magic, I was more powerful. I've been taught this type of magic during my royal classes, but nothing could prepare me for experiencing it without any guidance. My heart was erratic as I quickly reached the dark office, shutting the door behind me.

Falling into the office chair, it dawned on me that this office no longer belonged to my mother. I wouldn't see my mother at her desk writing in her journal with her coffee in her hand, nor would I see her arguing with my father. All I would have was past memories that I would never forget, like the picture of us on her desk. My parents and I went to the gardens of Paris one summer, and my mother made us take a photograph in front of her favorite flower, the Jonquil. Their sweet fragrance left us in a daze. I don't think I enjoyed another trip we took after that one, even though, at the end of the day, my parents ended up fighting behind their closed doors. To think their fighting was caused by a punishment for knowing the future. Now, I'm alone with just bitter-sweet memories. Youna! How could I live with myself? Tears welled, clouding my vision. My mother knew of her impending death, which made it worse. I've spent all this time running around when I could have been spending time with her.

Del slipped into the office without knocking. Her eyes squinted as she saw me sitting with a small, sad smile on my face in the dimly lit room.

"Are...you okay? Or have you gone crazy?"

I chuckled, but it came out as a choke as my throat tightened. "No, Del. I was just remembering the time we went to Paris. Trivial things."

Walking over to the bookcase, wedged between the wall and another golden bookcase that was never used when my mother was alive, was the entrance to her Enchantment room. Commanding my magic, it swept across the rows of books as they fell down on their spines with a clunk, causing Del to jump. The books will stay as is until I close the room. When the door popped open, so did my mouth. *What the fuck!* My feet stopped working as I stood in the room. Del's thin body collided with my back, drawing a small humph from me. "Oh, my Youna," Del muttered so low in my ears, ignoring me.

Yes, oh my Youna indeed.

This was what my mother did when she disappeared, leaving us wondering where she went. The medium-sized room held several rows of mason jars that were filled with elixirs on one side. From naivete elixirs to unmarked jars of white odollam and everything in between. In the distance, Del muttered, "And to think you went through the trouble of finding that Fae." But on the other two walls were stacked with knitting supplies and clothing. Color-coded, they formed a beautiful rainbow across the room, bringing the room to life. Soft cotton and silk glided over my palms as I ran my fingers over them. In the middle of the room was an old sewing machine with a large red wooden chair a box filled with scraps of vibrant fabric and the softest yarn known to the supernatural world on one side, and a box filled with a bunch of baby clothing. A letter sat on the top with my mother's perfect cursive handwriting.

To My Little Emerald Moon,

If you're reading this then that means that Youna has come to collect me. I've always dreamed of being there to see you grow with your own mini-moon. To help you along the way to motherhood, but that wasn't in the cards for me. What I can do is leave you with these pieces that I knitted when you were still in my belly and plenty more on my wall of love. Just like your paintings, these were made with love, tears, and an added special Mear la magie.

Love you to the underworld and back.

Hot tears soaked my cheeks and dropped onto the white page of the letter, smearing the words. Kneeling down to the box, my hand ran over the fabric. A calmness washed over me as my mother's Mear magic soothed me. Her presence was all over the tiny outfits. Would there ever be a time I would get used to them? Probably not.

Del sniffles rang in my ear, "That was so beautiful, KD. Did you know she loved to knit? She really wanted to see you pregnant."

Wiping my face as I cleared my throat, "No, I didn't know about the knitting. I just knew she kept spare elixir's in here." My voice clipped as I tried to avoid sounding emotional. "Let's grab the naivete elixir and go back to the office."

Del opened her mouth but closed it shut when I walked away from her. If my mother was here, she wouldn't want me to dwell in my sadness. I grabbed the jar off of the shelf, placing my hand over the small jar that was just enough for one. Echoing the ancient incantation in my mind, my magic slowly melded with the elixir's thick gray texture causing a dull grayish brown to formulate in the jar. With the warm elixir in my hand, I stumbled into the office with Del in tow. Locking the bookcase with a click, a knock at the door caused us to scatter around the office, fixing ourselves. I took a seat behind my mother's desk.

Del opened the door for Ms. Kincaid and dodged outside the door, "Good morning, Ms. Kincaid."

"Good Morning, Princess Kaydian." Ms. Kincaid's silver eyebrows bunched together on her puzzled face as she took a seat across from me.

"I won't keep you long since you're busy preparing for the harvest. Ms. Kincaid, your loyalty has been nothing short of a blessing. I hope you will keep that loyalty to all of the descendants of Youna for the foreseeable future."

Ms. Kincaid leaned close to the desk and took my hands into hers. "I'm sorry, Princess Kaydian. Youna has finally called for your mother. The Queen was counting the days when Youna would give you the strength to do what needed to be done. I remember trying to convince her that maybe she had it wrong, but your mother is like you, Princess. Hard to persuade." She paused, her watchful hazel eyes observing my every move. With a sad smile, she said, "I remember when your mother came home from visiting the three sisters. She was so excited for the future, not knowing that fate had already started to collect their dues. It was like night and day. That morning, your father's eyes sparkled, but by the end of the night, it was muddled like dirty water. Blinded by love...something I wouldn't wish on my worst enemy."

All I could do was nod and recite the story of last night including Greyson's death. By the time I got to my parents' death, the stones in my stomach got a bit easier. My tongue is less heavy. Confessing my sins, even if it were to my trusted follower, made the pressure easier. At some point during my confession, I had closed my heavy eyes as the words continued to tumble out like water. When I was done, I stayed with my eyes closed until the silence got to Ms. Kincaid as she cleared her throat.

"Are you not worried about the shifters retaliating? You killed their Alpha."

"It's not out of the realm but there's more turmoil between the small group that I don't think they will be a problem. Plus, Greyson's uncle was foaming at the mouth to be the alpha, but we will have to handle it another day."

Ms. Kincaid's keen eyes landed on me, and I took her silence as a chance to continue, "Loyalty is all we have in our world, and during my reign, I will make sure that is upheld." Smiling, I pulled out the small jar and opened it. "As a condition, I need to make sure that the truth of my parents' death will never make it out of this office unless I deem it necessary. Some folks wouldn't understand the complexity of the situation, and I would rather not have to deal with the outcry. You can understand that, right, Ms. Kincaid?"

"I can, but..."

Cutting her off, "I don't want to be rude, Ms. Kincaid, but there's no buts, just yes or no."

Defiance laced her hard eyes, but they softened after a moment. She took the jar from my hand.

Covering my hand over hers, I continued, "A promise to never speak of the past nights' events about Greyson or anything I deem not for the public's ears. The secrets we share are for our ears only."

My magic warmed her already dry hands, giving it a soft green glow until the binding was enacted. Ms. Kincaid drank the contents in one go until the thick brown substance was gone. While I watched, I almost told her to stop, but I knew this was the right thing to do. Hopefully, the elixir pulsed green around her unmarked brown skin until it faded away. A little shiver of power ran through me. I hate to admit it, but it gave me just a bit of a rush knowing she can't gossip, at least about this particular coven business.

"Good!" Clapping my hands together, "You will prepare one of the house staff to take the fall for my parents' death. It will be a sacrifice to Youna...oh, and pick one that's kind of simple-minded enough to go along with the plan, please. Del has taken my parents down to the morgue to start the process for their burial."

Ms. Kincaid's mouth dropped open to protest, but nothing came out of her mouth and only a tortured sound from her throat was heard. Her arm stiffened against her side. But I just smiled at her and waved her off. Ms. Kincaid, who I love dearly, always took a while to figure out when I wasn't budging on a subject.

"Ms. Kincaid, do you have something to say?"

When she opened her mouth, the words tumbled out. "Princess— My Queen, this is not right..."

"Ms. Kincaid, I mean no disrespect because I do value you and your opinions and the time will come when I need your valuable advice, but this is not up for debate. You have one hour to bring me someone..."

She stood erect. Her back is straighter than a board, with a slight red hue at the tip of her nose. But she nodded her head as she said, "As you wish, my Queen," when she exited the office until she stopped.

"I promised to show you where your grandmother kept her secret room. Your mother insisted that you would need it...I guess she knew hard times were coming. I'll get Ms. Pourciau. She should know as well."

Del returned, and we followed Ms. Kincaid to my family's prized chair in the sitting area. With one of my eyebrows cocked, I was about to ask if the elixir had caused some memory problems. But I clamped my mouth shut when she pushed down on the seat, causing it to hit the back of the chair with a soft thump, revealing a staircase to the unknown. Ms. Kincaid stepped away, leaving both Del and me in awe as the chair continued to transform. The seat railing was unlatched from one side, allowing someone to enter the staircase to the room.

My mind led my body before I had a chance to think about what may lay waiting for me down in the dark space. The steep steps caused me to turn sideways, and Del made a joke, saying it was because my feet were big. I guess she was right since I was the only one that had to turn sideways. I wouldn't admit it out loud. When I reached the bottom of the steep steps, I sent my magic out to flood the space, lighting up the hanging lights to reveal a small garden full of Cliff Fieldcress by the dozen lined the rows of dirt. My mother had enough of the red plant to help twenty royals for a couple of years.

"You're grandmother, may her soul rest in the underworld, saw the changes in your father and his frequent trips that kept him away. She figured your mother would need something to help tide her over until your father finally decided to come back home. So, she sent her men off to gather as much of the Cliff Fieldcress they could find."

Walking in a daze through the middle row, "There must be fifty year's worth of them here."

"One hundred years, my Queen. Your mother had been preparing it for a while now. Since you hadn't met your fated mate, she wanted to keep a hefty stock in case…"

"I know, Ms. Kincaid. It will be okay. Our coven will be okay. We have enough to see to that," I said with hope in my voice. Things were starting to at least look a little brighter than before.

"But your majesty, it's important that you remember if you do not check on them weekly and feed your magic to them. They will die quickly, and they do take quite a while to grow back."

"Right, we will come back weekly and tend to the garden."

Laying my hand on the edge of the brown dirt, I let my magic fill the interconnected rows of plants until they all glowed green and vibrant with power. Their red petals opened, showing their seedy yellow center, just a bit more than when we first got in. A musky aroma diffused throughout the garden, leaving me wondering how something so beautiful could smell so rank. Turning out the lights, we retreated back to the office. We walked around the chair while Ms. Kincaid pushed the seat down, closing the entryway to my family's garden.

Now, I knew why my mother hadn't wanted me to help her with the chair.

"Ms. Kincaid, can you tell Sir Reid to gather the coven and take them to the coliseum after you find a house staff."

"As you wish, your Majesty," She turned, leaving this time in a hurry.

"Del, could you take my parents to the morgue and tell them to plan for the burial? We don't have time for a big funeral, but we will make it grand. Send out the message to the other Royals and their covens."

"Got it, Kaydian…or should I say, Your Majesty."

We both chuckled, but it was then that everything truly hit me. I was the Queen. I finally made it without a mate. Do I really want another one? That was the question. Even though I knew my mother didn't have control over her fate, it made me think hard. What was the use of men outside of my guards?

Pleasure? I could go a while without that.

Money? I had plenty of that.

Power? I was consumed with it.

"Ha, I will always just be KD to you." I smiled as I touched her cheek. "Let's get ready. The funeral should start around eight when the sun has just settled down. That gives us nine hours to get everything ready. Have the cooks and your mother set the coven banquet tables outside of the coliseum. We will eat outside under the stars."

"As you wish, My Queen."

Watching as Del slipped out of the now quiet office, I couldn't help but shake my head at my stubborn friend. I thanked Youna for at least having one person to help me with the burden. Looking out of my window, which overlooked the coliseum and Tou-sin village... that was when I felt it. The unadulterated euphoric joy of my newly heightened power coursed through my veins. The ominous voice that I had become accustomed to screamed into my brain...

Mine!

Chapter 34

Kaydian

After leaving my mother's office—My office, I was thrown into a wind whirl of frantic staff and magic clouds. Literal clouds as the poor kitchen staff used their magic to shuttle the food and tables to the coven banquet hall. Chef Dubois almost crashed into me as he carted the items down the long hall. His face was as pale as his uniform. Call me prideful, but when he called me princess, I had to bite my tongue to prevent myself from correcting him. Nodding my head, I just watched as he and Clarissa fumbled down the long hallway like two peas in a pod.

Those were some strong, inept genes.

When I finally made it upstairs to my floor, silence greeted me like an odd friend. Goosebumps formed on my arms. I knew it was me being silly, but the halls that led to my wing didn't hold any warmth anymore. It all felt cold and sterile, like the shifter section of the dungeon. Or was it just me? I thought as I stood at the entrance of my mother's hallway. If I closed my eyes, I could almost envision her standing at the end of her wing, just coming out of her bathroom with her fluffy white robe and her dark curls wrapped in a bun as she'd done. Oh, so many times. She would turn toward me, sticking out her tongue while I followed her into her room.

Folding my arms around my body, I made my way towards my wing, leaving the cold hall behind. I'm not sure if I will ever venture back down the tan hall, but I knew I would have to get rid of the things in the rooms. Finally, making the castle mines. When I arrived in my room, I threw myself onto the bed, staring at the ceiling until the sharp lines of the paint blended and shifted as my eyes narrowed until I was fast asleep.

When I awoke, Ms. Kincaid was standing over me. Her hands locked onto her hips for dear life. She had the same cocked eyebrow look from earlier on, but this time, she had a smirk on her face. Groaning, I sat up and rubbed the kink out of my neck. Ms. Kincaid was dressed in her emerald house dress as she swept into my closet, pulling out the dress my mother and I brought on one of our trips. The long-sleeved silk dress, the same color as my eyes, sat in the back of my closet reserved for royal funerals.

"I have your bath ready, and I'll leave the dress on your bed. Or would you like me to wait?"

Without thinking, I hugged Ms. Kincaid. When I pulled away, she smiled. "Please wait. I think I will need help with the dress."

"Of course, my Queen." She paused. "I picked the staff. An older gentleman with no immediate ties to our coven, he's simple. I've asked Sir Reid to place him in the holding cells in the coliseum, and everything else is set and ready."

When I finished getting ready, I entered the room to find Ms. Kincaid folding clothes. I grabbed the silk dress off of the bed, slipping it over my head and over my body. Every curve that graced my body was highlighted in the dress. Ms. Kincaid finally stopped fussing with the scattered clothes, turned to me, and shook her head. "You're the spitting image of your mother," was all she said as she walked behind me. She made quick of zipping the dress up, helping me with my makeup, and helping with the last of my looks. A quick glance at the clock showed seven fifty-nine P.M.

"Thank you, Ms. Kincaid. Our guest and the coven are probably waiting for us. Let's not keep them waiting."

Without a second thought, a thundering noise made us jump as my white portal cracked the open space in the room. Both Ms. Kincaid and I jumped, staring at each other.

Ms. Kincaid humphed. "Well, someone's new power has gotten the best of them."

The shaky smile that settled on my face reassured Ms. Kincaid... or me, I wasn't sure. Hurriedly, I took her hand, and we crossed the portal into the entrance of the coliseum. Pushing down the wave of nausea that threatened to make its way up, Ms. Kincaid's gentle hand on the small of my back drew my attention back to my reality. Never let them see you with your crown down. Back straightened. I was about to make my trek to the coven circle when Sir Reid stepped into the small walkway. In his hand held my family's crown that had been worn by Youna. The emerald gem-encrusted crown was exquisite. Two medium-sized silver bands formed the base of the crown. Between them were rhombus-shaped gems the same color, with Youna in the middle of the crown valley of the crown, holding both in her hands on either side of her. She stood strong, commanding respect.

"Let me fix it for you. It's the least I can do for what you've been put through in the past couple of days. Remember, I'm always here to help you, my queen." Sir Reid's gruff voice vibrated through the empty walkway, shaking my already trembling nerves. I guess I could thank Ms. Kincaid for that. Since he always puffs out his chest when she's around. "Not all the covens are well versed in the old ways, fate, and so forth. I would suggest being conscious of what you're going to tell the coven. Your mother is going to be missed by many, and some may not take to the sudden change of power as they did with your mother. You and I both know that change is hard for the coven," Sir Reid mentioned.

"I agree, Sir Reid. That's why I had Ms. Kincaid find a prisoner." I replied, agreeing with him for once. His eyebrows scrunched as he looked at me, perplexed. I guess there was a first for everything.

"Smart." He nodded.

After he fixed the crown on my head, Ms. Kincaid made sure it didn't mess up my hair. When she came close, Sir Reid nearly jumped out of his army attire. If this was any other time, I would tease him mercilessly. Too bad it was past the start time for the funeral, gauging by the amount of chatter from inside and the magically induced instruments playing my mother's favorite songs.

"Let's get to it. Time waits for no one and especially not a Thibodeaux."

I took one last deep breath, standing by the entrance of the lion's den with the same straight statue as my mother had always taken. Ms. Kincaid shuffled out of the walkway to where the announcer sat, waiting for my arrival. His white suit made the emerald shirt stand out against the crowd of plain emerald-suited crowd and the light-colored wood stage meant for the equipment. The announcer's head bobbed as he fought to stay awake. By the time Ms. Kincaid reached the sleepy announcer, someone had knocked him awake. A sheepish smile and flushed face emerged as Ms. Kincaid whispered into the older man's ears.

Rushing to the stage, the old man almost tripped on the stairs to the stage, causing the equipment to stutter slightly. He paused as he played with the ends of his suit while letting the music end on a good note.

"Ladies and gentlemen, please welcome Queen Kaydian Thibodeaux."

The crowded arena became deathly silent as Sir Reid and I stepped into the elegantly decorated coliseum. Confusion had laced the massive arena as everyone watched my every move. A slight shiver passed through me. Could I do this? What if I've gotten it all wrong? **It's too late now. It's our time to shine.** Swallowing, I held firm with my head held high and continued down the white carpet leading to the royal table. As I drew closer to the Royal coven table, each golden army bowed slightly. The gold-colored walls reflected the hanging lights that brightened up the dark arena. White banners with Youna and her mates hung in the open spaces along the coliseum walls. Our royal table was made of black onyx marble in a u-shaped that sat high enough, bringing us level with the bottom row of the coven seating row that lined either side of us. House guards lined the steps to the seating area, one on each step for safe measures. Sir Reid helped escort me to the top of the stairs, leaving me to acknowledge each of the six coven leaders from their respective continents.

Turning to face the coven members, I stalled slightly as I looked around the rows filled with my people. Typically, they would be seated in front of me on the coliseum floor, but tonight calls for a unique arrangement. Folding my hands in front of me, "I'm sure you're wondering why you're all here. There has been a grievous event that took place today." Turning to Sir Reid, who stood next to me. "Bring out the prisoner and my parents, Sir Reid."

He nodded and sent the eight of the guards on the steps to complete my instruction.

"See, while we ate and slept, a treasonous bastard wormed his way into the Queen's chamber and poisoned my parents with white odollam tea." Pausing, the crowd echoed their dismay. Raising my hand, a hush silence fell over us. "I understand this comes as a shock to many of you... to me as well. We trust our staff, and to be repaid like this is unimaginable. Tonight is not only about redemption but celebration, as our Youna will have revenge for her blood."

Two guards returned first as they dragged the prisoner to the foot of the stage. He was an older man with raw skin around his wrists and ankles from the chains. My nail dug into my palm as the stinging pain helped to keep the acid in my stomach at bay. Once they reached the foot of the steps, the guards let go of the older man, as he dropped to his knees. Even from here, I could make out the white cast across his pupils. It became so thick that you could only see the faint edges of his retinas. The thick ball in my throat burned when I noticed the tears falling from his face. Ms. Kincaid, who stood by the announcer on the other side of the stage, held her head straight, staring off into the crowd. Out of all the people she could have chosen, she chose a blind man. I'm too afraid to look back at the other coven members for fear I may break out in tears and ask for forgiveness. Sir Cross most likely would make my life a living hell if that were to happen.

The low chatter quickly died as the Golden Army's heavy footsteps clunked across the cement floor. Funerals were the only time you will hear them coming and today I wish I hadn't. "Fix your face, my Queen," Sir Reid whispered low enough through his clenched teeth so that the coven wouldn't see me blink back the tears that threatened to fall. *Keep calm and never let them see you stress.* I repeated in my head until my mouth was in two hard lines.

More clunking resounded in the coliseum as the small guards reached the steps with my mother's casket. The Double casket, my mother's pride and joy, was made of gold with a full length painting of Youna on its side that I completed when I finished royal classes.

Embedded in the end was a diamond we painted emerald that was the size of my fist.

Pushing the small button embedded into the stage. The floor in front of the stage opened wide enough for the golden pedestal and the casket to emerge from beneath the arena. The golden army placed the casket on top of the wide pedestal and stepped back. Walking down the steps, past the kneeling prisoner. One guard waved their hand over the cover, and the casket caps opened, falling to the opposite side so that my parents were on full display to everyone, royal, and coven. Gasps, crying, and mutters of disbelief filled the building. Whether they were authentic, no one will ever know.

"This outsider has come into our village, our home, and desecrated Youna's bloodline. Afterward, we showed him mercy." Peering into the casket. My mother, even in death, looked beautiful in her emerald silk dress that almost matched mine with her pin of Youna. I remembered how her eyes twinkled when she found my size in the matching dress. Sniffing back tears, I thank Youna that the Golden Army would never react to me having a mini breakdown.

The coven grew impatient as they chanted *wase roe*. Kill him in what may be the last words they remember from the old royal language.

The dark green of my magic darted out, reaching the blind man before I could think, and dragged him by the casket. He screamed and cried some more as his legs dragged against the concrete floor, leaving a trail of blood behind. Flinching, I hadn't commanded my magic to do anything, but it seemed it wanted to put on a show for everyone. My magic dropped him right at my feet. Face first on the ground. Sir Reid pulled him up to his knees, and the prisoner's shackles clanged as he trembled.

"What's your name?" I asked low enough for us to hear.

"M-Michaël, M-M-My Queen." His stuttering was so bad that I almost missed his English accent.

"Why did you come to this coven when you're clearly from England?"

Michaël's face flushed pink, causing his sandy skin to darken. The clinking sound of the metal handcuffs filled the void between us. He was as nervous as I was.

"Speak your last piece, Michaël. Youna and the goddess will

welcome you with open arms." I said, but Michaël just stared straight through me. Clearing my throat, he snapped out of his trance.

"S-Sorry, my Queen. I only have one ear," he responded, turning his small head to the side. The dark puckered scar made Sir Reid's one look like a paper cut. With jagged edges that ran along his scalp all the way to the base of his neck, whoever did this made sure that he would remember them. This did nothing to help calm my churning stomach. Could I do this to a man who has lost his sight and hearing? Was I such a monster?

Repeating my last question into his functioning ear. His shoulders slumped. "I-I ran away from England..."

His confession made me find the jubilant coven leader of Europe in the royal circle. With my eyebrow arched. I watched as a small smile crept onto his face. Sir Cross was many things, but he was loved and cherished by the European Royal coven and the coven. Both his and mine. All eyes were on me and the prisoner. I wish I had time to learn more about him because I hated to be surprised in front of the coven and royals.

"For?" I asked, curiosity laced in my voice.

Michaël's bottom lip trembles, swallowing loudly. "Please, you have to understand... My Queen..."

"Michaël..." I said through my clenched teeth. With everyone's gaze on me, watching me. Judging me. The back of my dress stuck to my skin even in the cold winter air.

"I killed them. My family...they demanded too much of me, and I—couldn't take it anymore. I slit their throats and burned the house I paid for down." He wept. No doubt, Sir Reid placed a spell to regurgitate this horrid story.

It was as if time had stood still as I stared in disbelief. She couldn't have told him a better story. My eyes felt like cotton, dry, and itchy. When his grubby arms wrapped around my leg, soaking my skirt with his useless tears. The silk garment stuck to me, but I still hadn't moved as a state of shock washed over me.

"...I ran because I wanted a new life, and in return, the goddesses took my hearing and vision as punishment, but that's okay since I made it here. Where I found a better life alone."

To imagine Kaydian Thibodeaux, standing here in the middle of the stadium. The need to run away was quickly dampened by his omission. **Finish it! Its life should have been shortened, anyway.** My sympathy and tears for the witch were wasted on this despicable fool. Without a second thought, I unsheathed the guard's sword and dug my hand into the bastard's hair, pulling at the stringy, weak strands until he screamed. Thank you, Youna, for making me royal just for this. I used my strength to pry him from my leg and lift him with ease as I placed him over the opening of my mother's casket.

"Go with peace and take this offering to the underworld," I said the goddesses prayer in the Royal language. Unfortunately, my hand was trembling with anger as I lifted my heavy sword and dragged it back and forth across his meaty neck. Each pass of the sword caused the muscles and tendons to snap like a rubber band. I should have been appalled at feeling how much he shook while he screamed or the harsh snaps of his ligaments through my fingers, but it only made my magic ecstatic as it coursed through my veins, begging to help break the poor witch in half. But that wouldn't happen as the complete exultation I felt as this blood splattered the white lining of the casket, my face, and my silk dress as I sawed through his vertebra. The metallic scent filled my nose as his blood dried on my face. Halfway through his spine, my arms gave out from holding my heavy sword with one hand. The loud ringing sound echoed throughout the coliseum as the sword found its new home on the ground. Taking my leg, I placed my knee into his flaccid back, locking his lifeless body between me and the casket, pulling at the dangling link of bone until the sickening wet sucking sound as the last of his spine slid out of his body. A monsoon of his dark red essence soaked the floor and what was left of his useless body as I stood watching his lifeless remains slowly slide down the casket and the pedestal, kicking his body off of the pedestal and into his pooling river of blood.

"Go with peace and an offering. May Youna guide you to the underworld." The crowd repeated softly as I laid the head and spine in the casket between my mother's hands. My mother was saturated with his offering. Youna and the goddesses will guide my mother...and my father, for that matter.

Closing the casket lid, I spoke the goddess prayer over until I heard the loud click of the lid closing shut. The emerald gem in the middle of Youna burned bright green as it flooded from the sacrificial offering. A hushed silence fell upon the coliseum as I walked closer to the Youna painting on the side of the casket. My fingers felt for the incandescent button in the middle of her chest, and as I pushed, my magic added to my mother's stored magic. Green flames taller than I encased the casket, flickering and waving as the goddess claimed my parents' bodies. Through the green fire, I noticed Bernadette and two other coven ghosts paid their respect to my mother. Although I cast Bernadette out of the castle, she still gave me a sad smile and nodded to show respect.

As the raging fire dwindled, I counted in my head until the green flame flickers dimmed till there was nothing left but the smoky scent. Nobody made a sound, not even after I turned, stepping over the dead flesh and up the steps once again. Wringing my hands together, flakes of dried blood decorated the floor in front of me as I folded my hands in front of me. The house guards dragged the lifeless body by the ankle to the dragon woods. With a flick of my wrist, the pedestal lowered below the ground. The last resting place for the Thibodeaux's. Under the coliseum, where every one of royal descent could feel the soft hum of unbridled power that laced the tan building. A somberness fell over the royals and the coven as everyone turned their attention to the royal table. The loss of a royal from the second strongest family was a significant loss to every witch coven.

Turning to the Royal table, each Royal leader acknowledged me with a nod. Sir Cross stood from his position next to my seat, centered in the middle. His red suit stood out against his pale skin, which was usually pink, as his red cape trailed behind him. In the middle was a large silver pendant of Zadia, the goddess of life and death. The clanking of his shoes drew closer as I prepared for him to reach my side.

"Well, my favorite princess isn't one anymore." His somber tone seemed unnatural to my ears. He gathered my hand with my family's ring, giving it a light squeeze that tugged at my heart. "My condolences to you. I know Youna will be overjoyed to have another one of her children in her kingdom."

"Thank you, Sir Cross,"

"Your mother would be proud. You're a spitting image of her, and I look forward to seeing how you govern your people. Maybe it will inspire Liam to get his act together. Either way, you have my full blessings."

Sir Cross lightly pressed his thumb to the sharp point on my family's ring, filling the marquise-shaped ring with his Zadia blood, causing the emerald to turn a murky shade of green before it gave way to the painted green color. *Secrets among secrets.* I thought as, one by one, the Royal Coven leaders gave me their blessings with their offerings. Sir Muller was getting ready to leave when he muttered, "You did the right thing." In retrospect, he was correct. I did the right thing, but having it come out of the worm's slimy mouth left me with the need to choke him or any male that came my way. Of course, I couldn't because I had to keep up with a good appearance.

Grin and bear it...

One of my mother's favorite sayings.

I plastered on that forced smile and kept it on until I was seated in the emerald back chair used for special occasions. My mother used to complain that she would have to sleep on her stomach because the chair was so hard, and she was right, but I wouldn't complain. Not even throughout dinner, as I sat between Sir Cross and Sir Zheng from the Asian Coven. Where they played spit tag as they spoke around me. Did I complain? No. I couldn't stomach eating my food after I watched a wet glob of chewed-up food land in the middle of my plate.

Pushing away the dish, the young attendant hurriedly gathered them up and vanished before I could even thank him. Excusing myself from the overbearing table, I made my way to find some alone time, even if it was just going to the bathroom. All I could think about was escaping to my room and crying myself to sleep, but this will have to do for now. My throat ached from straining as I tried not to scream at the crowded table. After I was finished using the bathroom, I finally took my first full breath.

I can do this.

I only had a couple of hours left until everyone went home. With my blank face, I decided it was time to face the music and head back. The moment I placed my hand on the knob was when I heard some of the staff talking.

"...It's going to be a shit show," a male voice said. His voice sounded raspy, like he smoked. "She's unmated and ruling. That's a disaster waiting to happen."

The two men laughed as my nail dug into my wrist, fighting back the tears. It hadn't even been a good two hours since I buried my mother, and they were already gossiping.

"Youna must hate her. Imagine your ancestor is the goddess of fertility, and you have not even one mate to fulfill your family's legacy." A high-pitched voice said.

"What if her pussy is cursed?" Both men went silent before their laughs bellowed out throughout the empty hall. "Can you imagine... being from the goddess of Youna and being barren?"

"I mean, look at her mother. She waited until poor Frederick was balls deep in mermaid...heck, any pussy to have a child. I always wondered if Youna just gave her a child just for fun." There was a brief silence between the two. "And the disrespect for her father. Yes, he wasn't royal, but she could have at least shown him some respect. She was always running off, knowing her father would be furious. Fucking women. They don't know what's good for them."

"Exactly disrespectful bitch...I would put her over my knee and beat her. She does have the ass to handle a couple of beatings. Then I would fuck her until she couldn't walk or think. I always heard the bigger girls have the wettest pussy."

Standing against the cold bathroom door, paralyzed as rage ran through my veins. I waited until their footsteps and laughter faded into the background of the burial feast. Faint chuckles from the banquet hall drifted into the small bathroom, adding to my fiery mood. I've always held in my anger until I was alone, but one can only hold it in so long, and I was over the tipping point.

My heart pounded in my throat with each step I took back to the crowded, open banquet hall. Why do we really need men? I thought as I approached the royal table. Standing on the other side of the table, away from the rest of the coven guests, the scent of Fae wine thick in the air. It hadn't dawned on me that I, along with the African Coven leader, Queen Afolayan, were the only females in the Royal Coven. She hardly ever interacts with us, choosing to follow her ancestor, Uona, goddess of peace. As she sat there, her mouth slightly turned down in a frown as Sir

Muller and Sir Sladen drunkenly guffaw over whatever nonsense Sir Cross was saying. As if sensing me, her beautiful, warm brown eyes found mine with a raise of her eyebrow and sideways glance. Her full lips were pursed together. A grim smirk graced my face as I nodded to her.

With a wave of my hand, the instruments came to a halt as they plummeted to the floor, causing a loud clattering sound that ricocheted throughout the hall. Every eye turned to me, and if I wasn't already hot with humiliation, I would have cowardly backed down.

"Although it's late, I would like every one of my coven to meet me in the coliseum immediately," I said as everyone looked around. Ms. Kincaid came rushing toward me. I leaned over and whispered in her ears, "Please help get everyone to the coliseum and prepare for the accession ceremony."

"A meeting now with...surely it could wait until the mornin'." Sir Sladen said. His usual overzealous voice had a slightly slurred tilt to it.

"No, it can't, but I think you all had enough to drink. It's time to send you back home. You'll have a busy morning tomorrow."

I smiled, but it felt forced and unnatural.

" 'pose so. We will be in touch," Sir Cross said as he stood, stumbling a little as his housekeeper, a young man with green-tinged hair, helped him upright.

Twenty minutes later, when all of the Royal Coven leaders and their entourage were gone, I transported myself into the coliseum which Ms. Kincaid had turned back to the boring tan building. The table was gone and in place was the Emerald throne in the middle of the floor. It looked so dark that if I hadn't seen the gleaming green chair during the daytime, I would have thought it was made from onyx. All ten thousand of the coven sat on the green wooden chairs on the floor instead of the cavea. Some of them swayed, filled with Fae wine, while others gawked as I made my way down the rows to my appointed seat on the throne. The accession ceremony usually takes place in the morning after the burial, but I couldn't wait. I wanted to finish this night off right.

"Sera! Luc!" I bellowed. My voice dripped with magic as I used it to call my dragons. Within seconds, the heavy flapping of wings could be heard from behind me, and the hushed mutters of "Is she mad?" filled the coliseum. From my seat on the emerald throne, I could see fear laced throughout the sea of my people. My magic and I bristled at the fear because, above all else, fear was just as tangible as power. It felt better than anything to know they were afraid of me...well, some were, but only time will change that. Sera and Luc landed right beside me. One on each side of my throne. I trusted children. If I had no one else in this sordid world, I had them.

"Tonight, we celebrated the life of Celestine Thibodeaux by uplifting my ancestor Youna and her power of fertility by giving her back to the earth with a gift. Now it's time to redraw lines and reestablish loyalties." I paused to stroke Luc's blue head. The witches in the front row nearly tipped their chairs back as he inched closer to them.

"Sir Reid, please gather your men to the front." Sir Reid nodded from his position at the edge of the stage, beckoning the surrounding guards to fall in line. He, the Golden Army, and the house guards present formed five rows of gold and green armor-cladded warriors with Sir Reid at the forefront.

"As everyone knows, in this coliseum, no one is actually dead until they are given their send-off into the underworld. Death is inevitable even for an immortal, and although our body might die in this world, our tethered soul lives on in the underworld." Letting the words sink into the coven. "But as the door closed on one chapter ending my beloved mother's reign. A new day has come, and a new queen will fill the bestowed role that Youna had set for her bloodline. I, Kaydian Thibodeaux, will take my rightful place on the throne, and I will demand loyalty to a fault. And if that said loyalty is broken, then death would be the least of your worries. I make this promise to you we will usher Youna and our coven into a new era. A new beginning. A fresh start to a long and prosperous reign."

Sera laid her head closer to me, giving me a chance to think about my next words. "Many have questioned my inability to rule because I'm still an unmated royal, but rest assure. I've planned to make sure that I will uphold our family name and prolong our reign. I want everyone to know that my loyalty will be to our people and to no one else. Not the royal coven leaders. To every single person in here tonight in this coliseum." Turning my attention to the guards all lined up in front of the step.

"Like my mother, I demand nothing less than your ardent desire to protect Youna and her bloodline. Those who follow suit will be blessed by the goddesses with eternal life in the underworld."

My insides trembled as my magic rolled through me in waves of pent-up energy from earlier on.

Using my magic, I manifested my family sword from my enchantment room. With my palms open, the emerald hilt of my sword materialized into the palm of my hand. Unsheathing it from the scabbed. The usually soft green aura of my magic had turned a deep emerald green. I watched, mystified, as it warped around the silver metal until it turned green. Ms. Kincaid walked over with the golden chalice secure in her hands. The same cup Youna used to bind her heir's loyalist to our bloodline for all of eternity, which held telltale signs of its age with abrasions that cut deep into its surface. I held out my hand as my magic reached out, hugging the cup as if they were old friends. The tinge of green remained suspended, just high enough for me to feed the cup. With my sword in my free hand, I lifted it, sliding it across the fleshy part of my palms. My red essence, a mass as old as the goddesses, dripped into the golden cup. Repeatedly, my palm healed as I reopened it until the cup's gems shone against the coliseum lights.

In the back of my mind, I worried Sir Reid would turn me down. A silly notion in itself, but I couldn't help the doubtful voice in my head. Walking over to the man, I considered my family, his face blank and unreadable.

"Sir Reid, would you stay by my side and lead the Golden Army as you once did for my mother? And help keep Saint Youna coven safe?"

Sir Reid peered at me as if I were a hallucination. He thought this was a joke. I thought as a bead of cold sweat rolled down my back. If Sir Reid didn't stick by me, this coven may crumble. He was more than just my trainer and protector. He was my right hand—someone I trusted with my life. With my hand outstretched, with the chalice in my hand, I waited and waited until my foot tapped the ground. One black eyebrow cocked, and if I weren't going crazy, I would say he was going to laugh at me.

The maddening man leaned in close enough for only me to hear, "In order for this work, you need to be honest with me about everything.

And I mean everything. There are no more lies between us from this day on."

Balls of steel this man had, but I couldn't help but feel the balled up stress leave my chest.

"No more secrets or lies from this point on. We will tackle whatever together for as long as I have my sanity."

He shook his head as he grunted, "And I want to know the full story about your parents. My duty is to *you* before the coven, but that becomes tedious when I don't know the full story. We will plan accordingly for everything else."

With the chalice weighing heavily in my hand, I nodded while I held it out once again. His dark eyes landed on me once again. I was about to command my magic or Bernadette, who was huddled in the back, to shake him, but his large hand reached out and took the cup. He took a step back, downing my thick red essence in one gulp, leaving nothing behind. Sir Reid's pale skin engulfed my green glow as I watched with wide eyes. I'd never seen this take place, but I could tell he was enjoying the surprised look on my face as I watched a show only meant for my eyes. It made me realize how grateful I was for his support.

Sir Reid bowed. "I will and forever be a loyal servant to Youna Thibodeaux. As my father and his father and so forth, since the beginning of the first witches. I will serve you and your heirs until the goddesses determine its time for me to leave this world."

A knot formed in my throat, making me too afraid to speak. So, I just nodded, which caused a cacophony of metal clanging against the concrete as the Golden Army and house guards bowed to Sir Reid. It was a rebirth of loyalty. An applause broke out in the crowd from the coven, who looked half awake. Sir Reid bowed to everyone as a show of respect.

"May Youna bless everyone who attended today's royal funeral. You may now go home and rest. Tomorrow starts a new day for our coven."

Watching everyone filter out of the coliseum, I couldn't help but feel the tension leave my tight shoulders even if it was for tonight.

"It's going to be smooth sailing from here." My voice is filled with optimism.

Sir Reid snorted. He had moved over to stroking Sera as she rubbed her head into him, "I don't want to spoil your night or mornin', but I think trouble is on the horizon, My Queen, and it comes in the shape of two elder coven members. Sir Sladen mentioned they had some concerns about our coven, and they wanted to speak with the young new queen."

A deep groan fell from my lips. Running my hand down my face as my eyes shuttered closed.

We've only just begun.

My dark voice gloated. What else could go wrong?

About the Author

Teal Rose is a why choose paranormal romance addict that took her wild ideas from her hippocampus and placed them into her writings. She typically loves writing romance with a why choose, paranormal, and fantasy sub-genre. Teal's main goal is to share her vision of seeing Black Female's being loved, heavy on the love, in these spaces.

She's Pro-queer and everything she writes will have a representation of the LGBTQIA+ community. Hence her tagline, "Smut for everyone."

When she's not writing, we can find her in front of her TV, watching movies and shows about witches, vampires, and things that go bump in the night. You can also lure away her from her books with any Grand theft auto, the last of us, and any multiplayer game she can get her hands on.
Come stalk me!

Also by me
Ruined
Running from Love

But Direct Here